SUNDROPS AND SHADOWS

WOLF SHIFTER ALPHA KINGS

BOOK TWO

BELLA MOONDRAGON

For Jill

CONTENTS

1

CHECKED MATE

ESTRELLA

THE MORNING AFTER THE HAZE IN DUN'S CROSSING, MY BODY ACHES deliciously. The scent of my mate fills the tent–cool mint and that brown liquor they served at dinner here. After months of running out into the Haze back home, panting and wanting and finding no one, I am finally sated. I can feel my wolf inside me, grinning at the memory of last night. We are closer than ever, just like Mother promised.

My head slams into the ground as the warm pillow underneath me shoots back.

"Ow!" I sit up, rubbing my head. The blanket pools around my waist. I look toward the disappearing pillow.

And see the pale Dun's Crossing prince I met at the docks only yesterday. Anwen–that's his name. His naked body is all trim muscle, the line of his waist leading my eye to a thatch of light hair and the lengthy cock between his legs. I lick my lips. There is a welcome breakfast this morning—my parents and his brother decided attempting to fit a diplomatic meal in between the descending Haze wouldn't be clever—but I think there may be enough time for another round before we have to leave.

"Desperate, huh?" he says. "I knew you were a virgin."

Instantly, my mating bite burns. I yank my gaze up to his face. He's got diamond-sharp cheekbones, so different from what I'm used to in Sundrop Gem, but his ice-blue eyes are hard.

"What?" I ask.

He rolls his eyes. "Look, I don't know how you pulled this off, but obviously, this is a political ploy to strengthen the alliance. I'm not stupid, and I'm not falling for it."

His words hit like a slap to the face. Did he not feel what I felt last night? The Moon Goddess's hand was on my shoulders, pushing me toward him. I had never felt so close to Her, so right. I grab the blanket around my waist and pull it up to my chest, hiding myself from his eyes.

"If you think I affected the Haze, then you are very stupid," I reply.

"I would be careful how you speak to me." His voice whips through the tent with another pulse of pain from the bite where my shoulder meets my neck.

I put my hand on it. The skin is warm as if inflamed. "Turn around, if you're so certain. Show me you don't have the mating bite."

He spins insolently, and I wrestle my wolf not to look at his ass in the cold light of day. The more he speaks, the more I hope he's right somehow, that the Haze was manipulated. The man cannot be my mate.

But there, on the back of his shoulder, still surrounding the pink-red circle of teeth marks, is a pale sun. A mating mark. The same one I've seen on Mother's neck all my life.

"Well?" he asks roughly.

"It's not as if you don't know," I reply. "You can feel the pain of your own rejection."

He snorts and turns back around. "If you think that hurts, Princess, I'd love to have lived your life."

I told Father my thoughts when we received the letter. Everyone knew King Gavin was a monster. Even on the other side of the Lonely

Sea, the rumors reached us. We heard of the packs he decimated, one after the other, spreading across the land like a disease. I told him that nothing good could come of his son leading Dun's Crossing. A man like King Gavin could not have raised a better son. But Mother spoke to our holy woman, Yana, and she said the day we received the letter was a day of forgiveness. That if we did not reconsider the old feud, we would risk angering the Moon Goddess. And Father and Mother have always been two halves of the same whole, so when Mother believed it, the decision was made.

Finding my mate was supposed to be like that. I was supposed to fall into the arms of a man who would lead my people alongside me and love me. Not this hard-eyed prince that confirms all my worst suspicions about Dun's Crossing.

I stand, the blanket clutched around my chest. He doesn't deserve to see me. And I won't use my nudity like he is, like a challenge. "I am certain you would have loved to live my life, if even half the stories I've heard about your father are true."

He snarls at me, and it's like a knife through my mark. I nearly stumble with the pain.

"Don't speak about him like that." Anwen takes a step forward, mere inches from me. "In fact, don't speak about him at all."

My hurt and confusion starts to fade, and the pride my parents taught me surges in its place. I am the crown princess of Sundrop Gem. Our pack cares nothing for gender in our leaders, just the wisdom that comes with age. I am older than this sneering prince, who will only inherit if the child in Queen Raven's stomach dies. And he ought to understand who he's talking to.

I close the distance between us, the blanket the only thing separating our naked bodies. My wolf howls with want. His cool, deep scent threatens to overwhelm me. But I hold strong.

"You don't tell me what to say," I hiss. "In fact, you don't tell me anything at all."

Anwen glares down at me, fire finally burning in those icy eyes. He grabs my arm hard enough that I think it might bruise, and want coils between my legs.

"I'm going to walk out of here"—his voice is low and dangerous—"and sneak back to the castle. I'm going to cover my mark and tell every single person I see that I ended this Haze alone. If you like, Princess, we can find out who the people of Dun's Crossing believe more."

The pain that rips through me from his words is nothing like the sweet pain of his touch. It's sickening, knee-weakening. I slump in his grasp until he's the only thing keeping me on my feet.

"My parents would have you searched for the bite," I murmur.

"And I would pitch a fit until our healer got to do the inspection, and Fleming would hide anything I asked." He smirks. "So either we keep this quiet, or the rest of the world enjoys laughing at the mad, desperate princess of Sundrop Gem. Your choice."

He releases me, and I barely catch my feet before I stumble. Whatever else this prince might be, he seems to be right that the pain doesn't impress him. Only a sneer mars his expression. For a single moment, I wonder what growing up under a man who would burn his enemies to death must be like.

Then, Anwen sneers, and I decide that I don't care.

"That's a good idea." I straighten and turn for the spare clothes the prim people of Dun's Crossing leave in their civilized little Haze tents. Were we in Sundrop, I would march naked into my home, wearing my mark proudly, and my people would cheer. Everything here is twisted.

"Of course it is." Still, he sounds confused at my change of heart.

"Yes." I lift the simple dress and drop the blanket with my back to him. I couldn't care less if he looks at me. "I think there would be nothing worse for my reputation, or for the future of Sundrop Gem, than being mated to you." I slide the dress on over my head. "So thank you, Prince Anwen, for ensuring the safety of my pack with your gracious offer."

"Not wanting to throw my life away on a random virgin because a cloud told me to doesn't make me a bad leader," he splutters.

I turn to him with a soft smile that I have to hold onto by the tips of my claws. "The Moon Goddess told you to. And no, it's your reaction that tells me everything I need to know."

A bell clangs in the distance. Anwen jerks his head up.

"Fuck. That's the breakfast call." He lunges for the other pile of clothes. "We have to move. If we show up in these, everyone will know."

"I wish you luck with that." I curtsy to the man that should be my mate and step out of the tent with my mark burning. No matter what he wants, I'm not racing through his precious palace to change. I'll tell my parents I stayed in the Haze all night and claimed a tent to sleep if I must. I would rather do anything in the world more than please Prince Anwen Solberg.

But as I walk through a forest I don't know, foreign smells clouding my nose, the sounds of other couples fill the air. Laughter. A few soft moans. Happy, celebratory noises from people who found their fated mates and are ready to settle into a life together.

Tears fill my eyes, but I hold my head high. I am Princess Estrella Sollabella, and I have a breakfast to attend.

2

DISTRACTED

ANWEN

AFTER ESTRELLA LEAVES, I ABANDON THE MORNING-AFTER CLOTHES and shift. If the bell's already ringing, I'm fucked for time, so I'll be better off seeming like I stayed out all night and asking the gate guards for something to wear. I take a breath and start running. Today, even my wolf can't stop my racing mind.

Fuck, fuck, fuck. I can't believe I found my mate during my first fucking Haze! Sure, that happens for most people, but my first Haze had to fall the day after this stupid delegation arrives? That's the only situation that would've landed me here, biting my mate's head off for mentioning Father.

Pain rips through my shoulder. The things I said to her made her almost fall over. I watched a haze of hurt fill her gray eyes, and I damn near ripped my heart out of my chest and gave it to her in apology.

A howl tears from my lips, and I hope the Moon Goddess hears it. She's got a sick sense of humor, at least when it comes to the Solbergs, and I'm not going to be her laughingstock.

The plan is simple. We just can't be mated right now. This alliance is fragile, and I know Kieran needs it. But if we're not mated now, judging by the way Estrella tried to attack me, we never will be. So, I'll just avoid Estrella until her family leaves, and then I'll go to Fleming and figure out how to deal with the rejection pain for the rest of my life.

Simple. And goddamn lonely.

'*Anwen!*' Baz, my would-be Beta, calls through the mind-link.

I can taste the disappointment in his thoughts.

'*What?*' I snap.

'*No success, then?*' He sighs. '*Me either. You have something important, or can you go get drunk and complain with me?*'

'*Something important,*' I reply shortly.

'*Damn.*'

I wheel away from the gate. If I ask the guards for clothes, I'll have to shift, and Baz might see me. Good thing Father only bothered with me when Kieran was too busy doing kingly shit for someone else, so I spent my childhood learning this castle like the back of my hand. I lope around the outer walls, find a place low enough to leap over, take a different passageway than the one we used to re-enter the castle after Father's death, and creep up to my room.

A few minutes later, I've showered, dressed, and I'm skidding into the main dining room. Kieran and Bla—Raven are already there, wearing their royal robes.

"Any news?" Kieran asks. "Quickly, the Sollabellas are waiting outside. And the Winters so Snowcrest doesn't get the feeling they're being left out."

I wrinkle my nose. Nessa Winter has been quieter since Raven sent her ass down the hallway, but no less annoying when she does talk.

A small voice in the back of my mind suggests I could ask Kieran for advice on Estrella. He and Raven obviously didn't start out with a strong bond. But that suggests I want to try to fix what happened this morning, and I know there's no chance.

"None."

Kieran shrugs. "A mating bond with their princess would've made today easier, but perhaps it's better."

Raven puts a hand on his arm. "And your mate is not less important than the kingdom's politics, whoever she is."

Kieran inclines his head to her in agreement. I swallow an eye roll. Sure, I get why Raven's not grieving, but I'm tired of her magnanimous act. She made sure to tell me she forgives me for everything that happened before. I don't buy it, and waiting for her to crack is exhausting.

'Why am I here and not our other siblings?' I ask Kieran.

'You're the crown prince now,' he replies. *'And I know your ears. Listen, remember, try not to make an impression.'*

So, keep my mouth shut. That, I can do.

My mark aches.

Hopefully, I can do it.

Kieran and Raven take seats at the head of the table, and Kieran waves his hand. Servants open the doors as I sit to his right. Others bring in platters piled with food. First, Nessa and her father, Floyd, parade in. Nessa is wearing that awful, bright pink thing she insisted on buying when she was trying to impress Mother, but she keeps her head down. Floyd's been at our court long enough that he wears a doublet in our style, with only a light-blue sash to mark him as an envoy of Alpha King Andri's court. They greet us formally and sit on the left side.

"Thank you for this consideration." Floyd helps himself to some bacon. "I'm sure King Andri will be interested in the reintegration of Sundrop Gem into broader politics."

Kieran nods politely as he fills his own plate. I reach for the sausages and—

Her smell hits me, overpowering everything on the table. Something sweet baking and that flower I can't name. Every nerve in my body lights, and my cock responds. I cram one of my hands in my lap before anyone can notice.

The royal family of Sundrop Gem enters the room. Just like last time, King Isai and Queen Suniva are arm-in-arm. Are they really that close, or are they trying to seem like they're closer than they are? The two of them bow in unison, and the shoulder of Queen Suniva's wrapped, colorful dress slips. King Isai fixes it without a word. Actually close, then.

I force my gaze to Prince Castor next. He wears a broad-shouldered tunic like his father but in more sedate colors, jewel tones instead of bright ones. No crown, no obvious marker of status beyond his ramrod-straight bearing. But his bow is awkward. He's not used to being paraded around. Least-loved second son, perhaps?

There's no reason to look at Estrella. This morning, her gray eyes flashing, her luscious body hidden from me beneath that blanket, told me everything I need to know.

She sits down across from me. I nearly gag on my sip of coffee.

'All right?' Kieran asks.

I send him the mind-link equivalent of a thumb's up and struggle to listen to the conversation.

"So," Kieran says, "you mentioned an alliance on the docks yesterday. What does that mean to you?"

King Isai swallows a bite of bacon. "In truth, I'm not quite sure. We don't come with any great issue. Sundrop Gem thrives in isolation, and we're out of practice dealing with others."

"As are we." Kieran smiles. "Did the stories of King Gavin reach you across the sea?"

King Isai frowns. "Enough."

I glance down the table at Floyd. He's watching this back-and-forth with sharp eyes I've always found more ferrety than wolflike. Of course, his job is simply to spy on us for King Andri, a role Father allowed because Floyd likes the high life in the palace enough that he wouldn't do anything to jeopardize it.

"I learned of them recently myself." Kieran takes Raven's hand. "My wife is the crown princess of Escuro, one of the lands my father demolished in his quest for power. In falling for her, I discovered many new things about the history of this kingdom, and I wish to right them."

I clench my hands under the table. Father was cruel, and he fought dirty. I sided with Kieran for a reason. But Father did win. He did give us good lives. And no one seems to remember that anymore.

"Your letter contained the same sentiment," King Isai says.

"In the same words," Estrella adds.

My breath catches. Her voice is like a symphony, high and sweet with a tempting rasp.

"Forgive me," Kieran says. "I spent a great deal of time writing that letter, and I'm new to leadership. But, if it's not too personal a question, I can't help noticing you've got on the dress of someone who spent a night in one of the Haze tents. Have you mated with someone here in Dun's Crossing?"

I jerk my head up before I can stop myself. Her dark curls flow loose over her shoulders, tousled from a night in my arms like she didn't even touch them when she arrived back at the castle. Her heart-shaped face doesn't bear a trace of cosmetics, and her full lips look kiss-bitten. And she's still wearing the plain brown dress from the tent. My chest squeezes as she shifts in her seat and the neckline of the dress shifts to reveal the barest edge of the mark I left on her shoulder. It's like she's fucking taunting me, like she wants to get caught.

Estrella meets my gaze, her gray eyes hard. "No. But I had such a wonderful time running through your forests that I stayed out all night. I can't imagine how you spend your days inside when you've got such enchanting woods out there."

I swallow. Everything in me screams to leap across the table, yank her dress aside, and display her to the world as mine. But now we've both lied. And I know as soon as I'm out from under the influence of her eyes, I'll remember why lying seemed like such a good idea in the first place.

"You'll—" Raven pales and presses a hand to her mouth.

Kieran looks at her sharply, then nods. "Apologies. The early days of pregnancy don't agree with Queen Raven."

Estrella looks away from me, and the rest of the world fades back into focus. Nessa and Floyd are both watching Raven intently. Castor picks at his food.

"Come to my chambers sometime," Queen Suniva says. "I know a few tricks."

Raven smiles but doesn't look up from her empty plate. I cram food into my mouth, hoping that will dampen the fire that lit in me when Estrella denied me.

Kieran clears his throat. "Well, I suppose there's no reason to continue beating around the bush. Solberg family legend says there is a feud between our two packs."

"In Sundrop Gem, we go into a fair bit more detail than that." King Isai laughs. "But my queen tells me the day your letter arrived was a day for forgiveness. I don't care much for the arguments of our great-great-grandfathers. Do you?"

I study the king. He has Estrella's coloring—sandy skin, darker hair, gray eyes—and her same soft profile. He looks like a weak man, except for his eyes. They're not intense, powerful like Father's were, but they have a certain unshakeable confidence.

'He's not lying,' I tell Kieran. Part of me hopes I'm wrong. My very simple plan may become far less simple if our kingdoms become allies.

"I would love to know the story someday," Kieran says, "but I see no reason not to proceed."

King Isai laughs. "Our holy woman tells it better, but I'll answer any questions you have."

Across the table, Estrella won't look at me.

3

ALLIES

BREAKFAST FEELS LIKE A DANCE I DON'T KNOW THE STEPS TO. MY WOLF sings inside of me, begging for the touch of my mate again. Only a table separates us. And she won't listen to me when I remind her how he treated us. So we compromise. When he looks at his plate, I look at him. The way the towering windows pour sunshine over his fair hair, turning it golden instead of coldly pale. The elegant arch of his long fingers around his fork. The firm set of his shoulders in his fine shirt, promising the muscles underneath. My mouth salivates in a way that has nothing to do with the breakfast spread in front of me.

And with every move, my shoulder hurts. Answering King Kieran's question felt like choking on my own tongue. Sitting across from Anwen, so close and so far, is sickening.

The sooner we leave Dun's Crossing, the better.

I poke at my food while Mother tries to engage Queen Raven in conversation. The queen seemed so different than the rest of the Solbergs when we met on the dock, but today, she only nods and says a few words. Castor's in a sulk because, apparently, a few of the other

Dun's Crossing nobles made fun of him for not inheriting the crown even though I'm a girl, so he's useless. Father's deep in conversation with King Kieran, talking over what an alliance might mean for both kingdoms. Sitting in silence is agony, with Anwen's smell crowding the air between us.

"So, you're an envoy?" I turn to the girl next to me, whose name I don't remember.

She perks up slightly, then glances at the queen and wilts. "Uh, not exactly. My father is."

The gray-haired man next to her smiles politely in my direction, then turns back to the conversation between King Kieran and my father. He's not saying anything, just listening. Like Anwen. It's strange.

"Is that fun?" I ask awkwardly. After the years of isolation, I haven't met someone new in so long.

"Used to be." She fidgets with the sleeve of her vibrant pink dress. "Now, I'd give anything to just go home."

My heart goes out to her. Nobody has said anything at this breakfast that I agree with more.

"I love your dress, by the way," I say.

"Really?" She raises an eyebrow. "Everybody here thinks it's tacky."

My mouth falls slightly open. "Tacky? I'd give anything to get that color of pink into one of my gowns. Maybe not as a solid color, but a motif of it would be stunning. And it suits your complexion."

She puts a hand to her pale cheek. She has slightly warmer undertones than the rest of these frozen people. "Thank you. Maybe I should convince Father to be an envoy to Sundrop Gem next."

"You should." I lean closer. "I don't know if the colors here look good on anyone."

Nessa looks shocked for a second, but when I giggle, she laughs with me. It's almost like being back with Tess, my best friend who came on the trip but wasn't invited to this very formal breakfast. I think it might be the first time I've smiled where the royal family could see me.

At that thought, I risk a peek at Anwen. He's staring at a point just over my shoulder, a forkful of eggs suspended in midair between his mouth and his plate. Like he was watching me and looked away when I looked at him. I scowl and tear my eyes away. So he's an asshole and a coward. Or he thinks he can have me physically without the rest of it, a notion I'm happy to disabuse him of.

"Tell me more about Sundrop Gem," Nessa gushes. "When I heard you were coming, I looked in the library, but there were, like, two references. Is it beautiful?"

I hope he's listening.

"It's better than beautiful. There are no words." A soft smile curves my lips as I think of home. "Our palace is nothing like this. It's all light stone, open arches, airy breezeways. A million courtyards."

"How do you survive the winter?" Nessa asks.

"Our winters are mild." I shrug. "I've barely needed anything heavier than this dress, even on the darkest days of the year."

Her eyes grow wide. "I don't remember Snowcrest well, but even here, that would be impossible. Does that mean you've never seen snow?"

I shake my head. "I know it's some sort of cold rain, but that's all."

She laughs. "Oh, I have to see your face when you do. You're going to lose it."

"And that's… good?" My smile fades. Nessa speaks quickly, and without the polish of the people who come to the palace in Sundrop. She's very nice, but I'm struggling to keep up a little.

"I think it will be." She laughs again. "Goddess, this is going to be great. I'm taking you under my wing, okay? And I'm going to make sure you have the *best* time here." She leans close and drops her voice. "Or at least, as good of a time as you can in a place like Dun's Crossing."

We exchange secretive smiles. At least I have one ally in this palace, even if she belongs here as little as I do.

"What are you girls talking about?" Mother asks.

"Oh, nothing," Nessa trills. "Just how exciting it is for Sundrop to be re-entering politics."

I peer at her. Why is she lying to my mother? Nessa cuts her eyes at Queen Raven, who seems to be watching us, and the pieces fall together. If we told Mother how we really felt, we'd make a bad impression with the queen. Maybe I do need to be taken under Nessa's wing to survive. In Sundrop, I only had the same group of jealous families to worry about. Here, there are so many more dangers.

"Lovely." Mother smiles. "I'll admit a little girlish excitement myself. I haven't traveled since I joined Sundrop."

I smile. "But you came from Thunderpeak. You didn't even—"

"Can you pass the jam," Anwen asks abruptly.

Mother turns slowly. "Excuse me?"

"The jam." He points at a pot between Nessa and I. "Could I have it?"

"No, you mean to say excuse me," I reply without looking any more at him. "You've obviously interrupted a conversation. You ought to do so politely."

Anwen scoffs.

"Estrella," Mother murmurs. "Don't be rude. They may have different customs."

"Do you?" I turn to Anwen, my heart pounding. "Do you have customs that don't require you to display manners at the breakfast table?"

"Apologies," he says tightly. "Your conversation was so loud I assumed I was already a part of it. I assume it's customary in Sundrop Gem to yell over breakfast?"

I bristle. For the first time, my wolf snarls at him. "It's customary to make conversation, yes. I didn't know ears were so finely tuned in Dun's Crossing. I'll make sure to *keep quiet* going forward."

He clenches his jaw. That fire flashes in his eyes again. As furious as I am at his behavior, something low and wanting curls in my gut.

I crush it.

"Thank you," he says icily. "Now, may I please have the jam?"

I lift the pot and give it to him, then snatch my hand back before he can even brush my skin. When he begins smearing the ruby-red condiment over a piece of toast, I realize the table has gone utterly silent during our exchange.

My face warms.

Father laughs. "Perhaps we ought not make too many plans for our alliance yet, King Kieran. The next generation seems unready to give up old hurts, with your exception, of course."

Awkward laughter fills the room. Anwen mutters, "Sorry," in a tone that makes it very clear he doesn't mean it. I say something about a miscommunication that doesn't make any sense before it leaves my mouth or after.

What am I thinking? This is an important breakfast. As much as I think we couldn't pick a worse kingdom than Dun's Crossing to ally with, obviously Mother and Father feel differently. When I inherit the pack in thirty years or whenever they step down, I can make decisions about our allies. Until then, my role as the eldest is to support them. I take a deep breath, square my shoulders, and smile brightly at Anwen without meeting his eyes.

"I'm sure these little issues will smooth the longer we work together."

He nods wordlessly. I grit my teeth. It's like trying to make peace with a toddler.

King Kieran clears his throat. "Yes, well. With that in mind, I had a bit of a thought."

The whole table turns to him.

"What do you say we take two days to hammer out the rest of these details?" he asks Father, "and then when the sun sets on the third day, that anniversary you mentioned, we'll have a ball to commemorate the union of our two peoples?"

Father claps King Kieran on the shoulder. "A wonderful idea!"

A ball! We have all sorts of celebrations in Sundrop, but never a proper party like a ball.

'Can I be excused?' I ask Mother and Father through the mind-link. *'Tess and I need to plan our gowns.'*

Father smiles indulgently. *'Of course, my dear. Wow them.'*

I say my goodbyes, even to Anwen, and hurry out of the room.

4

PENT UP

Anwen

After breakfast, I give Kieran my notes. Floyd was nosy, as usual. The king and queen of Sundrop Gem seem to lead together. Prince Castor seems sulky. Nessa isn't trouble.

Kieran hums thoughtfully. "And Princess Estrella? She seems smart, involved."

"Yes," I say through gritted teeth.

"You don't like her." It's not a question.

Relief washes through me. If people think I hate her, perhaps they won't have to stick around. "Was it that obvious?"

My bite aches. That's fine.

Kieran snorts. "Get through two days without tearing her head off. Please."

I know the sound of a dismissal when I hear one, so I leave. Breathing clean air is a fucking blessing. I'm irritated all over again, certain that keeping away from Estrella is the right move.

'I know you're free,' Baz calls, his mental voice slurred with alcohol. *'Come get pissed with me.'*

He'll be in the Blue Slipper, our favorite tavern in town. And honestly, even though it's not yet noon, a little bit of fuzz around my thoughts doesn't sound too bad. Drinking is the only going out I do these days anyway. I turn on my heel and head for a secret passage that will take me directly into town. Fuck the ball. Maybe I won't even go. That ought to make it easy to stay away from her.

'Don't pass out before I get there,' I reply.

Baz laughs in my thoughts. *'Run.'*

I shake my head. If he has his way, I'll have the reputation of a playboy prince before winter comes. Not that that would require a change in my behavior. Just how careful I am.

Unbidden, my thoughts drift to Estrella, the night we shared. She showed her inexperience, but I'd be lying if I said I'd had a better orgasm. Is sleeping with other people going to be lackluster now? Have I doomed myself to life as a monk because nothing will ever be as good?

Instead of heading for Baz, I find myself pacing. He'll be expecting a bitter bachelor, and that means getting my head on straight.

Every time I run into Estrella, I just prove all over again why it would never work. When Kieran mated with Raven, he changed. Maybe not immediately. I remember the days of reports on his progress chasing her, Father stalking around the castle. We all believed him. But quickly enough, he staged a coup against his own father.

I march onto the upper balcony surrounding the ballroom, and conversation greets my ears.

"If he's going to treat you like garbage, he doesn't deserve you," a woman I don't recognize says.

I peer over the edge just as her partner speaks.

"But the Moon Goddess thinks he does," Estrella says.

Years of listening in corners fly out of my head in a single sharp exhale. Both of them look at me immediately. Estrella catches my gaze.

Her gray eyes are wet, like she's been crying.

My stomach churns. I'm the same Anwen that ran into those

woods last night. I am my father's son, and I intend to take my time burying the man. With any luck, I'll bury the parts of me that are with him. At which point she'll be lost to me, which is exactly what I deserve.

Estrella turns on her heel and strides away. "Come on, Tess. There are better places to walk and talk."

My temper flares as my mark twinges. How dare she walk away from me? What have I done to her, really? She's humiliated me in front of my brother, insulted my father, and had the damnable timing to show up in the first place! A few impersonal remarks hardly count against that. She's in my house, and she ought to realize that.

The door shuts behind them with the same hollow *slam* I remember from all the times Father took Kieran into his office to teach him how to leave and shut the door in my face.

I grab my head in my hands. It feels like I'm being pulled in a thousand different directions, and it's only been one day. There's only one thing to do.

'Get pissed enough for the both of us,' I tell Baz. *'I need to run.'*

I leap down from the balcony and land already shifted. There's something electric about shifting on the fly, the closest I think I'll ever come to having the powers so many people from other kingdoms possess. And there's a passageway in here I can open with nothing more than my nose.

In moments, the only things I can hear are the soft *thud-thud, thud-thud* of my paw pads on the packed dirt of the ground. The air down here is musty and stale, but I know what waits for me outside. The careful, politically masked Estrella I saw at breakfast today has nothing in common with the wild woman I tasted last night, but I agree with her on one thing: it's nearly impossible to stay in the palace all day with the forest outside. Everything makes so much more sense on four legs.

I burst out of the palace, into the midmorning sun. When I reach the walls, the guards open the gate without asking. I may have white fur like so many of our pack, but I lost the end of my tail in the first scuffle Father allowed me out on, so they know my profile from a distance. I pound out the back gate and into the welcoming trees, away from town.

The promise of rain hangs in the air. The last threads of the Haze, reeking of primal sex, drift in the wind. Fat, late autumn birds and rodents dot the trees. To my left, a ballsy herd of mist deer graze in a clearing. Out here, there are so many smells I can barely remember Estrella's.

As soon as I think that, I taste her on the wind and howl. The mist-deer leak fear pheromones.

Only a few wolves are fast enough to catch the beasts. But, unluckily for them, I'm one of the ones who can. I wheel in their direction, lengthening my stride and softening my landings.

When Kieran, Candace, and I were very young, Mother used to tell us bedtime stories occasionally. Bedtime story, really. After Finn and Ingrid arrived a few years later, she didn't have the time, but I can still recite the story off by heart because she retold it the day after my very first shift, and the rhythm of it is perfect for timing a wolf's strides.

When the Goddess makes a wolf, she gives three natures for Her three phases of the moon.

For the crescent, when She shows first glimpse, She gives scent. To hunt with eyes closed, with ears dead. Our gray wolves will always find Her.

For the gibbous, when She's near, She gives speed. To chase slickest prey, quickest enemy. Our white wolves will always catch Her.

For the full, when She bares Her face, She gives strength. To never falter, to fell great foes. Our silver wolves will always claim Her.

My breathing, my footfalls, even the extensions of my limbs fall into the old rhythm. All thoughts of Estrella fade away. My wolf slips over my mind with none of the animal hunger of last night. Just peace. I veer onto a hill that will let me overlook the clearing the mist-deer graze in.

Eight of them, and only one buck. His crystalline horns glint in the rays of sunlight that jut through the leaves overhead, casting rainbow patterns on his green-dappled coat. My stomach rumbles. I barely ate breakfast. I drop lower to the ground and prowl forward.

The wind shifts, and something new greets my nose. Not a prey smell. A predator one. Another wolf is out here, and not far.

That makes sense. Kieran said he invited representatives of other packs to the ball, and with Raven's power over animals, our missives arrive almost instantly. But something puts my hackles up. This wolf doesn't have the icy tinge of Snowcrest, the familiar grit of Dun's Crossing, or even the must of Escuro. I haven't noticed a throughline in Sundrop yet, but I know the four smells of their royalty, and it's nothing like any of those.

The wind shifts again, weakening their scent and ruffling my fur. And they take off.

I was preparing for a hunt.

I launch myself after the mystery wolf, pouring on all the speed I had saved for the mist-deer, who scatter as I charge. I half wish I'd brought Candace. Her gray wolf would sense things I can't even imagine. And she'd be able to hold the trail, despite the whipping winds that wreak havoc on my nose. I twist, run in one direction for a minute and then zag another way. The smell intensifies, weakens again. It's like chasing a ghost.

This wolf can't outrun me. No one can. But being fast doesn't make a difference if I'm running in the wrong direction.

When I look up, the sun nearly touches the horizon. I've spent hours out here, and I'm nearly out of mind-link range. My hackles raise again. If I were trying to set a trap, I'd do it exactly like this.

With a final, irritated howl, I wheel and head back to the palace.

5

A CATCH

Estrella

I stalk through the halls of Solberg Castle with an unfamiliar scowl on my face. Well, it used to be unfamiliar. After a full day in this palace, I'm starting to worry my face is going to be stuck this way. Father asked me to meet him after one of his endless meetings with King Kieran simply because we haven't seen each other for more than a few minutes since that breakfast yesterday. I suspect he's going to take me for a walk in what passes for a courtyard here.

A maid scurries past me with her head down, obviously frightened. I wince and try to soften my scowl. There's really no reason to be storming around like this, except that my mark has begun itching as well as hurting. It's like having a headache and a mosquito bite in one. I haven't seen Anwen since that breakfast, for which I'm very grateful. Occasionally, I walk through clouds of his stink. If it only worsened the pain in my mark, I think I might be able to handle it, but without fail, my knees go weak and my wolf howls with want.

Still, I keep walking around. I need to. Pacing is the only thing that keeps all my racing thoughts at bay, the only thing that tired me out enough to sleep without crying last night. Even Tess won't walk with me anymore.

Or perhaps that's because she's tired of hearing about Anwen. Tess became of age a couple months before me, and a Haze swept through Sundrop the week after. While I sat at home, smelling the air and wondering what it would be like when it was my turn, she found her mate, Orion. He's a bit lower ranked than her, but he's big, sweet, and he treats her like she's his world. They haven't married yet, but that's only because Orion is working up to a promotion, and he wants to be good enough for her. She's told him a thousand times over he is. Honestly, watching them together is enough to give a person cavities. When the Haze took me, Tess was completely convinced I'd come back just as happy as her. She hasn't really known what to do since Anwen rejected me. We're just trying to focus on the ball.

I enter a large room and nearly retch. There's his smell, mint and something fermented, powerful enough that I suspect he was here recently. It shivers up my spine. My wolf wants to tear my clothes off and track him down. But I know what to do. I simply pinch my nose closed with a wooden pin I found one of the maids using for the wash and keep marching forward. The hall Father told me to meet him in is this way. And Solberg Castle is so large I rarely ever see anyone but servants that I don't bring with me in its halls. I escape the room, but I know how his smell lingers, so I leave the pin on a moment longer.

And if I have to wipe a few tears from my eyes, it's only because the smell is so overpowering.

I turn a corner and slam directly into something. With my momentum, the abrupt stop sends me careening back. I try to catch the wall, but someone grabs me around the waist and pulls me flush against their chest.

"Thank you." I blink to clear my eyes. "And I'm so—"

The words die in my mouth. The person holding me, who saved me from falling, is none other than Anwen himself. There's a furrow between his fair eyebrows, like he was worrying about something, and I'm so close to him. My breasts are crushed against his chest, trying to escape the bodice of my dress. One of his legs landed smoothly between mine, just the suggestion of friction against the inside of my thigh, south of where my wolf screams for it. I can feel him hardening against me. His hand burns through the back of my dress, and his mouth is so close that I can see the fine, golden hairs of a beard that hasn't been shaved in too long. He stares into my eyes hungrily then drags his gaze down to my mouth.

His frown deepens. "Clothespin?"

And the brief hold the mating bond has on my thoughts shatters. I snatch the pin off my nose—his scent is too powerful, overwhelming —and stuff it into a pouch tied to my waist.

"I'm training my hearing," I lie. Anything is better than telling him how much he affects me.

I yank myself out of his hold.

"Interesting," he says, like he doesn't believe me. "Any particular reason?"

"So that next time my nose misleads me, I can think around it." I look him up and down before realizing what a mistake that was. He wears a pair of leather pants that cling to every inch of his legs, as well as what lies between them, and a tunic that's half-unlaced at the neck to show a tempting swath of skin. I swallow sudden saliva in my mouth.

He purses his lips. "Right. Well, good seeing you, I've got somewhere to—"

"Wait!" I grab his forearm.

He stops, even though he could probably tear out of my grasp easily. "What?"

At home, Rhys Ibarra always runs from me when he's up to something, but he won't actively disobey an order I give him. It seems like Anwen might be just susceptible enough to the mate bond that he'll behave similarly to my friend.

"You've been avoiding me. Why?"

Anwen turns back with a small smirk. "Are you sure you want to discuss this in the hallway, Princess?"

"Are you sure you want to take me into a private room?" I drop my gaze deliberately to the bulge in his pants. My wolf yowls for me to touch him.

His smirk drops. "I'm avoiding you because of the scene you made at breakfast. Clearly, you're unable to resist me."

"Resist you?" I laugh. "Resisting you is the easy part. Trying to figure out why you're so insistent on your secrets when your king seems all in on an alliance is the hard part."

"I thought you were protecting your people from me," he says, but he won't make eye contact with me anymore.

I've found something.

"So, you're not hiding us for political reasons." I smile. "What, then?"

"Leave it, Princess," he snaps. "I really do have somewhere to be."

I tighten my hold on his arm, more reminder than an actual stopping force. Just like Rhys would have, Anwen stays. My body lights with the rush of keeping him here through will alone.

That certainly never happened with Rhys.

I shove that aside. "I don't think you're the one who gets to be angry here. I've been shoved aside, made to feel like garbage, and you won't even do me the honor of telling me why. Are you that scared?"

"Scared?" That burning flares in his eyes. "I stood up to King Gavin. The one you're all so goddamn scared of you needed permission to go to a ball. Do you think a little thing like you scares me?" He snorts.

Tess's words from yesterday echo in my head. If he treats me badly, he doesn't deserve me. And she's right, no matter what the Goddess says—though I do offer a quick mental apology to Her for thinking that. I am smart, kind, and beautiful. Even if I weren't the crown princess of Sundrop Gem, I would deserve someone who treated me well. Everyone does. So I'm not going to sit around waiting for Anwen to pull his head out of his ass, lapping up scraps of affection when he gives them to me.

"You can keep putting me down." I force my voice even. "Call me a virgin, a mad princess, a little thing. But the Goddess put me in your path for a reason, and I think you know what it is. And *that's* what scares you. That I might really make a difference in your life."

I know Anwen's wolf is fast. I don't expect him to move just as quickly. He rips my hand off his arm, twists us around, and slams me into the wall.

"Keep talking shit." His breath is hot on my face. "All I'm hearing is that you need me to pay attention to you." He runs a hand up the outside of my thigh. "If I fuck you again, will you stop yapping? It's worked for a lot of other girls around here."

He's so close, his hardness pressed against my stomach, and no matter how much my wolf begs, I don't want a thing.

"Get off me." I shove him back.

To my surprise, he goes.

I straighten my dress huffily. "I'm so glad you stood up to your father. It's lucky Dun's Crossing has such different leadership now."

Before he can reply, I turn and march away. I am certainly asking Father when we're leaving–as soon as possible.

6

REFLECTION

"KIERAN SAID YOU HAD TO GO?" BAZ ASKS FROM WHERE HE SITS ON THE railing of the balcony attached to my bedroom.

"Those were his exact words." I scowl at my open wardrobe. *"Anwen, you have to go to this ball, or it will look bad for all of us.* Authority command and all. Who the fuck does he think he is?"

Baz snorts. "Sounds like he thinks he's your fucking dad."

I grab a shoe from the bottom of my wardrobe and launch it at his head. "Shut up."

He dodges, and the shoe sails off to land somewhere on the grounds. "Not to be a dick, but why are you so pissed anyway? You're the one who said balls are called that because that's what women show up looking for."

That makes me smile a little. I am funny.

"Perfect way to get over the Haze," he adds.

And I'm pissed again. I still haven't told him. I haven't told anyone. And I think if I show up to this party, and Estrella's there looking like a Goddess-damned dream, I might just explode.

'I have to tell you something,' I say, *'and it needs to stay secret.'*

Baz grins. *'I'll take the Beta's oath right now if that'll make you happy.'*

'It needs to stay secret even when you're drunk.' I turn and shoot him a look.

"I swear to the Moon Goddess Herself." Baz draws an X over his chest. "Drunk or sober, this one's staying locked up."

I look at him for a long moment. He's my best friend for a reason, and a lot of it has to do with our shared penchant for learning the right piece of information to put in the wrong ear. The court calls us gossips, Father called us spies when he was feeling generous, but I've always just thought of us as opportunists. Still, his gaze is steady on mine, not laughing for once in his life.

'I lied about the Haze.' I grimace. *'I found my mate. It's Princess Estrella.'*

"Oh, shit," Baz says.

"Swear to the Moon Goddess," I remind him. I don't like the light in his eyes.

He crosses his chest again, then hops off the railing of the balcony and walks inside. "There's a real chance I've finally drunk enough to become stupid, but why the hell is that a secret?"

"Because—" Because I don't want to be mated. Because Father hasn't even been dead a month yet, and no one cares. Because I pinned her against a wall, threatened to fuck her into silence, and she looked scared of me. "Because she asked for it."

He blows out a long breath. "You should've come to drink with me. That's the only thing I've heard of that might actually be worse than ending the Haze alone."

"You're telling me," I mutter. "Nobody knows except us. And, I guess, you."

"You haven't even told Kieran." He shakes his head. "I mean, you fucking gotta. She's the crown princess. You're gonna inherit Sundrop Gem."

Somehow, in all of this, I haven't thought of that yet. Me, an Alpha King. The thing I gave up when I turned my back on Father. I drop into the chair at my desk.

"Maybe that's why she's not telling anyone," Baz says. "She wants the whole place to herself. I mean, it's crazy she's inheriting at all. It should be her brother."

"She's going to be a fantastic leader," I snap as some feral protective instinct rears up inside me. "Castor doesn't know his head from his ass."

Baz puts his hands up. "Damn, you're really mated. I take it back."

"I am." I groan. "And I'm shit at it, and now I have to go to this fucking ball, and I feel like a girl because I don't know what to wear!"

As a testament to our friendship, Baz swallows his laughter. "I bet you're not shit at it."

"I am." Maybe I can't tell the truth about why, but that's easy enough to say to the guy who once dared me to shit over the castle wall and helped me back inside when I fell off in the process. Another secret we're taking to our graves. "Trust me. Every time I see her, I just get… feral. And there's no telling how that comes out."

Baz gets serious again. "You hit her?"

"No!" The idea makes me nauseous. "But I'm a dick. We can't talk without fighting, and I keep wanting to grab her and—"

"Enough details." Baz puts his hands up to stop me. "Look, you're just kind of an intense guy. Always have been. Maybe she makes that worse, so you just gotta channel it."

"Channel it?"

He nods, stands, and walks over to my wardrobe. "You remember Earson?"

"The etiquette tutor with the ears." I grin. "I think his name was Karson."

"Whatever." Baz starts pulling things out. "He was the one who kept saying a gentleman is just the cage around the animal inside. So channel into being the cage, not the animal." He throws an armful of clothes at my head. "Might look like shit, but you'll be dressed."

I roll my eyes. Baz wears all black so he "can't be wrong," and the outfit he picked out for me is more of the same. But I'm tired of going in circles in my head. I get dressed and look at myself in the mirror.

I look exactly like the portrait of Father when he took the throne.

Baz punches me in the shoulder. "We look like we could be twins."

He couldn't be more wrong. His hair is shorter than mine, straw-colored where mine is gold, and his eyes are dark blue. Plus, there's the time he broke his nose trying to run through the gate before the guards shut it and smashed right into the damned thing. But it's such a stupid thing to say that it startles a laugh out of me.

"There!" He grabs my jaw, pinning my mouth in a slightly open smile. "He looks like the crown prince of Dun's Crossing, not some sad fuck next to the king. All right?"

I shake my head as much as I can in his hold. "What would I do without you?"

"Drown in your own tears." He lets me go and thumps my back. "Now, let's move before my very good advice wears off."

We leave my room together and start heading for the ballroom. When we pass the spot where I cornered Estrella the other day, my whole body warms. If she'd even whispered she wanted me—hell, if she'd stayed still—I would've taken her. Right there in the fucking hallway, where anyone could see. And just because she pissed me off. Feral was the only way to describe it. If I'm scared of anything, it's that. What she does to me. How far she pushes me outside of the person I am.

Or maybe the person I want to be. Because I know one person who acted like that when challenged, and I'm a spitting image of his coronation portrait. I clench my fists hard enough that my nails draw blood.

That night, holding Kieran's arms, I made my choice. I decided I wanted to be king less than I wanted to stop hearing that door slam for the rest of my life. It used to haunt my dreams, echo in my thoughts every time I saw Father. When I turned on him, I said I wanted to be something more. Maybe this mess with Estrella is my chance to prove it.

Music leaks into the hallway as we approach the ballroom, and new smells are everywhere. Despite the late notice, at least half a dozen packs sent some representatives. Kieran thinks it's curiosity, but he doesn't mind that because he's going to prove them wrong. He really is going to be a different king than Father.

Fuck, maybe I should talk to Kieran. I don't know how he pulled the transformation off.

"Let's take this shit by storm." Baz pushes open the doors.

Inside, the ballroom is already half full. A page scrambles to announce us, but we blow past him. Baz splits off for a group of giggling girls from some new pack. I head for Kieran and Raven who are standing by the raised dais with the musicians.

'You're late,' Killian says.

'I was primping,' I deadpan.

Across the ballroom, I see him smirk.

'Primp faster next time,' he replies. *'The ceremony starts as soon as the Sundrop Gem contingent arrives.'*

I stop at their side. "And remind me what my job in the ceremony is?"

Raven puts a hand on her slightly swollen stomach and glances at Kieran. "To stand behind him and represent the future of Dun's Crossing."

There's an edge to her voice that makes me smile. She thinks she should have my job. Now, that's something I can understand.

"Silently?" I ask.

Kieran nods, but his eyes are on Raven like they're talking over mind-link. I scan the crowd instead. No sign of Estrella. A whole lot of signs of other women who haven't experienced my particular charms, but they don't hold their usual appeal. Even a redhead in an equally red, temptingly low-cut dress who would usually be my first target. This mating shit sucks.

The door opens again, and this time, the page is prepared. "From Sundrop Gem—"

I turn.

7

VERY FIRST PARTY

Tess stands behind me, pinning back sections of my hair in the setting sun. "I wish we'd been here longer already. I don't know any of their styles."

I frown at myself in the mirror. "I don't want their styles. I want ours."

"Isn't the point of this cultural exchange—" She catches sight of my expression and stops. "To show off the abilities of Sundrop Gem. Would you like braids?"

"Do we have enough time?" I look out the window of the chamber King Kieran gave me. It has a view over that wonderful forest of theirs, outlined bright orange as the sun sinks below it. We should've started this hours ago, but Tess and I have quickly learned that getting ready to get ready is just as much fun. My skin is silken after a perfumed bath, and every line on my complexion seems to have disappeared. Until the actual getting ready began, I was having a wonderful time.

But now, I can't forget what we're getting ready for.

"I think we will." Tess adjusts the pins so she only has one section of hair loose and begins braiding like the wind. "It's not as though they can start without the guest of honor."

I laugh. "I think that may be my father."

"It should be all of you." She shakes her head. "I don't understand the male supremacy here."

"It's strange to see how it affects the rest of their behavior." My mind drifts to the encounter in the hallway. I arrived at the location Father gave me breathless and out of sorts. I didn't even remember to ask him about leaving. All because I had the gall to come across Anwen in a hallway and ask him a few questions.

Tess raps the top of my head. "You're thinking about him."

"Apologies." I wince. "I don't mean to."

Her stern expression softens. "You can't help it. Do you remember how I was in the days after the Haze?"

"Yes." I groan, then say in a fluttery voice, "'I never realized how handsome Orion is. Have you seen him carry his sword? Have you seen his wolf? Have you seen his cock?'"

She laughs and swats me. "I did not sound like that! And I certainly did not ask if you'd seen his cock."

I shake my head very slightly. "I may as well have. You should have become a poet, Tess. Your description skills are unparalleled."

"Perhaps I still will, when you finally fill the position of hairdresser." She drops the first braid against my head.

"I've told you a thousand times that I can have others do this." I meet her gaze in the mirror.

"Never as well." She grins wryly. "And how else am I going to find space for myself in your busy schedule once you become Luna?"

"We have many years before we have to worry about that," I remind her.

Tess reaches around in the enameled box in which I packed all my hair things for travel for a few minutes before she finds the next pin. "Next time, a light would be very helpful."

I grimace. "I am certain it would be."

She looks at me. "Why are you making that face?"

"I did what you told me." I stare at my hands in my dressing-gowned lap. "I thought of the Haze, of the feeling it inspired, of the way the Goddess felt overhead. But I couldn't produce anything."

Tess hums. "Nothing? Not even a little spark or light?"

"No." My stomach sinks with the same shame I felt when experimenting under my covers last night. "Do you think I might not have any powers?"

"Nonsense." She tugs on my hair to make me tilt my head, and I obey. "You're a member of the royal family. There hasn't been a royal without powers in Sundrop Gem since… perhaps ever. If anything, I would guess this is because of the situation with Anwen."

My mate bite hurts every time I hear his name now, and the itching never abates. "That sounds like an opinion I would find in Dun's Crossing. Are you truly telling me you believe my powers are completely dependent on a man?"

She laughs. "Perhaps it's just a matter of timing."

"Perhaps." I open and close my hands a few times. If I were normal, I'd be able to light a whole room, or warm one. Instead, I can just stare at my useless hands. "Did your powers manifest immediately after the Haze?"

"Not immediately," she says in a way that tells me she's stretching the truth.

"How long?" I demand.

"About three hours," she admits. "But these things are never the same for everyone! And Orion and I didn't bother trying to deny the bond."

I groan. "I will have someone else finish my hair. I don't want to hear this again."

"I've got you captive now." She smiles mischievously. "I knew you'd want braids."

"Awful, awful friend." I shake my head just to mess her up.

"I only mean… well, you can feel it already, can't you? The mating bond?" she asks.

"I wish I could stop." I scratch the spot on my neck.

Tess knocks my hand away. "Don't. Every time you're with him, that stops, doesn't it?"

I shrug in frustration. "Sometimes, yes, but other times, he says something so horrible that it starts hurting all over again."

"When he says those things, it hurts him too." She steps around the front of my chair, between me and the mirror. "You can stop all of this."

"I will not force someone to be in my life, Tess." I cross my arms and look away from her. Tears well in my eyes. My heart aches even more than my mark. "If I tell my parents, they will tell King Kieran and Queen Raven, and within the week I'll be married to a man who hates me. I will not do that to myself."

She sighs. "You deserve better. I don't deny that. But the Goddess brought the two of you together for a reason, and I believe the only way you're going to find that reason out is if you force him to stop running away. You won't be able to resist the bond forever."

Someone knocks on the door. I scrub at my eyes as Tess goes to open it.

"Yoo-hoo, Estrella!" Nessa trills.

I turn around. The envoy's daughter twirls past Tess wearing another dress she said no one in Dun's Crossing liked, a rich, rusty orange that brings out the reddish undertones in her hair.

"You look wonderful," I say.

"Really?" She smooths down the skirt. "I've never even worn this one outside my room."

"Wonderful," I say resolutely. "Right, Tess?"

"I may be jealous of that color." Tess clasps her hands under her chin.

"Well, show me your dress," Nessa says.

I blink. Did she not hear Tess? Or is that another of those fast-talking Dun's Crossing customs that I'm not yet used to?

Nessa smiles warmly, and I realize it's silly to overthink. I stand and pull one of my favorite dresses from my trunk, a weaving pattern of purple, green, and yellow.

"Oh, you're going to look amazing." She touches the fabric. "And the braids are nice, but you're running low on time. Did somebody mess up your timing?"

"I did." I smile ruefully. "All your products tempted me."

"Apologies," she says a little teasingly. "But the half-head of braids might be cute. Can I try something?"

I shrug. I don't really want to be late.

Nessa pushes me back into the chair and begins pulling out the pins Tess was using to keep other sections of my hair aside.

"I'm going to go change," Tess says.

"Good luck!" I reply.

"Shush. You have to stay still." Nessa narrows her eyes critically as she adjusts, primps, pins.

Tess returns, but Nessa's too deep for me to look at her immediately. Behind me, I can hear Tess finishing her own getting ready alone. My chest aches a little, but Nessa's fluttering is so distracting that I can barely think of Anwen, so I let her continue.

Finally, she steps back. "Voila!"

The girl in the mirror looks like a strange blend of styles from home and those I've seen here. Nessa pinned the finished braids back along half my head, making me look almost as though I've shaved it, and left the other side loose in a waterfall of curls. The final effect is beautiful.

"Thank you," I breathe.

"Always." She dusts off her hands. "Now, hurry. We're running low on time."

I dress behind a privacy screen to hide my mark, and Tess helps me with the wrap. Nessa picks out a pair of shoes that I slide on without checking which they are, and we rush out of my room. Mother, Father, and Castor are already gone, likely waiting at the ballroom for me.

"I'll go ahead." Nessa winks. "You wouldn't want to create a political scandal by showing up with Snowcrest." She disappears down the hall.

"She is so thoughtful," I say.

Tess nods. "Ready for your very first party?"

"Ready for yours?" I grin.

She takes my hand, and we follow after Nessa.

8

GLOWING

Anwen

I look up the flight of stairs into the ballroom, my pulse hammering in my mating mark.

"Alpha King Isai and Luna Queen Suniva Sollabella," the page declares.

The king and queen appear in the doorway, smiling and waving, both of them dressed like they think any color they don't wear will disappear from the sky forever.

I squeeze my hands behind my back. They look good. I'm just—

"Princess Estrella Sollabella, and her companion, Tesandra!"

And there she is, like nothing I've ever seen before. Her gray eyes sparkle as she takes in the ballroom. The soft flush on her cheeks calls up fuzzy memories of the Haze. Her hair drapes over one shoulder, loose and curling like a new plant, like she wakes up in the morning looking like this. But the dress is what threatens to knock the breath out of my chest.

Around here, we mostly wear single shades, sometimes with a little embroidery. Estrella is a swirl of color and hue. Golds bring out

43

the warmth in her skin, purples turn her eyes luminous, greens harmonize with the other two and make her look like a work of art. The swaths of wrapped fabric highlight the plush curve of her hips, the soft swell of her breasts.

She curtsies then takes the arm of the woman next to her and hurries down the stairs.

'Pick your jaw up off the floor,' Kieran says wryly. *'Sleeping with her is only going to make a mess.'*

He has no idea how right he is.

Castor arrives, I assume, and I think I hear the page say something about Nessa, but I couldn't give less of a shit. Even with Kieran's warning ringing in my ears, I keep glancing at Estrella, talking to her parents across the ballroom. Then, it's time for the ceremony.

Kieran and I stand on the musicians' dais. Aylin, the holy woman, joins us, and so do King Isai and Estrella.

"The Moon Goddess rules many chambers of a shifter's heart," Aylin declares. "She gives us many gifts, but she also offers us the chance to stumble. A shifter's rage is often their greatest enemy, occasionally their greatest strength."

I glance at Estrella out of the corner of my eye. Up close, fuck, it's like she's glowing. My mouth waters.

"For too long, Dun's Crossing and Sundrop Gem have let their rage come between them." Aylin raises her arms. "Tonight, we celebrate the quiet of a new moon, the quiet of peace and friendship to come."

Kieran bows to King Isai, then holds out a bottle of whiskey. "In honor of the new moon, I offer you drink from our cellars, that you might never go thirsty."

Estrella looks at me, just for a second. As soon as she catches my gaze, her eyes go wide, and she turns back to her father. My mark pulses with want.

King Isai takes the wine, bows, and offers something folded in a brightly colored scarf. "In honor of the new moon, I offer you *aswore*, a bread my lady wife made in your kitchen, that you might never go hungry."

Kieran takes the bread.

"Now, partake of the others' gift, in view of those assembled, to show this is no mere promise but an oath to be honored," Aylin says.

King Isai uncorks the whiskey, and Kieran unwraps the *aswore*. Apparently, Queen Suniva made it recently enough that it's still warm. Its smell fills the air, and it has that same floral note as Estrella herself. Kieran rips off a piece and eats it, then offers one to me. It takes all my willpower not to devour the whole thing. The soft sweetness on my tongue reminds me so much of Estrella that I can't help but look at her.

With the bottle tipped to her lips, she meets my gaze and holds it. My pulse hammers in my ears. I have to have her. Once this ceremony is over, neither of us have any obligations. It would be easy to sneak off for a few minutes.

She finishes her pull and looks away from me. Aylin declares our houses forever reunited, says something about letting anger never separate us again, then proceeds off the center of the dais. I take a step forward, hoping we'll all follow her.

'Back the way we came,' Killian says.' *Apparently, it's bad luck to follow in the exact footsteps of a holy woman in Sundrop.'*

Fuck luck. Every fiber of my body screams for Estrella. I need to get to her before that moment between us fades.

But she's already walking after her father with her back to me, and there are a metric fuckton of dignitaries looking at me. I scowl at the floor and trudge after Kieran.

"I thought that went well," Raven says as we return to the floor.

I nod absently, scanning the thickening crowd for Estrella already.

"It's time for the first dance." Kieran puts his hand out to Raven. "My love?"

She takes it with a smile, and they leave.

Candace nudges me. "Do you think we're supposed to dance too?"

"With you?" I scoff. "If Kieran wants me to dance, he'd better let me pick my own partner."

Candace sighs. "Always wonderful talking to you, brother."

I wave her off and begin cutting through the crowd. All the

nobility worth knowing in Dun's Crossing are here, but there are more than enough strangers. It turns out if nearly a dozen packs send a couple of representatives, the place tends to get crowded.

"Prince Anwen!" Sybil, an Escurian woman I spent a brief night with, waves.

I'm about to brush her off when her mother, Luna Delaney's lady-in-waiting, steps up next to her. Even with Raven in the family, I can't forget the lessons Mother drilled into my head about who is acceptable to offend.

"Sybil." I bow deeply. "You honor us with your presence."

She curtsies, then puts her hand out for me to kiss. I oblige. Her mother smiles.

"I was just telling Mother how I wished we were here for the Haze." She flutters her eyelashes. "I heard you were not mated."

"Unfortunately not." My bite sears. "Perhaps next time."

Sybil doesn't take her hand back, and both women look at me expectantly. Hot frustration pours through my veins. I'm supposed to ask her to dance, with the taste of Estrella on my tongue.

"Will you come to the dance floor with me?" I grit out.

Sybil grins.

At the very least, Sybil is a half-competent dancer. The same is not true of Maia from Lilywind, to the east, or Ivy from Tansy Beach. All of them laugh in a register that grates on my ears and irritates me further. After them is the parade of Daniela, Gia, and Hope, all Dun's Crossing nobles or nobles-to-be that took our nights together far more seriously than I intended. I've been attending these balls for long enough that my feet usually don't hurt until the end of the night even if I spend the whole evening on the dance floor, but I think they must know how little I want to be here because they ache only an hour in. I make my apologies and head for the edge of the room where I'll hopefully be able to spot Estrella.

You look like someone asked you to walk over hot coals,' Baz says from somewhere else in the room. *'Loosen up, or the whole kingdom will know you're mated before we get to dinner.'*

I grimace. He's right. Asshole. I grab a glass of something alcoholic from a servant passing by with a tray and down it. The slight fuzz around my thoughts dampens Estrella's smell, reminds of me what really matters. This is a diplomatic event. And until the night ends, the most diplomatic thing to do, as always, is to make as many of the women in the room as possible think they have a chance with me. The more they believe it, the more they'll spill their secrets. I roll out my shoulders and throw myself into the party.

Paloma is a low-ranking noble from Whaleberry Harbor, and her father doesn't believe Dun's Crossing can change, but she's convinced after one dance with me. Nathalia of Redwood Nimbus is only here for the party, but her mother may have some sway with their Alpha, and she laughs at my jokes. Oakspring Dunes produces the lovely Lana, who believes in us even before our dance and is happy to inform me of their aging Luna. Apparently, she and the Alpha were never mated, so he may be looking for a new wife soon.

In the chaos, I pick up a scent. That wolf from the back woods the other day is here. The skin on the back of my neck prickles, but I force myself to relax before Noemi can notice in my arms. One of the packs probably just took a strange route to the castle. Very quickly. The music trills, calling for a spin, and I lose the scent in the crowd before I can even ask Lana to find out a little more.

The party wears on, and I allow myself another brief break from dancing. I'm leaning against the wall, nursing another drink and watching the crowd for any pack I haven't spoken to yet when I see her. Estrella. She's dancing with that woman she walked in beside, laughing as they both struggle with no one leading. My heart hammers.

Fuck it. I'm dancing with representatives of every pack. It would be strange if I avoided Sundrop Gem. I wait until she and the woman leave the dance floor, finish my drink, and stride over.

9

BEAUTIFUL

Tess laughs and pats my arm. "Now, you've shown everyone the real abilities of Sundrop."

"The real abilities to stumble all over each other?" I smile.

"Excuse me," someone says behind me.

I don't know who I think I'm kidding. I recognize Anwen's voice instantly, and even if I didn't, Tess's smile freezes on her face in a way that means it can only be him. I turn slowly.

My breath catches. In Sundrop, he would stick out like a sore thumb, but amidst the dour colors of Dun's Crossing, Anwen's all-black outfit is striking. It makes his pale features seem so much paler, like he's something plucked from the pages of a storybook rather than a real man standing in front of me.

"I'm glad to see you've learned some manners," I say, praying he can't hear the slight breathlessness to my voice.

Tess's grip on my arm tightens.

"Don't get used to it." He smiles teasingly.

Who is this man, and what has he done with the monster I've been avoiding these last two days? I've watched him flit from one she-wolf to the next like a bee gathering pollen, but he's never used this charm on me before. My wolf pants. Perhaps it's the night, the heat, and excitement of the party, but she's starting to make some sense.

"Estrella and I were just discussing leaving," Tess blurts. "We need to powder our noses."

I pat her hand on my arm. "But I've realized my nose is adequately powdered already. You can go without me, Tess."

'Are you sure?' she asks. *'If I leave you alone, I doubt you'll be able to resist each other.'*

'In a roomful of witnesses?' I raise an eyebrow at her. *'I believe I have more decorum than that, no matter what this bite does to my self-control.'*

Tess sighs but walks away without another word. Anwen watches her leave, then turns back to me.

"So, you have been avoiding me."

"After the stunt in the hallway?" I shake my head and wish I'd brought a fan to hide my expression. "You should be honored I'm not running from you now."

"You have my sincerest apologies for that." He sounds earnest. "In honor of the new moon, I was hoping to mend bridges."

I look him up and down, grabbing onto my self-control for all I'm worth. "And by that, you mean…?"

He swallows. "I mean that you look beautiful. And I'd like to dance with you before the night ends."

Nothing about the mating mark burning on my shoulder. Nothing about the fights we keep having. Nothing about the night we already spent together. I'd be a fool if I thought Anwen was offering anything more than a dance.

But the compliment sparkles through me like no one else's words have tonight, lighting up parts of my body that have lain quiet since the Haze. Perhaps, if I go into this with my eyes open, one dance can't hurt.

I hold out my hand, palm down, like I've seen the women of Dun's Crossing do when a man offers them a dance. Anwen grins, takes it, and brushes a kiss across my knuckles. His touch is like a lightning strike, and I never want to stop feeling it. He leads me onto the dance floor as a new waltz begins.

He moves with practiced, liquid grace. Somehow, he manages to twist the hand he's holding without an ounce of awkwardness, so we're properly positioned at the soft right angle Mother taught me on the ship ride over. His other hand, he slips around my waist, pulling me just a hair closer than propriety calls for. I place my palm on his right shoulder, and he spins us into the dance.

"Tell me," he says, "about *awore*."

I blink. "You want to ask me about bread? Now?"

"There's a flower in it." His grip on my waist tightens slightly, just enough that I can feel it through the layers of my dress. "I have to know what it is."

"Sweetcress," I answer. "But why?"

He dips me low and whispers in my ear, "Because you smell just like it."

My heart leaps into my throat as he pulls me up again. "You taste like that drink."

He smiles. "Is that why you looked at me?"

"I thought you wanted this kept a secret." I glance around at the packed dance floor. "We aren't exactly in private."

His gaze dips from my face to my chest. "We could be."

My body warms. My mark hums for the first time in days, and my wolf nearly screams for me to accept his offer. Perhaps, if I go into this with my eyes open—

Someone taps on Anwen's shoulder, and we both look up. Father stands there with a genial smile on his face and hard eyes.

"Mind if I cut in?" he asks.

Anwen glances at me, as if for permission. I am too busy trying to reclaim control over my wolf and pull myself back from what almost just happened to communicate anything to him.

"Certainly, Your Highness." Anwen releases me and steps back with a small bow. "Your daughter is an exquisite dancer."

He's being kind. If my disastrous galliard with Tess is anything to go by, our success on the dance floor was all due to Anwen's skill. But I can't say that with Father looking at me.

He offers Anwen a bow in return and steps into Anwen's place, holding me at the proper distance instead. Anwen melts into the crowd, and I struggle to quash disappointment I wish I didn't feel.

"I'm not surprised the prince sought you out," Father says. "You are particularly radiant this evening. You remind me of the portrait of my mother, in the east hall at home."

I smile. "You know that's my favorite one."

"Perhaps." He laughs. "Perhaps I'm merely honored to have such a wonderful daughter."

"Should I be worried?" I ask teasingly. "Usually, you only compliment me this much when there's a dull state dinner to attend."

"It does seem Dun's Crossing has mastered the not-so-dull state dinner at least." Father looks out over the crowd. "On the matter of the prince, though—"

"There's nothing between us," I say quickly. Pain lances through my mark.

"Of course." Father nods easily. "On the matter of men, then. Since we have now entered a world that has not always known the beautiful, smart young woman before me, I feel it bears saying that you should never accept anything less than worship."

"I'm sorry?" I frown up at him.

"You are the latest in a long, proud line, Estrella," he says. "If any young man does not fall at your feet, he's the fool. Do you understand?"

I meet his gaze and know that he knows. Hot shame washes through me, but he doesn't expect me to confess, not now. Father will wait until I'm ready, all while making the path ahead of me as easy as possible until I am.

"I love you," I say.

The song draws to a close. He smiles. "And I—"

Father lurches forward. Time seems to move in slow motion as we both look down.

A silver-tipped arrow juts out of his chest, at the center of a spreading red stain.

10

SCREAM

ANWEN

A SCREAM SPLITS THE AIR. IF I WASN'T ALREADY WATCHING ESTRELLA like a hawk, I would still look over just in time to see King Isai touch one finger to the arrow through the center of his chest, then slump. Estrella tries to catch him, but she's not strong enough to support his bulk, so they go to the floor together. Other nobles scatter back, ducking like such a perfectly placed arrow could be anything but an assassination.

'Who fired?' Kieran barks over mind-link. *'Find the shooter! Quickly!'*

I don't know if he's talking directly to me, but I know he relies on me for details like that. Still, I can't force my head to turn. My chest—my *heart* screams with pain like I was the one shot. Tears bead in the corners of my eyes, and I actually stagger. The mark pain, I could handle. It was nothing compared to what I've endured. But this? I have never hurt like this before, and I have no idea why it's happening.

Dun's Crossing soldiers slice through the parting crowd like knives. Handfuls of them trace the edges of the room, looking to the upper balcony I saw Estrella from only a few days ago. Others swarm around me, waiting for instructions.

I say the only thing I can manage. "To her."

They rush forward, and I let the wave of them carry me along. Every step I take closer, the pain lessens slightly. Just slightly.

I kneel across her father's body from Estrella. Her shoulders shake with sobs. Instincts pull me in a thousand directions. Touch her, take her hands, find the killer, protect her from another attack.

"This is too open." The words choke in my throat. "We need to move. Take King Isai, bring him to Fleming's room."

"No." Estrella's voice is ragged.

I blink. "What?"

"I said no." She looks up at me, the pain in my chest echoed in her gray eyes. "Find Mother. Find Castor. We're not going anywhere without them."

That goes against every inch of my training. Her mother and Castor are adults who can handle themselves. But I find myself saying, "You heard the woman. Locate the rest of the Sollabellas."

A few of the soldiers split off to search. The rest remain in a tight circle around us. A shield, in case the archer decides he didn't quite finish the job.

Looking at King Isai—which sends a fresh wave of pain tearing through my chest, though I barely knew the man—I can't imagine anyone thinking that. At least six inches of the arrow's shaft protrude from the front of his shirt, slick with blood. But even the blood can't disguise the distinctive shine of the tip. I can't know without touching it, but if I had to guess, I'd say it was pure silver. Overkill for an archer with this kind of aim. The silver wouldn't poison him like wolfsbane, but it would weaken his ability to defend himself, his natural healing. Father said silver weapons were for people who couldn't land a killing blow on their own, and that is obviously not true here. The king's face is ashen, and his eyelids flutter as he struggles to focus. Every movement sends more blood spreading across his chest.

"I'm sorry," I whisper. But I have no idea who I'm talking to.

The soldiers part, and Queen Suniva plunges to her knees next to her husband with a cry. Suddenly, I am in the way. I stand and back nearly into the circle of soldiers.

"Isai, please," the queen begs. "Hold on a moment longer. We can get you to a healer."

"Not until Castor's here," Estrella says savagely.

"Estrella—"

"I'm not arguing, Mother." She takes her father's hand and holds it so hard her knuckles turn ashen.

My chest aches with an echoing hurt. When Father died, everything moved so quickly. We had to run for the castle before news or escaping soldiers reached Mother. I sent everyone ahead and lingered for a single moment. If I buried him, I would never catch up, and in that moment, I thought I might have to save Mother's life. Maybe even Candace's, Finn's, or Ingrid's. But under an empty sky, an uncaring moon, I whispered a single prayer to the Goddess to keep him until we could bury him properly. I wanted one last moment with my family all together.

His body was gone by the time I went back for it. I understand Estrella's desperation all the same.

The soldiers part again, and Castor, looking alive for the first time, stumbles in and falls next to Estrella.

"I was in the hall," he whispers. "I didn't—"

"We have to move him," I say. "Now or never."

Queen Suniva smiles softly down at her husband. "I'm afraid, Prince Anwen, that we have already arrived at never. There's nothing your healer could do for him now."

Estrella closes her eyes, and fresh pain tears through me like the news devastates me. I stare at her. Am I… feeling her pain? But how?

Castor makes a choking sound like he's trying not to cry. "I'm sorry."

"You didn't know," Queen Suniva says. "We all wish we'd done something different."

She's not talking to me, but the words resound. Estrella is my mate. I should've been with her, protecting her and her loved ones, not flirting my way through a party to keep up appearances. Maybe I'll never be the man she deserves. Maybe it's too late for me. But I owe it to her to try.

"Father," Estrella says. Despite the terror and sadness of this moment, despite the screaming nobles around us and the sinking feeling I'm intruding, she looks golden. "We're all here. We love you."

"I—" King Isai coughs and spits up a mouthful of blood.

I wince. Queen Suniva is right. It's over.

"We love you," Estrella repeats.

She is beautiful even in her despair, like a single ray of sunlight has found her. Then, the ray of sunlight collects around her hands. I'm not imagining it or seeing something I want to see. Castor jerks his head up to stare at his sister. Queen Suniva's mouth falls slightly open. The golden glow increases, brighter and brighter, until it's like standing next to a tiny sun cupped in Estrella's hands.

"We love you," she says a final time, and the glow fades out. She opens her eyes.

King Isai coughs again, and his eyes flutter open. Pain pinches his brow, but his gaze looks mostly clear. What?

"Wh—" He glances around at his loved ones, then back at the arrow in his chest. "Ah. It seems the Goddess is calling me home."

"Don't say that, Isai," Queen Suniva murmurs. "If we have another moment, we can—"

"—say our goodbyes properly, my heart." His gaze is soft on her, but certain. Like Estrella, he is not to be argued with now. "I will love you until you join me in the stars, and for eternity after that. To be allowed to spend as many years as I have in your presence is my greatest blessing."

Queen Suniva lets silent tears fall down her cheeks. "And if I do not find you waiting, I will chase you through the sky."

"I would expect nothing less." He smiles and looks at Castor, near his feet. "My boy. I know this world stage has been unkind to you so far, but do not let them delude you into thinking you have no role to play in our future. You may not lead the pack, but you have a warrior's heart and an advisor's instincts. Help your sister, and never forget that you come from the same noble blood."

Castor makes that choking noise again and stares at his father's ankles. "Yes, Father. Of course."

"Estrella." King Isai says her name like that alone is a treasure, and I've never agreed with another man more. "The greatest pain of a parent, especially a royal one, is knowing that they are raising their children in preparation for their own death. I have spent your whole life training you for this moment, and my dear, I have never been less afraid for our future. You inherited your mother's heart. Love our people. I like to think you inherited my stubbornness." He smiles. "Stand beside them, no matter what comes. The rest, you will figure out along the way."

Estrella crumples in on herself with a sob. I feel like I've been stabbed through the gut. Even Father's death didn't hurt like this.

King Isai hacks up another splatter of blood. "I will see you in the stars."

He slumps like a puppet with his strings cut, and I know it's over. Queen Suniva wraps her hands over Estrella's. Castor slams a fist into the ground. It's like nothing exists outside the bubble of safety the soldiers carved out for them. My body burns, but I keep looking at Estrella.

The king was dead already. I knew it, and so did Queen Suniva. So what the hell did Estrella do with that light?

11

LUNA QUEEN

MY HEART STOPPED IN THE MOMENT FATHER'S DID. I HAVE A VAGUE AND distant sense of being moved—someone says Father may be crushed if we don't—but no idea where I'm being sent. The noise of the ballroom dampens. There's less screaming, or at least, less outside of my head.

Father is dead. Not half an hour ago, I was dancing with him. And now, he's a body on a slab. That's the only way to describe the surface the soldiers place him on. A plank of wood, like a bed stripped of all its dressings. There's nowhere to hide on the slab, nothing to disguise the chilling stillness of his body. Mother stands over him, weeping and stroking his face. Castor sits on the ground with his back against the legs of the slab. I have no idea what I'm doing, other than staring at them.

Father is dead. I am dead.

"Shit. I forgot—Father said I had to—" Castor closes his eyes and takes a deep breath. "As the eldest nonheritable Sollabella, I embrace the duty of announcement. Alpha King Isai Sollabella has taken his

61

place among the stars. I introduce to the world Dowager Luna Suniva Sollabella and"—he opens his eyes and meets my gaze—"Luna Queen Estrella Sollabella of Sundrop Gem."

My stomach drops to my toes. The rest of the room ratchets into sharp focus. Bottles of herbs and other, stranger things line the walls. Soldiers stand at attention throughout the room, especially at the door. Not just soldiers. Dun's Crossing soldiers. Men belonging to the pack that let this happen.

And among them, talking quietly to the group at the door, is Anwen. My unwilling mate who nevertheless saw fit to insert himself into the deepest grief of my life.

I stand—it seems I sat on the floor at some point—and curtsy. "Thank you, brother. I accept this responsibility with a heavy heart. And as my first act as Luna, I demand answers from the crown prince of Dun's Crossing."

Anwen turns. "I am working on getting those, Estrella."

"Your Majesty," I snap.

He blinks. I watch his gaze trail from my face to Father's body and back again. Finally, he bows. "Apologies, Your Majesty."

"That's insufficient," I snarl. All that dead numbness burns away into some emotion too intense to name. "We came here at your behest. The rules of hospitality dictate our safety is your responsibility. What do you have to say for yourself?"

Anwen straightens. "I would say that, while I am crown prince of Dun's Crossing, I do not answer for the whole pack. For that, you want my brother."

"I don't want your brother." I take a step closer to him, ignoring the way the front of my dress pulls stickily at my skin. "He's not here. You are, *Your Highness*, and I demand answers from you."

He meets my gaze steadily. "I've told you all I know, Your Majesty. What further answers to do want from me?"

Behind me, I can feel Castor and Mother staring. I am making a scene, disturbing Father's deathbed like I used to disturb his sleep. But it's not as if he'll awaken now. I have nothing to lose but the respect of a few men whose opinions I couldn't care less about.

I step closer to Anwen, and he backs up. The soldiers part for him without a word.

"I want to know who did this," I say coldly. "I want to know why."

"We're pursuing those answers, but wanting them doesn't make them readily available," he replies.

Another step closer. Anwen opens the door and lets me chase him into the hall. The storm of emotions in my chest whirls on, unabated.

"Then tell me who let this happen," I demand. "Tell me how in the Moon Goddess' light did your people—did you miss an assassin intent on my father's life. Was this the plan all along? Did your precious brother pen the initial letter always intending to end up here?"

"If you'd just *listen*—"

"No!" My voice breaks, but I plunge onward. "I am Luna Queen of Sundrop Gem. I will spend the rest of my life listening. But right now, Prince Anwen of losing your title to an unborn baby, you will listen to me." I poke him in the chest, and he takes a final step away, his back hitting the wall of the empty hallway. "My father is dead, and you are going to tell me who's responsible."

Fire flickers in Anwen's eyes, but for once, he doesn't unleash it on me. Instead, he simply says, "I can't."

The storm of emotions explodes from my chest, and I throw myself at him with no idea what I'm going to do when I reach him. Perhaps no one is more surprised than me when I crush my mouth onto his, lapping up the taste of mint and whiskey I've been craving.

Anwen grabs my shoulders and pulls me off. Hot shame burns through me. I'm so foolish. No, I need a stronger word than that. He doesn't want me, he may be part of a plot to kill my father, and I'm throwing myself at him. Of course, he would reject me.

He swipes a thumb across my cheek, and wetness smears. Part of me wonders when I started crying.

"Come with me." He takes my hand and begins pulling me down the hall toward a low cacophony of voices.

I'm going to look into the matter myself, I tell Mother and Castor. *You will know what I do.*

Before we reach the voices, Anwen leads me into a passage behind a tapestry which releases us into an empty hall I've never seen before. For a moment, I consider that Anwen is actually part of the plot, that he's pulled me away from my family to kill me next. Then, he opens a door and pulls me into an obviously unused bedchamber.

"The staff keeps a private room ready in case a member of the royal family ever needs it." He pulls me in and kisses me before I can ask anything else.

This time, when my dress sticks to me, I can't ignore it. A sob bursts from my lips.

Anwen pulls back. "Is this not—" He looks down at the bodice of my dress, where I can't look but know he'll see it stained bright red. "Turn around."

Following his orders is easier than thinking. He runs his fingers along the neck, clearly looking for the line of neat buttons I've seen on Dun's Crossing dresses. Still weeping, I grab one of his hands and put it on the last fold of my gown. He fidgets for a few moments, then manages to loosen the end.

My wolf howls, and I seize onto her wants. She can fall into his touch. She can let it swallow me whole.

My world narrows to the tips of Anwen's fingers as he traces the line of the folds. He's warmer to the touch than his icy demeanor suggests, and he's careful with my gown. Careful and decisive. With each tug, more and more of it falls away, becoming the length of fabric it truly is. His scent fills my nose. My mate, my one and only.

The silken fabric slides from my body, now little more than a loincloth. Crisp air whisks through the window and snarls in the cooling wetness remaining on my stomach. All that remains of Father.

My wolf slinks away, leaving me to myself.

Anwen sucks in a sharp breath, and I expect him to keep touching me. Instead, he shucks his jacket and black shirt, baring his chest, and wipes at the wetness. There's no doubt in his movements, just calm. I only know it's done when the air across my stomach feels the same as it does everywhere else.

I shove my hands into his hair and kiss him.

Now, in private, he responds hungrily. His teeth tear at my lower lip, his hands grope every inch of my bare body. My wolf roars back, and I throw myself at him. For every dazzling spark of pain he deals, I offer him one in return. I claw down his back, pull on his hair, bite him as he bites me. He hardens against me.

This is nothing like the Haze. I am completely present. Here, and now, and nowhere else.

I yank the final fold of my dress, and the fabric tumbles to the floor. Anwen growls into my mouth, then runs his hands down my back and lifts me by the underside of my thighs. I wrap my legs around him and rock against the ridge of his bare chest. Sweet friction.

He tosses me down on the bed, but he's on me before I even have a moment to miss him. He puts his teeth to my neck, and bright spots of aching pain bloom in his wake. Bruises, like the ones Tess sports after her nights with Orion. Anwen isn't being careful anymore.

That thought threatens to send me crashing from the bliss of his touch, and that's unacceptable. I shove my hand between my legs like he did that first night and try to find the spot that made me see stars. Anwen chuckles against my throat, scrapes my teeth over my mark. Until now, I didn't even notice it had stopped hurting.

"Here." He takes my fingers and guides them to a soaked nub of flesh.

I arch up into him with a moan as we make contact. Instinct takes over. I circle the nub in time with Anwen's racing heartbeat, pounding through his chest into mine. He drops his mouth to my breasts and wrings noises I've never heard before from my lips. Seconds turn to minutes, turn to days in that space.

"I think you're ready," he murmurs against my skin.

I nod. Anything that gets me more of him, that takes me higher, I want. He unbuckles his pants and drops them. The scent of him doubles, triples, and my mouth waters. Someday, I'll taste him. For now, his cockhead brushes over my knuckles as he lines up with my entrance.

He meets my gaze and sinks in. There's a tiny ache, barely noticeable between the other marks he's left and the throbbing heart I'm ignoring. And then pure pleasure. I have never felt more whole, more right, than when Anwen hilts himself inside me.

I roll my hips against his, begging, and he obliges. Shameless moans pour from my lips. I sharpen the tips of my nails and claw at him again, pulling him closer, lapping up his pleased hisses. Pleasure threatens to overwhelm me, to swallow me whole, and I throw myself into it.

His name is on my lips when I come. Mine is on his a moment later. But as the high fades, my heart takes up its ache all over again.

12

SATISFACTION

ANWEN

I BLINK AWAKE THE NEXT MORNING, SORE AND SCRAPED. FOR A SECOND, I stare at the ceiling, trying to remember who I fought. Then, someone shifts in the bed beside me, and everything snaps into place.

The assassination of King Isai. Estrella yelling at me. Falling into bed with her. And collapsing into sleep afterward without exchanging a word. A fuzzy corona of dark brown hair sticks out above the blankets, promising she's still there. I smile.

Last night complicated everything, I'm sure. She's Luna now, and I don't know if Sundrop has some extra traditions or rules about a Luna's mate. But all I can think about is the moment when she came at me, yelling, putting me down, and I didn't take the bait. I didn't snap back. I ignored all the voices in my head screaming that she couldn't talk to me like that and became the person she needed me to be.

If I can do that, there's no point in avoiding telling the world we're mates. Estrella is mine, and I need everyone to know it. I brush a lock of hair off her forehead.

She stirs, then shoots up, her eyes wild. I jump back to avoid knocking our heads together and barely stay on the mattress.

"Hey," I say softly. "I'm here. You're all right. You're in a private room in the east wing of the castle."

Estrella blinks a few times, and I take the opportunity to marvel at her in the morning light. Her gray eyes shine. One of the pillowcases left a jagged dent in her cheek that my fingers itch to smooth. A trail of purplish bruises in the shape of my mouth decorate her neck. She's just as beautiful as she was when she entered the ballroom.

And I don't even think the fact that she's topless is most of it.

She shakes her head. "Hours have passed. The sun is up. What have your men learned?"

I frown. "I haven't checked in yet. I thought we could—"

"Please check in." Her voice is sharp, tight.

"Of course." A milder protective instinct surges, reminding me I never want to be the one making her feel like that. Any conversation about our mating can wait until she's less upset.

'Baz?' I call across the mind-link.

Kieran assigned me to lead the chase on the trail a few soldiers picked up last night while Taner searched the castle. When it became clear I couldn't make myself leave Estrella, I asked Baz to chase it in my stead. He's a gray wolf, so he'll have a better chance of following the trail with his nose anyway.

'Took you long enough,' he replies. *'I was starting to think we should circle back and make sure a second assassin hadn't gotten you.'*

'It's barely after sunrise, you big baby.' I struggle not to roll my eyes with Estrella looking at me. Somehow, I doubt she'll appreciate that I'm irritated with Baz's antics and nothing more. *'What have you found?'*

'Less than I'd hoped. The fucker is fast, and he's smart.'

Swallowing my grimace is another fight. Luckily, the one useful skill Father taught me was hiding my expressions. *'Smart how?'*

'He peeled out of the ballroom, shifted, and only using hallways big enough for a wolf, found the royal escape tunnels.' Baz sighs over mind-link. *'I hope he's smart. Otherwise, he's damned well-informed.'*

The insinuation shivers up my spine. *'None of us had anything to do with this.'*

'Of course not,' Baz answers easily. *'Just strange. I thought nobody outside the palace knew about the tunnels. Anyway, I've still got the trail. We're on his ass, headed west. I'll report in when I know more.'*

'Thanks.' I look at Estrella, and that information doesn't seem like enough. Quickly, I reach out to Taner. *'Did you find anything?'*

'Nothing,' my brother's Beta replies. *'Suspiciously nothing. No bow, no quiver, not even a feather. The closest we've got to a clue is the arrow in King Isai's chest, and the family's not letting anyone near him yet.'*

'Dammit.'

"Well?" she asks. "If you're talking this much, there must be something."

I take her hands. "We've got people on the assassin's trail."

Her face falls. "So you don't have him."

"Not yet." I squeeze her hands. "But we've got our best men on this. Preliminary findings indicate the assassin was smart, so this wasn't some impulse killing. He took all his weaponry with him, and we don't yet know how he got in, but he got out using secret passages under the castle for royals to escape if we are attacked."

She pulls her hands back. "It sounds as though you're attempting to dress your grandmother up as a bride."

I blink. "What?"

"It's an idiom." She flips her hand dismissively. "I mean to say you have nothing, and you're pretending otherwise."

I swallow. In that moment of hesitation, a lance of pain rips through my chest, nowhere near my mark. I put my hand to it.

"Did you feel that?" I ask.

"Feel what?" She frowns.

"The pain." I rub my chest. "As if someone stabbed my heart."

Estrella stiffens, which has the lucky side effect of putting her breasts even more on display. Her expression tells me now is not the time to be thinking like that.

"Are you asking me if learning you've utterly failed to find my father's killer is painful?" she asks icily.

I shake my head. "I'm asking why—"

Thunderclouds gather on her brow. Maybe I'm better off not trying to solve the mystery of feeling her so intensely right now. Which means it also isn't the time to bring up the glowing incident.

"I apologize." I drop a kiss on her bare shoulder, scant inches from her mark where I know the skin will be tender. "I'll think before I say these things in the future."

Estrella leans away, and my mark aches.

"What?"

"Last night was…." She bites her lip. "Do you understand that I am the Luna of Sundrop Gem now?"

"Yes." I frown slightly, trying to understand. "You were quite clear about that, Your Majesty."

My teasing doesn't make her smile. She slides out of bed, gloriously naked in the morning sun. "So you understand that the situation has changed."

"What situation?"

"This situation." She gestures to the two of us, our marks. "The matter of us being mated."

"I agree!" I sit up. "You were right about me, but after last night, I—"

"Anwen," she says as gently as if she's talking to a child.

My stomach drops. I know that tone. I've used that tone on the dozens of nameless women that have passed through this bed before. It's the *I had a wonderful night* tone, the *I'm just not ready* tone.

"No." I cross my arms. "I was wrong to try to keep this a secret. We can't go back now. Goddess, look at your neck! You can't even walk through the castle without someone seeing those."

She grits her teeth, then turns to a polished bronze mirror on the wall. After a few minutes of inspection, she turns back with a sigh.

"I would be lying if I claimed to be pleased about those, but I own scarves." She shakes her head. "I don't know how to be clearer, Anwen. Sundrop Gem demands satisfaction from Dun's Crossing, and as Luna, I am Sundrop Gem."

My temper slips my grasp for a moment. "You could try not speaking in riddles."

"You're being childish," she replies. "This was your idea, don't you remember?"

"What was?" I demand. "I want to hear you say it."

"Hiding our marks." She meets my gaze steadily, and no hint of the pain she felt over her father sparks in my chest. "Denying that we're mates."

"I want to change my mind now," I say.

Hanging in empty air, it sounds exactly as childish as she claimed. I scowl.

"Perhaps princes have that luxury, but I am queen, and I intend to act like it." Estrella straightens. "Do we understand each other?"

I understand perfectly. I just feel like my skin is about to boil away into nothingness and leave the flesh underneath behind.

"What if I disobey, Your Majesty?" I ask.

"Then there will be war," she says simply.

That hits me like a blow without any of the magical force I've been enduring. War. Looking at her, naked and fearless, I don't doubt for a second that she would keep that promise. No matter how stupid a thing my mouth is to go to war over. I thought she wasn't stupid.

She lifts her chin a fraction higher, as if convincing herself of something, and I realize she isn't stupid. She wouldn't risk Sundrop over me. But she would risk Sundrop over this assassination attempt.

Estrella thinks Dun's Crossing was involved. Or that we might have been. That's why she's walking away, so she doesn't have to bear the shame of being mated to her father's killer.

A bright, beautiful path back to her illuminates in front of me. I squash my temper into a box—into a cage—and smile. "I understand. Rest assured, Your Majesty, I will be helming the investigation from here on out, and I won't rest until your father's killer is brought to justice. For now, there are spare dresses in the wardrobe."

Estrella peers at me, clearly wondering about my change of heart, but walks over to the wardrobe anyway. I take a deep breath. Now, all I need to do is prove my mate wrong.

13

ON ICE

ESTRELLA

I SCRATCH AT THE SECOND PLAIN, SHAPELESS DUN'S CROSSING DRESS I've worn in four days and try not to cry. My gown lies on the floor of that ridiculous room Anwen took me to, and as much as I'll miss it, I think I'll be happier if I never see it again. My scalp aches from leaving the braids and pins in all night. The soreness between my legs makes it impossible to forget what I did.

'Strella?' Tess calls. *'Your mother said you were looking into things, but I'm starting to worry. Just tell me you're not dead.'*

I swallow against a lump in my throat. My heart still feels like a dead thing in my chest, like it stopped beating with Father's. In some ways, I'm grateful for that. If it weren't frozen, I might have to deal with what just happened with Anwen.

The soft, fragile hope in his pale eyes claws at my still chest. It doesn't hurt any more than the mark on my shoulder, than the sinking feeling I've just left my mate for the last time. Tess will never understand. But I know what she's truly asking.

'I am alive,' I reply.

'Thank the Goddess,' she breathes. *'Have you learned anything?'*

That I cannot trust anyone here. That the Goddess has a cruel sense of humor. That Sundrop Gem is about to have its first unmarried Luna in a century.

'Nothing worth sharing.'

'All right.' She pauses carefully. *'Your mother and Castor are going to spend the day in your mother's chambers, if you find a moment to come by.'*

I let that message hang, unanswered. I have no idea where I am in this castle. And if I return to my family, I'll have to explain the dress, my absence, the sick nausea of everything Anwen told me. I'll have to take on the duties of Luna and lead my people.

The tiny handful of them here.

Last night, I manifested some magic. It washed through me with the Goddess' gentle warmth, just like Mother and Father always said it would. But instead of producing light or heat, I bought Father another few minutes, the minutes he needed to say his goodbyes. I've never heard of a power like that, but if it can restore things, I need it now more than ever.

I squeeze my hands into shaking fists, just like I did last night. No glow.

"We love you," I whisper.

No glow.

I clench my fists until my still-sharp nails draw blood from my palms. No glow. No feeling of the Goddess guiding me. Nothing. Whatever magic I held is gone.

Just like Father.

Footsteps echo off the walls ahead of me, and my heart hammers. I need to hide. No one can see the Luna like this. But I look around and find myself in a featureless hallway, without even a tapestry to duck behind like a child. I scrub my eyes and hope.

Nessa rounds the corner and sees me. "Oh, hon."

That breaks me. Everything hurts, and I am lost, and I am alone except for this strange girl who has been nothing but kind to me. Tears sheet down my face.

Nessa closes the distance between us and wraps her arms around me. "Just let it out."

My shoulders shake with ugly sobs, and Nessa simply strokes my frizzing hair. We stand there, entwined, until my tears dry up.

She pulls back and looks at me. "You stayed in my room all night."

I blink. "What?"

"I know that dress, hon." She strokes a few curls off my face. "So does half the castle. Which means you're going to come with me, get changed, and we're going to tell everyone you stayed in my room after Prince Anwen was needed for the investigation."

My cheeks burn. I had my suspicions, watching Anwen at the ball, but Nessa doesn't need to say another word to confirm every one. I don't even know if that room is kept for royalty in need, or just for Anwen to bed women he's too ashamed to bring to his royal bedchamber.

"Thank you," I say.

"You've been through enough." Nessa takes my hand and begins leading me through the palace.

Like Anwen, she takes a series of back routes and hidden passage-ways. Every time we hear voices, she knows the exact room to duck into for a moment of peace. We don't see a soul on the way to her room, for which I'm grateful. The soft pressure of her hand keeps me teetering on the edge of collapse in a way I know a Luna should not be.

Finally, she pulls me into her room. It's set up very much like mine—a few seats around a fireplace, a bed, a separate washroom—but it's smaller, less luxurious.

She nods to a door on the far wall. "That leads to Father's room. I think he's actually with your family, so there shouldn't be much to worry about, but it's way less soundproof than the rest of this place."

"With my family?" I eye the door and drift away.

"Mm-hmm." She opens a wardrobe to reveal a wide array of dull earth tones and a few bright ones at the end. "The Solbergs are running themselves ragged after the assassin, so in honor of King

Andri, Father took it upon himself to ensure you had company as well as an army."

I sink to the couch. "An army."

"That's sort of how the Solbergs solve problems," Nessa says. "Action first, emotions never."

I blink and turn to her. "It seems as though most of the normal diplomatic conventions have collapsed, so I'll just ask. At the breakfast, there seemed to be something between you and the king and queen."

"You're a little shorter than me, so I'm going to have to put you in one of my summer dresses. The winter ones will crumple right up," she says as though she didn't hear me.

"Nessa." I try to sound as important as this suddenly feels. "I am asking you as a friend, not as Luna of Sundrop Gem. I need to know more about our gracious hosts, and I suspect few others in this castle would tell me the truth."

She sighs and pulls a faintly purplish-gray dress from her wardrobe. "I don't like talking about this."

"And I apologize for asking." My eyes water. "But my father lies dead. I need to know."

"You can change behind that screen, if you like." She gestures to a folding screen, then pulls down the high neck of her dress to reveal four thin, jagged scars in a row. "Blanca—Queen Raven, as you know her—can control animals. Once, we were having a disagreement, and she sicced a cat on me. It nearly tore my throat open."

I gape. To have scars like that, as a shifter, Nessa must've been gravely injured. Or she wasn't allowed to see the royal healer and receive treatment.

She pulls her gown back into place. "But, truly, that was one incident. Queen Raven has very rarely attacked me since. Go, change."

I take the dress and duck behind the screen. "Very rarely?"

"There was a small encounter, following the coup against King Gavin," Nessa says reluctantly. "We never got along, and Queen Raven was enjoying her new power. She...blew me down a hallway. Told me never to bother her again or to leave the palace if I couldn't."

"Blew you?" I strip off Anwen's dress and pull Nessa's on over my head. "Does she have weather magic as well?"

"Powerfully," Nessa agrees.

I swallow sudden worry. Rumors of Escuro reached Sundrop Gem, but I had no idea what we were really dealing with. Mother has some magic, simple weather prediction and plant control from her original pack, and Castor hasn't come of age yet. We are outmatched, even though Dun's Crossing has no innate magic.

"And King Kieran." I step out from behind the screen. "He allows this?"

"He didn't used to." Nessa's smile wobbles at the edges. "When he realized the Moon Goddess led him to a woman he believed to be his sister, he spoke to me. Before the Haze, everyone expected—" She shakes her head like she can't say the words. "Well, I accepted the offer. It wasn't true love, but I thought we'd be happy together."

"And he turned on you." I cross the room to Nessa and pat her shoulder. I was right to warn Father. It seems the rumors of a new day in Dun's Crossing have been greatly exaggerated.

Nessa sniffs. "I'm sorry, I don't want to unload on you. You have enough going on right now."

"Perhaps it's the Luna in me speaking, but it's somewhat peaceful to immerse myself in other's problems." I offer her a soft smile. "If only for a moment."

She smiles back. "Thanks. But come on, your family is waiting."

* * *

In the bedchamber Mother and Father shared before last night, Castor sits on a couch in front of the fireplace, just staring into the flames. Tess and her father, Cristofer, stand against a wall like it's the only thing holding them up. Mother, still in her dressing gown, perches on the edge of the bed. Only Tess looks over when Nessa and I walk in.

'Are you all right?' she asks.

I nod to her then address the room.

"Apologies. I spent the night with Nessa after the investigation called Prince Anwen away, and I forgot to inform you." The lie burns slightly on my tongue.

"You scared me terribly," Mother says in a wispy voice I've never heard before. "You can't do that, Estrella. Not now."

My gut churns. I should have warned them.

"Do you know anything?" Cristofer asks dully. As my father's Beta, he'll be feeling the loss almost as intensely as Mother, Castor, and me.

"Not much." I tell them everything Anwen told me, but as if I learned it last night.

The room greets my meager revelations with silence. I don't truly know what else I expected.

"Where is Father?" I ask. "We have to prepare his body for burial before the journey home if he is to survive it intact."

Castor stands. His gray eyes look haunted, and dark bags speak to his sleepless night. "You were gone. Mother and I spoke with the envoy, Floyd Winters. As a Snowcrest Canyon wolf, he has offered to keep Father's body stable until the investigation concludes."

"Father's very good with his ice magic," Nessa says. "He'll make sure the king doesn't degrade from time or the ice itself. You'll be able to return him to the Goddess as cleanly as if he'd died the night before, no matter how long it takes."

Ice magic. Somewhere in this castle sits my frozen father, suspended as unnaturally as he'd been killed.

I look at my brother. "What are you saying, Castor?"

"We're not leaving until Father's murder is solved." His eyes burn with a hollow fire. "Until we get justice."

His words reignite the fire I felt staring at Anwen this morning and last night. Father deserves better. Sundrop Gem deserves better.

"I agree." I square my shoulders. "Do you have a culprit in mind?"

Castor grimaces. "Yes."

14

RESPONSIBILITY

KIERAN PACES BACK AND FORTH IN FRONT OF THE THRONES, HIS ROYAL robes flapping in a wind he's creating, a habit we both picked up from Father. The Sollabellas called a meeting with him to discuss the events of the ball last night, and Raven is too ill to do more than sit up in bed, so he asked me to join him. I fidget with my shirt, trying to stop it from scratching over the claw marks Estrella left behind. If I can't feel them, it's easier not to think about her.

"Last night was our first statement to the world," Kieran says. "Our first shot to declare that we're different from Father."

Your first shot, I almost say. Judging by most of the conversation I overheard last night, the rest of the kingdoms consider Kieran an outlier and hold the rest of us in suspicion. Raven is the only reason he's getting the chance he is.

"It needed to go perfectly." He stops and looks at me. "Instead, another king's blood stains our floors."

"I didn't kill him," I say automatically. Does everyone in this castle think I'm guilty?

79

Kieran shakes his head. "I'm not saying that. And when somebody else asks you, answer a little slower. You sound defensive."

I grit my teeth and clamp down on my temper. He's dealing with the humiliation of having failed with the world's eyes on him.

And I'm dealing with the humiliation of being rejected by my mate. Somehow, I think my mark's burn has gotten more potent. Or it just feels more personal, now that I want something else.

"I brought you here because there can be no mistakes in how we handle the rest of this," he says.

"So stand back, listen, report." I flip him a salute. "Heard and—"

"No."

"What?" I shake my head like I might've heard him wrong.

"I have to run the kingdom," Kieran says. "It's mostly paperwork and dull activities, but if it doesn't get done, the kingdom comes crumbling down around us. I can't lead this investigation and do that. And with the lingering confusion in the army after Father's death, Taner can't devote himself to it either."

Realization starts to sink in. "You want me to lead it?"

"And make the Sollabellas happy. It may have been irritating when we were younger, but you have an ear for things people don't want heard in this castle." Kieran finally sits on his throne, like the motivation driving him to pace was offering me this chance. "You're smart, when you apply yourself, and worse than that, you're clever. I think it's time you were given a chance to put that to better use than dicking around with Baz."

I blink. This is what I've been waiting for my whole life. The king —admittedly, I always imagined Father—looking at me and saying I have something to offer the kingdom more than a fallback Alpha. Something fizzes behind my ribcage in a way that makes me shift uncomfortably.

The phrase "make the Sollabellas happy" rings in my ears. I always intended to chase every lead in this investigation to its fullest, but Kieran is offering me something bigger. Something that will put me in direct proximity to Estrella constantly until this is over. For now, they may be the Sollabellas, but she's the real power in the group.

Luna Queen of Sundrop Gem. If I'm making reports to anybody, it'll be her.

"Well?" Kieran says. "I sort of expected you'd be kissing my feet by now."

I roll my eyes. "In your dreams. But I do… appreciate this."

He leans back like the matter is settled. For all he's changed, he has more of Father's mannerisms than he'd probably admit. "Wonderful. I didn't exactly have a second choice. Now, in terms of next steps—"

A trumpet blasts, and the door to the throne room swings open. Estrella, resplendent in a new dress that reminds me of the strip of fabric I unwound from her last night, leads her mother and brother into the room. Kieran straightens. I step up onto the dais with him but don't take the throne next to his. That belongs to Raven, whether she's here or not.

Estrella stops just past a respectful distance from the thrones, a subtle insult and insinuation of her rank, then curtsies. "Good morning, Your Majesty, Your Highness."

Kieran inclines his head. "I hope you've had as good a morning as you can. Please accept my condolences on behalf of the Solbergs and all of Dun's Crossing for your loss."

Castor scowls at that. Queen—Dowager Luna–Suniva simply stares at a spot between the two thrones like she's only half here. Estrella won't look at me.

"They are noted," she says. "First, we have an announcement."

Castor clears his throat. "Introducing Luna Queen Estrella Sollabella and Dowager Luna Suniva Sollabella, of Sundrop Gem."

"I wish I could offer you congratulations on your ascension." Kieran stands and bows, then sits again. "Instead, I offer any help you wish during this difficult transition."

"My entitlement is merely a matter of statecraft at this time," Estrella says. "Until we return to Sundrop Gem, and I undergo the coronation ceremony, the magic will not recognize me."

"When do you intend that return to be?" Kieran asks.

Castor clenches his jaw. Some expression flickers across Estrella's face and away again, too quickly for me to read, but the stab of pain in my chest tells me the question isn't a pleasant one. Automatically, I start to share the information with Kieran, then stop. The information I've learned from this strange bond is too private. And it might open up questions I can't answer.

"Promptly upon the conclusion of the investigation I'm told you're conducting into the matter of my father's death," she says crisply.

My stomach sinks slightly. As soon as I prove we have nothing to do with this, I lose her forever. That means I need to figure out a way into her heart before then.

"We are," Kieran says. "And we're extremely sorry about the way this has all gone down. I had the honor of speaking with King Isai often in his final days, and he told me a little of your legends of the feud. I'm taking strength from those now."

"Strength, Your Majesty?" Estrella asks.

"I assume you know the stories better than I." Kieran smiles wryly. "But I'll explain how they sound to new ears. King Isai spoke of a line of twin brothers who led Sundrop Gem in unison, the throne passing to whichever of them had a child first. As it always goes with brothers, one of them eventually grew jealous. The paler one." He holds up his hand. "And the one without magic. When the brothers fought, the jealous one decided it was a rift that could not be mended and fled across the Lonely Sea with his supporters." He looks at me. "If there is one issue I have learned how to mend, it's fights between siblings. I know no one of Dun's Crossing committed this atrocity, and that means our discomfort right now is nothing more than another brotherly squabble."

I suck in a breath as Estrella draws herself up, already knowing somewhere in the core of me that she won't interpret that little speech like Kieran hopes.

"I am so glad, Your Majesty, that you specialize in *squabbles*." Venom drips from her words. "Forgive me if I don't share your bird's eye view of the situation, with my father's blood still wet in the halls of a castle that offered us hospitality."

Kieran's smile grows stiff. "I meant no offense."

"I'm certain you didn't," she says.

My mark aches. She still hasn't looked at me.

'Fancy words aren't getting us anywhere,' I say to Kieran over the mind-link. *'Offer something real. That might go over better.'*

He clears his throat. "I am aware the envoy Floyd Winters is currently keeping your father from decomposing. Is there a reason not to conduct his funeral? Our holy woman, Aylin, would be honored to release the soul of such an impressive man to the Goddess. In accordance with the hospitality you mentioned, Dun's Crossing is also willing to handle any cost or inconvenience associated with transporting one of your holy women here, if that would be preferable."

Estrella lifts her chin and stares down her nose at Kieran. Still just Kieran. "Sundrop Gem appreciates your offer, King Kieran, but our traditions dictate my father must be buried in our own soil."

"We can transport him as well," Kieran says. "Or all four of you there for the ceremony and back to assist with the investigation."

Frosty silence fills the throne room. Shit. If there's one thing I've learned about Estrella, it's that actions mean more than words. But if this isn't the sort of thing actions can fix….

"Allow me to be clear, Your Majesty," she says. "Until the matter of this investigation is closed, Sundrop Gem will not be accepting any favors from Dun's Crossing beyond housing. We have had quite enough of your help."

The implication dangles in the air, cold and clear. She thinks—they all think–Dun's Crossing had something to do with this. Earlier, I thought she might've suspected as much, but there's no hesitation in her gray eyes now. She's settled in the matter, in her own mind at least.

"Certainly." Kieran stands, covering the upset and frustration he mind-links to me well. "Then I'll take this opportunity to reintroduce Prince Anwen, who will be leading the investigation. He will make regular reports to you, as you see fit."

"And if I see fit that your prince includes my father's Beta in the investigation itself?" she asks Kieran.

"I see no issue with it, and I doubt Prince Anwen will either." He looks at me. "Will you, brother?"

If being watched is what it takes her to believe me, I have no issue at all. "No. And I look forward to completing this investigation to your standards, Luna Estrella."

Finally, finally she looks at me. But it's like looking into the eyes of a stranger.

"We shall see."

15

NO CHOICE

Estrella

Tess pulls swaths of fabric out of my trunk, sorting through party dresses and everyday dresses for anything suitable to wear through the halls now that I'm Luna.

Luna. Fuck.

"I've always liked this one," Tess says.

I glance at the blue and purple damask over her arm. "I don't want to wear blue unless I have to."

"Because it's their color." Tess nods, folds her offering, and places it in the growing pile of rejected options.

This morning, I only needed to dress quickly and attend the meeting. Mother leant me one of her gowns, but she's taller than me. Dun's Crossing eyes might not notice the difference, but I could feel the bunched fabric and pins with every step I took. Certainly not a look befitting the Luna of Sundrop Gem.

"This one?" She holds out an orange, red, and yellow silk gown.

I run my fingers over the fabric, feeling the subtle difference in its weft and weave. Tears bead in my eyes. "Father bought that for me just before we left."

She rubs my shoulder. "It's beautiful."

"He had stunning taste." I smile tightly. "That was part of how he courted Mother, between their Haze and their wedding. He said she deserved to look like a queen already."

Someone knocks on the door, and I swipe the tears away. No one who would bother knocking can see me cry. Tess leaves me on my bed and goes to answer the door in the sitting room. Low conversation issues through the door she left slightly ajar, as she always does, but I can't make out anything they're saying.

She returns with a wooden board covered in an array of cured meats, cheeses, and fruits. "Snowcrest Canyon sends their regards again, in the form of a concern that the royal family may be avoiding public meals in their grief."

I smile wanly. Nessa's smarter than the Solbergs give her credit for. "We should send our appreciation. You can ask your father—" The words catch in my throat. Father asked Cristofer to learn all he could about other packs' customs before we left, but now, he's attached to the investigation. He doesn't have time to answer questions about appropriate thanks for Snowcrest diplomats.

Tess sets the board down on my nightstand, sits next to me, and wraps her arms around my shoulders. "I will find a way. Don't worry about that, in addition to everything else."

Easier said than done. I am the Luna now, and I have no Alpha to rely on.

"We should keep looking at dresses." My voice sounds thick. "This is a kind gesture from Snowcrest, but I won't have rumors swirling around this Goddess-forsaken palace that Sundrop Gem crumbles without its Alpha. I will attend dinner tonight."

If it kills me.

She shakes her head. "You should eat. I'll look at the dresses."

My stomach churns acidly. It feels like the last thing I ate was the dinner before the ball. I don't even know if that's true anymore. I haven't been paying any attention. But how can I eat when Father lies, cold as ice, on a slab? When his killer runs free, maybe even in the same palace I occupy?

Father's voice echoes in my mind. *You are the latest in a long, proud line, Estrella.* He was talking about Anwen, about how I didn't need to lower myself before him. But now, those nearly last words of his sound like an executioner's blade hanging over my head. I am not just the latest, but nearly the last. I love Castor, but he doesn't have what it takes to lead. He's impetuous, quick to anger. He'll be a dear advisor, reminding me never to take an insult we don't need to bear. But as Alpha, he would destroy the pack.

Just like Anwen, albeit in such a different way.

I can hardly believe only last night Father seemed encouraging about the idea of mating with Anwen. I've seen so many sides of the prince in the last twenty-four hours alone. He is obviously smart, a dexterous social manipulator. Perhaps he has a droplet of kindness in him—he did take me away when my emotions overflowed—but that kindness has never been nurtured, is a withered fruit on a dying branch. And he is a Solberg, a member of Dun's Crossing, the people my family believe murdered Father. I can imagine no worse mate, no worse Alpha for my pack. The mint of Anwen's scent was a promise. He is just as cool and slippery.

And still, I fell into his arms when I should've been with his family.

"Estrella?" Tess frowns. "Would you like space? I can go."

"Nessa lied," I blurt. "As did I."

Her black eyebrows shoot up. "What about?"

I pick at the edge of my robe. "I did not spend the night in her room."

Tess takes my hand and stares at our intertwined fingers, knowing truth sometimes comes easier when no one is looking at me. My heart throbs. There are so few people who know me well, but somehow, Anwen has quickly become one of them.

"I spent it with—" My tongue sticks stubbornly to the roof of my mouth. I cannot say the words, cannot admit my sickening betrayal.

I spent the night in Prince Anwen's bed, I tell her.

Tess's mouth tightens in a way I know means she's biting the inside of her lips to keep from having a reaction. My face burns.

"Say it." My voice comes out sharp and jagged. "There is nothing you can tell me I haven't already told myself. I know that it was a humiliation, a betrayal of Sundrop Gem, a dive to the depths of depravity the likes of which a Luna cannot—"

"I think it makes sense," she says quietly.

My heart skips a beat. My mating bite sears, but I've grown used to the pain. "Does it still make sense if I lied even now? If he couldn't be bothered to actually take me to his bed but instead stored me in some hidden chamber a dozen other women have obviously seen the inside of?"

"Yes." She squeezes my hand. "He's your mate."

I yank my hand back. "He's nothing to me."

"You keep saying that." Tess shakes her head, and I know there's an Orion story coming. "But the Goddess declared him your other half. He's the person in the world most suited to comforting you. Orion—"

My body burns with the rough way Anwen handled me, the fading bruises I covered with extra drapes of Mother's dress. "I don't want his comfort. I don't want anything to do with him."

"But you sought him out." Tess frowns harder. "After your night, did your bite not feel better? Did your bond not become undeniable?"

Nausea roils through me. I stand, hoping that will ease… something, but I'm forced to grab the post of my bed or tumble to my knees. Still, I stare down at Tess. Her heart-shaped face is almost as familiar to me as my own. I know the story of the thin scar on her jaw —a tree-climbing accident Castor goaded her into—and I know the worry painted across her features. What I'm experiencing right now is completely beyond her experiences, nearly beyond what she can understand.

Calm certainty settles over my shoulders like a heavy blanket. No, not calm, but at least numbing. Tess has never woken up next to her mate and wondered why. No one I know has. Perhaps no one in this whole castle, because I struggle to believe Kieran and Raven truly had no inclination they were not siblings. I struggle to believe anything the king and queen of Dun's Crossing say anymore. So I am alone. Just as I am alone in leading my people.

Father told me to rely on my mother's heart and his stubbornness. But he led a Sundrop Gem protected from all outsiders by ancient customs. He didn't—couldn't–understand that those traits must be reserved for our people, and our people only.

"Nothing is undeniable," I say, my voice infused with that same certainty. "Even the Goddess. We are given our free will. She only guides our choices, and sometimes, the right choice is to ignore that guidance."

Tess flinches back, though she keeps her hold on my hand. "You don't mean that. You can't. Because if you do, that means you're agreeing to a life of permanent loneliness, for you and Prince Anwen."

I meet her dark eyes. "I mean it with every bone in my body."

My mate mark has never hurt this much, not even that first morning. Only my hold on the bedpost keeps me on my feet.

Distantly, I understand Anwen a little better. He endured this pain without flinching the first morning. It's the only impressive quality I'll admit to just now.

Tess shakes her head slowly, wordlessly.

"I have to avenge Father's death," I continue. "I have to lead Sundrop Gem mere months after my birthday. The last thing I need in this life is a mate I cannot trust as far as Queen Raven's unborn child could throw him. And I have hope that my friends and advisors will not desert me in the years to come, so I will never truly be lonely amongst our people."

"I know you, Estrella." Tess stands and meets my gaze. "Do you really think you can handle all of this by yourself? Tell me once, looking at me, in the eyes, and I will drop the matter."

The promise springs to my tongue, fully formed, but I cannot lie to a face I know so well.

"No," I admit. "I'm not certain, and I doubt I'm ready. But"—I cup her cheek with my free hand—"I am certain I have no choice."

Tears fill Tess's eyes.

16

TIRELESS

ANWEN

DAYS PASS IN A BLUR OF ACTIVITY. EVERY ONE IS EXACTLY THE SAME AND just different enough to drive me crazy. I wake up reliably with the sunrise, something I've never done before in my life. My steward, Frazier, is shocked the first time he comes in to wake me up and I'm already half-dressed with a few pieces of dried meat dangling from my lips.

I have too much to do to lie around in bed all day.

Kieran happily sets aside an office on the same hall as his for me to work out of, and I usually arrive there before most of the castle finishes breakfast. With a mind-link to the team still chasing the assassin, my day begins.

I take a map of the forest surrounding the castle from the library and begin marking the paths different coalitions took. I spend hours running the forest myself, trying to find the exact spot where I caught that foreign smell. It's gone, and so are the mist-deer, but I think I've found the spot anyway. That goes on the map as a bright-red pin, and every route is compared against it.

Reports filter in from the team in pursuit nearly every hour on the first day, then every couple of hours, then a few times a day as the chase wears on. Every time, it's the same thing. The trail is growing fainter, but they haven't lost it yet. One by one, I interrogate every delegate who attended the ball, an agonizing process of dodging flirtations and trying to read through lies while also asking the questions myself. I'd give almost anything to feed someone else a list of questions and simply be able to observe from the back, but my sole attempt at that ended when every answer was addressed to me anyway.

Meals arrive at my office, and I take enough bites to keep going before promptly forgetting about them. When the stars hang high in the night sky, I write my own report of everything I've learned and send it via page to the chambers assigned to Sundrop Gem. To Estrella.

We're three days into the investigation, and I haven't received a response yet.

But if I do all of this, if I push myself to the point of exhaustion, I can fall into bed at night and just about sleep without my mark keeping me awake. It's enough to stay sharp for the next day, anyway.

On the fourth day, I sit across from Evangeline of Redwood Nimbus, mother of a woman I apparently danced with the night of the peace ball, trying not to roll my eyes as she natters on about choosing her dress. She has pull with their Alpha. I can't piss her off. At least she doesn't smell like that wolf in the forest, just like everybody else I've spoken to so far.

Anything? I ask the team in pursuit across mind-link.

The response is slow coming back, as it has been all day. They're at the edge of our mind-link range.

Trail faint but not gone, Whyte replies.

He's changed direction a couple times, but I don't see any pattern in it, a low-ranking soldier named Heath my father called "soft" adds.

Just like every other day.

Report if anything changes. I cross my fingers that the assassin is changing direction so my men stay within mind-link range.

Afternoon, Baz says tiredly.

I blink. His message lacks the resonance of a multi-shifter mind-link. He's talking to me alone.

What's up? I reply.

I don't think anyone else has put it together, but there's definitely a pattern, he says.

And it's something bad. I smile and nod at Evangeline, trying to keep her from noticing the mind-link look on my face.

He sighs. *It looks like the trail is looping back to the castle.*

My stomach drops. That means either the assassin is coming back for another swing, or—

Like they came from there originally, Baz says before I have to finish the thought.

I close the mind-link without responding and smile tightly at Evangeline. "My dear woman, I've had a lovely time talking with you today, but I've been informed of pressing business elsewhere. Could we pick this back up another day?" I offer her my warmest smile. "Say, over tea?"

My mark pulses painfully as she grins.

"I would love to." She puts her hand over mine.

"I appreciate your consideration." I stand, bow, and crush down the nausea churning in my gut. "I'll send a page with details."

And then, I escape to the hallway. My heart pounds unevenly, as it always does these days when I'm out in public. Estrella might be around any corner I turn. She hasn't been, since she left my bed, but that doesn't stop part of me from hoping.

Instead, I nearly run right into Floyd Winters, the ferrety envoy who seems to be everywhere these days.

"Ah, apologies, Prince Anwen," he says.

I shove past his pleasantries. "Have you discovered any more stable ways of preserving King Isai's body?"

He simpers. "Apologies, Your Highness, but my magic simply isn't powerful enough. There is no way for you to inspect the king's body without disturbing the ice, which—"

"Will damage the body before they can get it back to Sundrop

Gem," I snarl. "I've heard the speech before. Just"—I shake my head—"keep trying, I guess."

He nods and scurries off. I run a hand through my hair, trying to rein in my temper. I can't do anything to hurt Estrella, and harming her father's body would do exactly that. But fuck, this investigation would be a lot easier if I could look at the fucking victim. Maybe I can send to the Alpha of Snowcrest and get a more powerful member of his pack out here.

I stride off down the hall. Despite my hopes, I don't even catch a whiff of Estrella. If I didn't know better, I'd guess she's left the castle, but I saw the look on her face when she demanded satisfaction. Not even burying her father will pry her from these walls until his murderer is caught.

A dark, bitter part of me whispers that I could keep her here if I just drag my feet a little. If I took my time, missed a few pieces of evidence, maybe ignored a lead or two.

My mark burns through my body. If I won't risk a little bit of defrosting because it might upset her, I can't do anything less than my best on this investigation. It's what she deserves, even if I can't give her anything else a mate should.

I arrive at the dispatch tower, the organizational hub of the military within the castle and outside of it. Jase, the field marshal who manages it all, slumps in his comfortable chair, exhausted from always extending his mind-link to the edges of its range.

"I have a strange question," I say.

His eyes open slowly. "Color me surprised. Everything has been so normal."

Exhaustion also makes Jase sarcastic. There's a reason I don't come up here often. "Are all the palace guards accounted for? Everybody who would've been around, say, four days ago?"

Jase narrows his eyes at me but doesn't ask. "Let me check."

A few moments of silence pass. I drum on my leg, pace back and forth. Every second I spend doing nothing here is a second wasted.

"One," Jase says suddenly.

"What?" I ask.

"One wolf is missing, a man named Harper." He eyes me. "He hasn't been seen since before the ball started, and the last report has him speaking quietly with King Kieran."

My stomach drops. "Don't tell anyone else that piece of information, or I will find someone else with your stamina."

Jase's eyes go wide. I turn and march away before he can say anything else.

The threat was overkill. Jase has been a good, loyal soldier for half his life now. But I can't risk this getting out. If I learned this about anyone other than Kieran, I'd be sprinting through the halls to tell Estrella I'd found the killer right now.

But it can't be Kieran. His face, half-dark and half-golden in flickering firelight, bright with righteous anger from the night he gave the speech that turned the army against Father, echoes through my mind. He was so confident he would be a different king than Father ever was. Confident enough to convince me, even before I knew the extent of Father's crimes. I gave up a chance at the throne for that speech.

If there's one skill I've cultivated all my life, it's reading people. At first, it was an accident. I was always just out of line of sight, shunted half a foot off to the side so Kieran might stand in the center but still away from the ruckus of my younger siblings. It's a perfect position to watch from. Since I couldn't do anything else, I watched. I learned how people move when they're worried, when they're sure of themselves, when they're bluffing. I learned the palace inside and out, a warren of secret tunnels lost to history. And I learned my family most of all. Kieran believed every word he was saying in that moment.

And he believed them when he took the throne. And again, every time I've spoken to him about it. Kieran couldn't lie to me any more than I could lie to myself. He's turning himself inside out over this. There's no way he instructed one of our soldiers to kill King Isai.

But I can't give Estr—anyone else my knowledge of my brother. And my only other defense is that Father was a capable, careful enough murderer that his heir-apparent wouldn't be stupid enough to use his own men.

No, the information is better kept quiet until I know what it means. I just have to hope no one else tells Estrella.

96

17

WARMING UP

ESTRELLA

IN A BREAK BETWEEN MEETINGS, WHEN CASTOR REPORTS ANWEN IS shut up in his office with orders not to disturb him, I creep through the halls of the castle to visit Father. My dress, a re-dyed version of the purple and blue Tess offered is now purple and deep, dark red that reminds me of blood if I think about it for too long, swishes along the stones. It's already growing cold in Dun's Crossing. The sooner we are able to leave this place, the happier I'll be.

I pass a few nobles whose faces I've learned during endless lunches with Nessa, who seems determined to ensure I know every person in the palace with a square foot of land to their name before the week ends. In Dun's Crossing tradition, I wait for them to bow or curtsy first, since I outrank them now. In Dun's Crossing tradition, the moment of hesitation before they move makes me sick to my stomach.

Finally, I arrive at the room Father's body has been moved to. Apparently, that first room was their useless healer's office, and he needed it back for some purpose or other. Now, Father rests in an out-of-the-way guest chamber, watched over constantly by Floyd Winters or one of the two guards he brought with him from Snowcrest.

Today, Floyd himself stands in front of the door. "Luna Estrella. How are you today?"

I don't bother curtsying to the man who's done so much for our family. Our relationship goes far deeper than court formalities by now. "I have been better, but your Nessa is doing her utmost to keep my spirits high, as always."

He grins. "You know, I've never seen her quite like this before."

I raise an eyebrow. "Like what?"

"Is it trite if I say happy?" He shakes his head. "She had a group she used to go around with, but I haven't heard about them in a while, and she never came back from time with them smiling as often as she does time with you."

"She's a good friend," I say honestly. A little gossipy for my taste sometimes, but here, I need that. Nessa's kindness only barely outweighs her value as a never-ending source of information on this world I know nothing about.

"I'm glad you've got someone." Floyd's smile fades. "I can't imagine the weight of the world on your shoulders right now."

Most people here don't have the guts—or the stupidity—to say that to me, but I can see it in the eyes of every person I meet with. In some ways, it's refreshing to hear the words outright.

"Thank you," I murmur. "May I?"

"Oh, of course." Floyd steps aside, clearing the door.

I pull the ribbon holding the key off my wrist where I've been keeping it ever since Floyd handed them out to Mother, Castor, Cristofer, and me, then unlock and open the heavy door.

A blast of cold air rolls out. I step inside and rub my arms only after the door closes behind me. Floyd Winters is the kind man who, by necessity, has been privy to more of the inner workings of my father's assassination than normal, but I still don't wish him to see me any more vulnerable than he must. I run my finger over the thin rime of ice that lays over the empty wardrobe and desk in the room, dallying even though there is no one else to hide from in here. Floyd's magic is powerful. The ice covers every piece of furniture but a chair at the head of the bed. Mother, Castor, and I don't tell one another how often we occupy it. That allows us to pretend we can survive this.

I take a deep breath. A soft cloud exits my lips, and I rub my frozen hands together. Humiliatingly, since my second night with Anwen, I've manifested some slight heat powers, weaker than what Father had by far, and I let them flow over my skin now. The icy room loses its bite.

I'm wasting a sliver of time I've carved out of my day. I stride to the head of the bed and sit next to Father's body.

As always, my first glance hits me like a blow to the chest. He looks like a stranger. His warm, sandy skin, the same color as my own, is ashen. Lattices of ice climb his cheeks and tangle in his hair. Someone closed his eyes, a blessing, but I made the mistake of opening them once to see if they had survived the onslaught. I will never forget the frozen nothingness that looked back at me until the day I die.

At least the brown-gray bloodstain on his clothes no longer sends me spiraling back to our last moment.

I take Father's hand. "I wish I could warm you up."

In some ways, I could. I could brush my fingers over his ruined cheeks and return color to them. But with my weak abilities, I could do no more.

"Would you like that?" I ask anyway. "Then, we could change you into something a little more comfortable."

I wonder if Floyd can hear me through the door. I wonder if he thinks me mad.

I wonder if Mother and Castor talk to Father when they come to visit.

"I'm sorry," I reply as if he agreed. "I am less your daughter than you hoped." My voice cracks, and I swallow against tears. In a burst of frustration, I abandon the magic keeping my hand warm. If I can't do anything for him, I deserve to feel the chill of his icy fingers.

I have never been less afraid for our future, he said in his last moments. If only he could see how wrong he was.

Burning tears drop down onto my cheeks. "I can't fix anything, Father. There's no movement in the investigation, and no one will look at me with anything other than pity. Half of the formal invitations still arrive addressed to Mother. I miss you."

I imagine his frozen brow wrinkling in soft concern. I sound nothing like the daughter he raised. But I still think she died in the moment he did.

"I love you," I whisper.

Just like I did that night. These tiny heat powers I can conjure up on command are nothing compared to the warmth I felt that night. Like lava poured through my veins, hot enough to kill anyone but me in an instant. Like the Goddess herself cupped Her hands around mine and pushed. But then that faded, and nothing I've done since has conjured the glow again. No one has mentioned the incident since it occurred. Part of me worries I dreamt it in the fugue of loss.

"Did you feel the burning, Father?" I ask. "Do you know what it was?"

As always, he has no answer for me. This time, though, the room rings with a finality I may be imagining as much as the glow. There is no answer for me here. Perhaps anywhere.

I stand. I need to return to my room before an afternoon meeting. I'm dawdling here, indulging a childish fantasy that Father might return and make everything right again. I would do better to focus on things I can change, like the pace of the investigation. Perhaps avoiding Anwen hasn't been the right choice after all. I am growing tired of his nightly missives rattling off nearly the exact same information.

With my shoulders square and my chin high, I stride to the door and knock for Floyd to release me without even asking Castor over mind-link whether Anwen has moved. The door swings open noiselessly.

"Good visit?" Floyd asks.

I offer him what I hope is an enigmatic smile and don't pause. I need to seize this momentum before it withers.

The walk back to the room disappears in another flurry of curtsies. I unlock my door with the other key around my wrist and step inside.

A letter, sealed with the dark-blue wax of the Solbergs, sits on a shining tray on my receiving table. There's no sign of Tess, or any of the staff that always seems to flit around. I purse my lips, pull a letter opener out of the small drawer in the table, and slit the envelope.

Crown Prince Anwen Solberg of Dun's Crossing, lead investigator into the murder of Alpha King Isai Sollabella, requests the presence of Luna Queen Estrella Sollabella of Sundrop Gem at lunch tomorrow to discuss important discoveries and vital information regarding the investigation. If the Luna Queen is amenable to such a meeting, she should write back indicating what dining room she would prefer.

I bite my lower lip as a smile threatens. I've never heard Anwen talk like this before. It's very plainly his attempt to make a direct request to see me seem like official business, and the level of formality tells me in no uncertain terms that, while he may have some new information, he is at least interested in seeing me again.

My mark throbs. I rub my neck then pick up a quill to pen my response.

Luna Queen Estrella Sollabella of Sundrop Gem would find a luncheon in—

I grimace, trying to remember everything Nessa taught me.

—the solarium amenable at noon tomorrow. She will bring her attendant, Tesandra Solis of Sundrop Gem, to ensure no details of the meeting are forgotten, and she expects Crown Prince Anwen Solberg to bring an attendant as well.

I dot the final period, read my letter over, and smile. He wants a meeting? Fine. But I will be alone with my mate again over my own grave.

18

BREAKING DOWN BARRIERS

Anwen

I tap my feet against the solarium floor, fighting an instinct that demands I pace.

She's coming, Baz reminds me without looking away from the spread on the table in front of us. I called him back from the chase leading ever closer to the castle because there's no one else who could sit at my side for this. I'll send him back out as soon as we're done here, a piece of information he didn't take very kindly to.

A servant brings in the final few plates and squeezes them onto the table.

I may have overdone it with the food. The castle library didn't tell me anything about what Sundrop Gem eats for lunch, so I decided I'd rather not miss something important. At least a dozen plates cover the tiled tabletop, and more will be coming out as we finish these. Unseasonable fruits imported from distant kingdoms sit between hearty stews putting off steam. Three dishes of bread sit at one end of the table and three more on the other.

The glass door to the solarium opens, and only Father's voice

103

ringing in my ear keeps me from jerking my head up to look at her. Instead, I turn slowly from the papers I'm theoretically reviewing in front of me.

Still, my heart skips a beat. She wears a dress of some incredible fabric that looks like all the colors of flame at once and trails behind her like a cape. A simple golden circlet rings her head, drawing attention to the symphony of braids holding back her dark hair. Yet again, there's some woman next to her. Tesandra, I assume.

She starts to curtsy, then stops herself. Fuck, right. I hop to my feet and bow.

"Luna Estrella," I say. "Allow me to introduce you to my Beta, Basileos."

He stands and bows as well. "Please, call me Baz."

With a staggered synchrony half the nobles in Dun's Crossing haven't yet mastered, Tesandra curtsies, then Estrella. My mouth goes dry.

"Prince Anwen." Her tone is unforgiving. "This is my attendant, Tesandra, daughter of my late father's Beta."

"Tess," she corrects.

"I've enjoyed working with your father, Tess." I sit back down. "Help yourselves. The kitchen ran away with the request."

Estrella eyes the food on the table, then me like she already knows this is my fault. I hold her gaze. Days apart make her smell heady, nearly blotting out the food like it did at that first breakfast.

She sits directly across the table from me. Tess takes the seat next to her, across from Baz. When I sent the letter, I hoped I could keep my head, but that was stupid. Estrella's just too tantalizing.

'Does "help yourselves" extend to very hungry best friends who've been running for days?' he asks.

I barely don't roll my eyes. *'Yes.'*

He begins filling the empty plate in front of him with everything he can reach.

"Our cultural knowledge of Sundrop Gem is severely lacking." I pour myself a drink and sip it. "Do you have particular foods you prefer for lunch?"

"We tend toward two smaller midday meals before dinner." Estrella takes some fruit preserves and bread onto her plate. "However, you called this meeting to discuss the matter of the investigation. You said you had some discovery?"

Dammit. She's not going to be distracted easily.

"Yes, I did." I scrounge through my memory for anything important—or anything important that doesn't implicate Kieran. "Three days before the ball, just after invitations were sent out, I smelled someone behind the castle. Someone I didn't recognize. And I smelled them again for just a moment at the ball."

Her eyebrows tick up a single notch. "And you didn't see fit to mention this until now? What is the purpose of your exhaustive reports if not to tell me what you know?"

Wrong move.

"I didn't say anything because the smell could've been an early arrival, simply a member of a delegation with no connection to the investigation." The drink makes my thoughts swim. I grab a heel of bread and choke down a bite to sop it up before continuing. "Over these past four days, I have systematically ruled out every delegate invited to the ball. Whoever I smelled should not have been there. I strongly believe they are the assassin."

"He is," Baz adds through a full mouth.

Estrella and Tess wrinkle their noses very slightly in unison. So Tess isn't just an attendant; she's a dear friend for them to move so easily together.

"Apologies." I smile, trying to reclaim their attention. "Baz has been leading the chase, which is why I chose him as my second for this meeting. He means to say that he knows the smell better, and he's certain it belongs to a male wolf."

'Manners, jackass,' I snap over the mind-link.

He swallows. "Exactly that. And he doesn't smell distinctively like any of the royal families I'm familiar with either. We've got another gray wolf on our pursuit team—he's actually leading it while I'm gone —and he agrees there's no chance it's nobility from Escuro, Snowcrest Canyon, or Dun's Crossing."

"How lucky," Estrella murmurs.

The edge of disbelief in her voice stings. "Our gray wolves have the best sense of smell. You can trust that report."

"That secondhand report, corroborated by a wolf I don't even know by name?" She flicks her gaze up to meet mine for a split second. "Apologies, Prince Anwen, but I cannot rely on the word of anyone outside my own kingdom at this time."

My temper flares. "And what if someone from your own kingdom perpetrated the attack? Baz and his team didn't rule out Sundrop Gem. We don't know your smells."

Her grip on her utensils tightens. "My people would not do this. My father was beloved. We gain nothing from his death."

"Apologies, Luna Estrella, but I cannot rely on the word of anyone outside my own kingdom at this time." I smirk at her. "If you would give Baz some idea of what your people smell like, we could rule you out properly."

My pulse pounds. Blood rushes below my belt. Fighting with her is electric, and if I can push her off topic into scent—

"Many of us have the smell of something cooked, though it varies wolf to wolf." She clenches her jaw. "Father believed it was because our magic heated our very scent."

I inhale a deep breath of her cooked-sugar scent. Next to me, Baz does the same. I nearly clobber him. She's my mate! But I clamp down on it, reminding myself he's only gathering information.

"Satisfied?" She raises a single eyebrow.

The word "never" sits on the tip of my tongue. I swallow it.

"Heat magic, you say?" I lean back in my seat and take another mouthful of bread. "What's that like? Is it related to that glow at the ball?"

Estrella stiffens. Tess glances at her sharply, her eyes clouded with mind-link. There's a secret here.

"I wouldn't know," Estrella says tightly. "I've only begun to come into my powers. At this time, I can keep myself warm and sometimes warm things in my palms."

My mark pulses with more want than pain, for once. I smile slowly.

"In Dun's Crossing, we're not born with magic," I say. "I've always been curious. Could we get a demonstration?"

Estrella studies me then pours herself a glass of ruby-red fruit juice. She cups it for a moment and holds it out to me. I run my finger along it. As promised, the surface that should be cool is body-warm to the touch.

"Can you do it to people?" I hold my hand out to her, mentally urging her to accept.

She looks at Tess, who nods infinitesimally. After a brief hesitation, Estrella takes my hand.

Her fingers slide into position around mine like that's where they most belong, like puzzle pieces locking into place. The warmth follows immediately after, like the soft burn of a sip of whiskey, but spreading up from my palm. It's intoxicating, addictive, and I instantly want more.

Baz clears his throat, and I remember we're not alone. I pull my hand back, but slowly, lingering in the feel of her.

"Remind me to bring you along if I ever get tricked into visiting Snowcrest." I smile.

Miracle of miracles, she smiles back. "I think a much grander trick would be required to get me anywhere near those mountains."

"Maybe that could be arranged," I say softly.

'Trail just changed direction again,' Heath says over the mind-link to Baz and me. *'No denying it anymore. This bastard is headed back to the castle.'*

Motherfucker. *'Close distance and take him down.'*

Baz sighs. *'I'll wrap up and head out with Caden and Marko. Wait for me.'*

Caden and Marko are both white wolves and wicked fast. Exactly the role I'd fill if I was on the team.

"Something's changed," Estrella says. "What?"

"The team in pursuit thinks they've got the assassin cornered," I lie easily. "Baz has to go help with takedown."

He stuffs a few more bites into his mouth, stands, and flips a salute before marching out. Goddess, he's going to get his ass handed to him one of these days. I'm never taking him to a political meeting again.

I turn back to the table and discover the tiny inch of ground I gained with Estrella is gone. She's back to ramrod-straight posture and cool gaze trained on her plate. Fuck. Every glimpse I get of her without the hardened political shell makes me crave more.

I'm tired of resisting. Solbergs take what they want head-on.

"Tess," I say, "could I speak to your lady alone for a moment?"

Both their gazes go hazy, so I assume they're using the mind-link. Estrella frowns. Tess shakes her head very slightly.

Abruptly, her eyes clear, and she stands. "Certainly, Prince Anwen. Thank you for lunch."

"Not certainly." Estrella jumps to her feet to leave as well. "I indicated I would come with an attendant, and I don't intend to revoke that."

I shove my chair back as I get to my feet and find an unexpected word on my tongue. "Please."

So ridiculous. So vulnerable. So unlike the man Father raised me to be.

Maybe that's not the worst thing, though.

"As it seems you have no more to report, we will both be leaving." She turns toward the door coldly.

Vulnerability doesn't work. I should've known that. Father's lessons flow back into place, and my hand snaps out. Before I realize what I'm doing, I wrap my fingers around the soft flesh of her wrist.

Estrella whips back to me, her eyes flashing.

19

REVERIE

Estrella

I yank against Anwen's grip, ignoring the way my wolf howls for more. "Unhand me!"

He looks at me with those icy blue eyes, then turns to Tess. "I must insist you give us a moment alone."

My face burns. How dare he talk to her like I'm not here? I am Luna Queen of Sundrop Gem! I turn to Tess, expecting to see concern in her eyes, to receive a mind-link for a plan to get out of here without jeopardizing our standing in the castle. Instead, like she's hypnotized, she only looks at Anwen.

"Yes, Your Highness." She curtsies, turns, and leaves the solarium. The *click* of the door closing behind her echoes painfully.

Abandoned by my dearest friend, left to the whims of the monstrous mate the Goddess picked out for me. I have nowhere left to turn.

Anwen pulls aside the neck of his doublet, revealing the very edge of the sun-shaped bite on his shoulder. "We are mates, Estrella. Doesn't that mean anything to you?"

"It did once." I fight his iron hold. My skin bruises under his fingers. Sickeningly, that only makes me—my wolf—want him more.

"We need to be together." He jumps over the table and lands next to me without releasing my wrist. "It's written in our bodies. I'm tired of hurting."

"I am tired of you treating me like your equal." I stomp on his foot, but I've forgotten his capacity to endure pain. His grip doesn't loosen. "I am Luna Queen Estrella Sollabella, and you are nothing more than a soon-to-be contingency plan."

"Seems your father was right about your stubbornness, at least." Anwen snorts. "Titles don't matter between mates. We're made for each other." He strokes a finger down my cheek, letting his nail sharpen to a fine enough point to scrape.

I shiver. If I screamed, someone would come running. I could mind-link Mother or Castor, and they'd save me in a moment.

"I don't believe that anymore," I say, fighting to keep the quiver out of my voice.

Anwen's eyes flash. "I know a challenge when I hear one."

He tugs me into him, and our mouths clash. His taste spills over my tongue. He gropes my breasts through my dress, hungry and desperate. My wolf snarls, paces, fights my control. She wants to melt into him and become the perfect, sweet Luna he desires.

Never. I am Luna Queen.

"You're not proving much," I hiss between kisses.

His blue eyes burn, and I realize Anwen's control is as fragile as a moonbeam. I can push him into whatever I like. I sink my teeth into his lower lip until hot, coppery blood overwhelms his taste. Memories threaten to rip me away, but nothing can stop me now.

"You want proof?" He shreds the front of my dress and shoves the remaining fabric off my shoulders before I can even reply.

I am naked before him, before anyone who sees fit to pass the glass walls of the solarium, and I am burning. I stare up at him, defiant.

He snarls, turns away from me, and swipes an armful of dishes off the table. They shatter on the floor, food smells mixing with the heady scent of sex and him. He whips back, grabs me around the waist, and sits me on the cleared table. My wetness drips down my thighs as he pushes me around.

"I knew it." He swipes a finger through it and holds it up to the light. "You need me just as badly as I need you."

Not trusting my voice, I shake my head.

He growls. "By the time I'm done, you won't be able to remember anything but my name."

Anwen drops to his knees between my legs, and my heart hammers. Hazy flashes from our first night together remind me he's done this before, but not the details. When his tongue first touches my clit, it takes everything in me not to scream. I will not give him the satisfaction.

And I don't believe I want anyone to come rushing anymore.

I thread my fingers into his pale hair and hold on as tightly as I can. He pushes my legs wider and pins them against the table, the edges of the tiles scraping my soft skin. A soft whimper escapes through my lips.

I feel his smile against my inner thighs.

No. I won't let him believe he's in charge, that this moment is his. I fight his grasp again, but my legs are far stronger than my arms, and he is far more distracted. I manage to slip one out and wrap it around his head, pulling him ever closer and making it impossible for him to leave. He slides dangerously sharp fangs along my wet flesh, a threat more than pain. I only pull him tighter. Let him try it, if he thinks he can survive the consequences.

His fangs fade away as his tongue fucks into me. I stuff my free hand into my mouth to stifle the noises threatening to flow free. Anwen glances up at me, and his eyes become impossibly hungrier as he takes in the fingers between my lips. The apex of pleasure builds between my legs.

And if I allow it, this will end. Whatever spell exists between us will shatter, and we'll be forced to face what's happening. That is the one thing I can't control.

I unwind my leg and yank him back by his hair. He licks his glimmering lips salaciously.

"Not satisfied?" He smirks. "I usually get better reviews."

I don't want to hear a word about his other women. I pull him to his feet and shred his pants just like he destroyed my dress. His cock springs free, hard and proud.

"I'm happy to fuck—"

I drop to my knees in front of him and take his cock in my mouth before he can finish the sentence. If I allow him to bring me to those euphoric heights first, I will have lost. This way, he is the one wild with want, desperate and writhing. My wolf complains, as does the want between my legs, but I focus my attention on him.

His taste, his smell, is overwhelming with him in my mouth. Mint and whiskey, something gritty, and the animal stink of sex. I've never done this before, but like the first night, instinct guides me. Instinct, and his hands on the back of my head, pushing me further onto his cock.

"Just like that," he murmurs. "Use your tongue."

I scrape my teeth along him, a sharp reprimand for attempting to order me around, despite how much the order shivers down my spine. Giving myself up to him has never been so tempting. But I want to watch him come undone for once. Let him be the one who wants, who lies awake at night wondering what he did wrong. I bob forward and take more of him into my mouth.

He groans like music.

The rhythm isn't hard to find. Forward and back, forward and back, to the frantic beat of his heart. When I think he's forgotten, I do try using my tongue, swirling it around the girth of him. He slams into me with another groan, and I smirk. Hopefully, he feels that as I did. I drag my nails up and down the backs of his thighs, alternating between sharp and dull with my thrusts. His hips judder, struggling to maintain pace, and his words lose their shape. I look up.

The perfect prince I met on the docks—could it be only a week ago?—is a ruin. His golden hair sticks up at odd angles, shaped by my hands and legs. His pale mouth is open, exposing the hot, red inside of him. His doublet, the only remaining article of clothing between us, nearly slumps off his shoulder. He has never been more beautiful.

He sucks in a breath. "I'm going to—"

I pull back. He whines like a pup, and I drink in the sound.

My wolf prances, begging me to let him take me.

"No," he snarls suddenly. "You don't get to do this to me."

The dangerous edge to his voice is just as delicious. Perhaps my wolf has the right idea.

I move easily as he drags me off the floor and bends me over the table. The sharp edges of the tiles dig into my breasts, and my wolf howls. He yanks my legs apart, and I reach back to hold them in place. Anwen groans as he lines up.

"Perfect." He sinks into me.

The pleasure I delayed roars back to life like a stoked fire. I drip for him, enough that I feel it sliding down my thighs. He hammers into me, his hands bruising my hips. Harsh panting fills the air and mingles with his groans. I fight to stay quiet.

"Scream for me," he demands.

I shake my head. He slams me into the table.

"Have I not proven myself?" he roars. "What more do you need? Should I drag you into the throne room and fuck you just like this?"

The pleasure rebounds, redoubles, crests. I open my mouth and—

—shoot up in bed, soaked with sweat. I blink. Where am I?

A few rays of morning sun peek through the gaps in my canopy. My wrist aches dully, but only when I focus on it. I wear my nightgown, though it seems to have rucked up around my thighs. And I am very much alone.

Yesterday, at lunch, Anwen grabbed my wrist and asked me to stay. I reminded him I was a foreign royal and left with Tess because the thought of a moment alone with him sickened me.

Everything else was a dream.

I shove out of bed quickly, leaving the canopy drawn so I don't have to face any mess I made. In the real world, I was strong. That is all that matters.

Perhaps, by the time I go downstairs for breakfast, the nausea churning in my gut will believe that.

BREAK

Anwen

"...So I haven't discovered anything solid, but we're making progress," I report to Kieran the day after my failed lunch with Estrella. Raven sits next to him, nodding.

He taps on the arm of his desk chair. "All right. Would—"

'Got him!' Baz roars to all of us.

'Finally,' I reply.

'How close are you?/ Kieran asks. *'And is the assailant alive?'*

My heart skips a beat. I forgot to worry about Baz's fucking restraint.

'And kicking,' Baz answers.

I exhale sharply.

'Bastard took off toward the castle when we caught up. He'll be in the dungeon in ten.' Baz closes the mind-link, likely to focus on making sure his prisoner doesn't escape.

Kieran scrubs his hands over his face. "Thank the Goddess, this will finally be over."

Not something King Isai's killer would say. My confidence in him strengthens.

I stand. "Send for Cristofer. Luna Estrella prefers news from her own people's mouths, so he should monitor the interrogation."

Kieran stands as well. "And I'm happy to come help."

The second he finishes, he twists toward Raven, and mind-link distraction clouds them both. I'm getting pretty fucking tired of people having conversations without me.

"I don't need the help," I say loudly.

Kieran looks back at me. "Ah, If you're sure."

I snort and start to leave. "Enjoy your privacy."

"Wait!" Raven calls.

I pause.

"It wasn't my intention to leave you out, it's just"—she looks at Kieran, who nods—"I know we haven't been the closest, even since your father's death."

I hate the way she says "your father," like he didn't raise her too.

"But have you been in the dungeons, Anwen?" She meets my gaze and holds it. "They're cruel, inhumane, and your brother hasn't had time to clean them up yet."

I frown. "They're dungeons. I've seen them once or twice, but I can't exactly imagine a kind dungeon."

She takes a step closer. "Please just be careful down there. They twist people."

"Yeah, sure." Talking to her is just like talking to Mother: agree, and you get to leave.

Raven still looks worried, but neither of them say anything as I exit the office.

Baz reports that they've arrived just as I set foot on the top stair down to the dungeon. A thick, musty, underground smell drifts up, and I wrinkle my nose once. That's at least half the reason I've never spent a lot of time down here. Candace can't even walk down this hall without getting sick. But I am mere minutes from proving to Estrella that Dun's Crossing had nothing to do with her father's murder, so I square my shoulders and march down the stairs.

A heavy-jawed guard named Rohan I remember seeing down here nearly every time I've come greets me at the bottom of the stairs. "Catch of the day?"

I scowl at him. "I'm not here to waste time."

He scoffs, then turns and leads me deeper into the dungeon. My stomach churns until we pass the turn for Mother's cell. I really should visit her sometime.

"There." Rohan jerks his chin at a solid wood door and holds out a key. "Delivery team already cleared out, and the Sundrop mother-fucker is in there. You want advanced tactics?"

He means torture. My stomach churns all over again.

"Do you really think I need those to get results?" I unlock the cell door and stride inside.

A wiry, raw-boned man peers through a nest of dark hair and two black eyes at me. He's manacled to a metal chair—silver, perhaps—and flanked by another prison guard and the bulk of Cristofer. I bow briefly to the Beta, and he does the same. Rohan follows me and locks the door behind both of us.

"Come to dirty your knuckles, pretty boy? Catch a little scar to impress the bitches?"

My mark throbs. Estrella will be impressed, but not for any reason this monster can understand. I roll up my sleeves slowly.

"Do you have a name?"

Cristofer closes his eyes as if wincing very slowly.

"I'd say I do." He snickers. "First interrogation, pretty boy?"

Yet another answer he doesn't need. I channel the snippets of Kieran's lessons from Father I overheard and grab the back of the chair he's chained to, tilting it back and forcing him to look me in the eye. I wear gloves around the castle this time of year, but I can feel the dull sickness of silver even through them. This close, the assassin is obviously injured, but pity is the last thing on my mind. He killed a king.

"Tell me your name," I growl.

His smile grows. "Tell me yours."

Whoever gives ground first loses, Father says in my mind.

I drop the chair back to the ground so he's sitting upright again. "Kill him, dump the body somewhere the Goddess will never find him."

The assassin chuckles. "Pretty boy's got some balls. I like that. You can call me Birsha. But you need me too bad to drop me in the ground just yet, so let's keep playing."

One of the guards flanking him seems to smother a smile. My pulse pounds in my ears. I am failing, and I'm doing it in front of an audience.

"What pack do you belong to?" I demand.

"Packs are for sissies like you." Birsha puffs out his chest as much as he can in the chains. "I live wild, like a real man ought to."

A rogue. Fuck. Anybody could hire a rogue, even someone in Dun's Crossing.

"Did you kill King Isai?" I lean close again. His scent, wet mulch and sweet rot, chokes the air.

"I don't like you enough for that." Birsha leans back like he's avoiding my gaze, then whips his head forward.

A thick, hot glob of spit lands on my cheek. I scrub it away and lurch back. That same fucking guard chokes on a laugh. My temper rages in my chest.

I grab the laughing guard's chin. "Name."

He pales. "Kyle, Your Highness."

"Rohan, if Kyle laughs again, kill him," I say directly into Kyle's face.

"With pleasure," Rohan replies.

I release Kyle and turn right to Rohan. I don't want to see Birsha's fucking smirk.

"Tell me more about those tactics," I grit out.

Rohan pulls out a thick dropper, half-full of a bluish-gray liquid. "How's a truth serum suit you?"

"Pretty damn good." I grab the dropper.

Kyle grunts. "He really is King Gavin's son. Goes straight for his favorite."

"Don't be too quick on the draw," Rohan says. "Even the king and

Albatrose swore a single droplet sufficed, on the skin just after you ask something."

'Don't tell me what to do,' I snap over the mind-link before turning to Birsha, whose eyes have gone wide.

"What is that?" he asks.

"I second the question," Cristofer intones.

"Did you kill King Isai?" I squeeze a single drop onto the bare skin of Birsha's arm.

Birsha throws back his head and howls like he's in his wolf form. His skin sizzles, and an acrid stench fills the air, underpinned by something familiar and sickening. Cristofer vomits in the corner of the small cell.

Once, Mother took me into her private greenhouse, pointed me toward a stalk of blue flowers, and made me promise never to touch them or tell anyone about them. I agreed, as always. Though I didn't understand what she showed me until much later, I never forgot the smell.

Wolfsbane. In tiny doses, it hurts like a bitch and weakens a shifter's powers, even limiting their access to their wolf. In bigger ones—

Memories of my brief trip into Escuro flash through my mind. I turn to give the dropper back.

"Yes!" Birsha yells.

Everything slows. I turn back to him. "What?"

"Yes, I killed the fucking king!" he says. "Fuck, just stop that."

"How did you do it?" If he answers wrong, I'll know he's just agreeing to get me to stop.

Birsha rocks in his restraints. "Let me go. I'll tell you everything if you let me go."

"Tell me how you did it." I squeeze another drop onto his arm.

"Silver arrow!" Birsha screams as his skin melts. After a few breaths, he continues. "I've always been a crack shot, and the balcony was a dream. Please, just stop. I'll answer anything."

"I won't stand for this." Cristofer steps forward. "He may be a prisoner, but he's still a person."

I stare up at the massive Beta. Father was right about more than anyone's willing to give him credit for. With this, Birsha is putty in my hands.

"No," I say evenly. "He's not while he's in here. If you don't have the stomach to solve your Alpha's murder, listen from outside."

Something in Cristofer goes taut. He storms to the cell door, where a guard lets him out, and closes the door behind him. I have no way of knowing if he's still outside, if Estrella will believe anything I learn without him backing me, but I can't miss out on this opportunity. The thrill of the hunt sings in my veins, and I feel more alive than I ever have in my human form.

I turn back to Birsha. "Did you do it for yourself or because someone hired you?"

His eyes nearly bulge out of his skull. Rohan chuckles.

"Ask me anything but that."

"Tell me their name." Another drop.

"I don't know!" Tears roll down Birsha's face, cutting lines of paler skin through the layer of dirt. "I met this motherfucker in the woods, and he handed me a note."

"When did you meet him?" I've spent days tracking down the whereabouts of everyone in this Goddess-damned castle the day of the ball, so if we can narrow down the window, I can start ruling people out.

No answer. I move to his other arm and splash another droplet onto him. He screams.

"Day of the ball." His voice is ragged. "Sun was still up."

"Good." I take a step back, out of the wolfsbane fumes. Candace and Ingrid started getting ready four hours before the ball, and a dozen different servants report they didn't leave their room after they started.

"Was it before or after noon?" I don't wait for Birsha to hesitate before dropping more wolfsbane.

He writhes. This is no more than he deserves. He's a contract killer, and King Isai was a good man.

"After," Birsha finally gasps. "At lunch at the… I don't know, the fucking pub with the sign. Ask around."

I mind-link with Baz. *Take a team into town. Ask for a wolf meeting Birsha's description at all the pubs on the day of the ball. I need to confirm his timeline.*

'Get a new Beta,' Baz replies tiredly. *'After this.'*

I smile down at Birsha. Once Baz has that information, Ingrid and Candace will be cleared. Now, for the rest of us.

* * *

Huge, gray-red welts cover Birsha's now bare chest by the time I'm done. I ran out of skin on his arms before I even cleared Finn, and then I realized none of this would mean anything if I couldn't be sure about our Betas as well. But I've done it. With only a few drops left, I've cleared just about everyone.

Everyone except Kieran. Because Harper's still in the wind, and no one knows what they talked about.

Rohan claps me on the shoulder. "Hell of a job, kid. We'll make sure he lives through the night."

"I don't really give a fuck." I can't force the smile off my face. The rest of us are cleared, and I know Kieran didn't do it.

I have to go tell Estrella.

21

HAPPIER NOT KNOWING

ESTRELLA

THUD.

I sit up in bed, clutching the blankets to my chest. My heart races. Someone is attempting to break into my room.

The noise comes again, but this time, without the muffling of sleep, it sounds far more like a knock. I swallow.

Silly, I chide myself. *Even in a serpent's nest, paranoia doesn't help anyone.*

I slide from bed, shivering against the encroaching cold, and pull a robe on over my nightgown. The person outside knocks again, urgent but quiet. I hurry from my bedroom, through the sitting room with its low-burning embers in the fireplace, and open the door.

Anwen stands in the hall, hair and eyes wild. "Can I come in?"

I blink. "It's the dead of night. I was asleep."

"I'm sorry." He steps inside, even though I haven't given him permission. "I had to see you."

I step back and clutch my robe closer around me. It was a gift from Nessa, and I'm thankful for the thicker fabric now. Anwen's leather doublet hangs slightly askew, exposing a triangle of skin at his throat, far too near his mark. My wolf paces and howls, reminding me of last night's dream. I need the wintry wrap to keep myself away from him. My sleep-addled mind is obviously insufficient, if I'm noticing that bit of skin at all.

He shuts the door behind himself, intensifying his scent, and grins. The firelight shines off his teeth. "We caught the assassin."

My heart skips a beat. "Truly?"

"There's no mistaking it." He steps closer again. "The man confessed."

Thoughts tumble through my mind. Even before this, I was sleeping restlessly, like my logical brain was trying to keep me from another dream, so my mind is muddled. Emotions swarm like tiny fish, darting away from my grasp. A burst of relief washes through me, and for a moment, I think I must tell Father. On the heels of that, rage follows. I cannot tell him. This assassin took that from me. And though it all, a powerful thread of shock. Is this nightmare... over? Could I possibly relax?

"Who...? Why....?" No question seems sufficient at this moment.

"He is a rogue," Anwen says. "A hired thug, no one with any particular grudge against your people."

Like a cold wind against the rattling windows of this castle, despair sweeps through me, scaring off all the other emotions. I sit down heavily on the settee in front of the fireplace.

"So he's not the true villain," I murmur. "There's another one yet to find."

Anwen sits next to me. The firelight paints him even more golden than usual. He moves like one of the flames, flickering and strange.

"And I'll find them," he says. "But you should know that I've cleared my family. The rogue, Birsha, met with a messenger he described at a specific time. I know the movements of everyone in the palace on the day of the ball. Candace, Ingrid, Finn, Raven, myself...." He grins brightly again. "Estrella, you have nothing to fear from us. You can look your people in the eye and tell them the Solbergs did not kill their king."

Sleep hangs heavy off my thoughts as I try to review the list of his siblings, remember how many of them there really are. Has he said every name? Would he truly think me stupid enough that a simple omission would be enough to hide wrongdoing.

"Is this why Cristofer disappeared in the middle of dinner?" I ask instead.

Anwen blinks. "Uh, yeah. I guess. I figured, since you asked for him to be involved in the investigation that you'd want him to witness the interrogation."

That final word lands like a stone in the pit of my stomach. I am not naïve to the ways of government, the way traitors must be handled, but I will admit that I would rather live my whole life without knowing how Dun's Crossing handles such matters.

"I should wake him." I stand. "And Tess. I need more minds than my own, but I'd rather not excite Mother and Castor until I'm certain."

"Certain about what?" Anwen frowns. "I'm here telling you we made a massive breakthrough. That I am innocent. Don't you understand what this means?"

His frown calls the dream to the front of my mind again with a rush of heat. I tighten my robe at the waist, even though it shortens the arms and leaves inches of my wrists vulnerable to the cold.

"We can be mated publicly." He stands with me, his wild grin softening into something kinder. "There's nothing to worry about anymore. We didn't attack you, and I can't think of any better way to formally declare our alliance."

Publicly mated. Publicly tied to this man, son of the king who destroyed half the world in his quest for power. A man with a past I may never be able to fully understand, who will always be a part of my worst memory.

"It's late." I take a step toward the door that connects my room to Tess's. "Or early. I—"

"Please." He grabs my wrist again.

Pain like nothing I have ever felt before tears through me. It's as though someone managed to pour boiling sugar directly into the core of my bones, sickening and melting them in a single blow. A high, animal yelp tears from my lips, and I throw myself away from Anwen and stare at my wrist. There, just below the sleeve of my robe, is a line of smoking, black-gray skin. A stench fills the air between us, one Father had an apothecary replicate and taught me never to mistake.

Wolfsbane.

I jerk my head up to look at Anwen. He is studying his own, unmarred wrist. The pain starts to recede as the firelight grows brighter, and warmth fills me. It feels like—

The light catches on a damp patch on his leather sleeve, and the warmth flowing through my body instantly fades from my notice.

"How did you interrogate the rogue?" I ask quietly.

He glances at me. "I asked questions. He answered. Estrella, your arm—"

"Is none of your concern." I straighten as the pain becomes something I can live with. "Why did he answer? Wouldn't the sort of man you could hire to assassinate a king more likely go to the grave with his secrets?"

Anwen won't look at me now. The sickening feeling drains from my arm to my gut. I know the answer to the question, but a part of me needs to hear him say it.

"What do you know of what happened in Escuro?" I ask.

"I think that's unfair," he replies.

I shake my head. "They called for help. Missives arrived in every kingdom they thought wasn't already under King Gavin's thumb. Including ours. And do you know what it said?"

Publicly mated. Anwen did this, and he expected me to shackle myself to him for all eternity. I can't even see the golden tousle of his hair, the flash of hurt in his eyes. I won't.

"It said they were dying." I spit the words like my own poison. "Like the water was eating them from the inside out, and they needed supplies." I blink tears from my eyes. "Father wasn't fast enough. By the time we'd mustered our ships, they were already dead. When he taught me to recognize wolfsbane, he told me that story and called it the cruelest weapon to wield against our kind."

"I grew up with a different story." He stares at his hands. "That one… it makes me fucking sick."

"And yet you used it." I shake my head. "How could you?"

"How could I?" He whips a stare at me. "The rogue wouldn't answer any other way. I knew the second I looked at him that he couldn't have done this on his own. Was I supposed to just let the investigation die? Let you live out your days never knowing who killed your father? I was just trying to make you happy!"

His words nearly knock the wind out of me. If the wolfsbane hurt so much from the barest brush, I can't imagine what being questioned under its effects would be like. There is a man, somewhere in this castle, who knows because this prince thought it would please me.

There is no greater insult to Father's memory.

And my supposed mate dealt it to him.

"Is that what you're telling yourself?" I snap. "That you only resorted to torture because the mating bond drove you to it?"

"I don't get why you're so pissed." He throws his hands in the air. "You wanted answers. I got them for you."

"And I would rather not have them if they only come at the cost of this much suffering!" I roar. "There is nothing in this life that could induce me to cross that line. Nothing. So if you would truly like to make me happy, stop blaming me for you having given yourself the permission to be the man you wanted to be all along."

His mouth falls slightly open for a second before he clicks his jaw shut. His icy eyes light with cold fire. "You're going to have a bitch of a time getting that high horse of yours back across the Lonely Sea, Your Majesty."

"What does that mean?" I grit out. More Dun's Crossing idioms that he knows I can't understand.

"It means"—he takes a step closer, towering over me, the stink of wolfsbane clouding out his smell—"I can't wait to see how you lead a kingdom without ever compromising. It'll be a real pleasure, watching you come crawling back to us when you need help. Or do you have someone else do your dirty work, so you can keep being happier not knowing what goes on?"

I snarl, "Sundrop Gem doesn't need this violence to maintain itself, and I pity you for thinking we do."

"The strong lead. The weak judge," he spits. "I did what I had to do. And yes, I fucking did it for you. Forgive me for thinking you were a goddessdamn adult who could handle the truth."

"You didn't!" I close the final gap, smashing my chest against his and praying the robe is thick enough to protect me from any other splatters of the poison. "I had to discover the poison. You only wanted to tell me that you could finally make me yours, now that the timing is right for you."

His jaw works. "You keep pushing me away because you don't trust us. I came to tell you that you could."

"With poison on your clothes." I laugh, the sound strange and stilted. There's nothing left for either of us here, and I won't wake my family with our shouting. I storm to my door and hold it open. "You really are your father's son, Prince Anwen."

22

GROWING UP

Anwen

I stare at Estrella for a long moment, my blood boiling in my veins. She doesn't flinch, doesn't release the door.

"If you're not careful, you're going to end up your father's daughter." I storm out and slam the door behind me.

Does she think I'm fucking stupid? Wolfsbane isn't a mystery to me. I slam my fist into the wall, and my knuckles burn. I crossed the line for her, because I fucking had to, and because it fucking worked. Goddess, it was like she didn't even hear the part where I caught her father's killer. I do everything she fucking asks me to, and still, she kicks me out in the middle of the night like I'm some kind of monster.

The strong lead, Father says in my memory, *the weak judge.*

He was fucking right about that too. And I'm getting tired of pretending he was never right. I know he did horrible things. I sided against him that night, and I'd do it again. But dammit, we didn't bury his every teaching in his empty grave.

The castle walls start to close in on me. My skin itches. I need to fucking run.

Tonight, I don't waste my time with secret passages and hiding from guards. I'm the crown fucking prince, if anybody even remembers. I stride through the halls with my chin high and my knuckles weeping blood.

The first step I take out into the night, I throw myself into a shift. My wolf swallows me whole. Insects hum their evening symphony, too quiet for human ears to hear with winter on the horizon. Nocturnal animals rustle through the brush, tempting but always too small. All beyond the gate.

'*Release me,*' I yell at the guards manning the mechanism.

Finally, someone fucking listens. The gate opens smoothly, and I launch myself out. Rotting leaves crunch under my paw pads. The wind tears at my fur as I push myself fast, faster. My heartbeat hammers in my ears, nearly blotting out the other smells.

Maybe I can go fast enough that shit starts making sense again.

Trees whip past me. I don't pay attention to them. I don't want to see the spot we shared during the Haze. I don't want to know if it still smells like her, if I can even pick it out. I just need to run.

A smell catches my nose. Another wolf, this one familiar. Grit underpins moss. Kieran.

'*What the fuck are you doing out here?*' I ask over the mind-link.

'*Clearing my head,*' he replies. '*You learn anything?*'

'*Don't ask me that.*'

He lopes over to my side, his silver wolf a hand and a half taller than me. Just like Father. I would tell him to fuck off, but he doesn't ask any more questions. If he just wants to run, fine. I dash off, daring him to keep up.

Kieran's never been one to back down from a challenge, but he doesn't stand a chance against me at the moment. We whip through the forest, past boulders, streams, and ponds without a glance. When we were younger, we used to do this all the time. And every time, the rules were the same: first to the Goddess' Fist wins. It was the only time I ever beat him at anything, but I beat him every time. I didn't mean to run toward the old spot, but when I see the rock formation through the trees and realize my veins are finally more full of adrenaline than anger, I know what to do.

I touch the fist-shaped boulder with my nose then shift and collapse onto my back. Kieran rushes up a few moments later and shifts as well.

"Someday, I'll beat you," he says.

"You'd have to play dirty." I roll onto my stomach and look at him, leaning against the base of the rock. He seems tired. Then, his eyebrows lift.

"Your back," he says simply.

I start to twist to see what he's looking at before I remember. The fucking bite. The one I completely forgot about before going bare-ass naked in front of my brother, the king. I grimace.

"It's her, isn't it?" he asks.

"You're right, Nessa is actually my mate, and I was too embarrassed to tell anyone." I smirk.

"Don't be a dick." Kieran rolls his eyes. "Does she have anything to do with your midnight run?"

A ghost of my rage flickers back through my veins, but mostly, I can feel the eating-me-from-the-inside burn of the wolfsbane. My stomach churns.

"Did Father ever take you to the dungeons?" I ask. "When he was… working?"

"I had to stay until I puked." He sighs. "Did the guards—"

"I did it myself," I say.

Kieran exhales slowly. "Fuck, An."

"Do you even want to know if it worked?" I meet his gaze. "Nobody seems to give a fuck that it worked. That Father might not have been all wrong."

He doesn't flinch. He better not. Everybody walking around accusing me of being my father's son seems to have forgotten that Kieran used to run this place with an iron fist, that he used to get complimented for how like Father he was.

"A lot of Father's methods worked," Kieran says.

That knocks the wind out of me. I sit up and put my back to the rock as well, so I don't have to look at him.

"Then why are they so bad?" I ask quietly.

"That's not what you want to ask," he replies.

I shake my head. "Then why was he so bad? Why won't anyone even say his name anymore without insult?"

"Because he took the easy way."

I blink. "Have you seen someone under the effect of his truth serum? It seemed pretty damn hard."

"For them," Kieran says. "For you, it was fast. Simple. Painless." He cuts his eyes at me. "Maybe you even liked it."

I swallow. Estrella's words ring in my ears. I definitely didn't mind it by the end.

"Father's methods work because they put all the work, all the pain, on other people." Kieran tilts his head back and stares up at the night sky. "Just like poisoning Escuro instead of going to war like an honorable king. They're the cheap way out. You may need a little smarts, but you don't have to put anything on the line."

"How else was I supposed to get answers?" I whisper.

"With time," he replies. "By trying to connect with the assassin, make your arguments make sense to him."

And instead, I chose the option that asked the least of me. Isn't that what Estrella's been accusing me of all along? Of being too scared or selfish to choose anything but my own convenience? I close my eyes and lean my head back against the cold stone.

"How the fuck did you figure all this out?" I ask.

"Raven."

I scoff. He punches me in the shoulder.

"I thought we talked about you being a dick."

"Fine, fine." I hold up my hands. "Tell me your precious sister-love's words of wisdom."

"It's not like that." He sighs, obviously starting to get bored of my antics. "It's that our lives were fucking easy, An, and hers was fucking hard, but she kept trying."

"Your life was easy," I mutter.

'Look at me,' he says.

I open my eyes and meet his gaze. "What?"

"Our lives were easy," he repeats.

"Tell that to a lifetime of doors in my face." I shut my eyes again. "I had to work. I know every secret the castle has, and I found them out for myself."

"Fine. Why did you do that?" he asks.

"Because...." I shake my head. "Because it made me valuable." And if I was valuable, Father might let me into all those lessons he kept me away from.

"And you expected a reward for that."

"Fine, yes!" I explode. "I wanted to be just as important as you. Is that so bad?"

Kieran stares back at me evenly. "No, but expecting it is. Because he trained both of us—all of us to want the easiest path. To choose it whenever we could."

"How can you talk about him like that?" My chest hurts. "He raised us."

"Because I have to." He runs a hand through his hair. "Fuck, do you think I don't miss him? It's eating me alive. I killed him, An. But it's so damned easy to become him. That's the hard fight you have to choose if you want to be better."

I slump back against the rock. My eyes sting with tears. No one else has said that yet. Father's "funeral" was a couple muttered prayers around an empty mausoleum already dedicated in his name. No one cried, and no one's said a kind word about him since.

"I thought it was just me."

Kieran pats my shoulder. "That's the other thing. We've gotta talk to each other, too. Because we're nowhere near as special as we think, good or bad."

"Dickhead." I smile.

23

HEALING

ESTRELLA

I LIE IN BED WITH MY ARMS CROSSED, GLARING AT THE CANOPY overhead. Anwen Solberg may be the most stubborn, most callous man I've ever met in my life. How dare he call me weak? How dare he commit such atrocities in my name and then have the gall to act surprised when I show him the truth of his actions?

Thinking of him, at least, is easier than thinking of the man in pain, somewhere in this castle.

The candle next to me sputters, then pops. Three times. Which means I have been staring angrily at the ceiling for an hour and a half. I groan and scrub my eyes. Lying here is only likely to irritate me further, so with a sigh, I get out of bed. Dressing is difficult without a second set of hands, but I manage to get myself into something near-presentable before slipping out of my room.

Only the cold, stone hallways of the castle I've spent the last week and a half in greet me. It is too late and too early for servants, so I have the space to myself. My footsteps echo, lonely and uncertain.

Something in my chest pangs. I cannot imagine growing up here.

And I don't want to. This place makes monsters. I lift my chin and stride down the hall with no destination in mind. My dress brushes the inside of my wrist, and I brace for the pain.

Nothing comes. It hasn't hurt in some time, in fact. I step to the side of the hall and inspect my skin. Where the oozing blackish mark once stood, there is only my own unbroken, sandy skin. It healed.

My heart beats out of time. I run my thumb over the spot again and again, searching for any whisper of that sickening pain. Nothing.

I healed it.

The glow shines in my mind's eye, the one I dismissed in the room tonight and thought I may have imagined on the night of Father's death. There are stories, ancient stories, of leaders particularly touched by the Moon Goddess. Ones who channel her light, not into light itself, but into light for the body. Healing. Those leaders appear when… the voice of our holy woman, Yana, rings in my ears, but I can't remember what she said. These stories are told rarely. We haven't seen a leader like this since well before Dun's Crossing and Sundrop Gem became different kingdoms.

Could those be related?

Certainly not. Nothing healing has ever come from proximity to Gavin Solberg or his children. Anwen especially only causes pain.

An idea seizes me, and I turn on my heel. Anwen caused pain in my name. I did not ask him to, and I refused to accept it, but the pain was caused all the same. With this, though, I have some way to fix that and quell the roiling guilt in my gut.

I knock on Cristofer's door quietly. My father's Beta answers after a brief hesitation. He looks drawn, exhausted, but he snaps to attention.

"Your Majesty? Is everything all right?"

I nod. "I simply have a question. You were in the dungeons tonight, yes?"

His gaze slides away from my face. "Yes."

"I need directions."

"What?" Shock paints his face. "No, Your Majesty, I—"

"Directions." I try to infuse my voice with iron, like Father sometimes did.

It seems to work well enough. Cristofer looks away from me again as he mumbles a set of simple directions. I can only imagine what he saw tonight.

"The Goddess would not frown on you for taking a sleeping draught," I say by way of thanks.

He smiles wanly and shuts the door. I turn toward the dungeons. I've never seen him so tired. In my very first memory of the man, he's bent at the waist, laughing full-throated at one of Father's worst jokes during a luncheon. It was never easy to make him laugh, exactly—he took his duties as Beta seriously—but never was it too hard either.

Thinking of Cristofer leads me, as it always does, to memories of Father. Cristofer's hard-won laughter didn't stop Father from trying. A few months after Tess's mother and his mate passed, I remember Father pulling me over to Cristofer at an event and the both of us telling the silliest jokes we could think of until he cracked a smile. Later, when Mother complained we were being undignified, Father said that there was no point to being a king if he were not equally responsible for his people's smiles as their frowns. Then, of course, he tickled Mother in the spot at her side that always made her laugh, and the whole conversation dissolved.

My chest aches as I wind deeper into the castle. I doubt I'll ever be able to make people smile as effortlessly as he did, no matter how much I want to. I haven't managed it with Mother or Castor yet. Mother still floats around her rooms like a ghost, only putting on enough of a face that the strangers here won't realize that she's a shell of who she used to be. Gone is the vivacious, loving woman I grew up with.

With a stinging in my eyes, I suddenly realize I may not have my royal portrait painted by Mother. She brought her paints here, her personal promise that we would hope this trip succeeded until it didn't, but she hasn't touched a brush since the ball. And she always promised she would. Or, she has since the disaster of Father's royal portrait.

After he was crowned, he put off the matter of the portrait for years, claiming his princely portrait would do. So as the years passed, an image of Father at perhaps sixteen hung over his head, growing ever more out of date. On his thirtieth birthday, Mother put her foot down. He had to replace the portrait before he had lived as many years after it as before. He agreed—he always agreed when she put her foot down—and hired an artist. And then another. And then another. Every one came out "wrong," according to him, but he wouldn't let anyone see them. Finally, Mother declared the throne room closed for the day, sat him down, and painted him. He didn't even look at the piece before declaring it perfect and demanding it hung.

A small smile creeps across my lips. On my sixteenth birthday, Father showed me the room where he kept all the other portraits. Every single one was perfectly serviceable. And he told me, in a whisper, that he wanted Mother to do it all along but knew she'd refuse because she wouldn't believe herself good enough. Sometimes, he said, a leader must know his people better than they know themselves.

My smile dies. Knowing others better won't be hard because I don't know myself at all.

I turn a corner, and a damp smell oozes up from an open doorway, right where the entrance to the dungeons should be. My stomach curdles. I'm here. All I have to do is walk down those stairs and right a wrong I didn't create.

And face the man who killed my father.

Father believed in second chances. No jail term in Sundrop was ever more than three years, at which point the perpetrators were allowed a new trial, in which they might plead to atone for their crimes by helping the community instead. He preached constantly that this was the only way we survived. By believing in each other and the bond we shared. He would have no trouble facing down this rogue and offering him help.

Guilt and anger war in my chest. The wolfsbane was awful, monstrous. I didn't believe anyone deserved that. Mostly. But if anyone were to deserve it, it would be the man at the bottom of those stairs.

I have never been less afraid for our future, Father said.

In my heart, I know he planned those words for my coronation. His voice takes on a particular rhythm when he's giving a pre-written speech, and there's no other occasion he would have planned them for.

"I'm sorry." I sink to my knees with a sob. Father won't speak at my coronation. He won't ever speak again. And the man in the dungeon made that true, but I made myself the sort of daughter my father would be disappointed to look down from the stars upon.

Footsteps sound on the stairs. I try to convince my legs to stand, my arms to wipe my tears, but they won't obey.

"Oh," a woman says softly.

If the Goddess is truly with me, it will be Nessa. I pry open my eyes.

Luna Queen Raven stares up at me with pity on her face and a wooden bucket in her hands. I cannot imagine a worse witness to my failure.

"Apologies, Your Majesty." I fight for any shred of composure with my tears still flowing. "I—"

She sits on the ground next to me. "You know who's down there, don't you?"

I nod helplessly. Somewhere in the back of my mind, I note that she's wearing an even plainer dress than I've seen in most of Dun's Crossing.

"He's alive, if you're wondering." She sighs. "And hurt."

Nausea claws at my throat. "I can help him."

A hard, bright smile appears on her face. "You may have the biggest heart I've ever known. Don't worry, I was tending to everyone down there." Her smile turns wry. "Even my mother-in-law."

I blink and, humiliatingly, sniffle. "What?"

"Conditions are better than they once were, but there's still much to do." She pats her bucket. "I ensure they are fed and watered, unin-fected, the basics."

"Why?" The word stumbles over my lips before I can catch it.

She laughs in surprise. "They're people, aren't they?"

That startles me out of my sobs. The story of Luna Raven is quite clear. She's of Escuro, but she was raised here, under King Gavin. She should be like the others. But helping the prisoners... Mother took Castor and I to do that every month, and others tended them other times.

"Now, since I tended to him, can I help you back to bed?" Luna Raven asks.

"Yes," I say disbelievingly.

Without another ounce of pity, she helps me to my feet and leads the way back to my room. She's utterly silent, except for the few times she mutters the word, "Patrol," and changes direction. She's keeping me out of others' eyes.

"Thank you," I say when she deposits me at my door.

She smiles. "Any time."

I stumble back to bed, thinking perhaps the Luna of Dun's Crossing isn't quite as bad as Nessa says.

24

NIGHTMARE

ANWEN

PAIN SCREAMS THROUGH EVERY LIMB, STARTING AND ENDING IN THE center of my chest. Liquid fire burns through me. Someone is tearing my heart out.

I lurch up in bed, where I passed out after my run with Kieran, and find myself alone. Windows and doors all closed. I grope my chest. No sign of injury, but the pain isn't fading. For a moment, I think I've been poisoned. Then, the pain takes on the barest hint of a shape. It's not mine.

Estrella.

I throw myself across the room and out the door before I even have a second thought. The un-warmed castle hallways sink icy fingers into my skin. My loose, thin pajamas flap as I race toward my mate. Someone is hurting her, and I can't allow that. My teeth lengthen, and my nails sharpen. If it wouldn't slow me down, I'd stop in the armory for a blade. Anyone who touches her must die. I itch for the blood of the bastard causing her this pain and have to fight back a shift. In the tight halls and secret passages that shape the absolute fastest path to her, my wolf would only slow me down. I just barrel forward and curse whoever put the Sundrop Gem rooms so far from mine.

I burst into the hallway containing her room. A few servants preparing for the morning scatter. Fuck what anybody thinks, my mate needs me.

Her door is closed. I prowl closer, sniffing the air. No unfamiliar smells, though several of the delegates from other packs also sleep in this hall. No one I had marked as suspicious, either. I suck in a deep breath and rap on her door.

No answer. I press my ear to the wood, straining to hear anything. Nothing at all.

"Fucking human ears," I hiss.

I try the knob. Locked.

The tiny corner of my mind I still recognize begs me to knock again, to wait, to think about how this will look. The rest of me, all animal, roars that I'm wasting time.

It's an easy decision to make.

I back up to the far wall, lead with my shoulder, and charge. New strength infuses my muscles. No one touches my mate. The wood splinters just above the doorknob, but it's enough. I slam my fist into the splintered section, punch through, and unfasten the heavy bolt from this side. Then, I wrench the door open and race inside.

No one in the sitting room. The only smells in here other than hers are mine and her friend, Tess. Something creaks in her bedroom.

This door, I smash through without hesitation. It isn't even locked, something I'll have to talk to her about.

She yelps from inside her canopied bed.

For a dark second, I consider that Birsha might've escaped. That he might have disguised his scent and be finishing the job this very moment, and I might not arrive in time. But the pain threatening to tear me limb from limb continues, an agonizing promise that she's still alive. I have one last chance to make the apology I meant to give her over breakfast in the morning. I leap the final distance, arrive at her bedside, and yank open the canopy.

Estrella lays there, alone. The sheets twist around her body, and her eyelids flutter wildly. Her dark hair spreads across her pillow like a thornbush.

"No," she whispers.

I drop to my knees next to her. There are many witches in this world, and if someone has discovered a way to attack her in her mind, I need to know who.

"Father, I…." Her sentences dribbles off, then resumes with a groan. "—the blood!"

She's dreaming of her father's death. There's no attacker, no enemy other than the one I've been fighting all along. All my adrenaline melts away, alongside the lingering traces of my earlier anger. It would be easy to get mad at her and let her bear the brunt of the pain. I want to be better than that. For her. And, hell, maybe for me.

As gently as I can, I put my hand on her shoulder and wake her.

Her eyes fly open, bloodshot around the gray. "Duck!"

The pain stops like flipping a switch. I pull my hand back. "You're all right. You're in bed. It was just a dream."

"A…dream?" Her cheeks go blotchy. Tears gather in her eyes. "A dream."

"A nightmare," I say. "But it's okay. There are a few hours left until morning."

She looks at me out of the corner of her eye. "Anwen."

"That's me." I smile softly. "I, uh, felt you."

"Felt me." She starts shaking violently and pulls her knees into her chest. "I felt him. Die."

My chest aches, and I don't know whether it's an echo of her pain or my own heart breaking for her.

"I know," I murmur. "I'm so sorry."

She only shakes harder. Clearly, she needs something, but I don't know what. I pat her arm.

Estrella flinches away.

"Sorry." I wince. "Do you want to talk about it?"

She shakes her head furiously.

"Okay." I stare at the rug on the floor, racking my brains. All the information I learned, and I don't know shit about comforting people. "I can just talk to you."

She doesn't shake worse. She doesn't flinch. It might be the best I'm going to get.

Taking Kieran's advice, I go right for the hard stuff. Nothing I'd ever dream of bringing up with the girls I used to spend time with. "So, my mother's in the dungeons."

No response. That makes sense. I plunge forward.

"She has been for several weeks now. And I know that. I know exactly where she is. I could go visit her whenever I want." I sigh. "But I just haven't. I've been to my father's empty grave, but I've never visited her."

Estrella sucks in a breath. I pause, waiting for more from her, but there's nothing.

"My father… I knew exactly where I stood with him. We all did." I pluck at the rug. "Mother was—is different. I think Ingrid was her favorite, but I'm not sure. And, to be honest, I only really thought Father had anything useful to teach me. So I guess you were right about that."

More quiet, but her breath sounds a little more even.

"I don't want to be his son. But I never really was my mother's. I think she figured I was his problem. I don't know the woman in the dungeon, and her being there isn't really a great time to get to know her." I exhale in one big gust. "Shit. I didn't know that was the reason."

I look up at Estrella and find her watching me with wide eyes. I try a smile.

She seems to try one in return. Something in my chest flutters, fragile as a baby bird.

Goddess above, that's terrifying.

Estrella mumbles something.

I lean closer. "What?"

"Keep… going," she manages. "Anything."

"Okay." I nod. "I can do that."

I launch into a story from when Baz and I were young, one that doesn't make us look good. After that, I tell a couple stories about

Finn and Ingrid. When she still wants more, I just start describing the secret passages in the castle, where they lead, and who I think built them.

It's weird, but there's something freeing in just talking. I don't watch every word for secondary implications, don't keep my weaknesses close to my chest, barely even watch her expression for reactions. She wants noise. That, I can provide.

"All right," she says eventually. "I'm… all right."

I look up at her. Dark bags underscore her eyes, and she chewed her lower lip bloody. My heart skips a beat. She's stunning.

"Do you want a hug?" I ask.

She takes a deep breath and scans my gaze. She's clearly torn, looking for something. When did I get so good at reading her? Or has she dropped some façade tonight too?

"All right," she whispers like she doesn't want anyone to hear.

I stand, and she scoots a little back from the edge of the mattress. Making space for me. I take the spot beside her and wrap my arms around her shoulders.

Her smell enfolds me. I wait for the usual burst of lust, but something bigger keeps it at bay. Little shivers shake her body like an icy pond threatening to crack. Her knotted hair sticks to her cheek, and I can see new tears threatening in her eyes. She is just barely holding herself together, just barely all right enough to tell me to go.

"Lie down," I murmur.

She doesn't even ask why, just pulls out of my arms and makes herself comfortable. My chest aches, and this time, I know the feeling's mine. She looks so fragile, so small.

I slip into the bed behind her, curl my body around hers, and tuck my arm over her waist. She stiffens for a second then relaxes on an exhale.

"There's a little bit of time till morning," I say. "I want to make sure you actually sleep."

The ghost of a smile curves her lips. I wish I was a painter so I could capture the moment to have forever. But it disappears, like all beautiful things do. I just nuzzle into her hair and breathe her in. She twines her fingers with mine, and I have never been more comfortable.

In mere moments, her breathing evens out. She's asleep. Our chests rise and fall in rhythm, like we've done this a million times. I could do it a million times and want to capture that smile every single time.

But this morning, I watch the sky start to lighten, turning from near-black to pre-dawn gray to pinkish. When it reaches pink, I force myself to disentangle from her. She doesn't want to be publicly mated, and I won't force her hand. That means I need to get back across the castle before enough people wake to start a rumor.

I drop a kiss on her forehead and leave, feeling like my heart is sitting in her chest behind me.

'Hey,' Baz's voice is worried over mind-link. '*You might want to get to the west tower.*'

25

ARE YOU SATISFIED?

Estrella

"Yes, Mother." I prod at the toast on my plate. For the last week, that's about all I've eaten. I have no stomach. I just keep turning the night over and over again.

Castor shakes his head. "I don't believe you were even listening."

I glare at my brother, but in truth, I wasn't. I know I should be. Since the news of the assassin being caught, Mother has been a shade more herself, enough that she's managed a private, late-morning meal to discuss the transfer of power when we return to Sundrop. It's always *when* now, as opposed to her *if* of a few days ago.

"Apologies, Mother," I say, looking at Castor. "I don't believe he knows what he's saying."

She offers us a small smile, a pale echo of what she once was capable of, but brighter than yesterday. "Don't bicker. You know how your father hated that around the table."

Invoking his name even quells Castor. I return to picking at my toast.

"We'll have the… funeral first." The word puckers her mouth, like eating a lemon, but she plunges onward. "As the Goddess turns through Her phases, so must we finish one reign before beginning the next."

I nod. "And after… what will the changes be?"

"There is a magical element." She pats my hand. "Your power will swell. But beyond that, it's mostly administrative. I will still manage many of the details of our events, likely your calendar. Castor will serve as your right hand until you find your mate—"

My bite pulses. Anwen smiles in my memory.

"—and you will lead, as your father did." Mother sighs. "On the world stage, if you so choose."

"I cannot imagine Sundrop Gem returning to its isolation now," I say honestly.

"Nor can I." She stares at the table for a long moment. "Now, as for the matter of your coronation…."

Anwen's face floats through my mind again. Not the icy prince I've come to know, but the soft man who woke me this morning, who left before I woke with the grace of a wolf on the hunt. For a moment, after I found myself in an empty bed, I was devastated. But my mark didn't ache; my wolf didn't mourn. I ran my hands over the sheets, gathering the last of his warmth, and understood. If he left too late, the decision about us would be made.

That Anwen is the sort of mate I could fall in love with, not just fall into bed with.

"I spoke with Prince Anwen last night," I say. Luckily, reports from the lead investigator directly to the Luna raise no eyebrows.

Mother and Castor both turn to me.

"Did he have any news of the interrogation?" she asks urgently.

I stir my tea, sip it. Cristofer didn't answer my knock this morning, likely still under the effects of the sleeping draught, so I haven't been able to confirm Anwen's certainty that his family is innocent. But distrusting him, after all his care this morning, seems almost cruel.

"Some." I swallow. "He is certain the man they caught was hired.

He has begun the process of ruling out potential culprits, starting with his own family, to ease our mind."

Castor leans forward, rage in his eyes. He blames the Solbergs, I know. He wishes for any reason to attack them, get revenge for Father's death.

"He said that every Solberg had perfect proof of their innocence." I tap my spoon on the side of the teacup.

The door to the side dining room we have to ourselves bursts open. Castor leaps to his feet and draws the sword he keeps at his side since Father's death.

Floyd Winters hurries inside and shuts the door behind him, eyeing the blade. "Apologies. I didn't mean to startle you."

"Hold your temper, Castor," Mother chides.

Castor sheathes the sword and drops back into his seat. I study Floyd. His eyes are wide, his breathing labored. He looks as though he's had a terrible scare.

The hairs on my arms start to raise.

"I come bearing news." He folds his hands in front of him. "And I truly wish it was the better sort."

Mother goes ashen. "Has something happened to Isai?"

"Oh, my dear lady, I owe you my apologies again." Floyd creeps closer to our table, wringing his hands. "Nothing so disastrous as all that. But I do have news of the investigation, and if I may speak freely, it seems the sort King Kieran isn't likely to provide."

My stomach twists. I grip the arms of my chair. Anwen said—

"Early this morning, a body was found," Floyd says. "Looking to have been thrown from the highest tower in the castle."

"By the Goddess," Mother murmurs.

Castor just shakes his head.

"That of a Dun's Crossing soldier, one who had been missing for nearly two weeks now." Floyd tucks his hands behind his back. "A man named Harper. Had you heard of this?"

I shake my head, even as the muscles of my neck try to stiffen in place. Castor growls. My mark aches. Something is wrong, but I see no signs of dishonesty in Floyd. I never have.

"I am privy to this information only through a bit of luck. Maybe the Goddess' own hand." He smiles tightly. "I happened to be scheduled for an early meeting with the king that led me to his door while they discussed the details. I am obliged to inform you that the healer believes the body has been lying there, hidden in the brush, for a matter of days. Perhaps even the nearly two weeks the man has been missing."

I push my plate of food away. Floyd nods sympathetically. Yet again, I see no dishonesty in his face. There is no reason for this envoy, who has been nothing but kind to us, to lie.

"When I heard the rest, I knew what had to be done, in the name of Sundrop Gem's nascent alliance with Snowcrest, and in the name of your sainted father. I scuttled to the healer's chamber, where they were keeping the body, and took this." He produces a crumpled, bloodstained scrap of paper from behind his back.

I snatch it and read the handwritten note. Then again. My knees grow weak. My stomach sickens. I touch the blood, already dry.

"This…." I swallow down bile. "This is an order for the execution of my father. It names the time, the method, even the escape route. How—who—?"

"And we reach the reason why I thought the king might not see fit to inform you." Floyd bows deeply, as if in apology. "That note is written in King Kieran's own hand. I've seen it hundreds of times over—"

A roaring in my ears blots out the rest of his words. I don't know whether the sound is my wolf or my own heartbeat. King Kieran's hand. But that can't be true. Anwen said every sibling.

"Ask the assassin," I demand, unable to take in the shape of what he's saying. "If this is some conspiracy after the fact, the man won't know to lie."

Floyd grimaces. "On my race to reach you, I heard rumor that the rogue Birsha died in the dungeon last night.

"I'll kill them!" Castor bellows.

Mother already has a restraining hand on his arm, but she tightens it. "Peace, Castor. We cannot fight them here, not with our current numbers."

She's right, but my heart pounds like a war drum. The ground underneath my feet is unsteady. Anwen said—he *promised*, with that wild light in his eyes, named every sibling—

No, he didn't. A memory plays out in my mind's eye, listing every Solberg by name except one.

Kieran.

Something at the core of me boils. The softness of this morning shatters. Were it not for Luna Raven's confession, I wouldn't even believe his mother was being held in the dungeon. Last night, this morning, Anwen said nothing he has not been saying since the beginning. Nothing I did not watch him whisper in the ears of a thousand other maidens at the ball where his brother murdered my father in cold blood. I was a fool to let a single moment of care sweep me off my feet. Yet again, I've failed Father. He told me I deserve more, not to lower myself for Anwen, and I have done that ceaselessly. The answer is obvious. It has been all along. The war drums raise to a crescendo. I have no tears left, only a perpetrator to find guilty for crimes against my people.

The door opens again, slower. Mother releases Castor's arm. His sword catches the wan light streaming in through the windows.

Anwen steps inside. My heart climbs into my throat. He still wears the loose nightclothes I saw this morning, and his hair is rumpled. With his hands raised to show they're empty, he looks exactly like the man I shared my bed with.

I was wrong. It seems I do still have tears to cry.

2 6

HOUSE OF CARDS

ANWEN

THE TEARS ON ESTRELLA'S CHEEKS CATCH THE LATE MORNING LIGHT like diamonds, and I know I'm already too fucking late.

This is what I get for following my head, letting it lead me away from my mate. Baz's first call to the tower was fine. But as soon as I saw Harper's broken body at the base, I should've run to her. I should've seen what was coming and gotten out ahead of it. Instead, I let old loyalties distract me. I trudged through rescues and meetings and discussions like I didn't know exactly what was happening the second I smelled the old blood.

The smell sticks in my mind. So pungent, I caught it from the top of the tower, and Baz has three times the nose I do. Maybe I'm just looking for any kind of excuse, but I don't know how the corpse could've sat there for damn near two weeks without anyone picking up the scent.

All that flashes through my mind in the time it takes to blink, and then I'm rushing across the third dining room toward her. I can't see, can't focus on anything else.

Cold steel bites the flesh of my neck, more promise than injury, and I dodge back into a roll that leaves me on my knees. Castor stands between her and I. Pure, undiluted hatred fills his gray eyes.

"Stand and fight!" he bellows. "Defend whatever shit-stained honor you have left."

I hold up my hands again. "I'm unarmed. Shit, I'm in my fucking pajamas. I can't fight."

"Coward!" His sword slashes out, and a line of bright pain burns across my palm.

I don't wince. I don't even move. I just look at Estrella, my mate, staring past me as she cries. The pain in my hand is nothing compared to the searing in my chest.

A small, selfish part of me tries to calculate whether this hurts more or less than the nightmare that woke me.

"I know how this looks," I say as calmly as I can. "But if you just let me explain—"

"What could you possibly explain?" Dowager Luna Suniva rises from her seat, looking more like a queen than she has since her husband's death. "You lied to our queen. She was telling us of your successful interrogation, the proof it yielded, just as this news arrived." She flips her hand at a corner of the room that hasn't drawn my eye yet.

I glance over there, no idea what I'll find, but I'm certainly not expecting Floyd fucking Winters. Abruptly, I'm sure they've been presented the news in the worst possible light. The Lonely Sea connects to the Sapphire River, a direct shot into Snowcrest territory. The worse we look, the more likely Alpha King Andri gains a new ally of his own.

"Everything." I direct my words to Estrella. "If you'll just listen, I promise it all makes sense."

Castor tips my head up with the point of his blade. My temper rages, but I clench down on it. Let it burn my insides. Tears still steam down her face, sparkling like her eyes when she laughs. She still stares past me, almost blankly, but I can feel the pain ricocheting around her rib cage. Castor pushes the tip of his curved sword into the flesh of my neck. I swallow against it and feel a bead of blood run down my skin. No one else in the world could treat me like this, but for her, I'll do anything, say anything.

"You have one chance," he snarls like he's not half my size and two years younger.

That's all I need.

"I lied," I tell Estrella, "but not about this. Not like this."

"I told you!" Floyd crows.

"Shut up," I spit.

The blade bites harder. I wince.

Candace, Finn, and I used to play a game when we were too young to understand the suits and values on cards. We'd lean the tough little sheets against each other, one at a time, higher and higher, until we had a whole house of nothing more than paper. The slightest tap of the table sent the whole thing tumbling down.

When I decided to hide Harper's disappearance, I placed my first card. Now, I'm standing in a pile of paper I don't understand, wondering who tapped the table.

"I didn't tell you about Harper because I thought his disappearance looked bad but meant nothing," I say, hoping they'll understand the ring of truth in my words. "It was because of Harper that I couldn't prove Kieran wasn't responsible, but fuck, he'd never do anything like this. I don't know how, but it's a trick. I just know it."

Dowager Luna Suniva wraps an arm around Estrella's frozen shoulders. "Is that truly all you have to say for yourself? That we ought to trust your instincts?"

Yes. "No." I push myself forward, onto Castor's blade, trying to catch Estrella's eye. Still, there's nothing. My heart hammers. Take the hard path. "A month ago, I was a monster. My father's son."

Estrella shivers like she's been shocked, but she still doesn't look at me.

"And Kieran"—I swallow—"he's the reason I changed. He figured out what Father was doing and exposed him first to the men following and suffering under his orders. To those who needed the information most. That man, the one who tasted his own father's blood because that was what it took to rid the world of that cruelty, would never do this." I stare at Estrella, lower my voice. "I hid things, but only because I knew they would lead you astray."

"More pretty lies." Castor sneers down at me. "I've heard my fill."

The forge of my temper ignites. Someday, he'll pay for this.

Estrella makes a soft, hollow sound, and I tamp out the flames. Castor is a son, grieving a father he loved. Maybe, for her, I can make one exception. I just need her to look at me.

"Please." My voice breaks on the word. "Please, Estrella, trust the bo—"

She breaks her mother's hold, storms the distance between us, and backhands me with a sharp *crack*.

I sit back on my heels as my head snaps to the side. The hit is more noise than pain. I've taken worse, and anything she could dole out would be barely noticeable through the lightning storm in my chest. But the message is clear. She heard the word *bond* on my lips, and that was the one thing she couldn't tolerate. Not Floyd accusing me, not her mother demeaning our night together, not her brother threatening my life. The very idea anyone else might know what we are to each other. It hurts worse than a million slaps.

Estrella draws herself up to her full height and stares down her nose at me. Her mother steps up on her right, and Castor on her left. They still look like a puzzle missing a piece, but royal command oozes off them. Just like it used to Father.

I shrink. I know Floyd's here, and that fucking stings, but what the hell else can I do? My plan to get through a few days of their visit and live with the bite alone has never seemed stupider. When she goes… I don't know what'll be left.

"I, Luna Queen Estrella Sollabella of Sundrop Gem, formally revoke all alliances made with Dun's Crossing and anyone bearing the name Solberg before three witnesses and the Goddess herself." Her face is unreadable, whatever's going on in her eyes blotted out by the shine of the late-morning sun. "There are no *bonds* between us any longer."

There's no mistaking her emphasis. My mark burns like a brand, worse even than the pain in my chest. It's never been this bad before. Fuck, it feels like the wolfsbane.

"Envoy Winters, if you would be so kind as to send a messenger to the docks and inform the captain of *The Lady Suniva* that we'll be leaving in an hour's time, I'd be honored to consider a diplomatic visit to Snowcrest Canyon in the near future," she says.

The political dig sails over my head. So does Floyd's fucking response. My temper seizes onto him. He ruined this, made it so much worse than it had to be. The evidence against Kieran is circumstantial. I left out one detail. But the fucking worm had to make me look like the murderer somehow, and for that, he'll die. I'll make sure of it.

Estrella takes a step away from me. "Inform the Alpha King and Luna Queen of our departure, if you must."

"You can't leave." I toss the sentence like a lifeline.

She barks a laugh. "I said that I would stay until I was satisfied with the investigation. I didn't realize I was wasting my time when I said it, staring at the perpetrator all along, but you may consider me, Your Highness, satisfied."

Her first real sentence to me, not to the crown prince. It hangs from her lips like icicles.

"If *anyone*"—she looks pointedly at me, and her gray eyes are colder than the snow she's never seen—"attempts to halt or even delay our departure, I'll consider it an act of war."

She sweeps out of the room with her family and Floyd in tow, leaving me weeping blood on the floor.

Harper wasn't my first card. What the fuck was I thinking? The very first card, the first misstep, was in the tent that first day, when I told her we had to hide our marks. I should've marched out into the dawn, bare-ass naked, with her hand in mine. I should've told everyone what a fucking prize I won the second I realized it.

I always lost at the house of cards game. I always realized I was about to hit the table too damn late.

2 7

NUMB

ESTRELLA

I CLING TO THE SIDE OF *THE LADY SUNIVA*, LISTENING TO THE BIRDS' jagged calls and the rhythmic *thud, thud, thud* of the various ropes and riggings against the wood of the boat itself on the final day of our journey home. On the ride over, I was horrifically seasick. The waves are so much larger than those in the placid pond Tess and I sometimes row around on. This time, though, the sea doesn't touch me.

Nothing does. Ever since leaving Anwen sniveling on the floor like he had anything to be upset about, I've returned to the dull numbness that consumed me in the days following Father's death. It's as though I've died again. Or as though Anwen reanimated me in a facsimile of life, and now I've returned to my true self. There's something peaceful in this, at least. I haven't cried since that moment, either.

"We should see the coast soon." Mother steps up beside me. "Do you feel ready?"

The sea air has returned a little more color to her cheeks, though the rocking of the boat makes it impossible for her to sleep. And she's been doting on me as though I'm a child.

"I will figure out what I must," I say.

She places her hand over mine. "You were becoming friends with that prince, weren't you? Perhaps even falling for him?"

There is nothing under the moon I can say to that. And regardless, my throat fills with stones at any mention of him.

"I understand." She squeezes my fingers. "Before the Haze brought me to your father, I had a crush on someone in my pack. Eden. We talked ceaselessly, nearly courted. The whole kingdom assumed we would be each other's when the Haze came, including me." She smiles tiredly. "The feelings seemed very real until I met your father. So this will hurt, and I hope you talk to me, but something better will come to wash it all away."

I've never heard of Eden before. Normally, any new story of Mother's fills me with excitement. I wanted to see the world outside of our kingdom terribly. Now, it only adds more stones to my throat.

"Can I convince you to come sit with me?" she asks. "I thought I might paint the horizon, and I need someone to mix my colors."

All our best talks happen while I'm mixing her colors. It's a bit like drawing a curtain between us and the world, a private space where we are, briefly, nothing more than mother and daughter. Until this, I would've called it my favorite activity in the world.

I shake my head. Mother sighs, but she leaves without another word.

Next, like they've organized a rotation, Tess approaches. She alone knows just how much I lost that morning, and she has done me the honor of not mentioning it, but even the knowledge sets my teeth on edge.

"Have you eaten?" she asks.

"Dinner," I reply. That, at least, is a question I can answer.

"It's morning."

"I know that." I push my wind-torn hair out of my eyes. "But I'm not hungry. I need to be ready."

She looks over the edge of the boat where a dark spot has just come into view. Sundrop Gem, without an ounce of detail.

"We've got four hours before we dock." Her voice betrays her frustration. "The cook made fresh *aswore*, and I dug up a jar of orange preserves. Come eat."

My mouth waters. The acidity of the orange cuts the sweetness of the *aswore* perfectly. Tess knows that's always been my favorite breakfast.

"Where did you find preserves on a ship?" I ask.

She looks back over the side. "In the hold."

My gut twists. The hold is where Father's body lays, cocooned in a layer of ice so thick I can't make out his features no matter how long I stare. Floyd finally figured out a more stable method of containment, but it's horrifying to look at. The oblong block of ice is barely human, much less Father. I can't think about it for long, and I can't eat anything I know chilled in the sickening corona of his body.

"You don't have to say it." Tess leans her shoulder against mine. "Just promise me you'll eat something before the funeral."

I don't answer her. That seems more a question for the flurry of advisors and meetings I know await me when we arrive home.

＊ ＊ ＊

Tess stands with me for so long that I can nearly make out the palace by the time I'm alone again. A few moments later, Castor sidles up beside me.

"I'm sorry," he mumbles.

I glance at him. "Why?"

"I may not understand it, but obviously that… place meant something to you." He shrugs. "So I'm sorry their betrayal hurt you."

That comes the closest in the three-day journey to coaxing a smile onto my lips. Castor hates apologizing, mostly to me.

"Despite the fact you told me so?" I ask. I've been repeating that to myself for days.

"Exactly." He winces. "Except I want that to sound nicer."

There's a reason Castor will hopefully never be king of Sundrop Gem, and it's bigger than birth order. "Unfortunately, that is not a sentiment that ever sounds nice."

"Fuck it, then." He leans against the side of the boat. "I smuggled a *kras* board into my cabin. Would it make you feel any better to beat me before facing your people?"

The strategy game stands at the heart of a long-running competition between us. Castor has never beaten me, but he swears he will one day. For a while, I had to check his sleeves for spare hexagonal tokens before sitting down to play. Now, the idea lands hollowly in my chest. I am Luna Queen of Sundrop Gem, and that title will be mine forever in no more than a few days' time. What point is there to silly board games now?

Memories of Father teaching me and playing *kras* fight for my attention, but I push them aside. He was a different sort of leader than I must be. He had a partner to rely on.

"No," I say crisply. "I'm busy."

He looks at the empty waves I've been staring at for hours already, scoffs, and walks away. That doesn't matter. He's my advisor, whether he wants the position or not, and he loves this kingdom as much as I do, beneath it all.

"Lower sails!" the captain yells. "We're docking."

I squeeze the side of the ship my father christened so many years ago one last time.

* * *

I STEP ONTO THE SWAYING GANGWAY WITH MY HEAD HELD HIGH. Mother walks behind me, and Castor carries Father's body with three other sailors. The familiar smells of home—warm spices, astringent dye, and hot stones—thread through the salt air. I expect them to make me sadder, without Father, or to inspire dear memories. Just like everything else, they are nothing more than information. I am in Sundrop Gem, as I was in Dun's Crossing mere days ago.

As soon as I set foot on the dock, something changes. We entered mind-link range for the pack some hours ago, even across the sea. That felt like it always does—I was one grain of sand in an hourglass, one voice among a chorus. Now, I am at the heart of the network. The trunk holding all the leaves, rather than one of its rustling retinue. Voices whisper through my mind.

Luna Estrella.

So beautiful.

So young.

Is she ready?

Is she heartbroken?

I love you. We love you.

I sway and nearly throw a hand out for balance. But it wouldn't do for the first sight of their queen to be weakness.

I love you, I say to them all. *Make way for your fallen king.*

With a deep breath, I stride down the dock. The pack—my pack–shifts out of the way like choreographed dancers. I doubt I even had to ask them to move. Every gaze I meet holds the same admiration I saw so often pointed at Father, the same hope for an ever-improving future. My posture grows straighter under the weight of their expectations.

The long walk leads us to the mouth of the temple where Yana, our holy woman, waits. She must prepare Father's body before the funeral. Castor and the sailors lay his foreign, icy coffin at her feet. She stares at it with tears in her eyes for a long second, then raises her hands in prayer.

"May he find his place among the stars."

The refrain echoes through the crowd that followed us here, both out loud and across the mind-link. I barely repress a shudder. In Dun's Crossing, my people were a small handful of loved ones. Here, every wolf is painfully, palpably real. My footsteps pulsate through my mating bite, but for the first time in days, it is easy to put him from my mind. I owe them the future they expect from me, and I intend to provide.

Alone.

28
ACROSS THE LONELY SEA

ANWEN

THE DAY AFTER THE SUNDROP GEM CONTINGENT LEAVES, I SLEEP IN FOR the first time in days. When Frazier shakes my shoulder, and I open my eyes into the damn near midmorning light, pain rips through my chest.

Hers? Mine? Is there any point in asking anymore?

"Get the fuck off me." I rip Frazier's hand away. "Did I ask you to wake me up?"

"No, sir." Frazier bows. "Alpha King Kieran did."

"Tell Kieran to go fawn over his mate and his crown-prince-to-be," I snarl. "Leave me the fuck alone."

Frazier bows again and leaves. I grab a decanter I left on the side of my bed last night and take a few hearty swigs. A little bit of fuzziness in my mind can't hurt at this point. It's not like I have fucking anything to do today. The investigation's over. Kieran made sure to tell me that to my face yesterday. Even though he doesn't agree with the outcome, without the Sundrop people here demanding answers, there's "no point in wasting resources."

I hurl the half-full decanter at the wall. It shatters in a tinkle of glass. The stink of liquor makes it easier not to worry about smelling anything else, at least.

'Come to my office when you have a minute,' Kieran says through the mind-link. *'We need to discuss how to mitigate this problem with the other kingdoms.'*

His crap about taking the hard way echoes in my mind. Well, guess what? The hard way didn't work. It's bullshit. He can stick his hard way where the Goddess doesn't shine, and I'll handle shit the way I need to from here on out.

I ignore the mind-link, jump out of bed, and storm out of my room without getting dressed. What fucking difference does it make? Who do I have to hide from or impress?

The stone floor is cold on my feet, but it barely touches the storm in my head. She just fucking left. In every scenario I played out, every worst-case I imagined, this didn't happen. Not after the ball, not after our nights together. I can't live without her. And, fuck, is it so stupid to hope that she'd have some trouble living without me? That first morning, in the tent, she could barely handle the pain in her mark when I told her we should keep things quiet, but when she says she considers me an enemy, never wants to see me again, she walks out with her head held high?

I smash a vase off a plinth lining the hall to hear it shatter too. A couple of servants I didn't even notice before jump.

"Clean it the fuck up," I growl.

They still listen. I guess I've got that. All of this feels like absolute shit.

'What are you doing?' Kieran asks Goddess knows how long later. *'Lucias and Ifan are fielding complaints that you're cutting a path of destruction through the palace.'*

'Let them,' I reply savagely before closing the link. He wants to lead? Let him.

But his interruption shakes me out of my rage just enough to look up and take stock of where I am. Fucking pitiful. I've marched my ass right over to where she was yesterday. Not her hall exactly—like some part of me is still hiding our relationship for her fucking sake, like I give a shit what she wants or needs anymore—but the one where they put her father's body.

I pull up short. Not they, Floyd. Floyd kept King Isai's body here and guarded the door nonstop for my whole investigation. Bastard wouldn't even let me in to look at it through the ice. But when Estrella and her family want to leave, the body is stable enough for a three-day voyage? With an hour of fucking warning?

I slam my fist into the wall, and my knuckles spark with pain. Floyd was lying. I could've looked at the body the whole time, and he was keeping me out. The only question now is whether he did it because King Andri told him to sabotage our investigation or because Estrella asked him to.

Pain rips through me anew at the second thought. Fuck it. Fuck him. I'll look into it… later. Never. I don't fucking know, but if I track down the envoy of Snowcrest right now, I'll start an international incident before he finishes his first sentence.

'You wanna go for a drink?' Baz asks.

'Fuck off,' I reply.

Drinking sounds good. Going somewhere, talking to anyone? I'd rather have her slap me again.

A spear of pain shoots through my chest. Maybe that's not true, but it's damn close. I turn on my heel and whip in another direction. Anywhere other than her rooms, where I might be able to smell her and remind myself what I'm missing.

Not missing. Furious with.

I break another vase, a statue, tear a tapestry down. Every bit of destruction mutes a little of the storm, gives me something else to think about. And every time, the muting lasts for a handful of steps, until I come across some place I've seen her or smelled her or thought about her. She's all over this place. There's nothing left that's mine.

Avoiding every trace of her leads me, like everything fucking seems to, up the hallway that holds Father's office. When Kieran took the castle, he spent a day pulling everything he could need out of there then barred the door. Nobody's opened it since then. Once again, I stand in front of the closed double doors, knowing Kieran's a huge part of the reason I can't go in. The heir, the favored son, made the decision for all of us.

Well, I'm fucking tired of it.

My nails sharpen into claws, and I tear the bar from the doors in a flurry of violence. One of them swings open, loose on its hinges. Father's smell wafts out. And I stare at what lays inside.

The office I spent my whole life jealous of is in tatters. His desk is half-overturned, the drawers hanging out. The breeze from the door opening stirs the ashes in the fireplace, revealing half-burned books and pieces of paper. Tapestries hang shredded on the walls. There's a huge hole in one of the windowpanes, like someone put their fist through it. My temper flares. Kieran did this. It wasn't enough to kill our father, he had to destroy every memory of him, every piece we had left.

Then, a memory pops into my mind. The last morning, before Father sent Kieran and I off together. He summoned me to his office, and by taking a few of my shortcuts, I'd shown up early. Just in time to hear something crash behind the door, then watch Father step out, smooth himself down, and snap to a servant that he expected everything in their "perfect by the time this ended." I always assumed he had some kind of informant he was getting information out of, but there's no smell in here other than his. No blood. No nothing. Except a reminder that, every rare time Father didn't get his way, he stalked around the castle, snarling and destroying.

Just like I have today.

I blink, and like the Haze burning off in the morning, my thoughts clear. This is exactly what he'd do. And, by the Goddess, Estrella isn't the only reason I don't want to turn into him. She's just the best thing stopping me.

I know what I have to do.

'Where are you?' I ask Baz.

'Blue Slipper,' he replies. *'Why?'*

'Don't leave.'

I dart through passages and tunnels to the room the servants keep ready for when I have a girl and dress in my most casual clothes then pull a hood up over my head. At the last minute, I pull the spare dagger out from under the bed and strap it on. My heart pounds as I race outside without the guards needing to open the doors and head down into the city surrounding the palace.

Noises and smells surround me. Usually, I like the market—it's a damn good place to listen—but today, it feels like every shifter has been put in this city just to piss me off. It's an act of the Goddess that I can keep enough of a rein on my temper not to kill anyone. I just put my head down and slice through the crowd to our favorite tavern.

As always, Baz is sitting at the pitted bar, nursing a cup of rotgut. I don't know how he drinks the shit after growing up in the palace. I glare at the man on the stool next to him, and the idiot hurries away without a word.

"I've got a plan," I murmur.

"Better than scaring the shit out of half the castle?" Baz replies.

I punch him in the shoulder. Hard.

"No, you were a dick." He meets my gaze. "Ready to be different?"

Where the hell does he get off—

I swallow. "Yes."

Baz raises his mug with a grin. "Thank the Goddess. So, shall we drink away the pain?"

"I have a better plan than that." I lean in and whisper my plan, under the noise of the bar.

He blinks a few times, then shoots the rest of his drink. "You're one crazy bastard. Let's go get your girl."

* * *

"BUSINESS OF THE KING." I LIFT MY CHIN AND TAP MY FINGERS ON THE hilt of the dagger. "You wouldn't refuse him, would you?"

The merchant standing in front of me swallows. "*The Whirlwind* is halfway through a journey. I can't just abandon my cargo—"

"Then unload," Baz growls like he's some kind hardass. I almost laugh when the merchant starts trembling.

"You merely want the ship?" he asks.

"And three of your crew." I look him up and down. "Not including you."

He nods wildly and jumps into action. Crates and barrels disappear off the tiny merchant ship. I picked a vessel out that would only need a crew of five, the smallest in the port that I thought would actually get us across the Lonely Sea. And the vessel Kieran's least likely to notice missing. I don't give a fuck about politics or appearances right now, and I'm not going to be stopped.

As the whiny merchant and his people work, I lean against the side and stare at the horizon.

"You know, I've never actually left the kingdom before," Baz says.

I glance at him. His eyes glow with excitement, and he's nearly bouncing up and down.

"Me either," I mutter. Except for that rushed trip to Escuro–to murder Father.

But I don't share Baz's anticipation. I can't really think about anything but what awaits us on the other side of this trip—the twenty-four hour lead my mate has on me, and what I'm going to have to do to get her back.

29
CORONATION

Estrella

I SMOOTH MY HANDS OVER THE FABRIC OF MY SOFT, GOLDEN coronation dress, shot through with strands of color. Purple for the sky at night. Rich brown for the sand of the desert beyond our little oasis. Gray for Father's eyes. Red for the heart of our people.

The heart I hold in my cold hands.

"Isn't it beautiful?" Mother says.

I force a smile and nod. Father's funeral is already over. As always, Yana's words were beautiful. Between Father's remaining advisors and me, we managed to set up a showing most of the capital could filter through to pay their respects. I've spent the last four hours overseeing condolences, and my cheeks ache. But if my cheeks ache, I am feeling something other than the hollow ache in my chest.

"You're going to look lovely." Tess pauses braiding my hair to stroke the fabric. "I can't imagine anything better."

"Thank you both," I reply, rote and automatic. "Where did it come from?"

"My hope chest." Mother begins unfolding the swath of fabric, readying it to be folded into a dress. "After the Haze, but before I left Thunderpeak."

Coming back home, too, seems to have returned her more to herself. Perhaps it's simply the weather. Escaping the chill of Dun's Crossing should be a gift from the Goddess Herself. The pale stones under my feet are warm to the touch without any need of rugs, though several do still line the floor of my dressing room to show off our craftsmanship. I run one of my toes over the weave and remember the woman who gave it to us. To me. On our monthly market visit, the colors caught my eye. A silvery blue runs through the whole piece, rare in Sundrop Gem. As soon as the weaver discovered I liked it, she insisted we take it with us. I was young then, and happy to agree, but Mother insisted we pay her for her work, and Father had offered above asking if she would agree to make more for the castle.

Usually, that story makes me proud to be a Sollabella, proud to belong in Sundrop Gem. Tonight, mere hours from my coronation, it is simply another story.

"Tell me more about that," I say.

"About what?" Mother drifts over to the hanging display of my jewelry.

"Knowing you were to be Luna but not being one yet." I meet my own gaze in the mirror. The eyes staring back at me are barely recognizable.

"It was strange. I loved Thunderpeak—love, really—but the ways there are nothing like life here." Mother plucks a few pairs of gold earrings off the rack and looks out the window at the low-lying mountains that hide the kingdom she came from. "Everybody fawned over me ceaselessly. I couldn't turn a corner without some girl I'd spent half my life avoiding wrapping her arm around my waist and declaring us bosom friends. Quickly, I realized they all wanted to be brought to Sundrop as part of my retinue."

Tess tugs a braid tight and pins it in place. "Did you take any of them?"

Mother sighs. "I thought about it. I was terribly afraid of being lonely, even though I knew these girls didn't want me particularly."

This is the part where I ask what changed. My mouth doesn't move. Mother walks over to us and holds one set of earrings up to my lobes, then another.

"Then, your father came to visit me, the week before the wedding." Her smile is tired, sore, but present. "He was overflowing with love for me. Nothing in Thunderpeak shone like it did before. And his people were all just as kind, just as personal. They wanted to know me, not just their king's new queen. That was when I understood Sundrop for the first time." She sets the earrings down. "I thought the isolation made them standoffish, but it makes us rely on each other. There's real love between people here like I've never seen before. Remember that, Estrella, and you cannot lead them astray."

I stare up at Mother as much as I can with Tess still braiding my hair. Sleepless nights still darken her under-eyes, and a sallow tint remains on her warm skin, but there's something of the woman who raised me in her now. She is being reinvigorated by this place.

Why isn't that happening for me?

"It would be easier to remember, Mother," I say before I can catch myself, "if I did not have to lead them alone."

She blinks. "What do you mean?"

A confession dangles on the tip of my tongue. It would be best to make a clean break of things before my coronation.

Tess meets my gaze in the mirror, her eyes soft and almost pitying. I am in the company of two romantics, two women who have felt Goddess-given love so truly and deeply it affects their every choice. They could not understand about Anwen if I spent the rest of the night explaining.

"You were my age when you took the throne," I say instead. "But you had a partner in Father. Why do I have to do this alone?"

"Oh, my dove." Mother cups my cheeks, and I watch hesitation flicker in her eyes. I've asked her a question she doesn't quite know how to answer. "Didn't you listen to me? You're never truly alone in Sundrop Gem."

The bite on my neck itches. I scratch at it absently. In Dun's Crossing, I thought that itch meant Anwen was nearby, but I was obviously wrong about that. Like so much else in these last few weeks.

"Done with your hair," Tess says. "Dowager Suniva, have you picked earrings?"

* * *

Castor slips his arm through mine in the waiting area before the royal temple. On the rare occasions the reigning Alpha King and Luna Queen can retire, they escort the new leaders to the holy woman. Had Mother died, Father would walk with me. But Castor is the only other person alive with royal Sollabella blood running in his veins, so the job falls to him.

"You look nice," he says.

"You've never complimented my appearance before," I reply.

"Things are different now." He swallows heavily.

I tighten my grip on him. "I wouldn't like them to be. Not like that."

He sighs, and a bit of tension leaves his body. "You mean you don't want me to be a perfect, mannerly advisor?"

I offer him a wan smile. "If you transformed into one overnight, I'd worry we abandoned the real Castor in Dun's Crossing."

Real fury flashes across his face. Beyond the door, the drums and flutes climb to a fever pitch.

"We should kill them for what they did," he snarls.

My bite sears. "Perhaps. Someday. But for all they say they've changed, Dun's Crossing boasts the largest standing army in the world. If we attacked them now, we would be slaughtered."

Castor visibly forces himself to relax. "Perhaps it's good you're the eldest."

A high, trilling note rings out. That's our cue. Castor pushes open the door, and we walk arm-in-arm through a crowd of our people.

"Why is that?" I ask in the brief moment after we exit the crowd, before we reach Yana, on the altar.

"You can handle this," he says bluntly.

He releases me to face Yana alone and fades into the crush. For the first time since I realized how deep Anwen's betrayal ran, I want something. I want to ask Father for advice.

"The Goddess guides our footsteps, even in the darkest night," Yana declares over the noise.

The music softens. Even in the packed temple, no one says a word. I can barely pick out individual faces amidst the assembly.

"She does not abandon us." Yana meets my eyes. "She does not lead us astray."

I hear the meaning behind her words. I may be young, I may be alone, but the Goddess would not make me queen if I could not handle it. If only I could tell Yana what else the Goddess has asked of me recently.

"And as she dances from phase to phase, so must we in Her footsteps." With the introduction complete, Yana moves into the proper ceremony.

I've never seen a coronation, but I know the ritual by heart. I've been learning it since I was a child. The steps, the words I have to say, the candles and prayers echo in my dreams. I've always known I would have to endure them on nearly the worst day of my life.

In truth, I suspected the coronation would be worse. Yana's invocations of clear-headedness, of truth, of power wash over me like gentle waves. These are my people. I must lead them. There is nothing else.

A door at the back of the temple creaks open, and every head turns but Yana's. It is the height of disrespect to arrive late to such an event. I look, even though I don't expect to see anything over the crowd.

But two heads of blond hair in Sundrop Gem are impossible to mistake.

Emotions burst through my chest, hot and wild. Anwen is here. Anwen and Baz. I cannot think of anything else other than that they are here. The emotions are impossible to tease apart, to tell good from bad.

Yana grasps my wrist. I cannot stop the coronation, certainly not now. She lifts a curved, jeweled dagger.

"This blade was carved from the tooth of our very first Alpha King." She turns my hand over, exposing my palm. "These gems were mined from the home of our very first Luna Queen. Their blood flows in your veins. With this, I join you to their endless line."

Yana slices open my finger and drops the blood into the candle flame.

The emotions burn hotter, brighter. Like desert sand at noon. And then, I feel it. Just as the glow starts, a second set of hands around my own. Larger, warmer, softer. Smoothing over the cut, which heals instantly.

The Goddess is here.

30

LAST CHANCE

ANWEN

MY MOUTH FALLS OPEN. ESTRELLA'S WHOLE BODY IS CONSUMED IN THAT light, the glow I saw the night her father was killed. She tilts her head back with a beatific smile, and something in my ribcage heals too. I knew she was going to be beautiful. But the dress, her hair, the smile… it's all too much. She looks like the Goddess Herself, more beautiful if I won't be struck down for saying it.

The holy woman raises her arms. "Praise the Moon Goddess, our kingdom is made whole!"

Prayers whisper through the crowd around me. I push forward, Baz on my heels. I have to be closer to her. It's an animal need, just like in the Haze itself.

"Many long centuries ago, two families led Sundrop Gem. From the first brothers, Jasiah and Jadiel, our twin kings and queens were always born. They led our people in tandem, one heart beating in two chests," the holy woman says.

I keep pushing. It's a nice story, but all I can think about is her, the scent of her blood in the air, and no one seems to want to let me pass.

"Jadiel's line was blessed with heat and built the southern palace, where we now reside," she says. "Jasiah's line was blessed with healing and built the northern palace, long lost above the desert. For eons, our people were whole. And then, Alpha King Yair was born."

Murmurs fill the hall as I push ahead. My heart hammers her name against my ribs.

"Alpha King Yair was the first of Jasiah's line born without power. So instead of leading with his brother to the south, he grew jealous. War followed, and Alpha King Yair led his people across the Lonely Sea." The holy woman lowers her head. "Jasiah's power has never again been seen in Sundrop Gem, nor in Dun's Crossing. For it to return is an auspicious sign of a powerful queen and a peaceful future."

I arrive at the front of the crowd, and Estrella takes my fucking breath away. She is rapt on the holy woman, still glowing softly. The small cut on her hand is already healed. She doesn't look at me, but for once, I don't mind. Everything in me screams for her, but this is more important.

"I give to the Goddess Luna Queen Estrella Alana Sollabella, first of her name and destined reunion of Sundrop Gem," the holy woman says.

Estrella turns to look out over the temple. Her gaze catches on me for a moment then sweeps on. "I give myself to the Goddess, and I give myself to you, Sundrop Gem." She curtsies deeply. "With an open heart and a stubborn mind."

A small chuckle ripples through the crowd. My chest aches. She's going to be incredible.

"Now, let us honor the Goddess and our Luna with a celebration!" the holy woman declares.

The whole pack turns and floods out the door Baz and I came through. He nudges me as we are forced out with the tide.

'Did you know about that?' he asks through mind-link.

I shake my head. Walking away from her hurts.

'Hell of a mate,' he says.

'Hell of a woman,' I reply.

And she hates me. Fuck.

The flow of bodies leads us out to an open courtyard with a mosaic floor in colors as vibrant as the clothes. Spiced meats and that sweet bread perfume the rapidly cooling night air. Baz and I stick out like sore thumbs. There's no one as pale or blond as us for what seems like miles—we certainly didn't see any on our way up from the docks—and I suddenly get what Estrella was talking about, complaining that the clothing in Dun's Crossing was dull. I just sort of assumed the jewel tones she and her family wore were a marker of royalty. Instead, everyone here, from servant on up, wears the same rainbow colors. It kind of makes my head hurt.

Baz stares wide-eyed around the array. I know that look. He's itching to jump in.

'Go,' I tell Baz. *'Enjoy. But be ready to drop everything and leave.'*

'Sir, yes sir!' he replies.

I roll my eyes as he wades into the crowd. It won't be more than a minute before he has a dance partner and a drink. Once upon a time, I'd be out there with him. But I only have one person I'm looking for.

She appears at the edge of the courtyard, her glow slowly dimming, and everybody flocks to her. In a heartbeat, there's a crowd six shifters deep, vying for her attention. My stomach churns. I could announce myself, and there's no way that wouldn't clear a path, but I'm stuck with the fucking hard way. This is her night. She is a historic leader of her people, and I won't take that from her.

So I do what I'm good at. I get a glass of wine, pull my hood up over my head, and drift to the edge of the party. The courtyard is lined with columns that present a reasonable visual barrier, or at least the suggestion I don't want to be talked to. If I stare into my wine enough, people will assume I'm drunk. I consider sitting on the floor to complete the illusion, but I can't risk missing my moment.

That's what I need. A single moment alone with Estrella. A second to tell her it's not true and have her listen.

No, a second to tell her I'm sorry. That I know I can't live without her, and I'm willing to do whatever she needs—even sail across the sea on a stolen boat—to be with her.

From the shadows I grew up in, I watch her. She's nothing like the naïve, slightly awkward woman I met in Dun's Crossing. Here, she flits through the party like a butterfly. She never comes across anyone she doesn't already know by name, and most of them she greets with a specific question about something in their life she's already aware of. It's masterful work.

But as the party flows on, as she never so much as fumbles, I start to wonder if it really is work for her. I memorize facts about the nobility of Dun's Crossing to ingratiate myself with them, to seem pleasant and innocuous enough to loosen their tongue. Most of the things she knows don't really seem to do that. She asks a young man about his hopes for the Haze without a fluttering coquettish lash. She asks a child about their latest prank without their parents in earshot.

Realization dawns on me, and I feel like a moron. It's not work to her. When she says "her people," she means it. She cares about each and every one of them personally.

I turn away from the party and put my back to the pillar. Father barely cared about anyone other than Mother and his heir, that's simple. Mother cared about all us kids, in her own way. Kieran cares about the future of Dun's Crossing, about being an honorable king and restoring our name. Raven cares about protecting people who are being unfairly hurt, inside the kingdom and outside. None of them care about the citizens of the kingdom like... well, like their people.

Goddess above, Estrella is a miracle. An impossibility. There's no way someone like her will take another chance on someone like me. But fuck it, I have to try.

Finally, hours after the party starts, I find my moment. She steps away from a circle of admirers to refill her drink, then tilts her head up to the sky and takes a deep breath.

"Estrella," I say softly.

She doesn't jump. "What are you doing here?"

I had a whole speech planned. When I open my mouth, after watching her here, something else pours out. "I grew up alone."

She raises an eyebrow.

"That's not an excuse," I say quickly. "I just need you to know why

I did what I did." I shake my head. "I grew up alone with five siblings, alone in a castle full of people. Castor can probably tell you what it's like to be the backup heir. And care, attention, appreciation… those were things you earned."

"That's all very sad, but I have—"

I hold up a hand to stop her, wince. "I know. Give me a second."

She crosses her arms. "You have one minute."

"If you wanted to impress Father, you showed him finished projects. Nothing less. Certainly nothing he'd have to finish himself. If you didn't, he had no time for you." I shove my hands in my pockets, feeling like a raw nerve. "And if he had no time for you, you might as well not exist. I didn't tell you about Harper because I knew it was a false lead, but I couldn't prove it yet, and telling you would be like asking not to exist anymore."

"Thirty seconds," she replies.

Fuck, fuck, fuck. "And I know that's not good enough. It's the easy way out. But Kieran told me a couple days ago that Father trained us to do things the easy way, and most of the work of getting out from under him is learning how to do it hard. That's why I'm here. Baz and I stole a boat and snuck over."

Her mouth falls open slightly.

"No one knows where we are, just that we're safe, and them ever knowing is up to you." I squeeze my hands into fists. "I can't live without you. Tried. It sucked. So I'm here to say that I'll be north of the city at two in the morning. If you see a future for us, meet me there. If not, Baz and I'll leave in the morning, and you'll never see us again."

My mark screams, saying that. I really don't think I can live without her. But the hard way is giving her the choice, treating her like a real other person with a stake here, so I'm doing it.

"Your time is up." Estrella turns and leaves.

<h1 style="text-align:center">31</h1>

LAUGHTER

ESTRELLA

MOTHER KISSES ME ON THE CHEEK IN AN EMPTY COURTYARD. EVEN THE servants are gone, having carried all the remainder of the cleaning inside.

"You did wonderfully," she says. "As I knew you would. Now, sleep, and I will see you in the morning."

She leaves. I am truly alone. That hurts again, like it didn't scant hours ago. Before I saw Anwen in the crowd. Before he cornered me during the party and begged one last chance. I suck in a breath. The sound echoes around the courtyard.

Father told me not to lower myself for him. He betrayed me, dragged my name through the dirt, participated in the murder of my father.

And he came to me, without pulling the eyes of the room, and promised I'd misunderstood. A false lead, he called it. He's so sure King Kieran is not involved, but he hasn't tried to explain the note even once.

I've spent the last hours certain that, when this moment came, I would march upstairs and sleep peacefully, dreaming of him shivering in the cold desert night. But my feet turn toward the archway that leads out of the palace, out of the city.

I owe myself the chance to know if I truly have to spend my life alone.

I shed my coronation gown, fold it, and shift. North of the city, 2:00 in the morning. The stars in the bright, clear sky lead my way as I race to the point he described. Before long, I can smell him on the wind. It's so much more obvious here, where his scent doesn't blend at all. I could find him with no instructions at all.

When I pad up to him, he's in wolf form. A towering white wolf, outlined in the moonlight. A heartbeat passes between us. Will he shift, begin talking again? I don't know if I have room for more speeches. I've heard so many empty words today.

He huffs a great sigh and turns away. My wolf howls in betrayal and pain. Then, Anwen takes off running.

Memories of our first night together flood back, ones I'd forgotten. He chased me to the tent. Nessa said the white wolves were fastest in Dun's Crossing. Perhaps this is his way of spending time together without words.

Without words is all I want.

I race after him. Sand sprays up from his paw pads. He can't seem to find his footing on the foreign terrain. I leap ahead. These dunes are as dear to me as my family. Running across them is as simple as breathing. My muscles soothe, and my breathing steadies.

And then Anwen whips past me, the sand no longer slowing him. I throw back my head and howl. The bastard fell behind to watch me, to see how I'm navigating. He holds his paws at just the right angle and doesn't hesitate any longer.

Something bubbles in my veins. I prod at it, expecting fury or sadness or any of the emotions that have been my constant companions these last few weeks. To my surprise, I discover nothing more than the simple rush of competition. These are my dunes. If he wants a race, he has it.

I bite my howl over, duck low, and start moving. He may have speed, but I know the terrain. When he disappears over the top of a dune, I dodge to the side and circle around a particularly deep valley, the sort that slows even me. My heart pounds. My blood races. I veer around so he can see me at the mouth of the valley and—

He blazes toward me, somehow already nearly escaped. That's simply unacceptable. I lunge and catch his back leg between my teeth. He yelps in surprise, and I release him as he turns to look at me. Perfect timing. I burst ahead.

Mere moments later, Anwen catches up again, and this time, he nips one of my back legs before releasing with a short, sharp bark. The closest we can come to laughing in this form.

The world slows around me for a moment. When was the last time I laughed? When was the last time I played? I remember being the sort of person who did those things. Now, I'm the sort whose brother compliments them formally before state events.

Father laughs in my memory.

I launch myself at Anwen in a full-body tackle before I can think twice and hit him broadside. We tumble down another dune. He writhes in my grasp, biting whatever he can reach, never hard enough to hurt. I fight back, grab his tail, tug on his ears. When we stop slid-ing, I take off again, and he tackles me back to the sand. There's a rush in tussling like this, in not worrying about what I'm doing or why, just following my wolf I've been denying for so long. And if either of us rack up a few bright spots of pain where someone didn't guard their teeth as carefully as they might, I certainly don't mind.

A smell reaches my nose. Floral, deep. Dream thistle. I blink and look around as Anwen sinks his teeth lightly into my haunch.

I didn't think about the Haze often before Anwen. I knew the Goddess would take me by the paw and lead me where I needed to go. But when I allowed myself the thought, I hoped I might end up here. A tiny oasis, north of the city. Just large enough for a small pool of water, a sheltering copse of trees, and a blanket of dream thistle on the ground. The world has never looked so beautiful to me than it does here.

Anwen tackles me again, and we roll until he lands on top. The shift takes me almost before I know it's happening with a sweet shiver. I reach up and drag a finger along the soft fur of his snout. As soon as I take my hand back, he shifts as well.

There is nothing between us but night air and our own jagged breath. His body undergoes the same alchemy of everything in this oasis. He is even more beautiful, sculpted and moon-drenched. My core clenches.

Anwen opens his mouth.

Words will ruin this.

I surge forward and crush my mouth onto his then shove my tongue between his parted lips. He groans and wraps himself around me. His fingers seek purchase in my braided hair. I grab at his back, heedless of whether my claws are actually gone. Here, now, things feel just as simple and primal as they did the first night of the Haze. My wolf is free. I'll deny her no longer.

Anwen palms one of my breasts, kneads the soft flesh there. Want sends goose bumps over my skin. Already, my thighs are slick. He rocks up into me, rubbed his cock against my center with no real focus. I moan, and he slips his hand between us. When he brushes his fingers over the taut bud at the apex of my legs, I nearly scream in ecstasy.

I don't know what comes next for us. I don't know that there is a next. But we are keeping all of that outside for now. We are two wolves, two mates, finding each other in the night and wringing all the pleasure we can find out of each other's bodies. I push my hand between us as well and line him up with my entrance.

"Let's take it slow," he mumbles against my lips.

"No," I snarl. Saying anything else would break the spell.

Anwen hesitates, starting to pull back. My bite sears. My wolf howls. Not tonight.

I flip us over and pin his back against the ground. He stares up at me with wide, blue eyes, no sign of the ice I hated so much that first morning. But that's too much Goddess-damned thinking! I line his cock up and press my mouth to his chest. When I sink down, I bite.

"Fuck," Anwen groans.

He fills me up like puzzle pieces slotting together. I drag my teeth along his chest, his pale hair scraping my cheeks. His mate mark shouldn't be the only mark on his body. Right now, he's mine, and I need him to know that. I fuck myself on him and suck a series of bruises into his skin, haphazard and desperate. He fists a hand in my hair and chases my rhythm. I have never been so full, so free, so sure. The apex of pleasure races for me, and I sit up on his lap for a better angle. He sits up with me, crushing me to him, and finds that bud between my legs again. His fingers are so dexterous, so perfect.

As pleasure takes me, I sink my teeth into his mark once more. He stiffens and follows me over the edge a moment later. Thought, reality starts to filter back in as I fight to catch my breath, cradled against his chest.

"Are you done?" Anwen swipes his finger over that spot between my legs again. "Or can I fuck you slow now?"

3 2

SLOW THIS TIME

ANWEN

ESTRELLA ROLLS HER HIPS AGAINST MY HAND, AGAINST MY SOFTENING cock still inside her. I groan. I'll fuck her fast, slow, whatever she'll allow to just keep tasting her.

She starts to try to stand up, and I instinctively tighten my grip on her hair. She shivers—I knew she liked a little pain with her pleasure —but pries my hand free. Wordlessly, she walks into the tiny pool at the center of the little oasis we stumbled into.

I'm going to get that moment painted someday. Life-sized, if I can help it. Hang it over our bed where I can see it every single time I wake up. There's no way I'm ever forgetting this.

She glances over her shoulder, obviously asking if I'm coming.

If I'm lucky.

I scramble to my feet and follow her in. The water is warm like a bath, and the sandy bottom soft under my feet. It covers me up to my mid-chest. Her breasts float. I drift closer and drag my thumb over one of her nipples. It stiffens instantly, and she sucks in a breath. When I meet her gaze, her gray eyes are warm and heavy with want.

Slow isn't exactly my specialty, but for her? Anything.

I cup her other breast and play with them in alternating rhythms. Back and forth, slow, but never the same long enough for her to get used to it. Soon, her mouth is open, and low noises rumble up from her throat. I drink them in, wish I could add an audio component to my painting. She grabs my shoulder to keep her balance.

No need for that. I run my hands down her chest, grab her thighs, pull them apart, and wrap them around my waist. She obeys lazily, half holding on and half letting the water hold her. But she's at a height where it's all too easy to bend my mouth to her chest and taste her skin. The water of the pool is sweet, but I lap it up quickly. I want to taste her, nothing else.

She grinds against my core, already needy, but I ignore her. She wanted slow. Long minutes pass under the moonlight as I tease her higher and higher without ever touching her below the waist.

"Too proud to beg?" I ask, my breath ghosting over the shell of her ear.

She grinds against me harder. "My pride isn't the problem."

But isn't it? Hers and mine. Neither of us were willing to admit our connection to the other, what that meant. An idea blooms in my head. I am going to make her beg, and then I'm going to make her come like she's never come before. Then, we can talk on even footing.

I simply chuckle and return my attention to her skin. She's so delicious, the sounds she makes so perfect, that I'm happy to spend ages here. My cock returns to life after what feels like an eon and presses against her ass. I jerk my hips forward and she moans. Soon, I think.

Her hand lands on my side, then slides inward. She's trying to touch herself.

Fuck, I wish I didn't have a really good reason not to let her to.

I pull her hand away and swallow her complaints in my mouth. She rubs herself against me all the harder. I ghost my hands over her legs, her chest, anywhere I think she might want me and refuse to settle. When that doesn't break her, I take my cock in my hand and begin pleasuring myself. My knuckles graze her wetness with each stroke, just not enough to sate her.

"Please!" she finally says. "Please fuck me."

I grin. "Slowly."

She nearly cries when fuck into her as gently as I can with my own orgasm on the horizon. As much as I love fighting with her, the explosive passion that leaves marks for the next day, this is what she deserves. Someone to treat her softly, make sure she's safe and happy. She needs an Alpha King to her Luna Queen.

For her, I could be that man.

She falls apart on my cock seconds later. I spill inside her. Then, she climbs out of the water and lays, naked, on the not-quite-grass around the pool.

"Did your father tell you to lie to people?" she asks quietly.

My heart jumps into my throat. She couldn't have asked a worse fucking question. That's the only one that points the finger right back at me, that shows what a fucking monster I am. That maybe I would've been even without him.

She leans up on an elbow, her breasts swaying. "I need the truth, Anwen. I cannot spend—consider–my life with a mate I cannot trust."

Spend her life. She's thinking about a future with me. I swallow and leave the water, feeling a whole hell of a lot more naked than I was a second ago.

"No."

She takes a deep breath. "No, or not in so many words?"

"What do you mean?" I sit down next to her, close enough to touch but not yet.

"My father loved life." She smiles sadly. "He was always finding things to laugh about, ways to enjoy himself and coax others to do the same, even in the worst of situations. He never told me that I needed to laugh, but... I learned it all the same."

"Oh." I've never thought about it like that. There are just the things Father asked me to do, which I can blame on him, and the ones I can't. "Not in so many words, I suppose."

I wait for the disgust, but she just nods slowly.

She looks up at me. "You can ask me anything you'd like as well."

What are you thinking? Are you still mad? Why did we just have sex, and is it gonna happen again?

"Why did you ask?" I say instead.

"My mother, actually." She laughs quietly. "She taught me that there are no excuses for bad behavior, but that doesn't mean an explanation cannot help."

I lie back and stare up at the sky, thinking of the very similar conversation I had with Kieran. "Did it? Help, that is?"

"I'm not certain." She lies down with me. I can feel the warmth radiating off her body. "We buried Father."

"How was it?" Stupid, but I'm not sure what else to say.

"Crowded," she answers wryly.

It hits me like a punch. Suddenly, I'm back on that empty battlefield, searching for Father's corpse alone and finding nothing. There were other bodies. The stench of old blood hung heavy in the air. But I couldn't find him, and I'll never know what happened.

Estrella winces, then rubs her chest. "What was that?"

"One heart, two chests?" I suggest absently, fighting through memories.

She sucks in a breath of realization. I taste the cold dirt of that morning.

"Tell me what's hurting you," she says urgently.

I shake my head. "It's stupid. Tell me more about your father. He seems—"

"Like a good, brave man." She sits up. "But I strongly doubt this pain is… stupid."

I smile. She sounds like she's never said the word before.

"My father's funeral wasn't crowded. He missed the damned thing." I shake my head. "No one went back for his body fast enough. We buried nothing, and only the family and his Beta were there. He's not the kind of man you're supposed to mourn."

"And the chance to lead your people isn't supposed to taste like ash in your mouth." She takes my hand. "I don't know what I would do if my father's funeral was so poorly attended."

"He deserves better."

She squeezes my hand. "Yana, our holy woman, says funerals are for the living. Perhaps your father didn't deserve better, but you did."

I breathe in her words. They warm a cold, dark place inside of me. "Do you really think that?"

"That you deserve better?" She considers for a moment, which stings. "I do. Obedience, like so many other things, isn't an excuse. But it is a reason, and if you are truly trying to be different, it bears consideration."

"I am." I almost tell her the whole conversation I had with Kieran, but that contained as many of his secrets as mine. "I want to be. That's why I snuck off. If I told someone, either they would've stopped me, or it would've turned into a whole royal procession. I didn't want to be Crown Prince Anwen Solberg on a diplomatic mission. I wanted to be Anwen, your mate, trying to make things right."

A soft smile curves her lips. "That, I can tell."

I have to ask. "Does this mean you believe me? About Kieran?"

She starts to pull back.

"Kieran didn't do it." I hold onto her. "He wouldn't. I don't know who's doing it, but he's being framed."

She looks at the ground. "Anwen—"

"Do you believe me?" I ask.

33

BELIEF AND TRUST

ANWEN'S PALE EYES REFLECT THE STARS BACK AT ME. MY BODY HUMS with pleasure. In the wake of enjoying him, I feel the buzz of the healing during my coronation again, the guiding hand of the Goddess and Her whispered assurance that I stride the right path. Having him here feels nearly as good. I am half-drunk on his presence, so nearly out of my mind that I almost forgot why I left in the first place.

King Kieran stands accused—credibly—of orchestrating Father's murder. There is a note in his hand, a dead messenger who met a dead assassin at a time that makes King Kieran impossible to prove innocent. And I have heard story after story of King Kieran and Queen Raven's cruelty, though I'm somewhat less inclined to believe every story of Queen Raven after she discovered me at the mouth of the dungeon. In truth, if the evidence is to be believed, I have no idea if Anwen was involved in the planning, the murder itself.

But I want to believe him. The stars in his eyes look honest. He has nearly always looked honest to me.

"At your castle," I say slowly, "I often spent time with Nessa

195

Winters."

Anwen grimaces. "Why?"

I bristle. "Because she was kind to me when no one else was."

"Nessa's kindness comes with a price." He shakes his head. "Why are we talking about her now?"

"No one else would provide me with any information about the castle." I cross my arms across my chest. "She told me about King Kieran, how cruel he was. With all that, I find it difficult to discount his involvement."

He sits up. "Tell me what you heard."

"King Kieran asked her to pretend to be his mate when he believed Queen Raven to be his sister," I say immediately. "Despite that, he turned on her without warning and humiliated her before the court when he took the throne."

Anwen scoffs. "Nessa blackmailed Kieran and Raven into that arrangement."

I blink. "That doesn't sound like her."

"She caught them outside the tent in the morning and threatened to tell everyone they were mated to each other despite everyone believing they were siblings." He wrinkles his nose. "Unless Kieran married Nessa instead."

"He told you this?" I ask.

"Sure, and I trust him."

And I do not. Perhaps Kieran offered up a version of the story that makes him sound like a victim rather than a villain.

"She said Queen Raven viciously attacked her with a castle cat."

"True." He grins. "But did she tell you she hit first? Or that Raven didn't even know she could control animals at the time?"

I purse my lips. It's very likely Nessa doesn't understand what Queen Raven knew when, and it's often very difficult to tell who truly struck first in a fight.

"She said King Kieran hasn't spoken to her directly since his coronation." I pluck a dream thistle from the ground. "It's as though she's no longer good enough for him. She says Solbergs are all action first, emotions never."

"Kieran doesn't talk to her because Nessa bullied Raven nonstop for years. She used to run the castle, her and her little clique. He's just standing by his mate. As for the rest of it"—Anwen takes my hand—"I'm trying to change that, and so is he."

I study the fine, sharp planes of his face. He looks carved from stone, the pale moonlight washing all color out of his skin. There are a thousand ways he could be lying to me. A thousand ways Nessa could be lying to me. I have no proof other than the contradicting words of different witnesses. Nessa certainly seemed to take the king and queen's slights more personally than makes sense with Anwen's stories, but I only spent two weeks with her. And the man sitting before me now is the one who woke me from the nightmare and sat with me. The one I am gut-achingly terrified I may be able to love.

Selfishly, I am already tired of being alone.

"So." He rubs his thumb across the back of my hand. "The believing me thing. What are you thinking?"

"I am thinking that if I walk back into the city right now and announce I am mated to the brother of the man who killed their king, my people will riot," I say honestly.

Anwen blinks. A smile spreads across his face, slow like the sun coming up over the horizon. "Announce?"

"Perhaps." I fidget with the dream thistle, but his excitement thrills me. Despite everything, I want to be his–and him to be mine.

He laughs delightedly and drops back to the ground. "Shit. I was just hoping I might be able to convince you I wasn't hiding a secret plot to murder your father. This is way better."

I smile shyly. "I don't think you were involved."

"Hey, that's something." He studies me. "And Kieran?"

"Was the note truly in his hand?" I ask.

He shrugs. "Possibly. Everyone in the palace learns basic reading and writing from the same tutor. I'm not an expert, but it seems like it'd be pretty easy to fake."

I nod slowly. A new king—a new leader is susceptible to attacks from all sides. Several of Father's advisors have pulled me aside already to report the beginnings of what they feel may be plots against me. Attempts to impugn my ability to lead or to suggest I may not be the eldest Sollabella after all. There have been none since my coronation, at least. Perhaps the healing has allayed all concern.

Mother's words before my coronation come back to me. Sundrop Gem is a truly special place. I've known it all my life, but I felt it in the celebration more than I ever have before. I love these people, as they love me. Perhaps, if I simply tell them my love extends to this foreign prince, they will take me at my word.

Perhaps loving Anwen means taking him at his.

"The Moon Goddess does not make mistakes," I say slowly. "Yana said the leaders of Dun's Crossing and Sundrop Gem were once one heart beating in two chests. We could be that again."

He grabs me and kisses me, a short, sharp burst of passion. I drink in his taste and wish I could fall into him with no other complications. But our world is never that simple.

"Look me in the eyes," I say, "and promise me you believe every word you've said tonight. That there is no ounce of doubt in your heart that yourself or any in your family ordered my father's assassination."

Anwen drags his gaze to mine. My heart pounds. If I believe him now, I believe him. I am exhausted by living in this gray area, by never knowing. The Goddess brought us together, and She swore to me again tonight that She was right to do so.

He lays both his hands against the ground, palms down. "By the light of the Moon Goddess, in hardship and in ease, under pain of a thousand desert nights, I promise I'm sure no Solberg did this."

My mouth falls open. "That's our vow. How—?"

"I thought it might come in handy." He smiles. "Made a sailor teach me when Baz and I landed."

A laugh bursts from my lips, high and bright. There isn't a flicker in his gaze, not a second of hesitation. And he learned our words, my words, without even knowing what I would ask him. He sought out the way to commit himself without asking. I throw my arms around his neck and kiss him.

All along, he's smelled of mint and that brown alcohol. Gritty, earthy, and cold. But in this oasis, the one I've held in my heart for so long, there's something else, something new there. A familiar sweetness. Like he's becoming one of us. And there is something… missing.

Earlier, kissing Anwen felt like rebellion. As if it were the last selfish choice I was allowed before truly dedicating myself to my people and becoming the leader they deserve. But below all that sat a hardness deep inside my chest. Something jagged and cruel that sliced at me whenever I considered him, the mark on my shoulder, the way I am pulled into his orbit. It reminded me over and over that I was lowering myself, making a fool of myself, pricing myself too cheaply.

That feeling is completely absent now. Warmth—love?—floods in to fill the space it occupied. Wanting Anwen isn't a selfish choice, isn't a betrayal of my people. It's an acceptance of the truth the Goddess wrote in the stars for us both.

A thought, quiet and sad, worms its way to the front of my mind. Kissing him is not a betrayal of Father, either.

Tears prick at the corners of my eyes. I clutch Anwen closer and inhale another lungful. My wolf howls, pleading for another round here, but I ignore her. There is more to this moment than physical pleasure.

If I believe Anwen, then Father would be proud. He seemed pleased before I disagreed with him, said there was nothing between Anwen and me. More than that, he would want to see me happy.

Anwen makes me happy. I believe him. But I need the world to believe him as I do, and I need to find the real culprit, whoever framed King Kieran. They deserve my true wrath. Together, Anwen and I will ensure they get it.

I pull back. He smiles at me.

"Should I take that as a good sign?"

I nod. "But it means this chapter in our life isn't finished."

"Our life," he repeats as if tasting the words. "What do you mean?"

"I have the beginning of a plan, but it requires us telling everyone we're mated." I peek up at him shyly. "And… scheduling a wedding."

34

HOMECOMING

ANWEN

THREE DAYS LATER—FOUR, IF YOU COUNT THE FACT ESTRELLA AND I didn't go back to her palace until morning—I lean over the bow of *The Lady Suniva* and watch the towers of Solberg Castle rise over the horizon.

Baz claps me on the shoulder. "Someday, I'll get you back for only staying a day in that place."

I snort. "You can visit by yourself, you know."

"Ah, but then I don't get to say I'm the sole retainer of the crown prince." He smirks. "That opens a lot of doors."

I shake my head. To hear Baz tell it, he fucked half the kingdom on a single overnight. But I know from a drowsy mind-link he sent me as Estrella and I were stumbling back in that he loved the color, music, and culture at least as much as the women. There's something honest behind his party-boy desire to stick around.

"You're the Beta of the crown prince when we return," I say.

"The fine shores of home do offer their own pleasures." Baz waggles his eyebrows.

Home. It's a weird word now. If—when Estrella's plan works out, Dun's Crossing won't be my home for long. She needs an Alpha in Sundrop Gem, not a three-day trip across the Lonely Sea. I'll have a whole new palace to learn.

Every time I think that, it feels like knocking on a false wall. Something echoes, hollow and not quite right.

I stare down at my hands on the wood of the bow instead. Barely visible against my pale skin, a white tattoo rings my pinkie finger. It's a Sundrop tradition for married, but not yet mated couples, so we had to get them in secret.

'He's eyeballing you again,' Baz says through the mind-link.

I don't need to look over my shoulder. I know who he's talking about. When we wandered back into the palace that morning, Estrella insisted we have breakfast with her family. I sat through the whole thing awkwardly, picking at the fruit they still have at this time of year and trying to seem like the sort of man they should trust. But since her plan relies so much on tightly controlled information, I couldn't just tell the truth. No, we had to convince a grieving wife and son I came to Sundrop because I was pretty sure Kieran was being framed, which meant the real bad guy was walking free, and I couldn't allow that. Dowager Suniva came around sometime after the food had been cleared away, but while we were still drinking coffee. Castor… fuck, I don't think Castor has come around yet. Every time I see him, he puts his hand on his sword and glares at me like I'm two seconds from snapping and murdering everyone on the boat.

'Leave him,' I tell Baz.

'Fuck that,' Baz replies. *'He's got two hours before he finds out he's the jackass, and I think he could do that just as well with his teeth halfway down his throat.'*

'That's my mate's brother you're talking about,' I say with a flare of protective anger.

Baz rolls his eyes. *'I still think he's a dick.'*

Before I can agree, Estrella's smell blots out the sea air. I turn.

Apparently, she doesn't believe in wearing her finery while traveling. Called it a "ridiculous vanity" when I suggested we should look like royalty getting off this boat. So the fabric wrapped around her body is a thicker, rougher maroon without any other decorations, and she tucks it up between her legs, like a pair of pants, when she needs to help one of the sailors with a task. It's tucked like that now, and her hair is braided so tightly back from her face that her skin is pulled taught. Every time I see her in something new, I expect to feel differently, to find a way she's less beautiful.

It hasn't happened yet.

Even better, she's staring at me just like I'm staring at her. Like maybe the sun will go out, and this'll be the last chance we get to look.

"I say this with the utmost respect, Your Majesty." Baz bows. "But yuck. I don't think I'll hang out with the two of you until some of this sexual tension burns off." He hurries away.

Estrella laughs throatily. Since I said yes to our plan, she's been a little more back to herself. Well, back to the woman I met before her father's death.

"Is he always like that?" she asks.

"Or worse." I smile. "Hope that's not a dealbreaker."

"I think it may be a bit late for dealbreakers." She leans against the bow next to me, looks at the horizon and the approaching coast. "There isn't long left now."

I wish I could touch her. Yet another flaw in her plan. We haven't even been able to share a room, and sneaking through the tiny hallways of a ship is much harder than those of Castle Solberg.

"No, there isn't." I lean my shoulder against hers. The rocking of the boat might've pushed us together. "Are you ready?"

She chuckles nervously. "It may be a bit late for that as well."

The tattoo on my finger catches the light. "We hid our marks for weeks."

"No." She shakes her head resolutely. "I am not going to delay this any further because of something as simple as nerves."

"What's making you nervous?" I ask.

She clenches her jaw. "The reactions."

"So you think Castor's going to kill me too?" I smile, trying to lighten the mood.

I earn myself a faint laugh.

"I certainly haven't discounted the possibility," she murmurs. "But...."

"But you're more worried about my side." My mark aches, but it's the barest echo of what it was only a few days ago that I barely notice. Like smacking an old bruise against something. "I promised you could trust them."

"I know this."

I study her. The waves turn her gray eyes stormy, her shoulders bunch with tension, and a tiny wrinkle appears between her brows. Subtle indicators that she's losing her Goddess-damned mind in there.

"Is it the Nessa stuff?" I ask quietly. Now would be a great time for the mind-link, but we must have to actually go through with the wedding for that because it isn't working yet.

"Partially." She squeezes the side of the boat and doesn't elaborate.

Again, I wish her plan didn't rely on us going back to Dun's Crossing. I keep wondering if putting her back there, where Nessa can influence her again, is such a bright idea.

"I thought you trusted me," I say in the least judgmental tone I've got.

"I do!" she snaps.

Not non-judgmental enough.

"Then trust me when I tell you we can trust them." I bump her shoulder and burn to wrap my arms around her.

"I believe they have nothing to do with Father," she says like it's a mantra.

I'll take it. I have to.

* * *

THE SHIP DOCKS UNDER THE BRIGHT, NOON-DAY SUN. A FLOTILLA OF soldiers stands at the end of the dock. No sign of Kieran, Raven, or any of my siblings. Estrella visibly tenses.

"Not exactly the welcome we received last time," Castor mutters.

"Hush," Dowager Suniva says. "Your sister declared us enemies. It's only reasonable."

But she has enough of her daughter's tells that I can see the worry in her face too.

'Dammit, Kieran, couldn't you send Candace or Finn?' I ask across mind-link.

'Are you with the ship?' He demands in return.

Motherfucker. I forgot I was keeping that quiet too.

'I'll answer everything,' I say. *'Meet us in the throne room. Bring Raven.'*

'You'd better.' The connection goes dead.

It's not the welcome I was hoping for either, but nothing in Estrella's plan accounted for the fact that I've technically been missing for a week, and I didn't give Kieran any kind of clue I was coming back, with Sundrop Gem or at all.

"King Kieran and Queen Raven have matters keeping them inside the castle," I say with a smile. "They would be honored to meet you in the throne room."

Estrella nods. "Then meet them we shall."

And with her head held high, she takes the first step onto the gangplank.

Heading down into the city is never easy. Hooded cloaks have been Baz and I's friends for years. But I don't remember getting this many looks or whispers when I come down without a disguise at all. Every stall, every pub, every group of people walking down the street breaks out in conversation the second we pass. I have to order the soldiers not to surround us like we're prisoners being escorted to the dungeons twice. And the more they talk, the more Estrella becomes the Luna Queen. Her posture stiffens, her chin juts up, her warm face becomes icy. It's like I can see the thoughts in her head. She can't let them see her look vulnerable, but with every *'I thought they fled'* or *'takes some balls to return,'* sentiment from the people watching us, her defenses weaken, and she has to shore them up again. By the time we actually arrive at the castle, it's like walking next to a statue. At least they lead us into the throne room without making a fuss.

Kieran and Raven already wait inside, sitting on their thrones in their royal robes. Overkill. They're showing off just as much as Estrella is. Castor's hand goes to the hilt of his sword again, and he glares bloody murder.

"I'll admit an amount of surprise at your return, Luna Queen Estrella," Kieran says. "What brings you back to our shores?"

Estrella takes a deep breath. I step up next to her and hold her hand. There's a tiny, bright spark in my mark as I line up our matching tattoos.

The whole room seems to freeze.

35

TELL EVERYONE

ESTRELLA

QUEEN RAVEN RAISES A SLOW HAND TO COVER HER FACE. KING Kieran's sharp mouth turns down slightly at the corners. My pulse beats a warning in my ears. I trust Anwen. I want to trust Anwen. The stories he tells make far more sense with the woman who found me at the top of the dungeon stairs. But with horror, disappointment, painted so starkly on their faces, I cannot think of anything but the stories Nessa told. Queen Raven as a bully, King Kieran as a heartless monster. They look like those people to me now.

Anwen squeezes my hand. I can feel his pulse against the inside of my wrist—steady, sure. He's not scared.

I take a deep breath.

Mother steps around us, in front of me. I can no longer see King Kieran and Queen Raven.

"Does this"—she looks at our joined hands—"mean what I believe it means?"

For the first time in my life, I cannot read her face. That chills me to the core. When I told her the lie—half-lie—about Anwen believing

King Kieran had been framed, she gave me almost the same look. A careful, calculated blankness. Like she no longer trusts me with her expressions. Does she think believing Anwen, listening to him at all, is a betrayal of Father's memory? Does she think I'm abandoning everything we stand for?

My mark pulses painfully. I know I'm not betraying Father. I know what he wanted for me, for Sundrop, and this is the best way I can come up with to achieve it. I am no longer just my mother's daughter. I am also her queen, and I am choosing my mate.

"Yes," I say as proudly as I can muster.

Anwen squeezes my hand again.

Mother takes a step closer. "And does this make you happy?"

Still nothing on her face. But this question, at least, is simple to answer.

"Goddess, yes," I say. "Or at the very least, it gives me a path toward happiness, something I didn't see for myself before."

A heartbeat passes. Then, Mother enfolds me in her arms, a warm, soft embrace of acceptance.

I nearly crumple. But she is far from the fiercest dragon to face in this room. I stand strong.

"When I first woke up next to my Isai," she says, loud enough for the whole room to hear, "I was certain it was a mistake. I did wake up first, of course." She smiles. "King Isai would sleep the day away, if I let him. And I remember sitting on the grass next to the then-prince, just picturing his scowl when he saw me. I was some lesser noble from a distant pack. Surely, he'd want nothing to do with me." She laughs, but I hear a tinge of sadness. "Clearly, I did not yet know Isai. When he awoke, he smiled up at me like I was the most beautiful thing he'd ever seen and told me he already knew he loved me."

I glance at Anwen out of the corner of my eye. Nothing could be less like our first morning together.

Mother releases me. "I didn't believe him for months. Sometimes, love is slow-coming, even when it's in front of you."

I smile at her. That, I understand.

"Be happy." She looks at both of us. "However long it takes."

"Thank you, Moth—"

"What?" Castor demands.

I twist to look at him. Fury blazes in his eyes, but he is only looking at Anwen.

"You lied," he says disbelievingly. "You said this was about your brother, some half-baked story about a frame job…. Estrella, tell me you are not this foolish."

All the warmth of Mother's hug fades away as I face my brother. I knew he didn't agree, when that first breakfast ended, but I believed he was willing to see this out. To trust Anwen enough to explore the possibility. There is nothing of that in his face now.

"Please." His voice breaks as he looks between Anwen and me.

"Castor—"

Anwen squeezes my hand, then releases it to put himself between my brother and me. "In honor of your father's memory, I will not strike you down for talking about my mate that way."

"Your—" Castor's face starts to go purple. "That is my sister! I am trying to save her from being pulled in by your lies, from putting our whole people on the line for her heart!"

"No, you're not," Anwen says calmly.

Calmly! That may be more surprising than anything else that has happened in this throne room so far.

Castor sputters, unable to catch enough words to construct a sentence.

"If you wanted to protect her, you wouldn't have called her stupid." Anwen crosses his arms. "You want to protect your pride, which doesn't have anything to do with us."

"Our father—"

"Is dead," Anwen says coldly. "A devastating loss, and one I intend to revenge as much as I can. What does that have to do with our relationship?"

"You were involved!" Castor bellows, his hand going to his sword.

Anwen tenses. My heart leaps into my throat. They are going to fight, and I'm going to lose one or both of them.

"If you still think that, then you really do think Estrella's stupid, and I'll have to fight you," Anwen says. "Though I'll take the compliment."

Something in Castor deflates. "What?"

"Your sister's a genius for this whole leadership situation already." A soft smile curves his lips. "I haven't gotten a lie past her yet, and the one time I hid the truth, she was half-asleep and damn near caught me anyway. So thanks for believing I could pull it off, but the truth is, I don't stand a snowball's chance in hell against her. I'm lucky she'll let me stand next to her instead of against her because I was losing."

My breath catches. I put a hand on his arm, and Anwen turns to me with a wink. For a moment, I think that means he's lying, saying whatever he has to so Castor will relax. But his face is alive with warmth, with… love? He believes every word.

"We want to do this the right way," he tells Castor while still looking at me. "We want to tell you and get your approval. But I don't see your lack of approval stopping us any time soon."

After weeks of loneliness, of second-guessing, of pain, his words are like a magic spell. A balm to an ache I didn't even know I was carrying. We want to do this right, to use it to find the real murderer, but we also want to be wed.

How incredible to think that and believe it.

"Apologies," King Kieran says.

I whirl around to the foreign king and queen I nearly forgot about. They haven't moved from their thrones, and Queen Raven's hand still covers her mouth.

"But I must ask," he continues. "Does this mean you believe, or are willing to believe, that I did not hire that rogue to murder King Isai?"

Anwen opens his mouth, but I cut him off.

"Yes." My voice rings through the throne room, echoes off the walls. I hold myself with perfect posture, not a hint of hesitation. They are facing the queen of Sundrop Gem, and they should know it. "Anwen says the note was a forgery, and if that is true, any other evidence is circumstantial at best. I believe my mate."

Castor makes a soft, punched-out sound. I screw up every ounce of bravery, of confidence, of belief I have.

"The Goddess brough us together for a reason," I say. "And I believe there was more to that than merely the way we could make each other happy. My mate alone—Anwen alone—could convince me there was some other explanation for the events I've experienced in this castle, as if the Goddess knew I would need such a thing. So, I believe, and I will not rest until Dowager Suniva, Prince Castor, and all of Sundrop Gem believe as I do."

King Kieran exhales and seems to melt out of the foreign dignitary I've seen all along. For the first time, he looks like a man, like someone who will soon be my brother-in-law. "Thank the Goddess."

Queen Raven nudges him then stands. "I think what my husband meant to say is that we are honored by your belief and will do everything we can to prove you're right to give it to us." She smiles softly and holds her arms slightly out, as if offering a hug. "And welcome to the family. Believe it or not, you're arriving at one of its better times."

A wave of relief powers my steps and sends me into the queen's polite embrace. It's very strange, to be hugging like this in a throne room. Her formal clothes crumple under my arms, though I remember the dress she wore to the dungeons did not.

But this also seems right. This is a political maneuver, the first step in a quest for revenge, and the birth of a new family. It's a new future for both our kingdoms.

She releases me, and I step back. Castor is still glaring bloody murder, but he has released his sword. Perhaps that's all I can ask for at this time.

"Well, good," Anwen says. "I guess now's a good time to mention we need to schedule a wedding in the next month."

"And invite everyone." I grin hungrily.

3 6

CLEAN SWEEP

Anwen

Kieran leans back in the chair at his desk. "To get the sort of turnout the two of you are looking for, I've scheduled the wedding for the next full moon."

I suck in a deep breath and rub the pale tattoo on my pinkie. "Three weeks?"

"I know." He shrugs. "But everyone just went home after the peace ball. They need time to tend to their own kingdoms."

"I get that." Estrella's not going to like the news, but she'll understand too. "And Snowcrest?"

Kieran bares all his teeth in something that only barely resembles a smile. "After some discussion, Floyd agreed that the job of an envoy is, in fact, to carry messages to his king. He won't be back for at least a week, two if the Moonlit Pass is already snowed over."

The only reason he's not still raking me over the coals for my disappearing act is my Floyd theory. He'll do just about anything to prove I'm right about the bastard.

I want to be right. But more than that, I want to know if Floyd did this or if he's just covering for someone else. I won't let Estrella down again.

"And his guards?" I ask hopefully.

"With him." Kieran taps a letter on his desk. "The only member of Snowcrest Canyon left within these walls is Nessa."

I grimace. I haven't told him what Estrella said about Nessa, mostly because I can't convince her it might be safer for all of us if they stopped hanging out. She says Nessa's her friend, and aren't we an example of how hurt can reshape otherwise innocent encounters? So I've decided Kieran doesn't need another thing to worry about.

"At least you don't have to pretend to marry her." He smirks.

"I was smart enough not to get blackmailed." I turn and leave his office before I lose my chance. Nessa might be the only one yet, but she used to have a whole clique of friends. It wouldn't be hard for her to at least post a guard at the door King Isai's body was kept behind.

'Meet me in the east wing,' I say to Baz through mind-link. *'We've got a room to search.'*

'Be there in five.'

I can't walk through the castle without drawing eyes anymore. At least half the people I pass make sure to congratulate me on finding my mate and my upcoming wedding. Every time impatience bubbles under my skin, I remember Estrella. That's who they're talking about. And, of fucking course, they want to congratulate me. She's an absolute miracle. I don't know how I could see anyone with her and not say something.

And for the first time in ages, my bite doesn't even twinge. There's no hesitation, no worry. Just us.

Baz meets me out in front of the still slightly frost-covered door to King Isai's final chamber. "This mean Floyd's gone?"

"For a little while." I roll up my sleeves. "But Nessa's still around. Anyone see you?"

"Couple people." He shrugs. "I wasn't exactly sneaking."

Neither was I. She'll either know or she won't. I can't resist the lure of what Floyd might've been hiding.

"We should move quickly and take anything we find." I pull out two pairs of leather gloves and hand one to Baz. "Just in case anything's too cold to handle."

"Any idea what we're looking for?" He tugs them on.

"Anything." I push open the door.

A blast of cold air and a dribble of meltwater greets me. Floyd doesn't seem to have bothered to defrost the place properly before leaving, but without his magic to maintain it, the ice clinging to damn near every surface is slowly dissolving.

"Just another reason to move fast." I step inside.

Systematically, silently, Baz and I take the room apart. Nothing is sacred. Not the bedspread that still kind of shows a shadowed imprint of King Isai's body. Not the frozen bouquet of flowers on the nightstand. Nothing. And with every subsequent thing we turn over, I get more and more frustrated. It's like somebody already fucking did this.

No, not somebody. Floyd. Like he knew Kieran was getting rid of him on purpose, and he made sure there was nothing for us to find.

"Fuck!" I overturn the nightstand in a burst of rage.

"Chill out," Baz replies.

I drag my gaze up to him slowly. "I swear to the Goddess, if that was a pun, I'm gonna find a way to put your ass on cleaning latrines for the next month. The next fucking year."

He smirks. "You wouldn't."

"Try me," I snarl. "There's nothing here! If he wasn't trying to hide shit, wouldn't there be fucking something? Anything?"

Baz rubs his jaw and looks around. "It is weird. But I don't think furniture destruction is going to get us anywhere."

"It might," I grumble.

But the place it'll get us is having to clean the whole room back up or ask one of the staff to do it. It's the easy way.

"Fuck, all right. Where haven't we looked?" I ask.

He stares around the room for a moment. "Top of the canopy?"

"Stupid place to keep something."

Baz shimmies up the bedpost anywhere. "Clear."

I take a deep breath and try to regain myself. "Floyd's a lot of things, but he's not stupid."

"Pity." Baz grins.

I ignore him. "He wouldn't keep any evidence in his bedroom. That's why we're in here in the first place. But Estrella and her family were allowed to visit the king, so he couldn't leave it lying around in plain sight here, either. We've opened up all the usual hiding spots, and there are no secret passages in this room." My gaze lands on the fireplace. "But he was able to stabilize the ice around King Isai for the trip to Sundrop Gem, so he's more powerful than he claimed. He could've lit and snuffed a fire without anyone noticing."

Baz and I dart for the fireplace. Pokers, ashes…there! I snag the tip of the only thing in the scorched pile that isn't gray or black.

Half a brown feather, split down the middle and singed on one end, dangles from my fingers.

"This is fletching," I murmur. "From the arrow. It has to be. You see how cleanly it's split?"

Baz runs a finger down the feather's exposed spine. "So did he burn the arrow?"

"Must've." A slow grin slides over my face. "But he missed a piece. And good feathers for fletching are a bitch to find, so he wouldn't have burned this with it if it didn't mean something."

"Mean what?" Baz asks.

"I… don't know." I twist the feather, looking for any clues. There's some weird color fluctuation, I guess, but it kind of just looks brown. "I don't know anything about feathers."

Shit. The only clue Floyd left behind can't be a dead end. I can't go back to Estrella empty-handed. I just fucking can't.

An idea pops into my mind. "Raven does."

Baz raises his eyebrows. "She talks to birds; she doesn't memorize their plumage."

"But other birds do." I hop up, feather still in hand. "She'll know how to find out." And it'll be well worth whatever bullshit I have to endure to get it.

I race out of the room, leaving Baz behind. Like always at this time of day, Raven's in what used to be Mother's greenhouse. She killed all the plants she didn't approve of, and now she's tending new sprouts in the pots that used to hold poison. Stepping inside is weird, like walking back in time, but nothing can slow me down now.

Raven looks up, worry painted on her face, as I burst in. "Has something else happened?"

"Yes and no." I hold out the feather. "We found this in the room Floyd was guarding. Looks like arrow fletching to me, but I don't recognize the bird."

She takes the feather with a smile. "Thank you for coming to me."

Bravely, I don't even grimace. Maybe someday I'll ask how the hell she's so nice to everyone all the time. Maybe not.

She studies it carefully. My heart hammers in my ears. This is the only proof we have right now. It needs to lead to more.

"I'm sorry, I don't recognize it." She must see something on me face because she quickly says, "But I can find out. I'll ask the birds. Especially at this time of year, we've got a lot of migratory species. They should know."

I nod tightly. Not the answer I was hoping for but good enough. It has to be good enough.

"Seriously, Anwen." She puts a hand on my arm. "Thank you for trusting me."

Old lessons, punishments for talking to Blanca, harsh words and slammed doors, flash through my mind. I'm supposed to pull away when she touches me, remind her that she's the least of us.

Easy way, Anwen.

I pry out of her grasp slowly, trying not to hurt or offend her. "You were, uh, my first choice."

She glows with a smile. I guess I can kind of see what Kieran sees in her. But not with Estrella around.

"I gotta go." I step back slowly toward the door, leaving the feather with Raven. "Got a queen to keep up to date."

She nods. "Give her my love."

Doubtful. But I will walk through the busy corridors right to Estrella room, knock on the door, and stride inside without a care in the world who sees. Everything's been turned upside-down, but that is finally right.

37

FITTING IN

ESTRELLA

"THANK YOU," I MURMUR AS ONE OF THE DUN'S CROSSING seamstresses pins another fold of my skirt in place.

After a few days of what Tess deemed arguing, though I would more rightly call it standing my ground, the flock of women assigned to make my wedding dress have finally understood that I will not be —at least exclusively—wearing the dull neutrals so common in this kingdom. The head seamstress, ironically named Bright, in particular tried to put her foot down on a traditional charcoal-colored wedding gown. She now stands in the corner of the room with her arms crossed, eying the one pinning the swath of charcoal-shot purple and blue fabric of my skirt like a traitor.

"You look stunning." Tess clasps her hands beneath her chin, and her eyes sparkle as she looks up at me. Predictably, she has been delighted since Anwen and I announced our betrothal. To her, love has won, and no explanation about the plan underpinning our vows can sway her opinion.

In truth, when I look at myself in the three-paned mirror the seamstresses always bring to my bedroom, the plan does fade from my mind. I look like a bride, like the paintings I've seen of Mother on her wedding day, with a few twists toward Dun's Crossing traditions. Instead of a crown and a long, draping cape, Bright unwillingly produced a gauzy veil in all the colors of my gown. Instead of the scrolling colors I would usually paint on my hands with my nearest and dearest the day before the wedding, the seamstresses are embroidering them into the fabric of the gown itself. More of the folds are pinned and sewn in place rather than just cleverly wrapped. I look like someone who could be Luna Queen of both lands, or at least, of a Sundrop Gem which works closely with Dun's Crossing once more. I rub my thumb over the pale white tattoo on my pinkie finger. My wedding is fast approaching, and only when I am forced to stand still for these fittings, does that ring true.

Someone knocks on the door. I nod to Tess, and she opens it.

Without hesitation, Nessa sweeps in. She's been lonesome since her father left, but he ought to return soon.

"You're a vision, as always," she declares. "I swear, I need to post eyes outside of Bright's workshop. I can't risk one of these going by without seeing you."

I chuckle. Since my return, Nessa's been merely pleasant. She's barely said a word about the Solbergs.

"Isn't she just?" Tess replies.

Nessa doesn't take her eyes away from me, but before she can answer, another knock sounds.

I glance over my shoulder as Tess goes to open the door again. This time, King Kieran offered us different rooms. He assigned me—and Tess—quarters on the same hall as his younger sisters, Princesses Candace and Ingrid. Mother is but a turn away, and Castor a few more, alongside Anwen and Finn. But this closeness to the Solberg family seems to have created an odd coincidence.

"I heard there was some excitement in here." Princess Candace, Anwen's equally white-blonde sister, steps inside and curtsies.

And there it is again. Every time Nessa appears in my chambers, or nearly anywhere else I am in the castle, Princess Candace appears a scant minute later. Unless the walls have ears, I can't imagine how she always knows. She has the same eerily perfect neutral expression as her two older brothers, so I do not yet know her nearly well enough to be certain why she makes her presence such a constant.

"Princess." I curtsy as well as I can with a seamstress at my knees. "Lovely to see you, as always."

"Seconded." Nessa bobs a quick curtsy without truly looking at the princess. "We were just talking about how beautiful Estrella is in this dress."

"It's spectacular." Princess Candace drifts closer, Tess on her heels. "Have you thought about your hair at all?"

"I could do it again," Nessa offers.

I swallow. I've been thinking about my hair extensively, and I can't imagine walking through the temple with anything other than Tess's handiwork on my head. But I haven't found a way to explain that to Nessa yet.

"You're quite talented, but shouldn't she have someone who reflects either of the cultures she's uniting?" Princess Candace asks primly. "Tess, you do hair sometimes, right?"

The air crackles with tension. I have not yet figured out why Princess Candace keeps appearing, but it is obvious that she and Nessa do not get along.

Tess blinks. "Well—"

"I'm sure her lady-in-waiting does a palatable job, but shouldn't a queen have something special for her wedding day?" Nessa replies.

"Tess's work is far more than palatable," I say through gritted teeth. Nessa has been kind, but I will not allow anyone to talk about my best friend like that.

"You see?" Princess Candace waves a hand at me. "Luna Estrella knows what she wants, if you give her a moment to say it."

"She didn't say that was what she wanted," Nessa snaps. "She's just defending her people. I can respect that, but it doesn't mean anything about her hair."

"Or she doesn't know how to tell you it's what she wants." Princess

Candace folds her hands in front of her. "You do have a somewhat…
brash personality."

Nessa's mouth falls open, and there's a beat of silence. I meet
Tess's wide gaze. Both of us have been watching them go back and
forth like expert kras players, and my neck is beginning to hurt.

"Apologies," Princess Candace says. "I haven't been sleeping very
well, and my tongue got away from me. Spirited–the word I meant
was spirited."

"Spirited," Nessa repeats disbelievingly. "Horses are spirited."

"And very distinctive women." Princess Candace smiles softly. "My
mother was called that, in her younger years."

Nessa leans back as if Princess Candace just hit her. My mind
whirls, trying to keep up. Anwen mentioned their mother is impris-
oned in the dungeons I still haven't seen, and I can certainly understand why one would have a complicated relationship with such a
woman, but it is impossible to deny that Queen Rowena held her own
next to King Gavin, which is a feat in itself. A comparison to her, at
least in this matter, seems far from the most scathing thing Princess
Candace could've said.

Yet, Nessa turns to me and curtsies. "Sorry, I've just remembered I
have somewhere else to be. Father is supposed to return in a few
hours, and I have to get dressed for that."

Without another word, she scurries from the room.

This, too, is another "coincidence" that regularly follows Princess
Candace's arrival. I study the pale princess in the mirror. Her cornsilk
curls fold neatly into a complex bun that requires close inspection to
see the detail, just like the silver embroidery on her gray dress. She
always seems to wear that same faint smile, nearly beatific, and
Nessa's jabs never perturb her like hers do Nessa. There's certainly
something below her surface, and I can't deny a curiosity to discover
what it is.

"It'll be interesting to have Floyd in the castle again," she says.

Tess nods, wide-eyed. Last night, she confessed to me that
Princess Candace intimidates her a little.

"He is an interesting man," I say carefully. I believe she knows

Anwen's suspicions, but with all the seamstresses in the room, we can't speak openly.

"I look forward to hearing fresh news of Snowcrest Canyon." Princess Candace takes a few steps forward and plucks a bolt of fabric from a basket of alternate options the seamstresses brought along. "Stop me if I'm overstepping, but have you considered an overskirt of this?"

Bright makes a small, pained noise in the back of her throat. I study the slightly sheer, fragile-looking, rosy fabric in her hands. With the charcoal, the gown does currently lean darker than is usual for a wedding dress. And the purple in the current dress has red undertones that would match the pink well.

"Oh, that would warm your skin right up." Tess covers her mouth as soon as she realizes she's spoken.

Princess Candace nods thoughtfully. "You're right. I think an over-skirt might not be the right place, being so far from your skin." She hefts the heavy bolt easily and drapes it over my arms. "Here. You can do the embroidery in blue, tie the whole piece together, and it'll look like it's right on your arms."

I study myself in the mirror. The pink lightens the whole effect, and with a draping sleeve, it would look so much like the capes of home, I wouldn't even think to miss them.

"Sorry, this is how Ingrid and I work." She pulls the bolt away with a small, self-conscious laugh. "A dress isn't done until the party starts."

"No, I liked it." I catch her pale gaze in the mirror and smile.

She grins back at me, shockingly honest. "Well, good. I'm still getting my practice in at the sister thing. I've kind of always been the oldest."

"What do you mean?" Raven is the oldest daughter, and she has two older brothers. I know the situation with Raven was different with certain members of her family, but did Candace not think of her as a sister either?

"Oh, Mother and Father didn't allow us to treat Raven as a true sibling." Her tone is airy, but I can hear the sting of real hurt underneath. In that way, she's exactly like Anwen. "And the boys and girls got very different training. So Ingrid and I are thick as thieves, but I'm just learning to be Raven's younger sister." She smiles at me again. "And I guess I'll have to figure out a same-age sister as well!"

"I've never had a sister at all, unless you count Tess," I say, "so I suppose we can learn together."

"I'd really like that." Princess Candace sets the bolt beside the seamstress. "Can we stop with all the stuffy titles, then? I just want to be family."

"All right." I smile at her in the mirror. "Candace."

She giggles. "Now, Tess, tell me how you get Estrella's hair to do all these incredible things."

Tess turns ashen. "Well—"

I turn back to the mirror. I'm practicing believing anything the Solbergs tell me, so Tess must fend for herself. But as I watch Candace gesture broadly, sketching out the exact shape of her meaning, I can't help wondering how the same childhood produced both her and Anwen.

3 8

BECOMING ALPHA

Anwen

Kieran and I walk through the castle side-by-side, talking about the wedding. There's nothing else to talk about anymore. I swear to the Goddess, I heard a couple of maids chattering about it when I walked by the other day.

"Remember, there are still two weeks left," he says. "This likely isn't a full list."

"But I'd still rather know." I run a hand through my hair. "I want to know who thinks they can agree to attend a royal wedding with less than three weeks' notice, for one."

Kieran chuckles. "Fair. So, I've heard back from—"

He rattles off a dozen kingdoms. I recognize most of the names from my investigation after the peace ball. A few, I don't.

"And those are all coming?"

"They're all sending representatives." He shakes his head. "I've got all the furniture-makers in the city flat out trying to get enough places to seat them all in chairs that will be dignified for each of them."

"It's more than last time," I say. "Seems like, even with the assassination, the invitations have been accepted more than expected."

His answering smile is tired. For the first time, I wonder just how much turning around a proper royal wedding in less than a month is taking out of him.

'You look like shit,' I tell him through mind-link.

That surprises a real laugh out of him. "And this is why I don't come to you for confidence."

"What are brothers for?" I smirk. "But seriously, what the hell's going on?"

"What isn't?" he says wryly. "Raven is still struggling with morning sickness, but she's trying to push through to chase down that fucking feather. More kingdoms are showing up to a party after my reign has a death toll than after." He glances around and lowers his voice. "There's still the note—"

I shake my head subtly then pull him into a hidden passageway behind a tapestry.

He stares around in awe. "I didn't even know this was here."

"It's not on any maps but mine." I shrug. "Not the point. We can talk in here without being overhead. There's a little old magic on the tapestry which is sound-dampening."

He nods. "The short version is that it's hard to sleep at night knowing someone very effectively framed me for murder."

"I never thought you did it," I say.

"Really?"

"Really." I look up at the jagged rock that comprises the roof of the passageway. "You know, I found this one when you were on that table-topping kick."

He laughs, then grimaces. "Sorry about that. Taner was too damn good at setting himself up behind people."

"Right, blame the Beta." I offer him a sarcastic smile. I've got too many memories of Fleming's noxious headache treatment after he shoved me over his kneeling best friend's back to forget after such a shitty apology.

"Fine, fine, it was my idea." He holds up his hands. "At the time, I thought seeing people go ass-over-teakettle was about the funniest thing possible."

"That was very clear." I shake my head. I really hadn't even been looking for this one, but I could hear teenage Kieran's mocking laughter echoing off the walls behind me, and I knew he was smart enough to open all the regular doors. It just seemed like the safest bet to check all the most common ways of hiding passages, and I stumbled on this dead-end hallway. "I figured out it was sound dampening when you and Taner barreled past, and I couldn't stop myself from yelling that you were assholes. You didn't even hear me."

He chuckles. "Fuck, we were holy terrors."

"You can say that again." I shake my head. "Not that I was much better."

"None of us were." He sets a hand on my shoulder.

I raise an eyebrow. "Ingrid?"

"Okay, Ingrid was pretty good." He smiles. "*Is* pretty good."

I nod, and silence falls between us. In just two weeks, I'm going to be leaving all of this behind. The current plan is that Estrella, her family, and I leave for Sundrop Gem the day after the wedding. Her people have been without their queen for too long. No more turning a corner and being confronted with the door Father used to slam in my face or the corners I hid from Kieran in.

No more finding the place I taught Finn how to spar, though, either. Or where Baz and I finally got our ale-pulley to work, for all of about five minutes before Father shut us down. I might be leaving all my worst memories behind, but I'm leaving the best ones too.

"Still with me?" Kieran asks.

I blink. "Yeah, of course. You didn't mention Snowcrest. I know Floyd got back a couple days ago, but I'm avoiding him like the fucking plague until this is done. My hold on my temper isn't reliable enough yet."

"Alpha King Andri said he would attend with his family and a small retinue." Kieran peers at me. "But that's not what you were thinking about. Getting cold feet already?"

"No fucking way," I spit. The only good thing about any of this is how it's forcing Estrella and I together. Sure, there's a bunch of political crap to wade through, but at the end of it all, I get to spend my life with her. If we could have the wedding without any of the scheming, I'd do that in a heartbeat.

"What, then?" He leans back against the wall and crosses his arms.

I know him well enough. He thinks I'm hiding something from him.

"Nothing about the case," I say quickly.

His posture relaxes slightly.

"It's just…." I sigh. "A lot's changing. Fast. And in ways I never really expected it to–for me."

My mind drifts immediately to Father's empty grave. When the Haze descended, I was so sure I didn't—couldn't–meet anyone because that image loomed too large in my mind. Now, I not only have to leave the empty grave behind but the battlefield where I lost him. I don't want to be the man he wanted me to be, but I don't quite know how not to be his son yet.

"You really never expected this?" Kieran asks.

I raise an eyebrow.

"Becoming Alpha," he says simply.

He doesn't need to spell out the rest. He's asking if I didn't think I was going to kill him for the throne someday. A refusal springs to my lips. It's dark in this passageway. He'd barely be able to read my face, probably never know I was lying.

But that's taking the easy way. Fuck.

"I guess I did expect that." I wrap my hands around my belt and stare at the floor.

"I expected it too."

I look up at my brother and find him smiling. "You're a freak."

"Guilty as charged." He lifts his hands. "I was already auditioning secret food tasters. I figured you'd go poison, when you did. It's what Father would've done."

The "when" stings until I register the past tense. "Not anymore?"

"Should I still be?" He meets my gaze and holds it.

All of us inherited Father's ice-blue eyes. Mother's are blue, certainly, but much truer. Father and my siblings are the only people I've ever met with this exact color. Even when Kieran's trying to reach out to me, to give me a chance to be someone new, I still see coldness in his eyes. Is that what Estrella sees when she looks at me? Can I ever really outrun it? Or is the ice Father raised us with something I'll have to fight for the rest of my life?

Estrella's soft, gray gaze appears in my mind's eye. If it's a permanent fight, it's worth it. For her. Just like leaving behind my home.

"Nah." I try to sound casual. "Raven ripped up all of Mother's best plants."

Kieran laughs, and the tension between us shatters. Just like he didn't have to say he thought I was going to kill him, I don't have to say that I can't imagine doing that anymore. He just claps me on the shoulder, and all is understood.

"I'm not worried about allying with Sundrop Gem anymore either," he says. "Now, can we rejoin the land of the living, or are we gonna die in here?"

"It's a tapestry, dickhead. Just pull." I grab the edge.

'I found it!' Raven shouts through the mind-link. *'Coming down from the dovecote. Where are you?'*

Kieran sighs. "Seems like we'll have to give dying in here a shot. It's much closer than my office."

I laugh as he mind-links directions to Raven. A few minutes later, the tapestry pulls back tentatively. She stands in the opening, her hair tumbling out of a messy bun and her cheeks flushed.

"Get inside!" I hiss.

She crowds in with Kieran and I. "Sort of cramped, isn't it?"

"We were already talking." I shake my head, my heart hammering. "It doesn't matter. You found it? The feather?"

She nods so enthusiastically a few more hairs come loose. "It comes from a collared tern."

"O…kay?" I exchange a confused look with Kieran.

Raven huffs a sigh. "Terns are mountain birds, almost never seen outside of Snowcrest Canyon or what used to be Starfall Mountain."

My stomach sinks. "So it doesn't tell us anything."

"Collared terns are more specific." She grins. "They only like a couple of peaks, especially this time of year. And all those mountains are within walking distance of the Winters' manor."

Something warm expands slowly in my chest. "Tell me Winters isn't just a common name in Snowcrest."

"Not common enough!" She shoves some hair out of her face. "We're talking about Floyd's ancestral home."

I laugh, loud and long. We've got him. We've fucking got him!

Now, I just need to make sure no one else in Snowcrest was involved.

3 9

THE EVE OF THE FUTURE

ESTRELLA

"AT LAST." I SMILE ACROSS THE TABLE AT ANWEN. "WE'RE ALONE."

He kisses the back of my hand. "Tonight, but probably not again until this is over. The other kingdoms' delegations arrive tomorrow."

"And a week still separates us from the wedding." I groan in a very un-queenlike way and slump slightly over my steaming bowl of stew. "Your customs are barbaric. Why can you not just sleep in my room?"

He laughs. "And scandalize all the fine court ladies showing up to celebrate us? I barely recognize you."

"We don't bother with this false modesty in Sundrop Gem," I grumble. "A mated couple is understood to be just that: a couple. Wedded or not."

"Soon." His smile sparkles in the low light. "But we have tonight, and I got you a little surprise. Two, actually."

I glance around. The small dining room attached to my chambers looks the same as always. "What is it?"

"First, take a bite." He gestures at the stew.

I gather every ounce of will I have and spoon up a bite. The preparations have kept me busy enough that I can almost forget how little I like the bland food in Dun's Crossing, but their so-called stews are the worst of all. Mush on mush, without an ounce of spice to brighten it. When this is over, I think I'll miss the stews the least.

The bite crosses my palate, and it's… fine. The pale green stalks they call celery actually retain a bit of their uncooked crunch, the meat has a pleasant gaminess, and there's a tiny spark on the back of my tongue, the barest suggestion of spice.

Anwen watches me intently, clearly waiting for a reaction.

"Did you do this?" I ask rather than telling him my exact feelings.

"Yes, I did." He leans back, looking proud. "I memorized everything you said on our walk the other day and took it right to the chef."

I splutter a laugh. "And how did the chef feel about that?"

"I've definitely seen Magritte happier." He rubs the back of his neck. "But I want you to be able to eat when we visit."

The easy way he plans our future warms a spot in my chest Magritte's paltry imitation of spice can't reach.

"Did he pull it off, though?" Anwen asks.

"Why don't you try it and see?" I gesture to his bowl with a smile. The surprise is sweet, but I make a mental note to seal the alliance between our two kingdoms with a basket of the spices Nasir grinds and mixes himself for our food. Perhaps then, Magritte will have more success.

Anwen takes a bite with a huge smile, then shoots back from the table, spluttering. His nose runs, and his eyes tear. My heart leaps into my throat. It's another assassination attempt. He's being poisoned! I start to reach for Tess, Cristofer, anyone through the mind-link.

A faint burn takes up residence in the back of my throat, like a bit of pepper gone down the wrong way. I blink. I am no expert in poisons, but I'm reasonably certain they tend to hurt a good deal more than that.

Anwen thumps his chest. "Goddess above, Magritte took my intervention like shit. Seems like he really overdid my bowl as some kind of revenge."

"That is awful." I steal a bite from Anwen's, half out of curiosity and half to still the terrified pounding of my heart. It is exactly as spicy as my own.

He wipes a tear. "You see?"

I cannot help it. I burst into laughter so wild I have to clutch my sides and cover my mouth.

"What?" he asks, almost wounded in his confusion.

I only laugh harder. That first morning, in the tent, Anwen seemed like a bulwark of ice, an impossible-to-reach, heartless monster. Goddess, I remember the way he bore up under the bite pain that nearly knocked me to my knees. But a bit of black pepper and some laughter, and there's no sign of the cocksure prince I hated so much. Tears run down my cheeks from sheer, overwhelmed amusement.

"Well, maybe I won't give you your second surprise," he says sulkily.

"No, no." I shake my head. "Give me a moment, I just… oh, the stew is barely spiced, much less spicy."

He blinks then chuckles. "I guess I'll have to build up my tolerance. I can't exactly do that at a state dinner."

That sets me off again, picturing him spewing the barely seasoned rice we make for children in Rhys Ibarra's surprised face. Long minutes and several sips of rich wine pass before I can breathe normally again.

"Apologies, truly." I pat Anwen's hand. "I do not mean to insult you."

He smiles at me indulgently. "It's just good to see you laugh."

I wipe the last of the tears from my eyes. "It is good to laugh. Father would have wanted me to."

"Speaking of"—Anwen takes another very small bite and immediately chases it with bread—"I have some news."

"Oh?" I should've known he would take my laughter as a challenge. He only grimaced this time.

"I told you about the feather."

"The tern, yes?" I stomach another bite just as bravely. It really is still mediocre. "What about it?"

"It's native to the region around Floyd's manor, and the rogue,

Birsha, said his employer supplied the arrow. I figure that's as close to damning as we're going to get." He sops up some of the liquid with his bread and eats it without grimacing at all. "But Floyd isn't the only Snowcrest noble with holdings in that region. I don't want to get cocky and count the rest of them out."

Exhaustion drags on my limbs. So many weeks of running around like chickens with our heads cut off, stealing moments together when we can, and we spend nearly every one of them discussing the investigation. I want to discuss it—I want to know what is happening, how close we are to catching Father's true killer—and I love that Anwen is as dedicated to the task as I am. But all the lightness and laughter disappears from the room as soon as the conversation begins.

"I was not intending to," I say. "I simply do not know all these court politics as well as you. Is there anything we can do beyond keeping our guard up?"

"I've been thinking about that." He sits back in his chair. "Kieran's making sure no one's allowed on the ballroom balcony this time around, just in case."

I nod.

"But on the ground, I was thinking about potentially holding an archery tournament in a few two days. Just a little sporting competition between the kingdoms." His eyes glow. "If we provide the targets, then we can collect the arrows and—"

Abruptly, it is all too much. Castor would adore an archery tournament, but he won't participate here, and he'd be even more against it if he learned it was Anwen's idea. And that cannot even matter because the tournament, like the rest of our wedding planning, is about the moment my father's blood was spilled.

"Stop," I say.

Anwen snaps his mouth shut.

I don't want to be the newly crowned Luna Queen Estrella, bridge between two kingdoms. I want to be a woman with the man I love. There was a whisper of that feeling in the air when I was laughing, but the last time I truly felt it was in the dunes outside of the capital.

"If our wedding wasn't part of a scheme"—I trace my fingers over the back of his hand on the table—"what would it be like?"

"Oh." He pauses for a minute, and I can almost see the thoughts churning through his mind as he changes direction. "Um, I don't know. What would you want?"

"I asked you." I study his face, the small wrinkle between his eyebrows. He's startled, confused.

"I've never really thought about it." He shakes his head. "As in, with anyone. Planning a wedding… well, that's the sort of thing women do."

I smile dangerously. "And running a kingdom is the sort of thing men do?"

"Now you're putting words in my mouth." He grins back at me.

"Put your own in, then. I asked you a question." I cross my arms and stare him down.

"Shit, okay." He runs a hand through his hair. "I'd invite everybody to arrive a lot closer to the actual event, not a week early. Then, you know, ceremony, reception, wedding night. The usual."

"That's trite, and I know you're more clever than that." I trace the band of his tattoo. "Think about it. This is the moment that tells the Moon Goddess Herself we'll spend the rest of our lives together. All you really want is a bit more unstructured time?"

He blows out a long breath. "No laughing this time, okay?"

"By the light of the Moon Goddess," I say with a small smile.

"Honestly, I wouldn't just have them arrive closer to the day. I… wouldn't have them arrive." He shrugs. "If we could really do whatever we wanted, I wouldn't have anyone there but us and a holy woman. That's all it's about, right? We've already announced what we need to the world; the rest is personal." He glances at me and away again, almost shy. "I'd take the holy woman out somewhere. Maybe that oasis back in Sundrop. And I'd speak our vows where only the Goddess could see us."

My chest aches, and for a moment, I think it's his pain. But it's well and truly mine. Since I was old enough to understand, I knew I would have a huge wedding someday. In Sundrop, it's a seven-day ceremony for royalty, and each day has its own outfit or three. A parade of drinking and dancing and politicking. Always politicking. I've never considered anything else. But now that Anwen's said this, my chest aches with how badly I want it. One private moment in our public lives, between us and the Goddess alone.

"Fuck, I'm sorry." Anwen swipes a thumb over my cheek, and something wet smears. A tear. "Did I say something wrong? I want the big party. I love the big party."

I grab his wrist to keep him there, against my skin, and shake my head. "You didn't say anything wrong at all. That sounds wonderful."

"Okay." He frowns, clearly trying to understand why I'm crying.

That ache in my chest cracks in two like an egg, and from it, something warm and fragile hatches. I have always loved people who work for the things they have. I may have inherited my title, but any skill I have, at leadership or otherwise, I've trained to develop. It's a point of pride. And Anwen is always working harder than anyone I've met before. He works to understand me. To make me happy. To be a man he was never raised to be.

"I love you," I murmur wonderingly.

Anwen kisses me, the faint heat of the stew lingering on his lips. "I was waiting for you to catch up."

4 0

THE WELCOME BALL

Anwen

I rap on Estrella's door, the hallway behind me humming with activity. All the delegations are here—including Snowcrest—and the servants race around like ants in a colony, completing final preparations before the welcome ball just getting underway downstairs.

She opens the door.

"Fuck," I mutter.

"I am going to take that as a compliment." She puts out her arm for me to take.

"You should." I shake my head to clear it. She's beyond stunning. Candace told me tonight's dress was her concession to Bright's near conniption over the rest of the wedding clothes, but Bright seems to have lost anyway. Another wrapped dress drapes over Estrella. The base fabric is a dove gray that almost perfectly matches her eyes. Over it, though, is a rainbow riot of decoration. Jingling beads, dancing embroidery, everything I could imagine to liven up the Dun's Crossing gray I never thought was boring until I met her. Tiny jewels

237

in a thousand colors glimmer in her hair. Tonight, she wears it loose in curls that flow over her shoulder.

And, okay, her breasts look spectacular. These wrapped dresses really cup her every curve, but this one is cut a little lower than usual, revealing sandy swells of skin. It's gonna be a fight to keep my attention on the ball with her next to me like this.

She shakes her head. "I could arrive in a nightdress, and you would still stare."

"Most of your nightdresses are sheer." I grin.

She elbows me, and we begin walking down the hall together. It feels like we're dancing already, or like someone replaced the stone floors with clouds. I'm escorting my mate, my soon-to-be-wife, to a ball celebrating us. No standing across the room pretending to flirt with strangers all night. Just her mouthwatering smell and puzzle-piece curves. It's better than my birthday.

"Perhaps I should've dressed down." Her smirk belies how much she likes the attention.

I pinch her ass. "Just try it and see."

She squeals and swats my hand. "Anwen! There are people everywhere."

"They're servants, and they all know we're headed to a party celebrating our wedding." I push her against the wall, cage her in place with my arms, and kiss her soundly.

For all her protestations, she arches up into me and bites my lip. I hiss softly and pull back.

"I believe part of the plan includes me talking all night." I touch my lip and check my finger for blood.

"You fuss too much. You're fine." She smiles as she tucks her arm back through mine. "And I don't suppose you are unfamiliar with marking one's territory."

Goddess above. If weeks of planning didn't rely on us showing up downstairs, I'd drag her back to her room and fuck her right now.

I glance at a clock on one wall. Maybe we could sneak back and just—

"We are already running late to our own party." Estrella marches inexorably forward. "There is no time, and you shouldn't have started something you couldn't survive leaving unfinished."

"I can't believe this is going to be my life forever." I force my tone to be sullen, but I still feel like I'm walking on air. This, this woman, is my life forever!

She laughs. "Assuming we survive this week. To that end, what do you know about Alpha King Andri? Does he have a queen?"

"I met him once when I was, fuck, eight? Diplomatic visits were for the crown prince." Bitterness leaks into my voice, and Estrella squeezes my arm. I shake it off as quickly as I can. "Luna Queen Lara Kar died a little over a decade ago, which was the one time I managed to meet him."

"Her funeral?" Estrella frowns sympathetically.

I nod. "They were mated, so he never remarried. Only had one son, Hollis, a little younger than us. I don't remember much about the king other than he's a fucking wall of a man, topped with the first red hair I'd ever seen. I think I might've asked if he was on fire."

She giggles, a sound I can't wait to hear every day. "I'm certain that made a good impression–at his wife's funeral."

"Hey, I think he smiled," I say. "Or ordered me to stay quiet for the rest of the service."

She giggles again. My heart's going to beat out of my chest and move into hers if she keeps doing that.

"He was obviously the kind of man willing to ally with my father," I say quietly. "But Snowcrest has never been an expansionist kingdom, at least as far as I've heard. There was a rumor going around for a while that Snowcrest basically showed its throat as soon as Father set foot on the border."

"So he may have allied himself out of survival, not any desire to be connected to King Gavin." She nods seriously. "Are they active in politics?"

"Very." I roll my eyes. "If there's one thing Snowcrest loves, it's embedding an envoy in foreign courts. Floyd's not the only one—I wouldn't be surprised if you left tonight with an offer of the same in Sundrop."

We round the final corner and see a stream of well-dressed nobles flowing into the ballroom, pausing only briefly for the page to announce them.

I bend down and whisper in Estrella's ear, "Last chance. We could always run now, elope, live the rest of our lives on the run."

She sucks her lower lip into her mouth like she's seriously considering it, then shakes her head. "Father deserves better. But perhaps talk to me when all of this is done."

I laugh as we stride into the crowd. It parts for us like tall grass, and we reach the page within seconds.

The page blows a long, loud note on his horn. "Crown Prince Anwen Solberg and Luna Queen Estrella Sollabella, the guests of honor!"

Arm-in-arm, we descend the wide steps together. Damn near everyone in the ballroom turns to look at us. Estrella was being dramatic when she said we were late. The ball started maybe ten minutes ago, but most kingdoms have stricter rules about tardiness than Dun's Crossing, so the room is packed. It feels like the eyes of the whole world are on me. An old instinct I thought was dead—the same awkward impulse of a kid who thinks they're invisible suddenly discovering they're wrong that made me ask if King Andri was on fire —rises up in me. I want to squirm, to duck my head, to do anything but watch them watch me.

Estrella straightens even further as I start to shrink into myself, and it's like a bucket of ice water on my head. I don't need to watch them. I can just watch her. I know every inch of this castle like the back of my hand. Her skin glimmers in the firelight like she's covered in fairy dust, but there's a smudge missing where I cupped her face in the hallway. I marked my territory, in my own way. I smile.

Suddenly, we're on the floor, just two amongst the crowd. The tension in my shoulders releases. This, I know. I've been attending balls since I could walk. I guide Estrella quickly away from the bottom of the stairs so the next pair doesn't run into us. We nearly careen into Nathalie and Evangeline, the mother-daughter pair from Redwood Nimbus and the peace ball.

"Prince Anwen! We were hoping to see you again." Nathalie curtsies.

Her mother follows suit. "We were just talking about it, weren't we?"

"How thrilling to see you both." I bow. "This is my mate, Luna Queen Estrella."

Estrella curtsies. "Lovely to make your acquaintance. How did you meet Prince Anwen?"

Nathalie titters behind her hand. "Oh, the last ball, Your Majesty. I'm so sorry I didn't get to meet you then as well."

"You should be. She was ravishing that night." I wrap an arm around Estrella's waist and pull her close then murmur in her ear, "Keep the talk light until people have time to get drunk. Questions that require specific details are tactless."

She nods.

"You lovebirds are sweet," Evangeline coos.

We trade pleasantries back and forth for a few more moments, and Estrella seems to be finding her feet. I promise to speak to Evangeline and Nathalie again later then drift away. There's much bigger game to hunt tonight than a no-name pack like Redwood Nimbus.

"Is there anything else I should know?" Estrella asks tightly.

I hum. "Questions like that are best left for after the second drink is done, but before the third, while they can still remember the details. Ask about anything you know about their kingdom. It makes people feel special. Never say goodbye, always promise to talk later, even if you're not going to." I glance around the flow of people. "If you want to talk to someone privately, ask them to dance but know that's going to create some gossip."

"That is not—" She pauses, shakes her head. "Thank you, but I would not like to be corrected while we are in the middle of a conversation."

I cross my heart dramatically. "There's a reason I didn't offer these tips beforehand. I know these big events aren't exactly your forte, but I trust you. Even if you don't nail all the courtly manners, people are going to love you."

She takes a deep breath. "I will endeavor to 'nail' them anyway."

I kiss her on the cheek, and we join another group of people talking.

The rhythm of the night takes over. We drink; we dance; we chat. Estrella stumbles a few more times, but she corrects herself quicker every time, helped by the fact that whenever we leave a slightly awkward conversation, she demands to know what she did wrong. I'm not stupid enough not to realize that, as much as the party's relaxing me, it's tensing her up, but I'm not sure what to do. Balls aren't difficult, just complicated, and I know she's smart enough to get the hang of it. She just needs a little more practice.

While deep in conversation with a couple of Dun's Crossing noblewomen who keep insisting they have to dance with me at "my last ball as a bachelor," no matter how many times I refuse, I look down, and realize Estrella's no longer at my side. Did she leave without saying anything? Is she all right? I instinctively start to reach out through the mind-link, but the Goddess-damned wedding is still a week away.

"Prince Anwen?" Gia puts her hand on my arm. "You seem distracted."

"I'm fine," I reply absently then inhale as deep as I can, searching the room for Estrella's scent. If she is hurt, I'd feel it. I just need to know she's still here.

There. If she weren't my mate, I'd never be able to pick her out in the crowd, but I can't mistake her scent for anything. She's over by one of the large windows that looks out over the main courtyard. Probably just needed air, and I didn't hear her say it. Completely understandable.

I smile. Let her relax. I'll manage the room for the both of us.

41

THE PERFECT PRINCE

I stare across the ballroom at Anwen, surrounded by gorgeous women. A brunette throws her head back in a laugh and starts to put her hand on his arm, then pulls back. If I wanted to be kind—if I hadn't already spent three hours stumbling through conversations like some kind of backcountry rube—I would assume he didn't see the hand in time to pull away. But I know how perceptive he is. It's one of the things I've grown to love about him. And it means that any plausible deniability is impossible for me to extend. I sip my drink.

"Luna Estrella." A man about my age with jet-black hair and green eyes bows. The woman next to him, of similar age but with pale blonde hair, curtsies.

I scramble through my memories to place their faces. What gives the man away is the line of polished silver badges on his chest. He is Hollis Kar, crown prince of Snowcrest Canyon and famed archer. Apparently, the badges represent his success in Snowcrest's very strange custom of occasionally hunting in human form. The woman takes a moment longer, but eventually, I recognize Lady Sarachi, one of the most prominent members of Whaleberry Harbor's court.

"Prince Hollis, Lady Sarachi." I curtsy to both of them. "Are you enjoying the party so far?"

They exchange a quick, furtive look. Damn it! Anwen said I wasn't supposed to ask if they enjoyed the party so far because it's bad luck, implying the party might soon go wrong.

"I am." Hollis sipped his own chalice. "You make quite a splash, Your Majesty. I was surprised to receive the news."

A splash is... good? I lift my chin and try to seem like panic and rage aren't braiding in my veins. Floyd is at the heart of my anger, but it's difficult to assume honesty of this snide prince.

"Thank you," I reply. "But I cannot imagine why you are surprised. There's nothing more natural than those joined by the Goddess marrying in front of the world."

Lady Sarachi titters. "Of course, you're right. It's just that, well, Sundrop Gem isn't exactly the sort of place people think of as being part of the world."

Somehow, her saying that to my face is more socially appropriate than me asking about their enjoyment.

I'll be back in Sundrop Gem soon.

"I would call those people short-sighted," I say. "Sundrop Gem may not have engaged in your politics, but that does not mean we've ceased to exist."

"Certainly not." Prince Hollis raises his glass to me. "And we are truly honored to make your acquaintance because of it."

I raise mine in turn—refusing a toast is the height of insult, apparently, even when you'd rather slosh the drink in their faces—and he grins at me.

"We will be seeing you." He bows again, and the two of them drift off into the crowd.

Irritation bubbling in my veins, I stride to the wall and position myself there firmly. I am a queen, and no one has failed to treat me as such, but Goddess above, I haven't tripped over my tongue this much since my very first ball. There are just so many inane little rules, the indulgences of a network of kingdoms who care more about state-craft than leadership. It is simply exhausting to keep up with.

Anwen's scent catches my nose, and I twist to find him on the dance floor. My bite burns. The woman in his arms is stunning. I'm not sullen enough to lie about that. Her red hair flies out behind her as they spin to the music, a flame that matches the brightness of her laughter. And Anwen is laughing with her!

I force myself to look away. I am being childish. He is my mate; he swore himself to me, and I don't think he could have lied the night he came to me in Sundrop Gem. Anwen simply looks so… at home here. The endless rules come as easy to him as breathing. And the small army of women following him around makes it difficult to forget the implication of that room he took me to after our last ball. I would be a fool to assume Anwen had tasted none other than me.

"He looks good tonight," a woman I've seen around the castle says to her friend as they pass me.

"Who?" the friend replies.

"King Anwen—Prince, I guess." She giggles. "For now."

The two of them move off, but the implications ring in my ears. King Anwen. That will be his title, when we wed and return to Sundrop. But if we had never met, had never mated, he would only ever be the prince. In a few months—I glance at Queen Raven, swaying slightly in King Kieran's arms, her belly already slightly distended with child—he wouldn't even be crown prince any longer.

Only after Father was murdered did Anwen soften in his treatment of me. Only when marrying me would grant him the one title he was destined not to have.

My stomach flips. My bite burns. I cannot think like this. I've decided to trust him. I need some air—

I turn and nearly run into Nessa, resplendent in a bright-red gown.

"Whoa!" She catches my shoulders. "Are you okay?"

I shake my head, unwilling to trust my voice.

"Shit." She frowns. "Is it the Solbergs? I tried to warn you—"

"I do not wish to talk about it," I say thickly.

She nods, smooths the sleeves of my dress. "Gotcha. Um... I never asked you about the boat ride back to Sundrop."

Her awkward attempt scares a small smile out of me. "Less nauseating, thankfully."

"Goddess, I hear you on that. Father always tries to convince me to take a river boat home, but no way." She grins. "I'd turn greener than Queen Raven's dress."

I chuckle. "Father was the only one in our family who didn't have at least a little of that curse. But I had the rare pleasure of growing up in a desert. He liked the occasional ride, but he couldn't get one without entering the Lonely Sea."

"Lucky." Nessa clucks her tongue. "I'm surprised to see you without Princess Candace. She always seems to be around these days."

I nod. "The princess has been very kind to me as we drift ever closer to becoming family."

"Lucky for that, too." Nessa can't keep the bitterness out of her voice.

My chest aches for her. As much as I might worry about my perfect prince dominating the dance floor, she knows what King Kieran thinks of her. His heart belongs to another so truly I could see it at that first breakfast.

"The next Haze." I rub her arm. "I am sure of it."

She offers me a tired smile. "Definitely."

A trio of women march up to us, all Dun's-Crossing pale.

"Nessa!" the one in the front trills. "I thought you were gone with your father."

"My father returned days ago, Joli," Nessa replies. "And I never left."

"Right." The woman, Joli, taps her lower lip as if in thought. "I just basically haven't seen you anywhere since King Kieran and Queen Raven took over."

The women behind her giggle. My instincts tingle. Something is happening here that I lack the context to understand.

"I've been busy." Nessa curtsies. "With Dun's Crossing opening its borders, an envoy has a lot more to do."

"And so does his daughter?" Joli watches Nessa but doesn't even approach curtsying. "Here I thought you were banned from court life for, what was it?" She turns to the women behind her. "Girls, help me out."

"Queen Raven said she could either shut the fuck"—the second blonde lingers over the curse word—"up about the Solbergs and Queen Raven or leave the castle, Joli."

"That's right." Joli snaps her fingers. "And you don't exactly have much else to say."

Nessa's jaw tenses infinitesimally. "I don't have much else to say to you three. Sorry if you thought that meant I disappeared. As you can see, I've made better friends."

All three women look at me then freeze for a second before dropping into some of the lowest curtsies I've ever seen. Joli babbles apologies. Nessa touches my elbow, a brief apology, and walks out of the ballroom altogether.

My heart goes with her. These women are monsters—and, if I had to guess, the old friends Floyd mentioned when I spoke to him outside Father's frozen chamber.

"Stand," I say imperiously.

They obey in unison. I consider several responses, different ways to humiliate them. In the end, simplest seems best. I turn on my heel and leave after Nessa without another word. Let them tell that story and seem like the heroes.

Luckily, Nessa is not hard to follow. I trail her red dress through the crowd and to a small door, away from the general hum of the party. With a deep breath, I knock.

"Occupied," she calls tearfully.

"It's me," I reply.

There's a heartbeat of silence. Then, Nessa opens the door. Her pale skin is blotchy, and a few tears line her cheeks in the harsh light of the powder room she's hiding within. She grabs my wrist and tugs me inside before shutting the door.

"Old friends." She dabs her face with a towel. "If you can believe it."

"I can." I pry the towel from her hands, wet it with cool water from a pitcher in the corner, and start dabbing myself. "I made it very clear what sort of treatment they will earn from Sundrop Gem if they treat people that way."

Nessa laughs wetly. "Maybe I should've stuck around for that."

"Perhaps." I smooth some of her hair back into place. "Personally, I believe they already humiliated themselves."

"Good luck convincing them." She shook her head.

"I don't much care to." I smile at her. "I care to convince you."

Nessa stares at me for a long moment, searching my face. Thoughts churn behind her eyes, but I cannot guess what they are.

"Your father was killed," she says, low and urgent. "Why are you helping *me*?"

I start to tell her why Father would've wanted me to, but then the piece that fills the gap in her statement snaps into place. She would only ask that question, only about her, only like that if she suspected some of what we suspect. If some part of her knows of her father's involvement in the death of mine. My stomach drops. But there's no fear in her gaze, just confusion. The last worry that she may be involved melts from my chest.

"You have been through enough," I say, as she did to me in her room so long ago.

Nessa grins.

4 2

ALREADY IN BED

ANWEN

ESTRELLA NEVER COMES BACK TO MY SIDE. AT FIRST, I'M WORRIED—DID something happen? Has Floyd moved from murder to kidnapping? But I would feel her pain, and I know she wasn't having a good time. Plus, I'm used to running these events on my own. It's easier to float through unattached, saying whatever each person needs to hear without worrying about another person keeping up. And Baz needs someone to cart his sorry ass out before he throws up in the punch bowl.

When I'm done depositing him in his room, I hesitate in the hallway. If I turn right, I can head straight for my room and pass out before the meeting about the archery tournament I have tomorrow morning. King Andri's going to be there, so I have to be on top of it. But if I turn left, the hall will take me to Estrella's room…

The ball went damn well. We're making progress, and King Andri seemed about as pleasant as he ever is. I deserve a reward. And to make sure Estrella really is just tired. I take off to the left.

A little walking, and I knock on her door. No response. But we

249

agreed, since customs in Solberg Castle dictate we can't actually share a bed until we're married, that I could just walk in whenever I wanted to see her. She has nothing to hide from me anymore. So I pull out the key, unlock it, and stride in.

Her front room holds nothing more than the usual furniture and a fireplace burning low to keep just warm enough overnight. She's already asleep? Her scent is thick enough in here that I'm not worried she's anywhere else, but the ball is still ongoing downstairs. I just wanted to leave before people started pairing off. How is she already asleep?

I creep into her bedroom. Here, too, the lights are low, the curtains drawn. But her canopy isn't pulled tight around her mattress, so I can see her, wearing only a nightgown with her hair loose around her shoulders, staring down at a book in her hands.

"I lost you out there," I say.

"You seemed to have it well in hand," she replies cryptically.

"You didn't want to say good night?"

She turns a page in her book. "Good night, Anwen."

Fuck, what I wouldn't give for a mind-link right now!

I perch on the edge of her bed. "It seems like something is wrong."

"Really?" she replies acidly.

"Really." My temper bubbles under the surface of my skin. Why the hell am I putting in all this effort if she's just going to freeze me out?

"I'm surprised you noticed, through your crowd of admirers," she says.

Clarity dawns. "Are you jealous?"

"No."

I slide along the bed toward her, trying to catch her eye. "You are. You didn't like seeing me dance with other women. If you'd said something—"

"Saying things was working so terribly well for me, after all." Hot color rises on her cheeks.

"What?"

She daggers me with her glare. "Prince Hollis thinks me an idiot."

"I'll set him straight." I crack my knuckles. Hollis has always been cocky for my taste.

She grabs my hands as I do, utterly unromantic. "I do not want you to fight my battles for me."

Something in my chest aches. Maybe it's my newly discovered protective instinct. "Right."

"I mean—" She shakes her head. "I do not know what I mean. You should go. I'm in a foul mood."

"I don't think so. We're doing this the hard way." I cross my arms. "You have to talk to me."

"I do not have to do anything." She tries to draw herself up, which only makes her nipples poke against the thin front of her nightgown.

My mouth waters. Between my cock and my frustration, my patience for doing things properly is quickly fading.

"Fine," I growl. "We'll do it the really hard way."

I lunge for her. She tries to scramble away, but as always, I'm faster. I grab her wrists, pin them to the wall overhead, and toss her book aside. Her chest rises and falls rapidly, and her pupils grow.

"Tell me why you're upset," I repeat.

She eyes me for a moment. "No."

A true growl tears from my lips, but I recognize the small sparkle of amusement in her gaze. She's toying with me.

I'll show her what it means to be toyed with.

I shred her nightgown down to her waist and don't even let her finish gasping before my mouth is on her. The skin of her breasts is warm and soft, obviously perfumed from a bath. How long has she been up here? Did I really forget about her for that long? She'd be right to be pissed, if so. But right now, I can barely think about anything beyond the taste of her, the kisses I'm brushing against her skin.

Estrella arches up into me. She rotates her wrists in my grasp, struggling to escape, but I hold fast. Clearly, she wants my touch just as much as I want hers. I circle one nipple with my tongue, scrape my teeth across it, pluck the other like harp string. Groans tumble from her lips. She'll tell me the truth eventually.

Abruptly, I pull back. "Why were you upset?"

"Were?" She barks a laugh, a real smile on her lips. "I still am. Release me!"

I believe she's still upset. But I also feel her grinding against my leg, desperate for any kind of friction. It's always stubbornness and pride with her. I grin hungrily.

"I will when you talk to me." I rip the covers off her and loosen my grasp on her wrists just enough to spin her around until her face is in the pillow and her ass in the air. The fire turns her nightgown sheer, the dark shadows of her legs clearly visible through the white fabric. Just as visible as the wet spot she left on it, right between her legs. I drag my tongue across it, making her moan, then destroy the rest of the dress.

"Nothing to hide anymore, right?" I grip her ass to watch the flesh jiggle.

She jerks back into my palm, begging for more. "Yes!"

"Then tell me." I press kisses along the line of her back and palm myself through my pants like I'm not already rock fucking hard.

"I—can't!" she groans. "It is ridiculous."

"Never to me." I sink my lips into her ass cheek and pull another moan from her lips.

"Liar," she hisses.

She always needs more. Luckily, I'm happy to provide. I shove my pants down to my knees, line up my cock with her weeping entrance, and shove inside. Estrella nearly screams with pleasure, but her body accepts me easily. I fuck her hard, bend over her back, and palm one of her swaying breasts. She is so perfect, so beautiful underneath me like this. Exactly how the Goddess wanted us to be. How fucking stupid to have waited this long.

Estrella clenches around me, a sure sign she's approaching orgasm. I gather all the willpower I've ever had and pull out.

She keens, high and pitiful. "What are you doing?"

"Incentivizing you." I grin even though she can't see me. "Tell me, and I'll fuck you."

She fights my hold on her wrists harder, which I didn't expect.

Stupid. Of course she'd choose to fight before giving in. She manages to slip a single hand out and shoves it between her legs, furiously chasing the orgasm I denied her.

By the Goddess, I almost let her. I've never seen anything sexier in my life than my mate, wet and panting, trying to finish herself. But that's the easy way, and I'm not supposed to be doing that anymore.

Tonight, I'm fucking loving her the hard way.

I rip her wrist away, one in each hand now, and flatten my whole body over hers so she can't reach anything else. Our harsh breathing rings in my ears, mingled, thwarted want. My cock rests against the curve of her ass.

"I made a fool of myself," she murmurs. "I had no idea how many rules there were and… and you abandoned me."

"Abandoned you?"

She rolls over beneath me so we lay chest to chest. "I said I needed air, then asked if you wanted any. You said no. You never came looking for me."

Memories filter back in proving every word she's saying. I wince. "I didn't realize that meant you wanted me to leave with you. I was talking to—"

"The tall, beautiful redhead?" She frowns. "Or was it one of the many brunettes?"

"I'm not going to lie about my past." I kiss the corner of her mouth. "I had a lot of women before you. But they're all that—the past."

She studies me for a long moment. "You are not marrying me to become Alpha?"

I laugh. "I don't know if I can handle the job."

"At the next ball, I will ask you for a walk around the garden when I want you to leave with me."

"I will teach you everything I know about the court." I drop kisses along her jaw. "And send out a public announcement that I'm a one-woman man."

She sucks a deep bruise into my neck. "Perhaps that announcement is unnecessary."

I shudder. "Deal."

Together, we line back up, and I slip into the warm heat of her again. Estrella seems determined to cover me in so many bruises no one will see my skin again, but the pace is slower, less frantic. I don't have to force anything anymore. We careen over the edge together, each other's names on our lips.

43

A CRACK IN THE DAM

"My hair wouldn't stay. It's too fine." Candace runs her fingers through her cornsilk tresses sadly.

"You've never had your hair braided by Tess," I say. "She is simply a genius for it. Allow her to try, and you'll be surprised."

Tess smiles shyly. "I am happy to make an attempt."

Candace grins. "I guess now's as good a time as any to try. It's not as though they can start this Sundrop bridal shower without the bride."

"Exactly." I push her onto the stool in front of the mirror.

Tess begins braiding. Ever since Candace insisted I stop using titles, Tess has been a little less intimidated by her, which has made everything much easier. I pad over to the array of jewelry I brought and stretch before sorting through the pieces. Anwen stayed for three more rounds last night, and sleep drags at me, but I cannot miss my own bridal celebration. Even if it's going to be mostly peopled with diplomats I've never met before and made a fool of myself in front of last night.

My gaze catches on a scroll Anwen sent over before I even woke this morning. It's a simple diagram of all the kingdoms which sent delegates and a brief rundown of specific customs relevant to each, the sort of reference I've been trying to make for myself all along but have utterly failed at. My chest aches sweetly when I look at it. If I am tired, to have created that, he must be exhausted. And he chose to do it all the same.

"What do you expect today?" Candace asks.

I sigh. "I have no idea. Floyd is an envoy. He could be working with any number of people."

Candace starts to shake her head, but Tess grabs her and holds her in place. I watch my best friend panic as she realizes what liberties she's taken, but the princess barely seems to notice.

"You would be right, but Floyd got sent here as soon as he was assigned the position. He's barely better traveled than I am." A bit of bitterness seeps into Candace's voice there. "No, if he has any partners, they're in Snowcrest."

"Not here?" Tess asks.

I bite my lip. Her, Cristofer, and Castor maintain a worry that, even if the Solbergs can be proven innocent, there are many other Dun's Crossing nobles who might've participated.

"To be honest? Before everything that went down with Kieran and Raven, I'd be worried, but not anymore." Candace sighs. "Floyd became a pariah with Nessa, as much as he could without irritating King Andri."

"Do you think that's fair?" I ask quietly.

"Yes." Her reply is fast and uncompromising.

"Why don't you like her?" I return to the table where Tess is braiding Candace's hair. "Nessa, that is."

She exhales a long sigh. "Nessa... reminds me of someone I don't like very much."

I meet Candace's gaze in the mirror. She's obviously holding something back.

"I thought we were family," I say. "Anwen and I have agreed to keep no secrets between us, and I'd love to have the same with you."

Candace's mouth twists wryly. "I barely recognize either of my older brothers these days."

"I think that's a good thing." Remembering the cold, cruel prince I woke up next to after the Haze isn't pleasant.

"It certainly is." She takes my hand. "I'm different too. And that's… that's the problem with Nessa. She reminds me of a me I don't like."

Before I can ask what she means by that, someone raps on the door. Tess looks up at me, her hands snarled in Candace's hair. I nod and go to open it.

Nessa stands outside, her eyes and cheeks puffy like she either slept less than I did or has been crying for hours. Her hair is a mess, and she's wearing the plainest dress I've ever seen her in.

"We have to talk," she says.

"Certainly." I let her in, my heart hammering. "Is this about Joli and the rest?"

She shakes her head and opens her mouth, then catches sight of Tess and Candace in the other room. "Are we—can we go somewhere private?"

"Tess is my dearest friend and confidant. Anything I know, she knows within the hour." Candace's words ring in my ears, but she was just so honest with me. This affects her family too. "And Candace is my sister in marriage by the end of the week. We are already somewhere private."

Nessa swallows painfully. Tess and Candace drift out of my bedroom, Tess still braiding as she goes.

"Okay." Nessa nods. "I guess I have to get used to doing things a little differently."

"Differently?" I sit on the couch in front of the fireplace.

Nessa starts pacing. "It's not about Joli. Shit, I wish my biggest problem right now was Joli."

Candace winces slightly at the curse but settles on the opposite couch so Tess can keep working.

"Tell me." My heart climbs into my throat. Something is severely wrong. I've never seen Nessa so agitated. "Whatever it is, I can help."

"I'm really counting on that." She laughs and lets out a sob. "Just let me get through everything before you talk, okay?"

I fold my hands in my lap and wait.

"Father arranged King Isai's assassination," she blurts.

My skin goes hot, then cold. My pulse roars in my ears. Anwen was right, and Father's killer is inside this castle right now. My wolf snarls, and my claws grow without my permission. But I swore to let Nessa finish, and in exchange for all she's done for me, I'll give her that at least.

"He was ranting and raving after Kieran took power. Said he humiliated our family, all of Snowcrest. Him and Raven. So he wanted to destroy Kieran's reign before it even really started." Nessa's pacing picks up speed, like she can outrun the very words she's saying. "And he needed my help. I was supposed to become your friend, show you what kind of people Kieran and Raven really were before they could trick you, and gather any information we needed."

My one friend in this Goddess-forsaken castle, and she was using me to murder my father. I have never felt so stupid.

"He hired this rogue he knew from home, had me forge a few documents in Kieran's hand because we grew up with the same tutor, and paid one of the castle soldiers to carry the message. It was supposed to be perfect." Tears filled Nessa eyes. "And I went along with it because, fuck, Estrella, I was mad. Father was worried about our reputation, but I'd just lost everything. *Everything*. I wanted revenge."

My voice creaks out of my throat. "Wanted? Past tense?"

She drops to her knees in front of me. "Last night, when you came after me, I realized how stupid the whole thing was. I was just feeding into Father's hate instead of seeing the good things I could have in my life. I was going to become sad and bitter, just like him. I'm so, so fucking sorry for everything I did. But that's why I'm here now—because I'm sorry, and I want to be different, and I know the next part of his plan."

Next part. There's more. I will never be allowed to rest, as long as I am in this castle.

Before I can pity myself or allow exhaustion to overtake me, a burning rage demands my attention. Floyd Winters murdered my father for no reason. Or at least, no reason to do with Father. He didn't care that Father was a benevolent leader, a beloved parent. That he made Mother laugh, that he took Castor on daily walks about the courtyards to ensure he never felt too left out, that he taught me everything I knew. He just killed him to sate a petty grievance against someone else.

Floyd Winters will die for this. If it means that Sundrop Gem never deals with Snowcrest Canyon, so be it. My claws jut into the backs of my hands, the pain an important reminder that I cannot kill Floyd now. I have to attend a ridiculous party. A party! But Nessa is here. Nessa, I can handle quickly.

"So?" Nessa says. "What do you think?"

I stand. "I think you are a traitor. A liar. And—"

Her lower lip trembles as I tower over her.

'Punishment is not justice, restoration is,' Tess says to me through the mind-link.

One of Father's favorite quotes. If I follow my heart, call to Cristofer, even kill Nessa myself where she kneels, he would be humiliated. Disappointed. I swallow hard.

"And the fact that you want to be better must always hold meaning," I say through gritted teeth.

Tess exhales sharply. So does Nessa.

"Tell me the rest of the plan." It is as close to restoration as I can come in this moment.

"He's hired another assassin," she babbles. "A local rogue who's already down in the city somewhere. The night before your wedding, he's going to kill your mother and brother in their beds and make it look like Dun's Crossing wants you alone. Dependent on them for support."

Hot fear spikes through me. I grip the back of the couch to keep my feet. Danger surrounds us on all sides. Different pieces of information buffet me, and my mind swirls uselessly.

Candace, her hair half-braided, puts her hand over mine on the couch. "I'm telling Anwen now."

A lighthouse in the storm. I am not alone. Together, we will save what's left of my family.

44

KEEPING COOL

Anwen

'Nessa just confirmed everything,' Candace says through the mind-link.

'*What?*' I reply, trying not to look like I'm talking to anyone.

"If we put the targets in the west field, the sun will be in everyone's eyes by noon." Taner, Kieran's Beta and representative at the meeting, taps the rough map of the castle laid out between dishes on the breakfast table before us. "No, I think the south field's the ticket."

"The south field is where your men usually train, is it not?" King Andri asks, his voice dripping with suspicion.

'*Floyd killed King Isai and framed Kieran because he was mad about the fake-mate thing,*' Candace says.

My gaze snaps to the shifter across the table from me, Floyd him-fucking-self. He's staring at the Goddess-damned map without a care in the world. My canines lengthen as my blood turns to fire in my veins. Murderer. Shitty, petty murderer.

'*Anyone else involved?*' I snarl.

"Just because it's the best spot," Taner replies. "We all agree the north field is too narrow."

Maybe I'll kill everyone in the fucking room, just to stop them from talking about fucking archery fields. The tournament was a stupid idea. Doing anything but throwing Floyd in the dungeon until Estrella and I can go down there and slaughter him together was a stupid fucking idea.

Just Nessa,' Candace replies. *'But she's coming clean, telling us everything, so we don't have to worry about her anymore.'*

Why the fuck is Nessa turning on her father?

"Too narrow for you," Prince Hollis scoffs. "We offered our short-range bows."

"Which no other kingdom is trained on." Taner glances at me. "Prince Anwen? This was your idea."

I fist my hands under the table and force myself to answer. "The east field. We'll have to move the short-term stables, but it's the best compromise."

Everyone turns back to the map.

I snap at Candace, *'You can't actually believe her.'*

'She's got all the details right.' Candace sighs. *'And she's got information on the next attack.'*

Now, I'm going to kill him. I have to. *'On Estrella?'*

'No.'

The tiniest shred of my murderous rage eases.

'He's got an assassin set up to take out Queen Suniva and Castor. I can give full details later.'

"We can offer men to move the stables," King Andri grumbles.

"You could put those in the north field," Floyd offers.

My entire body tenses. I remember the pain tearing Estrella apart the night King Isai was killed. He did that to her. Shitty little weasel of a wolf.

'Details now.'

I can almost hear her rolling her eyes. *'The assassin is named Dorian Meadows. He's staying at some inn, but Nessa doesn't know which. Aren't you meeting with King Andri?'*

'Fuck,' I reply.

Taner nods. "The north field is a good idea. We should get started today. The tournament is in two days, right?"

"Right." I am barely not snarling. Taner glances at me, but I ignore him. Repeating the news will only make me angrier, and Kieran's Beta is too busy organizing palace events to help with this even if I wanted him to.

King Andri nods and glances at his son. "What will you do?"

"Practice." Prince Hollis smirks. "Lady Eva has been quite clear I have to win this for her."

Eva, his promised. They're not even mated, but the Kar family and hers have been intertwined for so long that they have already agreed to a marriage. The bland political details keep my fury from boiling over. Barely.

"I hear that." Taner grins. "Ayla says I have to give her a favor and everything."

Prince Hollis offers him a flat smile. "Do you usually win these? I am quite famous for it at home."

"This is one of our first." Taner glances at me again. "It was Prince Anwen's idea, spirit of cooperation and all that."

"Then we are done?" King Andri starts to stand.

"In Dun's Crossing, Your Majesty, a breakfast meeting continues until the participants are done eating breakfast," Floyd says.

"I'm still going. Lady Eva and I have plans." Prince Hollis stands, bows, and marches out.

King Andri drops loudly back into his seat. I nearly lose control. Of course, Floyd wants to stretch this out. The son of a bitch knows what he did. I bet he's fucking gloating behind those ferrety little eyes of his.

Fuck it. If I can't kill him right now, I'm going to destroy him.

"We can talk of more pleasant things for the remainder," I say as grandly as I can. "Envoy, I haven't seen your daughter recently. How is she?"

Floyd flicks his gaze up to me. "You haven't?"

"Why not?" King Andri asks.

"She's been keeping to herself lately." I shrug like I have no idea what could be causing that. "I worry."

King Andri looks severely at Floyd, who swallows visibly.

"She's been under the weather," he says. "I will have her pay you a visit soon."

I incline my head. "Much appreciated."

'What are you doing?' Taner asks.

'Making conversation,' I reply.

He shakes his head and takes a bite of his food. The conversation turns to another topic. I bide my time, just like Father would have.

Floyd leans forward. "I was speaking to King Kieran the other day, and—"

"You were?" I ask coolly. "When?"

He looks at me. "When the king asked me to deliver the invitation to your wedding."

"Three weeks ago, then." I nod. "Sorry, I was just wondering because I meet with him almost every day, and I haven't seen you around in a bit either."

King Andri looks at me sharply. "Is your king disinterested in alliances?"

"Certainly not." I gesture at the map. "We invited people from every kingdom for a reason. The doors of Dun's Crossing are more open than ever. Perhaps Kieran has simply been meeting with so many people that time must be fought over in a way it wasn't before."

He narrows his eyes at Floyd. I don't need to say a single word directly to imply Floyd could only handle this job when it was easy. Let King Andri fill in the blanks himself.

"But tell me more about what he was saying." I fold my hands and smile at Floyd.

As we eat, I nod to the servants to fill Floyd's glass most often. Like nearly everyone from Snowcrest, he drinks a fairly weak wine with breakfast, but even weak wine affects the tongue after a while. His movements grow looser, more fluid. His sentences drag on. For the first time, doing something Father would've done doesn't tie my gut in knots.

"It truly is an honor for the Goddess' will to be so clear that we can predict it," Floyd says at one point. "And Lady Eva will make a beautiful bride."

"I'm sure she will." I smile. "Will you return to Snowcrest for the wedding? I know how you love them, and it doesn't seem that another will be happening here soon."

His jaw tightens. "I honor the will of King Andri, whatever it is."

"Why no further weddings?" King Andri asks.

I shrug. "We've had two Hazes in Dun's Crossing in the last few months. It merely seems unlikely another will come soon. A more formal bond between Snowcrest and Dun's Crossing would be great, but Nessa—" I bury my face in my own cup, which I started filling with juice a long while ago.

"Nessa what?" This, King Andri addresses to Floyd.

"She is not interested in marrying outside the mating bond," he says stiffly.

"Anymore," Taner mutters.

I could kiss him. Maybe I should be filling his cup too.

"Then the rumors are true." King Andri scowls. "I had hoped it was southern trash."

I shrug again, letting him think whatever's pissing him off like that. "Floyd does his best, Your Majesty. There's no new suitor that comes to court who doesn't receive a visit from him." I pause deliberately. "For Nessa's sake, of course."

The gears spin visibly behind King Andri's eyes, wondering what the hell else Floyd could be meeting with people about. Now, if I could just punch that smug bastard in the face, this breakfast won't have been a complete waste of time.

"And for Snowcrest's!" Floyd blusters. "There are so many kingdoms here, making connections only makes sense. I've got a foot in the door with Sundrop Gem already."

I grit my teeth and let his sentence hang, unanswered, silently questioning exactly what kind of foot he has if I, the mate of their queen, has no opinion on the matter.

King Andri harrumphs. "This breakfast is another southern indulgence. I have better ways to spend my time. Taner, I will send you the men for the stables." He looks at Floyd. "You, come with me."

Floyd stumbles slightly out of his chair and trails after the visibly furious Alpha out of the room.

"What the fuck has gotten into you?" Taner asks.

"I'll tell you later." I jump to my feet and race out a different door. Somewhere else in this castle, Estrella just received the news that her father's killer is here, and someone she considered a friend helped. I need to reach her. The only way we can solve this is together.

No matter how fucking good raking Floyd over the coals like that felt.

45

STAYING BEHIND

Candace jerks in her seat. I look up from where I'm pacing the room to see a grin spread across her face.

"He's on his way," she says.

Tess, who long ago finished braiding the princess's hair, squeezes my hand. I don't need to ask who's coming. My heart thuds like a racing horse. Soon, Anwen will be here.

Nessa squeaks softly and draws her knees up to her chest. I still cannot look at her without my stomach threatening to turn inside out, but she is no longer the target of my rage. Most of it, at least. Shuffling her new stories together with her old creates a picture of a very lonely woman, convinced by a bitter, withered man to do awful things. Someday, I will forgive her. But not today.

The door bursts open, and Anwen and Baz dart inside. I throw myself into Anwen's arms before I can think twice about the show of affection. He wraps his arms around my waist and drops soft kisses on my hair.

"It's him," I hiss. "You were right about everything."

"I didn't kill him," he murmurs. "For you. But King Andri isn't going to be giving him another envoy detail any time soon."

His scent, his warmth surrounds me, and the slight to Floyd is the last anchor I need to tie me back to the earth. For the first time since Nessa arrived at my door, I can think clearly. Slowly, I release my mate.

"Have you told anyone else?" Anwen asks.

I shake my head. "Mother and Cristofer would struggle not to tell Castor, and Castor would charge off without a second's thought or an ounce of support."

"And Kieran said this was your investigation," Candace adds.

He nods. For a moment, silence reigns as we all consider that eight people in the whole world know of this plan, and two of those are its architects. I clench my fist and release it slowly, trying to bank the flames of my anger.

"We're going after the assassin, right?" Tess says. "Dorian."

Everyone turns to her. She stares back at us, unflinching, rage like I've never seen in her before bubbling in every inch of her posture.

"What about Floyd?" Baz asks. "He's the real problem."

"Going after him causes problems with Snowcrest," Candace says slowly.

"Maybe not anymore." Anwen snorts.

"I don't fucking care!" Tess shouts.

I dart to her side and put a hand on her heaving shoulders. I've never seen her like this at all.

'He wants you alone,' she says. *'What do you think that means for my father and I?'* Her mental voice breaks. *'How much will he take from us?'*

The realization hits me like a bolt of lightning. Nessa only mentioned Mother and Castor, and in the storm of emotion, I couldn't see any further. Floyd could intend to leave me well and truly alone.

"We go after Dorian first." I turn to Nessa. "Do you have any idea where he's staying?"

She shakes her head. "But I know the inns Father likes. I can help."

Anwen cracks his knuckles. "Thank the Goddess. I was worried we were going to need another involved political plan."

Baz grins hungrily. Candace stands. Tess crosses her arms, highlighting the muscles she's developed over the years. We cannot possibly leave without Castor—he might truly kill me—but solidity and certainty flood through me. I thought I was alone before Anwen arrived. I was surrounded all along by people who would help me save my family and my people.

I step to Anwen's side. "Merely allow me to"—my stomach drops —"change."

Horror dawns on Tess's face in unison. Candace takes a moment longer but catches on.

"What?" Anwen demands. "What am I missing?"

I run my hands down the simple gown with its wide, split sleeves. "I—we are dressed for my bridal party."

His pain curls in my chest. "Which you can't miss because every kingdom is sending a delegate. Because we told them it was too important to miss."

"It would cause an international incident that could ripple for centuries." My wolf screams. I am so close to justice, to peace, and something as foolish as a party stands in my way! "If I weren't Luna —"

"But you are." Anwen grabs me by the shoulders and kisses my forehead. "A damn good Luna, too. Which means you know that leadership is about delegating."

I stare up into his blue eyes and wonder how I ever could've found them cold. They have all the warmth of an oasis at noon, the sun's rays trapped below the surface of the water.

"I love you." I drop a kiss on his lips. "And, Goddess forgive me, I trust you. But you must take Castor."

Anwen grimaces. "Will do. The rest of the women should stay here with you."

Tess makes a disdainful noise.

"I can't leave her unprotected," he tells her.

I twist and watch my best friend soften. A small part of me wants to deny that I need any protection, but I've grown all too tired of loneliness. I will take company, even if I'm certain I could fight off a single wolf on my own.

"Me too?" Nessa asks.

"Make a list," I reply before Anwen can say something to irritate her. "The inns your father prefers. Anything else, and he may notice something has changed."

She nods. Tess scurries off to get her a piece of paper, and Anwen dips me in a deep kiss. Baz hoots childishly.

"I love you too," Anwen says. "I'll keep your family safe."

"I know you will." I simply need to convince my nerves of the same.

* * *

A SCANT FIFTEEN MINUTES LATER, TESS, CANDACE, NESSA, AND I parade into the solarium set aside for my bridal shower. This, like everything else, is a combination of Dun's Crossing traditions and Sundrop ones. At home, this event would take place the day before the wedding and would mostly be comprised of my loved ones painting the temporary star maps on my body that Bright's embroidery mimics. Here, this should be occurring both the day we became engaged and the morning of the wedding itself. The first, apparently, includes a slew of presents and a few games, and the second, an evaluation of the dress itself. Today's event—which I was looking forward to this morning—combines the games, a bit of painting on the hands alone, to be washed off later, and the final dress fitting.

After Nessa's confession, I cannot imagine anything I'd less like to do.

Still, I walk in with my head held high. The solarium's glass walls nearly bulge with how many women are gathered within, and any concern I had about using the room as we near winter disappears.

"We were waiting for you!" Queen Raven sweeps up to us and wraps me in a hug, then leans in close to whisper, "Is everything all right?"

"Behaving normally is paramount," I reply. "Ask Candace across mind-link, if you must, but trust all will be explained soon."

"I trust you." She releases me with a wide smile that gives no indication of the conversation we just had. Queen Raven is a political operator to be contended with, I cannot forget.

"Come on, ladies. Let's get started!" She claps her hands.

I am spun into a whirlwind of wedding activities. The game is foolish, just a series of questions to prove how well I know Anwen, with answers procured from him ahead of time. Queen Raven visibly —to my eye—changes the answers a few times in order to make mine correct, which I refuse to take personally. I know what truly matters. Anwen and I have a lifetime to learn each other's favorite foods or colors. And I am distracted. Castor informed me Anwen had come to him and that they were leaving, but I haven't heard a word from him since.

The presents are somehow more foolish, a parade of nonsense luxuries, half of which cannot even be used in Sundrop Gem's desert. My smile strains at the edges. At least tearing into the flamboyant packaging gives me something to destroy.

Finally, the horde of strangers staring at me are given pots of sacred paint to, humiliatingly, doodle upon each other while I change into my wedding gown for the final fitting. I step behind the wooden divider, where a sullen Bright waits with two other seamstresses. They slip the dress over my head then begin folding the few final panels into place. I close my eyes and let them fuss.

Bright nudges me. "Time for the show."

I take a deep breath and step out onto a small, raised platform in front of a full-length mirror. Gasps and soft, pleased noises echo off the glass walls. I have a moment to myself while Bright and her team make their final adjustment, just staring into the mirror. Anwen's voice echoes in my mind.

I'd take the holy woman out somewhere. Maybe that oasis back in Sundrop. And I'd speak our vows where only the Goddess could see us.

The dress is a perfect compromise. It is exactly what the Luna should choose. And in that moment, I hate it.

Pain tears through me. A thousand tiny points and one sucking hole in my chest. Anwen's pain.

46

ON INSTINCT

ANWEN

WITH NESSA'S LIST IN HAND AND ALL THREE OF US DRESSED IN PLAIN, heavy clothes, Baz, Castor, and I sneak down into the city proper, through my favorite secret passage so even the guards don't know we're gone. My whole body hums with adrenaline. I couldn't—can't kill Floyd. Not yet. But this fucking assassin, Dorian? He's already a bloody smear on the street in my mind.

Castor tips his head to the sky as we emerge into the market, sniffing. I grab the back of his skull and yank him back down. He tears out of my grasp with a glare.

"You remember walking through this place the second time you arrived?" I hiss.

He purses his lips, obviously playing back the stares and whispers. "They weren't talking about me."

I snort. "You don't understand court gossip. You're as recognizable as any of us now."

He grips the hilt of his sword. "That does not give you permission to touch me."

Baz sighs. "We've got a different guy to murder, remember?"

I roll my eyes. *'It's not like I'm starting it.'*

'You sound like a six-year-old,' he replies. *'Show me the list.'*

I pass the piece of paper to Baz as freezing rain starts spitting down on us. Castor tries to hide his shiver, but he's got enough of Estrella's habits that I see it anyway. Even for someone who grew up here, this sucks shit.

"This one." Baz taps one name on the list. The Iron Squid. "This is the place that recognized Birsha's description. Ten to one, he's there."

"It's a start." I adjust my hood to keep the rain off my face and lead the way toward the dive.

After a short walk and an honestly pretty cheap bribe, we stand in front of the innkeeper as she slurs her way through a description of the man staying under the name "Meadows."

"Stinks o'rogue." She gestures broadly, meaninglessly. "Hair's red as embers. Big. Stank o'trouble, too. Tweren't for t'other one, I wouldn't 've lettim stay."

A growl builds in my throat. "This *other one*. Did he have kind of a ferrety look?"

She slams her hand on the bar. "That's it! Couldn' put me finger on it for the life."

I thank her for her time, slide one more silver coin across the bar, and head back outside.

"What are you doing?" Castor demands as soon as we step into the rain. "We should go back, get his room number!"

"And lose our numbers advantage in a cramped space?" I shake my head. "We'll wait. Out here's where we want him."

Castor slumps against a wall, sulking. I shoot Baz a look, which he ignores. It's hard not to forget the kid's younger than either of us when he behaves like this.

The rain doesn't let up or get worse. It's just a constant, plinking nightmare that'll stay in my dreams until the day I die. Minutes fade into hours, and Castor's plan starts sounding a hell of a lot better. A man steps out of the tavern, and I glance up hopelessly. He's only the millionth to do that.

Just before he pulls his hood up, I catch sight of his bright red hair. "Got him," I hiss.

Castor leaps to his feet and draws his sword.

"Fucking relax!" I grab his arm.

He turns to me, eyes blazing. "That man has been paid to take my life. I will stall no longer!"

Fuck, his way is tempting. But I know it's the Goddess-damned easy way. And Birsha being murdered right under my nose when he obviously still had information still stings.

"We're going to follow him, shithead," I growl. "See where he's going, learn his plan, *then* fucking kill him."

"Give me one reason why I should listen to the likes of you," he snarls in return.

Baz snaps his fingers between both of our faces, and I realize how close to Castor I've gotten. "How about, shut the fuck up; he's leaving?"

I take a step back. Just like Baz said, Dorian's dark cloak has almost disappeared in the crowd. Castor straightens and sheaths his sword.

"Someday," he mutters as we peel off from our waiting place in unison.

I do Estrella the honor of ignoring him.

Baz and I have years of practice blending into the city crowds, mostly sneaking down to the Blue Slipper. I slouch, stuff my hands in my pockets, and duck my head like I'm hiding from the rain. Baz bobs and weaves like he's drunk, mumbling absently but not actually knocking into anyone. Castor... well, he walks like a fucking prince sneaking through a city. He hunches forward, visibly balances his steps with his hands, and keeps tapping the hilt of his sword like he's checking that it's still there. I suck in a deep, calming breath and walk in front of him. Birsha was fast and well-informed, but I've met more dangerous people. Dorian Meadows might be—

Floyd's fucking ringer. At the first corner, he does the subtlest check over his shoulder I've ever seen, catches sight of Castor, and takes off running.

"Shit!" I sprint after him, unable to do anything but hope the other two are following.

People scatter out of my way with small shrieks. I skid around the corner. The cobbled streets are slick under my feet—damned rain—but I'm faster than most white wolves, forget other shifters. If Dorian would just leave the city, I could really let loose. And this street leads to one of the gates out of the village.

Like he can read my fucking mind, he hangs a hard right into a narrow alley with a standing market. Vendors in layers of mismatched clothes crowd the tiny space. Speed won't help me here. I could throw back my hood and demand they stop him as their prince, but—

"Allow me." Castor breezes past me into the alleyway.

Where I ducked and wove, he barrels. I wince, thinking how much this is going to piss Estrella off, but then I see it. He's not just plunging through, he's strong enough to actually move shit—tables, people, wares—out of his way instead of slamming into them. I laugh out loud. I guess he and Estrella really did have the same father. Baz catches up, and we tear along the path Castor clears.

We reach Castor quickly. I could've found him by the trail of sweat alone. He's huffing and puffing, obviously not used to doing this much in human form. The three of us will catch Dorian eventually, but I don't think we have the fucking stamina to do it the regular way.

'Split up,' I tell Baz. *'I'll stay with Castor. Flank him. Head for the east wall.'*

He nods and peels off as soon as we reach the end of the alleyway. Castor shoots me a look.

"Trust me." I smirk.

He scowls, but he has no choice. Just like Estrella, I have to convince him to accept what's good for him.

And I have to stop fucking thinking when I should be running.

Dorian is fast, but he doesn't have shit on me, even with his unerring sense of the crappiest alleys in the city. And that perception works against him when he spots Baz, always to his west, always right before a turn we need him to take. Still, even my lungs are burning by the time Dorian whips around the final turn and realizes he's at a dead end.

A lesser man would pause, curse, think over his options. Dorian just tears a short sword from a holster on his back, whirls, and throws himself at me. I roll to the side, and he meets Castor instead. Despite his heavy breathing, Castor manages to get half his sword out of its scabbard before Dorian strikes, just enough to block the blow. The rogue grunts. I pull my two daggers and leap to my feet, diving at his back. Dorian parries my blade, then shoulders me out of the way and backs up.

'Soon,' Baz calls. '*Had to take the roofs.*'

'*Aim for the end of the alley.*'

Two on one, for now. Castor and I advance.

Dorian fights like liquid, his short sword somehow holding up against both Castor's heavier weapon and my daggers. I roll, dodge, try to get inside his guard. He dances back and forward, anticipating my moves before I make them. Castor swings crushing blows, takes a few on his leather armor, and still barely manages to nick Dorian. The message Floyd's sending is clear: Birsha couldn't get the job done. I'm not missing again. After the run, I'm nowhere near as fast as I should be. Castor's moving like molasses, and his armor is nearly shredded. Dammit, we need Baz.

I dip right, my daggers flashing. Instead of dodging, Dorian presses forward. I leap back just in time for the tip of his blade to barely graze my tunic. A familiar smell catches my nose. What the fuck is that?

'*Incoming!*' Baz yells.

Time to push my luck. I toss my daggers aside and lunge forward to shove Dorian full in the chest. His mouth opens in real surprise, and he starts to tumble, arms wheeling. Castor sweeps his ankles just as Baz lands at the end of the alleyway. Dorian collides with the soaking ground hard, wet garbage smearing on his cloak, his sword clattering out of his hand. Without needing to say anything, the three of us advance as one. I smile hungrily.

Dorian doesn't scramble. Scars cover his skin, like most rogues, making his expression almost impossible to read, but his gaze goes to the sky. The hair on the back of my neck prickles.

'Baz, how did you—'

The assassin leaps to his feet, twists, and slashes a second sword I didn't even fucking see across Baz's chest. My friend topples with a yelp, and Dorian sprints over his body to the fucking trellis at the end of the alley, the one Baz climbed down to get here. I snarl and coil my muscles to launch into another chase.

"Fuck," Baz says in a voice I've never heard before.

The stink of blood, thick and coppery, reaches me through the rain. Too much of it.

Time slows. My mind tears in two different directions. Catching—hell, killing–Dorian is what we came here to do. It's what I promised Estrella, promised everyone. It's the smart move. The political move. I can find another Beta.

But I can never find another Baz.

I whip around to Castor, trying to put every ounce of confidence and fury pounding in my veins into my voice. "Help me help him. I will find another way to get Dorian. Under pain of a thousand desert nights."

Estrella's younger brother clenches his jaw, stares over my shoulder at Dorian. I don't touch him this time. I don't think I need to.

He snarls, then sheaths his sword. "It's what Father would've done."

We run to Baz, lying in a puddle of his own blood. My stomach drops. My heart gives up the ghost. He's going to die.

Unless we can get him to Estrella fast enough.

47

REGRETS

Estrella

'My room!' Castor shouted through the mind-link. *'Now!'*

I turned and sprinted out of the solarium without a second thought, leaving the party behind.

I hurtle down the halls of Solberg Castle, the veil of my wedding dress flapping behind me like a broken wing, without a thought in my mind but Anwen and the debilitating pain in my chest. He went after the assassin without me, and he got hurt. If he dies—

My bite burns like wildfire. My wolf screams. I cannot think like that.

I slide up to Castor's door and find it already slightly ajar. My heart hammers in my throat as I push it open.

Anwen squats beside Castor's couch, his hands, arms, and right side covered in blood. He looks up at me as I enter. There is no true pain in his blue eyes, only concern.

He's uninjured. Or at least, not terribly injured. I will evaluate the little aches later. As the taut anxiety releases in my shoulders, I take in the rest of the room.

Baz lies on the couch in front of Anwen, bleeding heavily from a gash across his chest. Castor, far less bloodstained, tosses logs into his fireplace with an abrupt sharpness I recognize as anger beyond words.

"Can you help him?" Anwen's voice is ragged, halfway broken.

I blink. This is why he called me. The coronation, the glowing. Father.

Baz coughs up another gout of blood. The wound is bad enough to reach his lungs. There is no apothecary in the world who could fix this.

I race to his side and kneel next to Anwen, heedless of the blood. "I would rather try anything than allow someone to die before me, but for this, I owe you."

Baz chuckles, more wheeze than laugh. "Fuck that."

"Shut up," Anwen says through gritted teeth.

Another log lands on the fire behind me. Castor would only be this angry if they failed. But I cannot think about that either. I cast my mind back to Yana's words during my coronation. For the gift of healing to return is an auspicious sign of a powerful queen and a peaceful future. I take a deep breath, tasting blood, and will the glow into being.

Nothing comes. My chest squeezes. I should be more powerful now. I hold my hands over Baz's split chest and close my eyes.

A voice I know in my bones and have never heard before whispers the answer in the back of my mind. Prophecies, signs, power, none of those will save the life of my mate's best friend. All I can rely on now is belief.

And love.

The Goddess guides our footsteps, even in the darkest night. She does not abandon us. She does not lead us astray. Even when it seems like She has given us a mate that could never love us. I reach everything I am out to her.

Behind my closed eyelids, the glow begins. Emotions boil in my chest. Everything I've felt for Anwen, everything I felt leaning over Father's body, the shock and fear and rage of the last months. And the Goddess's hands are around mine, guiding my fingertips over the split in Baz's chest.

Something tugs at me—us, slows us. Like a knotted thread, or a leaf caught between teeth. He will not come together exactly right.

"Shit," Castor blurts.

I open my eyes. The golden sun of my hands nearly blinds me, but I can just make out what caused his reaction. Baz's side is bubbling.

Ice creeps through my veins, dimming the glow. I suck in in a deep breath. There, beneath all the blood, I can just make out a sickening, herbal scent.

"Wolfsbane," Anwen breathes.

I grit my teeth, shut my eyes once more, and focus on the look in his eyes when I walked in. He will be destroyed if Baz dies. I may not feel the same love for the man, at least not yet, but that love still exists. It still matters.

The glow fades. I have done all I can, and so has the Goddess. I open my eyes.

Anwen pulls Baz's blood-soaked tunic away to reveal closed skin, but only barely. A thick scab winds over the man's ribcage, already cracked and bleeding in a few places, blackened as if from the wolfsbane in others.

"Damn," Baz mumbles. "Helluva a girl you got."

His eyes close, and his breathing evens out. A little color even returns to his cheeks, as much as anyone has in Dun's Crossing. I am no apothecary, but he looks as though he's going to survive. I saved his life.

I burst into tears.

Anwen wraps his arms around me. "I'm so sorry. I don't know how exhausting that is, and—"

I shake my head furiously. "I killed him."

"What?"

"Father." My shoulders shake with sobs. "I *knew* the bond would make me stronger. Strong enough to—to—"

"Oh, love." Anwen kisses my cheeks.

I tear out of his arms. Everything is too loud, too much.

"Don't say that about yourself," Castor says roughly. "You couldn't have done anything. You didn't know."

"I should've!" I curl in on myself. I let Father die. There's no way to know that declaring Anwen and I right there, in the middle of the dance floor, wouldn't have changed anything.

Anwen kisses the top of my head and leaves my side. Quietly, I hear him say, "Let me handle this. Why don't you go tell Dowager Suniva and the others what happened?"

"She's my sister," Castor replies. "I should—"

"Protect your mother, who has a hit out on her," Anwen says firmly. "Please."

There's a pause. "She likes sweets when she's tired."

Castor's heavy footfalls promise he's left his room. Anwen rejoins me on the floor. I rock helplessly back and forth. If all I need is belief and love, perhaps the belief wasn't the trouble.

"Did I not love Father enough?" I gasp.

"You and I both know that couldn't be it," he says quietly. "Everything you've done since that arrow was for him."

"That's not love." Tears sheet down my face.

"Then what is?"

I shake my head. "I-I don't know. I don't know if I've ever known."

"I do." He takes my hand, a warm promise. "It's the pain that keeps you up at night, thinking about him. You'd only hurt that much if you loved him just as much."

"That's guilt." My lungs burn. Everything burns.

Anwen takes my face in his hands and forces me to look at him. "You want someone to be at fault for this? Someone other than Birsha and Floyd? Fine. Blame me. If us not coming out and declaring our bond right away is the problem, I decided on that. I forced you into it." He sucks in a deep breath. "If you're right, I killed your father."

My whole being recoils from that. This Anwen, my mate with the soft blue eyes and hard features, did not do that. Could not.

"And I killed mine." His voice is harsh. "I sided with Kieran, who killed him. So blame me for all of it. I already feel guilty enough."

"Absolutely not." I sniffle, but the next sob lodges in my chest, not quite big enough to shed. "You chose to do the right thing. You shouldn't feel guilty about something you had no idea would produce the outcome it did."

Anwen raises an eyebrow, and I realize what I'm saying. But real guilt and shame burn in his eyes. This has been eating him for a long while now.

"You cannot be blamed," I say quietly.

"For what?" His smile is wry. "I did a lot of it."

"For your father or mine." I fill my lungs with bloodstained air and try to believe the words I'm saying. "And perhaps… perhaps neither can I."

"Perhaps." Anwen takes my hands and kisses the backs of them. "As for the rest, I've been meaning to say this, but… I'm sorry. For that first day. I was too caught up in my own shit to recognize the blessing the Goddess gave me." He smiles softly. "I should've told everyone right away. Not even for your father, though that would be a benefit. I just don't ever want you to think I'm not proud to be with you." He swallows. "To be yours."

The room is warm and close. My gown clings to me, and I want nothing more to be out of it. No, I want one thing more. I want my mate to believe me.

I lean in to kiss him, intent on making my point however I must.

Someone knocks on the door. Anwen pulls back with a groan.

"Neither of us are exactly presentable." I smile as much as I can.

"I'll see who it is. I could've been hunting." He shoves to his feet, crosses the room, and opens the door. After a moment of quiet conversation, he returns with Nessa in tow.

"Oh, your wedding dress," she gasps when she sees me.

I look down at myself. The gown is soaked in Baz's blood and my tears. I didn't even remember I was wearing the damned thing.

"You said you had news," Anwen says impatiently.

"Oh, yes!" She shakes her head as if to clear it. "Father must have some way to communicate with Dorian that I don't know about because he just fled the castle."

48

SETTING UP CAMP

ANWEN

"ARE YOU SURE OF THIS?" KING ANDRI RUMBLES.

I hold the massive Alpha's dark stare. "Someone working with Floyd on the whole plan told us everything. I'm sure you understand why I can't tell you who."

"You think you cannot trust me." He studies me.

I hold my straight-backed posture. The king of Snowcrest doesn't scare me—in a fight, I could outlast him easily—but he radiates power just like Father used to. Part of me wishes I took Kieran up on his offer to have this meeting with me. But if he gets involved, it's a formal accusation. A prince telling a king one of their envoys is a piece-of-shit murderer creates a little less of an international incident.

"Good." King Andri's mouth twitches in what might be a smile, under his massive beard.

I exhale slowly and try not to show my relief on my face. "Great. Then can we count on your support?"

"I cannot go against Floyd Winters publicly. His family is old, if no longer powerful." King Andri nods slowly. "Everything else is yours. Snowcrest does not form alliances this way."

Questions about Father jump to my tongue. I swallow them down. If this all works out, hopefully Kieran will be able to make an actual alliance with Snowcrest, and I can ask later.

King Andri and I exchange formal goodbyes, and I dart out of the side chamber I asked him to meet me in.

One wild card down. That just leaves missing Floyd, missing Dorian, and Nessa.

'What's she doing now?' I ask Baz through mind-link.

'Still walking with Estrella to the meeting,' he replies. *'You do know I can actually do shit, right?'*

I blow out a breath. *'There's no shit to do.'*

Estrella believes every word Nessa's saying. And it's not like I have any proof she's up to something. Her information about Dorian panned out, even if we didn't catch him. She tells me more than I want to know every time I ask her a question.

But I can't shake this hairs-on-the-back-of-my-neck feeling that we can't trust her. Why did she come clean now? The story about Estrella and Joli is sweet, but it's not enough.

I smooth a hand over my hair and turn toward the war room Kieran set up in a hidden chamber I pointed him to. I'm letting Father's paranoia control me. He always said there was no such thing as a good deed. The point of this war room, of meeting in there at all, is to make that part of me shut up. We're finally going to settle on a plan solid enough that Dowager Suniva could be a traitor and it still won't fall apart.

We have to. The wedding is tomorrow. And fuck all this, I'm not missing it.

I check my surroundings. Completely alone. I depress three stones in a seemingly random wall in order, and it slides to the side. Warm, musty air spills into the corridor. I duck inside.

The war room is impressive for how little time we had to set it up. A huge table sits in the middle of the room, covered in maps that detail every square inch of land between here and Floyd's ancestral home and surrounded by mostly full chairs. Flickering fairy-lanterns light the space. The scraps of evidence we have lay on the back table, marked and labeled with everything we know. A blueprint of the temple where Estrella and I are going to get married covers most of the back wall.

Kieran stands as I step in and shut the door behind me. "King Andri?"

"On board." Since Floyd disappeared, we haven't wasted breath on anything other than what we absolutely have to say. "Enough."

Baz leans back in his chair, trying to balance a quill on his nose. Tess watches him with taut interest. Taut everything. I don't think a muscle in her body has relaxed since we came limping home without Dorian.

"What does 'enough' mean?" Dowager Suniva asks.

I circle the room and take my seat beside Estrella. She grabs my hand underneath the table.

"He can't denounce Floyd, but we've got him behind the scenes."

Nessa nods. "That makes sense. King Andri's grandfather loved my grandmother, and she's the only one living at home."

The door opens again, and Castor walks in with King Isai's burly Beta, Cristofer. They fill the final two seats.

"Right." Kieran sits. "Everyone's here, so let's get started. Anwen, give a quick rundown of what we know."

Baz drops all four feet of his chair onto the floor. Everyone snaps to attention.

"Floyd disappeared from the castle before we got back from fighting Dorian." I draw a line along the map, tracing secret passageways that aren't marked but I know by heart. "Since he got Birsha in and out without anyone noticing, we can assume he and Dorian took a similar route, but we didn't find any proof."

Baz nods. "I could smell he'd been down there at some point, but no clue when. It was too wet."

Dowager Suniva furrows her brow and looks at Estrella, who nods. My chest warms.

"And we know his plan. The night before the wedding, he plans to isolate Estrella and make it look like we did it."

She squeezes my hand tightly.

"Nessa?" Kieran says.

She brightens.

Maybe that's why I'm having a hard time trusting her. She lights up every time he looks her way.

"I know Floyd pretty well, but you're the expert. Do you think he left because he's giving up?"

She laughs then covers her mouth. "No. Father's… I've never seen him give up on anything. He's probably just changing the plan, now that he's lost the element of surprise."

That, too. She's weirdly calm for having turned her back on her father.

Kieran said I was projecting when I told him my worries.

"Can we not just track both of them down and end this?" Castor demands. "I know how to track. So do many of your men."

"That is too risky, my dear." Dowager Suniva puts her hand on his. "If you take yourself and so many soldiers away, those that remain will be left vulnerable."

Estrella smiles wryly. "This is why you always lose at kras. The better's gambit is called that because it's risky, not because it is always the right choice."

He rolls his eyes.

"Floyd's smart, but he never checks his work," I say before the siblings can start bickering. "We should use that against him."

Estrella nods. "He will assume we are proceeding mostly as planned without ensuring that's actually true. What would be the normal procedure for a situation like this?"

I exchange a glance with Kieran. Father would turn the whole might of the army to destroying anyone who dared do something like this in his palace.

"The most up-to-date procedures dictate that we place additional guards on your rooms until the threat is either passed or eliminated," he says carefully.

"A lockdown?" Tess's eyebrows shoot up. "We won't simply wait to be killed."

"No, we won't." Castor palms his sword. "We will be armed, ready."

Estrella's younger brother has all the patience the Goddess gave a hummingbird, but fuck if his plans don't start to sound pretty good after a while. I imagine all of us sitting in a single room, at the ready. Estrella and I tearing into the men who did this to her, to us, until there's nothing left.

"No, we will be elsewhere," Estrella says.

Everyone turns to her.

"The simplest plan is the best, for the speed we have to work at. We have one day until the wedding." She stands, pointing to a dense cluster of trees just north of the palace. "Everyone in danger will stay here. It's out of the way, and nothing Floyd would think of. And while those people are being kept safe, King Kieran and King Andri can ensure the temple is safe for the wedding."

I swallow. "And who is everyone?"

"My father and I," Tess says.

"Me." Nessa stares at the tabletop.

"Mother and Castor," Estrella adds.

Dowager Suniva sighs. "I hate to say this, but if we take away all of Floyd's most preferred targets, will he not just choose another? Say, a bride on the eve of her wedding?"

"Kill Luna Estrella, cut off Anwen's access to becoming Alpha." Kieran nods slowly.

Icy fear squeezes my ribcage. "That'd be a great way to make you look like the bad guy."

Estrella scoffs. "I'm not running."

"Like hell you aren't." My voice whips out, sharp with worry. "It's the only smart move."

"Am I running?" Castor asks.

Estrella grits her teeth. "Your life has been threatened."

"I love you." I sit, staring into her eyes. "Shut up."

She glares back at me for a long moment. "I love you too."

* * *

WIND WHIPS THROUGH MY FUR, AND I WISH I COULD ENJOY IT.

A bag of camping supplies bounces against my back. The whole group of us heads to the gnarled part of the forest Estrella indicated on the map. Kieran insisted on sending a guard of half a dozen soldiers with us, and I insisted on leading it. In addition to the Sundrop Gem contingent and Nessa, we have almost fifteen people.

This isn't exactly how I pictured the night before my wedding.

At least I get to watch Estrella's warm, brown fur shine in the setting sun. She's beautiful in every form.

Aldritch, the gray wolf leading the group, stops. *'We're here, Your Highness.'*

I nudge Estrella, and she slows. The rest of the Sundrop contingent does immediately after.

Nessa stops last with no mind-link warning for her. The closest member of Snowcrest is back at the castle.

We hope.

I shift, pull on some shorts, and scan for any sign of other people. There's no smoke rising over the trees, no torn, abandoned clothes. I don't even see the ring of stones rogues tend to leave in their wake.

The soldiers transform, shrug off their own packs, and begin setting up camp. I'm about to join them when the air shimmers, and Estrella's scent intensifies. She just shifted.

Fuck, knowing my soon-to-be wife is naked behind me makes my mouth water.

"I'm not looking," I mutter. "Your family's here."

"And you can't contain yourself?" I can hear the smile in her voice.

"Around you? Never."

She laughs quietly. I hear her get dressed before she calls, "I have a map to the nearest river. Anwen and I are going to go find it and ensure we have fresh water."

"Please be safe," Dowager Suniva replies.

"Of course, Mother."

Estrella takes my hand and tugs, spinning me around. She's

wearing a sliver of clothing, and the sunset looks better on her than any dress. Forget my mouth watering, my cock hardens just looking at her.

"It's the night before our wedding," she murmurs. "Do you really want to spend it with my family?"

I stumble after her, deeper into the trees.

49

THE NIGHT BEFORE

ESTRELLA

I TUG ANWEN THROUGH THE FOREST. WHILE I DO HAVE A MAP IN THE bag strapped to my back, I don't pull it out. The bag is heavy because King Kieran packed us enough fresh water in canteens to last a week.

I need a moment alone with my mate.

The twisting, winding roots guide my steps deeper. The forest just outside the castle had a certain appeal, but there's a wildness here that tugs at me, urges me to forget everything and lose myself in it. As if I were in the Haze all over again.

"How far are we going?" Anwen laughs.

"As far as I like." I smile. "I don't intend to keep quiet, either."

He swallows visibly. Ever since Nessa confessed, since Dorian escaped, we have been nothing but business. Who needs to be saved? Where should that happen? How can we prove everything we suspect? Our wedding, from beginning to end, has been planned with others in mind. Some of that, we owe our people. But a night of keeping careful distance from each other before we are bound as tightly as any two people can be? That is one exchange I will not make.

But perhaps walking into the forest until no one could hear us scream was a silly idea.

I shrug off my pack, drop it, and kneel on the slightly softer surface. Anwen threads his fingers through my hair and smiles softly.

"You don't have to—"

"I want to." I meet his gaze, trying to force everything I'm feeling through my eyes alone.

His grip on my hair tightens as his cock hardens. "Then take it."

I tug down his shorts. My whole body lights as he thrusts forward. Pain skitters down my spine to gather in my gut. I open my mouth, tongue flat, and take him.

His taste swirls through me. I hollow my cheeks, roll my tongue along his underside. He fucks into my mouth, hard and fast like he's worried someone will come looking for us soon. Here, surrounded by trees and what feels like the very breath of the Goddess, I don't care if they do. Let them see my mate, turned golden in the setting sun. Let them watch his mouth go slack with want, hear my name mumble from his lips. He is beautiful, and he is mine.

Just as I am his to wring pleasure from.

"I'm close," he groans.

His hands in my hair loosen, and I know he is giving me a moment to pull back. To let him finish himself.

Nothing has ever been less appealing. I press forward. My nose scrapes against the rough hairs between his legs. His cockhead brushes the back of my throat, and I moan.

"Estrella!" He spills into my mouth.

I start swallowing even as the taste overwhelms me. All the words, the comparisons I've assigned to it fall away. This sensation on my tongue is simply him.

He pulls back abruptly, and a few droplets spill from my mouth. I reach up to catch them, but before I can, he kneels in front of me and kisses me.

I gasp up into him. His grip is rough, taking the kiss more than giving it. I mold myself to his body, slide one of his legs between mine. The first press of friction is a lightning strike, and I pray he swallows my moan.

"Too good to me," he mutters against my mouth. "Pay you back."

I grind my hips against him. My dress is bunged up, so my wetness smears on his leg. He trails his lips away from mine, onto my neck, and bites. I hiss as sweet heat courses through my system. An image of myself throwing back my bridal veil to reveal a neck purpled all over with his bites sings in my mind. All the nights of resisting, restraining ourselves, would be worthwhile for that.

They are worthwhile regardless. At the end of them all, Anwen will not be leaving my bed for a week. I've already arranged matters with my advisors not to need me.

"More," I moan.

I feel his smile against my neck. In his next bite, the sharp sting of his teeth joins the slight pain. I hum.

He pushes me down, slowly, inexorably. My head lands on my pack. The roots scrape my spine, the backs of my knees. He slides one hand up my leg with his mouth still on my neck, and I part for him. The first brush of his fingers over my wetness is loud enough to hear in the nighttime quiet. I murmur his name like a prayer. Firelight dances off the furthest leaves I can see, a reminder of how close we are to camp.

"You deserve better," he says.

I shake my head, start to refuse. He pulls back and covers my mouth.

"Than these last few months." Anwen meets my gaze, his blue eyes alive with hunger, a smirk on his lips. "I've seen your worst moments. Now, I want to know how good it gets."

"Wh—"

He circles the nub at the apex of my legs, hard and fast, then thrusts a finger inside. My body contorts with the rush of pleasure. When he returns his mouth to my skin, he pushes my dress down and takes one nipple between his teeth instead. I moan, all thoughts of camp forgotten. His touch is irresistible, as overpowering as his come in my mouth. I hurtle toward the edge of pleasure.

"Close," I manage to nearly sob.

I expect him to let off, to string out this beautiful torture as long as he can like he seems to prefer. He doesn't even hesitate.

My orgasm rattles through me. I clutch his bare shoulder, and the scent of his blood licks the air as my claws extend for a better hold.

He fucks me through the aftershocks. I fight to catch my breath.

"I'm finished," I pant. "Slow down."

"No." His smile shines as the last rays of sunset disappear.

My mouth falls open. He takes it in a kiss and pushes another finger into my entrance. My body clutches him, trying to slow his pace. My wolf howls for more.

I join my howl with hers. I trust Anwen. He will not take me past what I'm capable of.

And if I hold out until his cock is ready once more, I can have everything I want.

He plucks my nipple between two fingers, scrapes his teeth down my other breast, fucks me fast and hard. My body melts into nothing but sensation. I exist in the breaths between his touches, few that they are. He is everywhere, and he doesn't seem to want to let me go.

When he thrusts the third finger inside, my second orgasm hits, sudden as a summer storm. I make a high-pitched keening noise until he covers my mouth with his again. His taste tints his lips. I kiss him just as hungrily as he fucks me.

He lines up a fourth finger before the second orgasm fades out of my limbs. I squeeze my eyes shut. I am so deliciously full already. But I want all of him. His thumb teases that bud, coaxes more wetness from my body. He soaks his hand in it.

I gasp as he slips inside with a burn that only makes me crave more.

"So beautiful." He grins down at me, just as wild as I am.

I roll my hips against his hand.

"And greedy."

He curls his fingers, and a third orgasm explodes through me before I can suck in a breath. There's so much of him. I shake, tears gathering in my eyes.

His thumb presses harder, and the next wave of pleasure is jagged edged. I am coming up to the extent of what I can handle.

"You can take one more," he says. "My thumb, or my cock?"

If sweet exhaustion wasn't winding its tendrils through me, I would laugh in his face. I have never been presented with a simpler choice.

"Your cock."

He smiles indulgently and pulls out one finger at a time. Each loss stabs through me. I whine until his cock brushes my entrance.

"I'm going to fuck you until I come." He says it like a statement, but I can hear the private question. He wants to know if I can handle that.

"I am not running." I smirk.

"Like hell you aren't." He slams into me.

We fit together like puzzle pieces. I consider wrapping my legs around his waist, keeping him close, but they still shake with the remains of my last orgasm. He bends low over me, and I capture his lips instead.

The rightness I've felt every time I've been with him fills me, and my tears spill. It should have been like this from the beginning. A perfect union of body and soul.

Anwen looks at me worriedly. "Too much?"

"No," I say.

No, it wasn't. The man in my arms, between my legs, did not exist before we became mates. And the version of myself I am now did not exist either. We could not have been happy, been perfect fits, without the intervening pain.

He kisses me again.

My orgasm comes slower this time, without his talented fingers pulling it out of me. I wrap my arms around his neck, breathing in the scent of his hair. When he mutters that he's close, I can seek the peak, but I am not there yet.

Like he can sense it, he stuffs a hand between us and teases my bud. I race to the finish line with him. He groans, spills into me, and his hand goes stiff.

That is what I need to careen over the edge with his name on my lips.

When I finally catch my breath, I realize how long we've been gone. It's well and truly night. The firelight through the trees is far brighter, a beacon guiding us back. Anwen leans on one arm, watching me.

"Ready to go back?" he asks with a smile.

My stomach wrenches at the idea of him being any farther away.

'We found a cozy spot for two,' I tell Tess. *'Well within earshot. And we have our packs. We are going to sleep here instead.'*

'Have fun,' she replies, amused.

"Not tonight." I wind my arm around his waist.

5 0

AMBUSH

Anwen

'*Wake up!*' Candace yells through mind-link. '*Right fucking now!*'

I shoot up. Candace doesn't curse. She's never cursed before.

'*I'm here. Who are you, and what did you do with my sister?*'

'*Shut up. I had a dream. You need to move everyone.*'

'*Your dreams are bullshit,*' I reply. '*You can't see the future.*'

Drowsy, I rub my eyes and look at Estrella, curled naked on the blankets we pulled out of our packs and wound into a lazy nest.

'*We don't have time to argue. Just answer me one question: are you willing to be wrong about this?*'

Estrella's skin is warm and golden in the pre-dawn light. Vulnerable.

But Father always said Candace made up the shit about her dreams because she wanted to feel special. There were a few spooky coincidences, but nothing more.

'*I—*'

My ears prick. There, just barely audible. The rhythmic *ka-thump, ka-thump* of paw pads over dirt. Someone's running toward us.

Fast.

I grab Estrella by the shoulder and begin shaking her. "Get up!"

'Aldritch, everybody, get the fuck up!'

She blinks up at me and frowns. "Hush. You kept me awake too late."

"We're being attacked." The words scratch out of my throat.

Instantly, the tiredness disappears from her face, replaced with the distant haze of a conversation happening through the mind-link. People start rustling behind us, in the camp we abandoned.

I meet her gaze. "Don't be a hero. People need you."

She scoffs. "Can you make the same promise?"

I grit my teeth. There's no good way to say, *not if you're the one in danger*. At least, not one she'll accept.

A howl splits the air, and I throw myself into a shift. Fur sprouts, claws and teeth extend, and I hit the ground running.

Aldritch and the other guards sound off as they wake up. Daz, who slept in the same tent as Dowager Suniva, is already dead. I heard the second team arriving.

My own howl pierces the morning.

Side-by-side, Estrella and I skid into the clearing we left behind. A dozen or more strange wolves brawl our group. And judging by the reek of blood in the air, someone is already losing.

I'll be damned if it's us.

I leap for the nearest wolf I don't recognize, a mottled silver-white, and catch him in the side. We tumble over each other, scrabbling for purchase.

'The wolf on top is the victor,' Father says in my memory. 'Always.'

He lost to Kieran. Just like I always used to. And I don't have the fucking time. Before we roll to a stop, I wrench one of my legs back, time the angle, and slash my claws across his throat. Blood sprays, and he goes limp underneath me.

One down.

I slam my body into another coming to check on his fallen friend. He skitters backward into the low fire the night watch maintained.

His tail catches becoming a bright brush of flame. His yelp hurts my ears.

My shoulder burns, but nobody's hitting me. I whip around, looking for Estrella.

A reddish-orange wolf sinks his teeth into her shoulder.

The exact same goddamn color as Dorian Meadows' hair.

I launch myself across the clearing, heart hammering in my ears. He's fucking dead. Saliva drips from my maw, and the rest of the carnage fades away. Nothing matters but the bastard who thinks he can take a chunk out of my mate.

A dust-gray wolf collides with me, and the guard who tackled him hits a second after. We tumble to the ground in a scratching, biting pile of limbs. Someone sinks teeth into my flank. I try to angle my claws again, but the guard is always just in the way.

'Get his fucking ass,' I snarl. *'HIs head is mine.'*

He obeys immediately, twisting away from the rogue's slavering jaws to catch the gray tail between his teeth. The rogue whines and loses focus. I tear his throat out with my teeth before he can regain it.

'Prince Anwen!' Aldritch calls. *'Southeast tent. Defending the Dowager Luna.'*

I'm gone before the dead rogue hits the dirt.

Father trained Kieran, Finn, and I nearly every day to be able to defend ourselves. But where normal soldiers went on their first missions at thirteen or fourteen, he insisted princes didn't need to face bloodshed to understand it. To conquer it. I didn't kill anyone until I was eighteen, when Baz and I snuck out and got in a bar fight that went south when the dickhead recognized me.

I've never killed as much as I am right now. Never as quickly. The air around me goes red with gore. I catch sight of my own side at one point and nearly mistake it for a stranger's. The pink tint of my fur is unnatural. I don't know if I'll ever escape the metallic taste of blood. But every Goddess-damned time I turn around, someone else needs my help. Someone yells, or I see them through the fighting. Castor's strong, and he's fucking angry, but he's obviously never been in a real fight before. Dowager Suniva is visibly out of practice, off balance without her magic to rely on. Tess isn't a fighter, so her father devotes most of his energy to protecting her. The guards do their best, but they were at the front when the ambush hit. Most of them are already injured.

The clearing becomes my racetrack, and I'm darting side to side, slaughtering one rogue only to dodge a vicious attack from another.

And I haven't seen Estrella since that rogue knocked me off course. Or Dorian Meadows.

She's not injured, I think as I suck in a deep breath. *I would know.*

The tide of battle shifts, and her smell wafts toward me in a gust. I whirl.

At the center of the clearing, Estrella brawls with a group of challengers. Her fur shines. Red spittle coats her teeth. Her eyes glow. She lacks technique, but whoever taught her obviously knew how to lean into her strengths. She's fluid, fast. She doesn't push her advantage when she's not sure she can keep it. Her enemies fall for every feint like they've never seen it before.

Cuts and scrapes line her pelt. She's not killing anyone, and she's not good enough to survive this unharmed. But she's a fucking miracle of movement all on her own.

A reddish pelt appears at the back of the pack, and I snap back to focus. Dorian's fucking sneaking away!

Coward.

I lower myself below the height of the scrum and creep along the ground. Blood smears in the dirt. I fill my lungs with Dorian's scent. He can't escape me here. These are my fucking woods. And for all he thinks he's so Goddess-damned smart, he's still slower.

By the time he reaches the tree line, I'm within striking distance. His muscles bunch under his coat. He's about to take off.

I remember Estrella shaking in my arms after Nessa finally told us the truth.

Never again.

I throw myself at him just as he leaps, when his weight is most off-center, aiming for a thick pine behind him. He can't escape, but he's not my kill either.

We slam into the tree. My ears ring, and my vision shakes. Dorian hacks out a breath and snarls up at me, fury in his eyes.

He's still conscious. For now.

I twist then pound my back paws into his skull, smashing him into the tree. He rips at my hold, tears chunks out of my ankles, but I don't release him. I can't.

Estrella's smell intensifies. I look over my shoulder, and there she is. Backlit by the morning sun. I nod at Dorian, display his neck to her. We don't need to use the mind-link for her to know what I'm telling her. She looks at me, then at the weak, bleeding Dorian in my grasp. The sounds of battle dim behind us.

She shifts back into human form, and my heart hammers. She's so vulnerable like this. Blood oozes from the bite on her shoulder.

"No," she says.

I cock my head to the side.

"I do not—" She shakes off her hands, flinging droplets of clinging gore. "There is no relief in killing. Certainly not a hired hand, and one who hasn't done anything to me yet."

She didn't kill anyone. Even though they attacked us while we slept. Even though they were all hired by the same motherfucker who killed her father in the first place. She just looks down at Dorian in my grasp with something like pity.

The towering mass of her mother looms over her shoulder, no reluctance on her face. I present Dorian's neck again.

Dowager Suniva tears his throat out with a vicious snarl.

Everything falls silent, except for a couple of birds in the distance. People shift back slowly. None of the ambush party lived. Daz is dead, and one of the other guards is seriously injured. Estrella heals him while everyone else watches.

The energy of pure life spills from her hands. It's just as incredible as the first time I saw it.

After that, there's nothing to do but clean up. Almost everyone has a few injuries. Estrella's shoulder is the worst, and she smacks me when I try to kiss it. My ankles are a wreck, but somehow, I'm still in the wrong for playfully smacking her when she heals them.

Everyone is injured except for Tess and Nessa that is. Cristofer's worse off than most, obviously from protecting his daughter, and Nessa... shit, I didn't see her. But it's not like the ladies of the castle are raised to be these incredible fighters. I doubt she's ever been in anything like this before.

We use the ripped tents to bury the rogues—they're not good for anything else anymore. As I stand next to Estrella, holding her hand and looking down over the corpses, a mind-link comes through.

'Everything's ready,' Kieran says. 'Come home. It's time for your wedding.'

51

EXCITEMENT

ESTRELLA

DRIED BLOOD ITCHES UNDER MY FINGERNAILS. A FEW STICKS SCRATCH the back of my neck where they're caught in my hair from sleeping under the moon. I cling to Anwen's hand as he leads us through a series of underground tunnels back into the castle.

I've never been in a fight like that before. Never looked in the eyes of someone trying to take my life. I haven't stopped shaking yet.

"King Andri had one of his courtiers spread the rumor that we left to carry out some secret Sundrop tradition," he says.

Mother nods. "We will demur if asked."

A vision of her tearing the would-be assassin's throat out flashes through my mind.

I take a deep breath. In the forest, with the Goddess's voice whispering in my ear, I understood. There is no justice in death. Only peace of mind, if you can forget the smell of the blood you've spilled. But I will not judge Mother for doing what she needed to do.

Anwen pushes open a door I can barely see through the gloom, and we step into a hallway.

"Thank the Goddess," Raven says. "That took longer than you said."

Kieran puts a hand on her shoulder, a silent reminder of the story we all must tell. Raven nods and schools her expression.

"Congratulations on your wedding," Kieran says stiffly. "Everyone but the happy couple, if you step into the room behind me, you'll find baths and your own fresh clothes. Clean up quickly."

They file away, and I wish I could go with them.

"Is it done?" Anwen asks quietly.

Kieran nods. "But King Andri wants to meet with both of us to go over the final state of things."

Anwen grimaces. "Now?"

His brother laughs. "A couple more hours, and then you have the rest of your lives together. You'll survive."

"Am I not to come?" I ask.

Raven wrinkles her nose. "Sorry, you have to go get ready. Delegates from all the other kingdoms are waiting already."

Exhaustion ripples through me. I want to collapse in bed and let whatever protections exist do their work until I am rested enough to make a good impression once again.

Anwen takes my other hand and catches my eye. "You were beautiful out there."

My stomach churns. "You were impressive." He tore through the battlefield like a storm, always with an eye to who was in the most danger. With him by my side, I may never need to fight for my life again. The thought warms me.

"But I can't wait to see you in the dress." He grins then kisses me softly. "Go. I'll be the one next to the holy woman."

His excitement is palpable. The air between us sparks with it as he lines up our tattoos. And I have to force myself to smile.

* * *

"Oakspring Dunes has our own wedding tradition," a pretty brunette produces a small comb of what looks like carved blue stone. "For cloudless skies in your future."

I smile and accept the gift. Just like I have every other so far. Expensive trinkets pile between pots of cosmetics and hairpins. Seemingly every kingdom has a tradition they simply must include me in. I'm only happy their excitement to open alliance negotiations with Sundrop Gem has blinded them to the bags under my eyes I haven't yet had a moment to cover.

The brunette flounces off into the swarm of court ladies flitting around me like colorful butterflies.

Tess tugs a few strands into place, and I feel the tremble in her fingertips. She is acting far more like herself since the bath, but our bloody wake-up call has left its marks on her as well. Part of me is grateful. At least with her around, I know I am not insane.

Candace steps up next to us with a redhead I also don't recognize. I've simply given up on that this morning. Either the women will introduce themselves, or I will talk around my ignorance. I'm a blushing bride, after all. Some distraction must be forgiven.

"Good morning." Candace's smile is taut. "I'd like to introduce you both to Lady Eva of Snowcrest Canyon. She's really made a splash here already."

Her words seem strange. I peer at her face, see a little of my own exhaustion within, then look at the redhead again. Sharply pointed nose, high forehead, taller than most—the name clicks into place, as well as the other detail. Lady Eva is promised to Prince Hollis in some Snowcrest tradition I don't understand, and Candace would only be making such a point to introduce us if this was the woman King Andri had had spread the rumor.

Tess does not move. Lady Eva curtsies. I incline my head.

"It's wonderful to meet you," I say. "I have heard only the best about you."

Some tension in her releases as she realizes I know. "Thank you, Luna Estrella. It's my honor to help you. Get ready, that is."

Candace's smile softens too. "When all this is done, we have to talk. You're going to love Eva."

Lady Eva blushes prettily. "When there is a moment. I am perfectly happy to wait."

Candace nods enthusiastically as they step away. It seems, in our absence, she's become fast friends with Lady Eva. That's a promising sign. Despite our fears, it seems most of Snowcrest can be relied on.

More delegates murmur soft compliments and congratulations. More gifts collect in teetering dunes. My body aches.

Bright claps her hands loudly. The whole room turns to her.

"Time for the dress," she declares.

Tess slips a last pin into place then leans over my shoulder. "I love you, and you are beautiful. I just—"

I lean my head against hers. "I know. Me too."

Bright claps again, insistent, and I force myself to stand. Was it really only a couple of months ago that Tess and I sat on the other side of this castle, giggling to each other as we readied for our first real party? I always imagined we would laugh like that on my wedding day. But today, neither of us have the energy.

Mother, Raven, and a small army of seamstresses wait for me in the smaller, second room designed for changing clothes. The dress hangs on a hook at the back. I step inside and close the door behind me.

All the seamstresses pounce. One holds my hair aside. Another waits with the veil. A third removes my robe. Bright stands in front of me the whole time, arms crossed and lips pursed critically.

"Aren't Mother and Raven supposed to be here to help?" I ask from the center of the storm.

Bright sighs. "Yes. Dowager Suniva, could you fold her skirt? And Luna Raven, if you could handle the veil?"

A small smile tugs at my lips. Mother at my back, representing my past, and my future in Raven at the front, was agreed upon almost two weeks ago. It's almost pleasant to remember the ridiculous power struggle the dressmaker thinks we are caught in.

Her assistants slide the dress over my head and begin making final adjustments.

Mother steps behind me. "Your father would be so proud of you."

My throat grows thick. In all the chaos, I haven't even been able to think about him.

"Father would have snuck away from whatever the men are doing to wait for the dress," I reply.

Mother chuckles. "And he would weep when he saw it. I may be able to fulfill that role for you."

He would call me beautiful in every language he knew then hurry off to make sure Anwen knew at least as many. Tears prick at the corners of my eyes. He should be here.

"Ah!" A needle pricks my ankle where one seamstress is fixing a hem, and I flinch away.

Bright towers over the offending woman "Be more careful! You—"

"There's no need for that!" I say quickly.

"She injured—"

Before she can finish her sentence, I reach out to the Goddess. The power springs to my command, easier and easier every time. My hands glow, and so does my ankle under the dress. When the feeling of pain fades, I lift my skirt to show the unblemished skin. "You see?"

Bright purses her lips. "Fine."

The seamstress shoots me an appreciative smile.

"You can heal?" Raven asks breathlessly, the veil delicately draped over her arms.

"Yes?" I furrow my brow. "Why?"

"Just yourself or others?"

"I haven't met anyone it doesn't work for, but I have only tried shifters from here and Sundrop Gem." I study the other queen's face, alight with excitement. This doesn't seem negative.

"What about animals?" She steps closer. "Or land?"

"I haven't tried. The power is fairly new. Please, can I know why you're asking?"

Raven grins, wide and unpracticed. "I've been trying to figure out how to help Escuro. The land itself. It's still sick, after what King

Gavin did. I've found a couple of potions that work on an extremely small scale, healing one plant at a time, with the books here, but that's not exactly something you can do to a whole kingdom."

Embers of something bright kindle in my chest. "And you want to know if I could heal the kingdom."

She nods. "If you'd be willing to even try."

"Veil," Bright snaps.

Raven closes the distance between us and lowers the gauzy fabric onto my head. The embers burst into flame. Her excitement is contagious, electric. Could I heal a whole kingdom? Perhaps I am not blessed like this only to reunite Sundrop Gem and Dun's Crossing, but other kingdoms as well.

"Yes," I say. "Of course. We can start as soon as this is over. Or, if we have a little time—"

"Mirror." Bright snaps her fingers.

We have no time. I have a wedding to attend. I turn and behold myself. The woman in the mirror looks like Luna Queen of Sundrop Gem, ready for her Alpha King of Dun's Crossing. That, I suppose, is the point.

"Oh, Estrella," Mother breathes.

Raven nods. "You look amazing."

I smile and accept the compliments just as I did the wedding gifts. After a few more fusses, Bright opens the door and nudges me out to show the whole swarm of delegates.

Some women gasp. Others coo. Excited chatter fills the room.

I want to take the dress off and see what Raven has been working on. Or simply lay down for a while. Whatever excitement these women feel, I can't.

Just as I couldn't feel Anwen's excitement.

"Show's over," Bright bellows. "Luna Estrella needs to finish her preparations in quiet."

I can't feel Anwen's excitement because I'm tired, and the women filtering out of the room have overwhelmed me. Nothing more.

Raven squeezes my hand. "Kieran needs me to finish some stuff up, but I'll come talk to you at the reception."

Mother beholds me for a long moment then kisses both my cheeks. "Castor and I are leaving for a different part of the forest to seek the final blessing. We will return in time."

"May you hear Her voice." My smile strains.

She, Raven, and the seamstresses leave with the rest. Only Candace, Nessa, and Tess remain, as I asked. Now that I'm dressed, they all glow with excitement.

An excitement I still do not feel.

5 2

SMOOTH SAILING

Anwen

Kieran pauses outside the door to his office and looks at me. "This part's almost done."

"What part?" I ask.

"The bullshit part." He smiles. "I know the Goddess steers us all to our true mates during the Haze, but people who claim that means you're perfectly matched from the start are fucking stupid. She knows that you can be happy together." His smile grows a little bitter. "We're just not the kind of people who can be happy right off the bat."

I laugh. "And now? With Raven puking up her guts every morning?"

"I'm happy," he says simply. "Now, game face. King Andri and Prince Hollis are… interesting to work with."

"What?"

Kieran opens the door and pushes inside without another word.

King Andri sits in the chair Kieran set up next to his desk for Raven, and Prince Hollis stands next to him.

"Good," the king says. "You are late."

"Transit delays." Kieran takes his seat.

I stumble over to stand next to him, a mirror of Prince Hollis, with half my brain still outside the door. Maybe this is the bullshit before the good part. It certainly feels like that, with Estrella on the other side of the Goddess-damned castle when all I want is to never let her out of my line of sight again. But the idea that after this, we're just going to be… happy? Forever? In all my best versions of the future, now and before Father died, I never imagined that.

King Andri harrumphs. "Your life to play games with."

Prince Hollis glances at me coldly. The first-prize medal for the archery tourney gleams proudly on his chest. He earned it, sinking three arrows into the bull's eye without breaking a sweat. But he barely talked to me the whole time, which everyone else in the castle has been tripping over themselves to do since they arrived. And it's not like he doesn't talk. I've seen him laughing with Lady Eva, chatting with other Snowcrest nobles. One night, I even found him, Candace, and Lady Eva walking the grounds together, so it's not just that he talks to Snowcrest people. I don't fucking get it.

"Anwen's and Luna Estrella's," Kieran corrects. "Let's start with the basic arrangements. You're going to get married in our temple." He gestures through the window where I can just see the spire of the temple poking above the rest of the castle. "Ayia's conducting the ceremony. You'll come in first, then Estrella. Floyd seems to want this marriage to happen, so there's no reason to worry about either of you being targeted. And he hasn't been seen since his initial disappearance."

I nod. I was pretty sure we already agreed on all of this.

"Three problems there, yes?" King Andri says. "Your temple is nearly tall enough to scrape the sky."

"In honor of the Goddess, we reach part of the way," Kieran says tightly.

I glance at him. A muscle twitches in his jaw. He's pissed. What the hell happened between him and King Andri while I was gone?

King Andri inclines his head. "Its height creates shadows a killer could hide in, and both families intend to stand at the front. Clearly visible from any of the windows on the spire."

"So we melted them shut," Kieran says. "No magic, just good, old-fashioned blacksmithing."

"What if someone tries to shoot through the glass?" I ask. "Or punch through it and then shoot?"

"That's what I said." Kieran looks at King Andri. "So we've also added a silver mesh over the windows themselves. An assassin would have to break the window, pull the glass out, then figure out how to cut through the silver without hurting themselves. We also meshed a couple of other relevant windows around the castle, just in case."

"This creates time." King Andri nods. "Any who are in danger can hide."

I grin, picturing my wedding being interrupted by the shittiest assassination attempt ever. If I were Floyd, after that, I'd leave the kingdom. Fuck revenge, I couldn't show my face again.

"Great, but I don't need to know that for it to work. There's other stuff, right?"

"My son commands the domestic army from which we gathered our guard." King Andri looks at him.

Hollis sighs. "We've added our guard to yours. Everywhere."

I nod.

He just stares at me with those eyes. They're almost too green. It makes him hard to read. That furrow in his brow could be boredom or irritation or a headache, but I can't look at his eyes long enough to tell which.

"Anything else?" I ask.

"What more do you need? If you see someone in Snowcrest green and gray, don't shoot."

I actually almost raise my eyebrows. Who the fuck does he think he is? He's in my fucking castle. I'm about to become Alpha King of Sundrop Gem. Hell, it's my fucking wedding day!

'Now, you see what I've been dealing with,' Kieran says.

'Any clue why?'

'They're not working with Floyd, if that's what you're asking.'

King Andri clears his throat loudly. "In Snowcrest Canyon, it is rude to have a private conversation in public."

"Apologies." Kieran dips his head, but I catch the scowl he's hiding. "Prince Anwen was curious about how Prince Hollis came to hold such a position of power."

I smile as surprise washes through me. Kieran hasn't lied—that I've noticed—basically since he took over from Father. But for this, he bends the rules.

Maybe he felt the same thing I did about crushing Floyd at that breakfast. Like there's times and places for the things Father taught us. And if he thinks it, fuck, maybe it's actually true.

"My father trusts me." Hollis smirks at me.

A current of irritation swallows anything else I'm feeling. He doesn't need to finish the thought—clearly, Father didn't trust me.

"It's actually too big of a job for one person in Dun's Crossing," I say. "We have four people to manage our at-home troops."

Hollis' smirk dies. Good.

"So, guards, mesh, what's the third thing?" I ask brightly.

"Your temple sits the crowd away from the altar. This is good. But the gap is not large enough." King Andri steeples his fingers. "It is nearly perfect for a wolf to jump in a single bound."

"That's actually how we measured it." I smirk at Hollis. "Is it too long for you?"

'Watch it,' Kieran warns.

I ignore the mind-link. He deserves it.

King Andri holds up a hand before Hollis can reply. "Snowcrest Canyon surrounds a series of caves, carved by a falling star, which have power the likes of which we cannot dream. We do not control this power—it is too old, too faded, too strange. But there was once a group who could, and they left behind their texts. Some of their rituals can be recreated on the eve of the full moon."

"Holy shit," I mutter. "Wordsworth was useful?"

Kieran covers a laugh with a cough. The only reason he hasn't kicked the old magician out is because Wordsworth has nowhere else to go, and Raven feels bad."

Hollis snorts. "Your man was a waste of time."

"That sounds more like him." I try turning my smile on Hollis. Maybe, if we can actually fucking agree on something, he'll soften up.

No dice. He looks back at me blandly.

"Daya has warded your temple until the full moon fades from the sky," King Andri says. "While inside, none can shift."

I blink. "None?"

"None." His voice is like a cell door slamming shut.

"This is what I needed you to know about," Kieran says. "If shit breaks bad, we're going to have to fight as humans."

I suck in a deep breath. Father made sure I could fight no matter what, but I massively prefer claws and teeth to my daggers. I'm faster as a wolf, tougher.

"What happens if you try to shift?"

King Andri shakes his head.

Shit.

"Someone has to warn Estrella," I say. "And everyone else."

"That's the problem." Kieran frowns. "The ward is only effective if Floyd doesn't know about it. King Isai's murder proves it's not hard to kill someone in human form, just harder."

"Telling anyone is telling everyone." King Andri crosses his arms.

Hollis nods. "There's a reason Lady Eva was able to cover your tracks. Gossip is the beating heart of this place."

"And here I thought your promise was just good at what she did." I smile tightly.

"Like I've been saying"—Kieran shoots me a look—"if that were true, the secret would already be out. I knew the whole time, and now so does Anwen."

"I'm telling Estrella." I stare down my nose. "Try and fucking stop me."

Hollis's lips flatten into a thin line.

King Andri grunts. "As I've told my son, the bond between man and wife is different. You ought to tell her. But no one else."

Something flashes across Hollis's face too fast for me to make sense of.

"All right, that sounds like a plan." I bow to them and smile. "If you don't mind, I actually have to go get ready for my wedding."

King Andri stands and clasps my hand in one of his massive ones. "May the Goddess smile upon you both for the rest of your lives."

I shake his hand once, firmly. He's still huge, even now that I'm an adult, but there's something in his grizzled old face. Fuck Hollis. King Andri seems intense, judgmental, and fucking stubborn, but ultimately like a good man.

Which is probably why Kieran didn't kill both of them when we left him alone with them.

King Andri releases me. I nod to Hollis—he returns it coldly—and leave. Every inch of me screams to go to the dressing room Raven set up for Estrella and all the court ladies. I rub the tattoo on my pinkie. A couple more hours, and then it will be real.

I square my shoulders and head to my bedroom.

53
IF YOU WANT SOMETHING DONE RIGHT

"What more is there to do, truly?" I ask. "I am dressed, my hair is done, my shoes are chosen."

"Jewelry!" Candace lifts a glittering box with a grin. The sleeves of her pure-white dress still droop so low they nearly drag on the floor.

"There's nothing to decide." I slump in the chair in front of the mirror. "I am going to wear my mother's lucky earrings and the bracelet Queen Raven gave me a few days ago."

Tess rubs my shoulder. "No necklaces? And you don't have to wear only one bracelet."

I glance at the armful of bangles she added during the brief break in fluttering over me they took to put on their dresses. "Is that so?"

She laughs and rattles them on her bare arm. Despite the weather here, she wears the traditional simple, sleeveless white robe from home. "I understand you chose all three of us to be your moon maids, but surely, I need something to make me stand out. The other two are new!"

Candace nods seriously. "Yeah, I'm honored, but Tess has seniority."

"Then shouldn't I get something above Candace?" Nessa fluffs the elaborate skirt of her white dress, nearly twice the circumference of her natural waist. "I've got, what, a month on her?"

My stomach twists. "A month in which you lied to me and worked with your father to assassinate mine."

The mood in the room dies a slow, painful death.

"I said I was sorry," Nessa mumbles.

"She still has the right to be upset," Candace says immediately.

"I would be." Tess winces. She hates conflict.

"Candace is just looking for a chance to be upset," Nessa spits. "You—"

I stand. "This is my wedding"—as much as any wedding of mine could ever be—"and I have chosen each of you because you are important to me. Tess, you are my oldest and best friend, but you're also the woman who sprinted away from her mate as soon as you woke up after the Haze to celebrate with me." I smile. "I almost didn't even mind that I hadn't found someone."

Tess bumps me with her hip. "You most certainly did. But I couldn't have done anything else. There's no part of my life I won't share with you."

Tears sting my eyes.

"Candace, I may not know you as well as I'd like yet, but you are hard at work on fixing that. I want you by my side because of how easily you cut through the formalities and open yourself to people. My father had the same skill." I blink quickly to catch my tears. "I would like to develop it someday."

She grins. "I'd love to help."

"And Nessa—" I look at her.

Her gaze burns into mine, begging me to say something that will change Candace's mind. Maybe change everyone's mind.

"When I arrived here and found myself alone, you promised I didn't have to be." I take a deep breath as the truth spills from my lips. "While I bind myself to this place permanently, I want to remember that promise. No matter what secret intent it held at the time."

Nessa raises her eyebrows. "Okay."

I look at each of the three of them in turn. "Promise me, at least for today, that you will see these things in each other. We are ending a centuries-old feud. I wouldn't like to start another."

"I can do that," Tess says slowly.

Candace nods. "Me too."

"Yeah, of course." Nessa shrugs.

"Good." I sit back down. "Now, if someone really believes I should wear a necklace, make your arguments."

"Yes!" Candace grabs the jewelry box again.

Someone knocks on the door. Tess wrinkles her nose, shoots the jewelry a longing look, then walks over to open it.

"Sorry," a voice I don't recognize says, "but I was sent here for Tesandra Solis, and I don't actually know what she looks like."

"She looks like me," Tess replies. "What do you need?"

Tentatively, Candace shares the jewelry box with Nessa. Good.

"Dowager Suniva and Prince Castor sent one of their guards back with a message." Paper crinkles.

A few beats of silence pass. Candace holds up a necklace, and Nessa shakes her head.

Tess sighs. "All right. Give me a moment."

She steps back into the room. I catch a glimpse of a man in green and gray at the door. Snowcrest Canyon?

"Your mother and Castor forgot the ritual candle," Tess says.

Without it, they cannot complete the final blessing. I would have to marry without full permission from the Moon Goddess.

"I can ask someone else?" she says uncertainly.

I shake my head. "I don't trust anyone else. Go."

She leaves with the guard. Nessa and Candace join me at the dressing table.

"I like the silver with your eyes," Candace says. "Nessa thinks something simple is just going to disappear in your gown. So what do you think about these?"

She offers three necklaces. Unsubtly, Nessa gestures to the leftmost one, with a nearly fist-sized red pendant. It would completely suit her and look terrible with my dress. Perhaps I'll choose it anyway. The longer I wear the dress, the less I like it.

I point to the middle necklace, a silver chain with a smaller, blue stone pendant. "That one. If I must."

"Fantastic." Candace grins as she plucks it out.

Another knock on the door. I frown. Candace hands me the necklace and goes to answer it.

A woman's voice, almost familiar. "I thought we were going to—"

"Oh! Right." Candace glances over her shoulder. "Do you need me, or can I steal half an hour?"

I chuckle. "I cannot say no after complimenting you like I did."

"I've got this," Nessa says.

Candace whisks out the door.

Nessa lifts my hair and places the necklace around my neck. "You're so lucky. This is the part I was looking forward to the most for my wedding."

I hold the chain so she can fasten it. "Which?"

"The getting ready part." Her smile is soft in the mirror. "Everyone around, laughing, talking, helping."

"I suppose yours would have been a bit less overwhelming."

"Barely." The clasp clicks into place. "Kieran was crown prince, and the first of the Solbergs to mate. Father was talking to King Gavin about inviting people from all over."

"I do not believe you missed much, in that regard." I smooth my hair down. "This morning was awful. Just an endless stream of strangers who hold unknown amounts of power."

"All trying to impress you." She leans against the table. "It's hard not to enjoy being the center of attention like that a little."

The dull lack of excitement in my chest throbs. "Not for me."

"No?" She shakes her head. "I can't imagine that. I still have dreams about my wedding."

"To Kieran?"

"Sometimes." Her smile is bittersweet. "We'd set a date, you know?

Bright just finished making my dress, and it wasn't perfect, but it was mine. I loved it."

"You can love it still," I say. "A dress is a dress, and I am certain you'll find your mate soon."

She laughs sharply. "I don't know if I could wear it for someone else."

"I'm sorry." I offer her a comforting smile. "If your time comes, and you discover you cannot, I will bring my personal dressmaker to you wherever you are."

"You really are sweet." She looks at me for a long moment then shakes her head. "But I don't have your hope."

I frown.

"I don't think there is someone else." Her eyes grow bright with unshed tears. "Or, if there is, that they'll want anything to do with me. I mean, you said it yourself, right? There's no one who's more willing to make friends than Candace, and even she can't stand me."

The secret Candace confessed to me burns my lips. But I won't tell someone else's story.

"The Goddess chooses people She knows will love each other. Nothing else matters."

"See? Lucky." Nessa shoves off the desk and starts pacing. "I guess you're going to remind me what happened with you and Anwen now, right? How you fought for a while, but it all worked out?"

Goose bumps pimple my skin. Nessa isn't just upset, wishing for a different path in life. There's no mistaking the tension in her stance, the jaggedness of her movements. She is furious.

I stand. "I—"

"No, sorry, you're too *smart* for that." She waves my words away sarcastically.

Twenty paces to the door. Ten to the window on my left, but we're at least thirty feet off the ground. Even if I shifted the drop might still kill me.

"Did your father have some words of wisdom you think I should know instead?"

Hot anger sears through me.

Father would rather let someone insult him than risk my life.

I turn for the door.

The temperature in the room drops. Ice climbs out of the stones around my feet, encircles my ankles, and freezes me there. I try to yank them out, but the frost is already too thick. I can't move.

But she was foolish enough to use ice.

Nessa laughs cruelly. "When I realized Anwen suspected something, I thought the jig was up. But Father was right. You fell for every word, even after I *told* you I lied."

I twist back to her. She grabs the necklace she liked best, the red pendant, and fastens it around her own neck like I'm not even here.

The moment of distraction should be enough. I reach for the weak sparks at the center of my chest, where the heat magic came from.

There is nothing there.

I haven't tried using it since I understood my healing. I don't even know if it's still there.

Nessa glances at me. "I'm kind of disappointed. I thought you were going to figure it out a couple times. Father said I'd get to kill you if you did."

Tess! I scream. My heart hammers against my ribcage. Mother and Castor are out of range of the mind-link, but Tess just left. *Come back!*

Complete and utter silence greets me.

Fuck.

Nessa pulls a pair of gloves out of a drawer in my dressing table then saunters over to the nearest window while pulling them on. "Nothing to say for yourself? You haven't shut up since you got here."

"You are making a mistake," I say. "You can still change your mind."

"After the only good thing you could say about me was that you really liked a lie I told?" She scoffs. "Yeah, right."

She unhooks a strange metal mesh over the window and opens the pane. Floyd leaps inside instantly, a wickedly sharp knife in his hand. My stomach plummets.

"Finally," he says. "I was getting tired of holding onto the fucking roof."

"Be quick. Somebody else pulled Candace away before Wil could, and she said she'd be back in half an hour." Nessa kisses him on the cheek, then leaves.

Metal groans. I glance over my shoulder and see shards of ice jutting through the lock and around the outside of the door. I am frozen in with him.

Floyd lifts the blade. "It's like I told Nessa. If you want something done right, you have to do it yourself."

5 4

MELTDOWN

ESTRELLA

MY HEART THUNDERS AGAINST MY RIBCAGE. MY PULSE ROARS. MOTHER, Castor, Tess—all gone. And with the wedding in an hour, I cannot yet mind-link to Anwen. I am alone.

With the man who murdered my father.

An oil-slick smile splits Floyd's face as he circles me. The dagger in his hand shines. I lift my chin, and fear burns into rage. Floyd does not check his work when he's confident. I merely need to buy myself enough time to identify what he's missed.

"You pretended to be our ally," I say.

"Not true." He shakes his head slowly. "I would've been your ally. Once you realized the Solberg snake for what it is."

"You *lied*." The word whips out from between my teeth.

My wolf screams, and I feel the beginning of a shift start to take me. But there's a pressure on my skin. Like a net, or the change in the air before a storm. I do not know what protections King Kieran laid upon the castle. With all the willpower I have left, I force the shift down. I will not risk this chance to end Floyd Winters.

"That's politics." His smile grows. "Or did your father not teach you that?"

Fury bubbles through my veins. Were we at home—had Bright ceased fighting me for a single moment—I would have the ritual dagger Yana used during my coronation on my belt. Dun's Crossing traditionally prefers their women useless. I am unarmed.

"Do not speak to me of him with his blood on your hands."

Floyd studies his palms mockingly. "I don't see it. Yours, though...."

"Was one Sollabella life insufficient?" I ask. "How many leaders will you slaughter in your quest for petty revenge?"

He chuckles. "Don't oversell yourself, Luna."

"What could that possibly mean, coming from an envoy who has not held a valuable position at his home court in years?" I ask.

He scowls and lunges, blade a hairsbreadth from the tip of my nose. "Nessa said you were fucking uppity, too."

I breathe in slowly. There is a smell, but I cannot think about that. I cannot flinch. Not in front of this man. His gaze darts over my face, clearly watching for signs of fear. He is savoring this, deep in the pit of his sick heart. I will starve him.

"Would you like to know what else Nessa said?" I grit out. "I wonder how much of the show she put on for us rings true."

His jaw works. "What do you mean?"

A crack in his armor. I should press my advantage, use those little tricks and tactics that come so easily to Anwen. None of them spring to my tongue, staring into the eyes of this murderer.

"She said my father's death was incidental." Fire burns in my veins. Why will it not burn on my fingertips where I need it? "That my family is nothing more than pawns in your game against King Kieran."

Floyd pulls the dagger away, throws his head back, and laughs, his greasy hair catching the light. "Of course, you'd take that personally."

A lance of hurt spears through my chest. Father's life was a card Floyd played. Something he took as easily as breathing. As if it never mattered at all.

Not as long as I have a say.

"He loved going out on the canoe, even though it made the rest of us sick," I murmur.

"What?" Floyd furrows his brow.

"His favorite fruit was a particular type of grape that only grows in Thunderpeak, so Mother would have a bushel delivered in secret for his birthday every year." My voice grows louder. Tears sting my eyes. "Wordplay made him laugh like nothing else, and he loved to laugh."

Floyd opens and closes his mouth a few times. "I—you're joking, right? You think fun facts about your father are going to change anything now?"

"Contrary to what you seem to think, I'm no fool," I snarl. "But that doesn't mean you shouldn't feel what you've done. You killed a living, breathing man with likes and loves and a family."

"King Isai was incidental." Floyd leans in close enough that I can smell the sour liquor on his breath. "But you? You're on purpose, you little bitch."

I haul back and snap at him. My teeth scrape his grizzled cheek before he dodges out of the way. I spit his taste onto the floor, and the cold bites into my ankles.

The cold. If it hurts enough, Anwen will feel me. He'll know. And he'll free me from this Goddess-damned ice so I can tear Floyd Winters limb from limb, as he deserves. That's what Floyd missed.

I grind the tender flesh of my ankles against the jagged edge of my prison.

"You're barely fucking civilized!" Floyd yells. "I'm doing the world a favor, putting you down like a fucking dog."

He advances on me with the dagger out, and my heart leaps into my throat. Rage will not save me. Fury, revenge—they only lead to standing in front of a woman who wanted nothing more than to save her father's life with a dagger.

Punishment is not justice. Restoration is. I cannot restore Father— I cannot even restore the months Floyd took from us with his lies— but I can make sure I am around to see the world restored. I will not let Floyd turn me into a mirror of himself.

Whatever it takes. Even finding a way to fit Anwen's words into my mouth.

"What was Nessa wearing before she left?" I blurt.

Floyd slows. "You can't stop me."

The ice starts to shred my ankles. And I've got a plan.

"Indulge me. A last wish." I swallow down a smile. "What was she wearing?"

He shakes his head. "Some fucking dress. What does that have to do with anything?"

"What does she do in her spare time?" Fighting the smile is getting harder and harder. "What is she looking forward to, after this?"

"I—who fucking cares?" He waves the knife wildly.

"Nessa does." Pain skitters along my skin. Anwen has to feel it soon.

"What are you talking about?" Floyd shouts.

"My father had a man in his court named Moses. A good, loyal man. Until the day someone walked up to him and suggested that he might be Alpha." My grin slips free, wide and wild. "Moses tried to kill Father the next day. He didn't get further than the doors, but all the same, he tried. Isn't it strange how sometime, someone only needs an idea suggested for it to take root and flourish?" I lean forward. "Who suggested that Nessa pretend to betray you to us after all?"

Floyd's eyes go wide. His pale skin turns a sickening, mottled red.

"Shut up!"

He slashes wildly with the dagger, and time slows. Even with my limited training, I can see the instability in his stance, his weak grip on the blade. My next move should be simple—duck and roll to the right, toward the smaller dressing room, where I could at least gain a modicum of cover. Father taught me most of all how to avoid an incoming strike, how to disarm opponents and purchase enough time to flee.

None of my trainers ever instructed me on how to dodge with both my feet frozen to the floor.

The dagger connects. A bright line of pain sears from my sternum to the bottom of my ribcage. My vision swims, and I crumple to the floor. The jagged ice at my ankles barely pulls my notice.

Floyd cackles. "You want to talk about your father so Goddess-damned bad? Enjoy talking to him when you meet him in the sky."

From a weapon that small, the cut is long but shallow.

"You are"—my breath rattles up my throat—"a fucking fool."

I reach for the power I know is there, the scrap of the Goddess hiding behind my breastbone, waiting for the chance to heal. My body heats as it leaps to my call. I begin to glow, brighter and brighter. With one palm on the slash across my chest and the other on the patch of ice, I close my eyes and—

"Ah!" The pain doubles over itself, deepens. My stomach lurches. The burn turns from fire to something corrosive, eating into my skin.

That smell. Stronger, now, under the stink of my own blood filling the room. Herbal and sickening.

"Come on now." Floyd leers down at me. "Did you think I wouldn't come prepared?"

The blade is coated with wolfsbane.

Ice turns to water around my feet, but the gash merely bubbles black and red. My vision starts to go gray at the edges. With the poison coursing through my veins, with blood pouring over my wedding gown once again and taking my life force with it, I cannot heal myself. Not fast enough.

Anwen, I call weakly, as though he can hear me. *I need—*

55

ONE HEART

Anwen

I pluck at the neck of my wedding clothes and look at myself in the mirror.

"You look like shit," Baz says from the bed behind me. Despite Estrella's efforts, he's still healing.

"Thanks." He's right, though. Sundrop's bright colors just kind of make me look sick. And the damned thing is so starched, it crunches every time I try to move my arms. I don't know what I pictured wearing to my wedding, but—

"Fuck!" Heartrending pain rips through my chest. I grab the mirror for support and still almost keel over.

Baz pushes himself up and wobbles closer. "What?"

I claw at my shirt, but I already fucking know. It feels like something is eating me from the inside out, but I'm going to be uninjured.

Someone is trying to kill Estrella.

I roar as another wave of agony washes through me.

"Get—someone. Anyone," I spit.

"What's hap—"

I don't stick around to hear the end of his sentence.

The shift takes me mid-stride away from the mirror. I don't give a shit that the castle hallways are too small, that everyone in the whole Goddess-damned world will be walking through them, trying to get to the ceremony. Someone is trying to kill my mate, and nothing else matters. I charge through my own door, shattering it off its hinges without a second thought.

People scream as I run down the hall. Baz says something through the mind-link. I put my nose to the air.

There. Cooked sugar and sweetgrass. Above me and east.

Every step burns through my limbs. My stride wobbles. I try to hold onto the old story, but it's too fucking long. Spots dance across my vision. Estrella. The pain. Estrella. The pain.

I try to take a corner too fast, and my paws skid. My shoulder slams into the wall, and my howl sounds like a human scream. This is fucking torture. I need something.

The holy woman from Sundrop's voice rings through my mind. *One heart beating in two chests.*

One heart. Two chests. It's simple. Clear. And just rhythmic enough to hold onto.

I scramble to my feet and pound through the halls of the castle toward the other half of my heart.

Her smell grows stronger as I round onto the right hallway, but now it's mingled with blood. And this hall is completely empty, of course. I should've fucking known when Kieran said she was getting dressed in a tower away from everything and everyone else.

The door where her scent is strongest looks like any other for a second. Then, I see the fucking ice coating the lock and handle. If I gave a shit about things like sneaking in or using my hands or protecting a single fucking inch of the castle over Estrella, that might matter. But Floyd has underestimated me for the last fucking time.

I back up a few steps and charge. The bastard's not smart enough to have reinforced the door. It shatters away, and the impact crashes through me with a burst of pain that knocks me right off my fucking feet. I tumble into the room.

Floyd gapes. "How—"

I scramble to my paws and search for Estrella. My stomach drops.

Blood gushes from her chest. Thin, black veins spider out from the injury.

He fucking poisoned her.

I brace to throw myself at Floyd, but Estrella's eyes flutter open, and I wrench to her side.

"Right about… Nessa…." she says weakly. "Love… you."

No.

Floyd laughs and drops his dagger. "This is perfect. I'll call the Snowcrest guard so everyone can see who really killed Luna Estrella." His gaze goes hazy with the mind-link.

Instinct swallows me whole. There's no training in my lunge or snapping teeth. Just pure, primal fury at the motherfucker who dared to touch my mate.

Floyd dodges back and collides with a dressing table that crashes onto the floor. The mirror shatters. I charge him again, barely noticing the glass shards slicing my paws.

"Fucking animals." Floyd scrabbles along the floor for the dagger he dropped. "All of you Solbergs. Fight like a man, or give up all your fucking castles and pretending."

The idea I would give a shit what Floyd fucking Winters thinks of me is laughable. I didn't give a shit when I thought he was just some ass-kisser. I swipe out and catch his cheek with my claws. He dives for the dagger.

The reek of his blood spurs that animal rage higher. I am on the fucking hunt, and my prey is already injured.

Behind me, Estrella sucks in a breath. Fabric rustles. Every instinct screams to keep my eyes on Floyd—

I glance back at her. She is pushing into a sitting position. The black veins climbing up her throat threaten to choke me, but she nods. Sways, nearly falls, but fucking nods and picks a piece of glass up off the floor.

Hope courses through me, and her vision clears a little more.

One heart, two chests. Why the fuck would that only allow us to share pain?

"Mates only make you weak. Why do you think I left mine at home?"

I whip back to Floyd as he brandishes the dagger and grins like he's got the upper hand. Moron. I swing between him and Estrella to block his view of her and feint for his throat. An animal like me should always go for the killing blow. When he brings his arm up to block, I sink my teeth into my real target and bite down.

Bone crunches. Blood spills over my tongue. Floyd screams.

I spit his arm, still holding the dagger, onto the mirror shards between us.

"Fine," Floyd snarls.

He explodes into his own black and gray wolf. A few other tables crunch under his paws. There's barely enough room for one wolf here, much less two. And keeping him away from Estrella is nearly impossible. I can't give him a fucking second try.

I barrel into him, heedless of the open window behind us. I don't think we're small enough to fit through it anymore.

We slam into the wall and wrestle for dominance. He scrapes his claws along my back leg, but that doesn't even come close to hurting as much as the wolfsbane in my chest. I almost get my teeth around his throat, but he knocks me away with a paw and rolls to gain the upper hand.

Cold wind gusts through my fur. We're so fucking close to the window. Distantly, behind the fury pounding through my veins, I'm aware there's a plan there somewhere. A plan I'd come up with on another day. Today, I rake my claws along his spine and open my mouth to taste the blood still dripping from his face.

Floyd yelps and wriggles to escape my grasp. At the worst fucking time, the agony in my chest intensifies, and I lose him. He whirls around and pants something like a laugh.

He saw her.

I scramble to my feet, but I'm so fucking slow. She wobbles in the center of the room. The black veins cup her cheek. It's impossible to believe I was ever proud of my speed. Floyd leaps for her, mouth open, claws outstretched and shining with my blood.

She pulls out the shard of mirror and jams it into his open jaw.

He tries to snap his mouth shut fast enough to catch her wrist, but the glass holds for a second. Just long enough for her to move, for me to get my fucking paws underneath me. I sink my teeth into his flank. He tries to make a sound but only manages to spatter blood and pieces of glass on Estrella. I yank him back, and he slides, landing in a pile at my feet.

There's no time to save the kill for Estrella or even offer it to her. I believe he called the guard, and that means the clock is ticking. As soon as he's within range, I catch his throat between my jaws.

But I bite slowly. Savor the sour taste of his blood. I want undeniable fucking proof that Floyd is dead, that I've destroyed the threat to my mate, her family, our life together. A sandpapery whimper escapes his throat the second before he goes limp.

All his planning, all his smooth fucking talking, and Floyd Winters died as a wolf who couldn't even howl.

I drop his body to the floor and shift smoothly. My wedding clothes are a bunch of scraps, somewhere on the other side of the castle. Estrella's are covered in blood. The wedding's in an hour, and I can't bring myself to give a single fuck about any of that. All that matters right now is me and my mate, celebrating the victory we've fought so Goddess-damned hard for. I turn to Estrella.

Just in time to watch the black veins creep up to her eye. They flutter closed, and she topples, boneless, to the floor.

56

ANYONE

ANWEN

SOMEONE SCREAMS. I THINK IT MIGHT BE ME.

I slide across the glass-covered floor to Estrella's side and wrap my arms around her. My heart hammers.

"No, no, no," I mumble. "You can't—not after—*please.*" My voice breaks on the last word.

Her body is still warm. That has to mean something. It fucking has to. Agony rumbles through me, just a promise of what's to come if—

There are other people in this castle. Healers. Apothecaries. I need someone–anyone with a fucking power or a wish or a prayer of helping. I struggle to my feet with Estrella in my arms.

Her head lolls back, and it damn near kills me. My feet skid across glass and blood as I begin running out of the room as fast as I can under her weight and the staggering pain.

Father's voice echoes in the back of my mind. *Ask for help and admit your weak points.*

Goddess above, why did I want his respect so badly? Why did that make any sense to me? My mate is bleeding out in my arms. Weakness, future attacks—none of that fucking matters unless I can face it with her.

'*Help!* 'I scream through mind-link to anyone within range. '*Luna Estrella was attacked. We need help, and we need it fucking now.*'

'*Where are you?*' Jase demands.

'*East tower, third floor,*' I bark to everybody in range. '*Running down.*'

Let them all know. If Floyd has another fucking assassin, if he managed to turn anybody from Dun's Crossing, let them come. I'd like to see any wolf under the fucking moon take me on right now.

Holy shit, Candace says over mind-link. '*What—I'm so sorry, I'm just downstairs. I thought she would be fine.*'

I fix Estrella's head so it's not bouncing as we run. Faint cosmetics kiss her features—her lashes are darker, her mouth redder. Her hair is an artwork of braids, now frizzy. I didn't even think to look at the fucking dress. My bride. My stomach lurches. At least she's not frowning anymore. Her perpetually furrowed brow is smooth for once. Her pain still ripples through me, but maybe she's not feeling it.

Small fucking miracles.

'*What happened?* Baz asks. *I'm on my way, just fucking slow.*'

'*Floyd,*' I snarl. '*Wolfsbane.*'

That, too, goes to everyone. I need healers, not killers. I already did all the killing we need. Estrella takes small, weak breaths. My skin goes cold when she inhales, burns when too long passes between one and the next.

'*I can help,*' Raven says. '*Trust me and come to the greenhouse. But it'll only work if you move fast.*'

My heart skips a beat. Three beats. Twelve. Trust Raven.

Estrella makes a small noise, and I can't remember why that was even a fucking decision. I wheel for Mother's—Raven's–greenhouse.

The castle spreads out before me like a map in my mind. Every hidden passage, every shortcut ever drilled into these walls. I can do this. One last trip through the castle I've learned so well.

'*Okay.*'

I plunge through tapestries, slam hidden buttons, shoulder open secret doors. Estrella's blood leaks over my fingers. My own smears on the floor as I run. Staff and delegates alike scatter out of our way on the rare occasions we actually use main hallways. Through the mind-link, I hear the running updates of our location—*north tower, second floor, main castle, private wing.* Clanking, armored footsteps chase us, but I'm not going to slow down for fucking anything. I will not let hesitation take my future from me.

We burst into the greenhouse. Raven and Kieran both look up from a bench along one wall. Something puffs smoke behind them.

Wordlessly, Kieran sweeps potted plants onto the floor to clear another table for Estrella's body. Raven doesn't complain as they shatter. I run the last few steps and lay Estrella on the filthy table.

Her face is nearly covered with the veins now. I twist away and throw up on the floor as pain and fear wrack me.

Kieran drapes his royal robe around my bare body. I ignore it and turn to Raven.

"What do you have?"

"A cure." She lifts a bubbling vial of burgundy liquid off a small flame with a pair of tongs. "I hope."

"You hope?" Anger tinges my voice. I could've gone somewhere else. If this is her last fucking revenge for the way I treated her, I'll—

"I've only tested it on plants so far." She nudges me out of the way, completely unafraid.

Like she should be. Fuck. If Estrella is already gone somehow, already looking down on me, and she sees me abandoning all the progress I've made the second she's not watching, she's going to find a way to become a ghost just to kick my ass.

I start pacing. Raven takes a dropper of the liquid, winces slightly, and leans over Estrella. My heart damn near pounds out of my chest as I lose line of sight. I don't want to ask if I got here in time. I can't.

"Floyd's dead upstairs," I spit. "And he called the Snowcrest guard, so they're going to find him first."

Kieran nods. "Don't worry about that right now."

More smoke, or steam, or *something* gasps up from behind Raven's body. Estrella moans softly.

My laugh scrapes out of my throat. "Done. What about Nessa? She was in on the whole fucking thing, and she's missing."

"I'll have people look for her." He shakes his head grimly. "And I suspect King Andri will be more than willing to help."

My eyes burn. Everything burns.

"Her family is in the woods," Kieran says. "For some final ritual. I've already sent people to get them."

"We played right into his fucking hands," I mutter. "No one was with her when I found her. Where did they all fucking go?"

He shrugs. I force myself to take a deep breath instead of screaming at him. That can't be the first thing Estrella wakes up to. But, fuck, I wish the pacing was helping. I wish I could shift without destroying everything in here—and if this works, I can't do that to Raven.

Maybe I can't do it regardless.

"For the last bit, she was supposed to be with just her moon maids," Raven says carefully. "Candace, Tess—and Nessa."

Candace's apology snaps into focus. She let this fucking happen.

Estrella moans again. Raven hisses. I clench every muscle in my body to keep from shifting.

"Tess is in the woods too?" I manage. A stupid, shitty distraction.

Kieran frowns. "I don't know."

My stomach swoops. "I can't let her find out her best friend is dead. I have to—"

Kieran grabs my shoulders, halts my pacing. "You have to stay here and shut up for a fucking second. She can't wake up without you, right?"

Something in my chest splinters. She can't. She might not be able to wake up with me out of my fucking mind either. Hope was the thing that strengthened her upstairs. Hope, and believing I was going to win.

Goddess above, how do I believe that now?

I sit on the ground between mounds of dirt and pieces of broken pots. No more pacing. No more shifting away. Hurt, fear, and rage crash over me. Kieran sits next to me.

"She's not going to die." The words echo hollowly off the glass walls.

"I agree." Kieran smiles comfortingly. "My wife can do anything she puts her mind to."

Raven's answering laugh is strained.

It's impossible that Kieran and Raven got together. Even more impossible that they're happy. But here they are. Because the Goddess said so.

For the first time in a long time, I pray.

I've never been much for religion. We don't have magic here, and the Goddess never really seemed like someone who gave too much of a shit. All the people who claimed to "hear" Her were quacks or fuck-ups like Wordsworth. And then Estrella. She believes wholeheartedly. She almost makes it make sense. The Goddess isn't an almighty bastard in the sky I can blame when shit goes wrong. She's like... well, like what I've heard a parent's supposed to be like. She lets us make our own mistakes, but She guides us. She wants us to be happy.

I don't know all the words to make this reach you, I think. *But I know I need her to be happy. There isn't a me without her. Not anymore. So just... please.*

Silence follows. But for Estrella's sake, in Estrella's name, I put everything I am into believing I reached Her. Believing She gives a fuck. Believing this isn't all there is for us.

Believing Estrella's going to wake up any second now, look at me, and ask why I'm crying.

Because, if all that's not true, I'm going to tear Snowcrest Canyon apart, brick by fucking brick, and I'd like to see the Goddess Herself try to stop me.

5 7

THE WEDDING IS ALREADY PLANNED

I FLOAT FOR A LONG TIME IN DARKNESS. NOT EXACTLY HERE OR ABSENT. Not exactly comfortable or in pain. Not very much at all.

Then, my whole body flames back to screaming, torturous life at once. I am the heart of an inferno, consuming everything that I am to produce the flame. A hoarse, ragged scream tears from my throat. I lurch forward, trying to curl in on myself.

Something restrains me. I lash out, swinging wildly, and someone catches my hand.

"…strella," someone says. "Estrella, it's me. Anwen."

I blink. Tears slip down my cheeks instead of collecting in my eyes, and a few shafts of green-tinted light make it into my mind.

Leaning over me, blood smeared on his cheek, is a blond man. My shoulder pulses. No, not just any blond man. Pieces of myself slide together underneath the pain. He is Anwen. My mate.

I burble something meaningless.

"Hi." He sits, rests his chin on the edge of the painfully uncomfortable bed I seem to be lying on. "I love you."

I nod, which sends bolts of agony through my skull.

"Don't move." He glances off to the side. "This cure was made for a plant time scale."

Cure. Plants. I… know something connected to those. Somewhere.

Anwen takes my hand, and it feels like running ice over a burn. Where he touches me, I am something other than pain. It's enough to allow me to notice the silver cloak around his shoulders and his bare chest underneath. What is he wearing?

The last thing I remember is calling for him. Between now and then, there are only flashes. Something shining. Something gray. Pain, endless pain.

And the healing. I can heal. If I've survived, which I seem to have because death isn't intended to hurt this much, then I should be able to heal myself. I pull my hand from Anwen's with a hiss and start to reach for the power.

"Don't—" a woman says.

Anwen grabs my wrist, clearly trying to be gentle, so I bite down on the scream of pain.

"You can't yet." He glances over his shoulder. "Like I said, it's slow. You're still tapped."

Tapped? I tap my fingers on the back of his hand, and he smiles.

"Spent. Fucking exhausted, if you prefer." He kisses my forehead. "Raven says the wolfsbane will leave your body over the next couple of days. After that, patch yourself up whenever you want."

Queen Raven, whom I spoke to about healing Escuro earlier—today? I open my mouth to ask how long it has been, but the words won't come.

"Just relax." He kisses me again. "Please. I can only sprint through the castle so many times."

I glance around the room, expecting the small chamber Floyd climbed into. Instead, plants and glass greet me. I'm somewhere I've never seen before. Panic trickles through my veins. Then, I meet Anwen's eyes. He looks just as tired as I'm supposed to be, as if anyone could rest in this inferno, and nearly overwhelmed with relief. He believes we are supposed to be here. That's enough for me.

"Here." Raven offers him a cup. "She should drink something."

Between the two of them, I sit up just enough for Anwen to tip the cup to my lips. Cool, sweet water flows down my throat, soothing the burn. I close my eyes and just enjoy the feeling.

More pieces of memory return. Black veins on the backs of my hands, clutching a shard of mirror. Knowing, deep in my bones, that I was going to die, and Castor was going to have to figure out how to lead our people. Being angrier than I was disappointed in myself. The Goddess owed me more, after all I'd done for Her.

It seemed the Goddess intended to carry out that promise.

I open my eyes as Anwen takes the cup away and lowers me back down.

"Castor," I rasp. "Mother. Cristofer. Tess—"

"All safe." He cups my cheek. "I knew you'd kick my ass if they weren't."

My smile splits skin, or perhaps everything hurts like a new injury. Still, it is worth it. Floyd threw everything he had at us, and he lost.

I do not need to ask if he lost. If there were any concern for myself, for my family, Anwen would be running out the door, if he was here when I woke up at all. Relief dances along the currents of my pain. I no longer need to manage everything with him at my side.

Anwen returns my smile full force.

A door creaks open, and voices fill the room.

"Estrella!" Mother shrieks.

Kieran says, "She's o—"

Mother throws herself down at Anwen's side, sobbing, and reaches for me. I tense, anticipating the pain. She stops.

"Can I—are you—?" Her voice breaks off on another sob.

'I'm going to be all right,' I tell my family. *'In a few days.'*

Mother cries even harder. Castor, Cristofer, and Tess crowd into the sliver of the room I can see without lifting my head. My chest squeezes.

'*But I could endure one hug now,*' I say.

They swarm me as Anwen steps aside to give them space. Mother wraps her arms around my searing chest. Tess circles around to the other side and drapes herself over my legs. Castor manages to hug Mother and I at once. Even Cristofer pats my shoulder, a gesture both painfully awkward and comforting in how simply *him* it is. Seeing them all, inhaling their familiar smells, knowing beyond a shadow of a doubt that Floyd failed, is worth the cascade of agony it sets off in my body.

Anwen grunts in pain. "Okay, that's enough."

"Just a moment longer," I plead.

Out of the corner of my eye, I see his indulgent smile.

After another moment, my family unwinds themselves from me. I exhale in a gust as my pain becomes manageable again. Tess perches on the edge of the seemingly wooden table I lay on. Mother remains kneeling at my side. Castor drifts back and forth between mere inches from my head and over by Raven's bubbling table of ingredients I know he's desperate to ask about.

"Thank you," I say to Raven through the crowd of my family. "I am sorry you had to waste your components on me."

"It wasn't a waste." Her voice is thick with emotion. "You said you wanted to help in development, after all."

"How—" My voice cracks, and I clear my throat. "How long has it been?"

"Four and a half hours," Anwen answers immediately. "Since you blacked out. I don't know what you remember."

I struggle to sit up. "The wedding—"

"Was canceled." Mother takes my hand in her own soft palm. "Your gown is ruined, if nothing else."

I look down at myself. My gown is ruined, far beyond whatever magic Bright used to clean it after I healed Baz. The bodice splits jaggedly to expose my naked flesh. A few scabs cling to my skin, but more remains wet and raw.

And the sick gray-black of wolfsbane reaches mere inches away from the injury itself.

My laugh is just as ragged as the fabric of my gown. I lay back down, fireworks of pain exploding behind my eyes.

"What if I wouldn't like to cancel the wedding?"

Mother, Castor, and Tess exchange looks.

"I… suppose we could come up with something from your closet," Tess says slowly.

"The delegates are here." Mother worries her lower lip.

"What? No," Castor says. "You have to rest. I'm not having your life saved by some magic potion, only for you to get sick while healing."

Painfully, I brush my fingers against his wrist. It's all I can reach. "You misunderstand me."

He frowns.

"Anwen?" I ask.

My mate, the other half of my heart, sits at my side once more. This time, there's no mistaking it—he is nude under the robe. I will ask about that later.

"Our wedding was part of a political plot to capture the man who murdered my father," I say.

He swallows. "Right."

I muster my best smile. "I would like to marry you because I love you."

His whole face lights. "I—"

"And," I interrupt, "I would like you to lead Sundrop Gem with me, as my Alpha King."

He blinks. "Isn't that automatic with the marriage?"

"The offer is supposed to be witnessed." I smile. "Is that a yes?"

"Of course." He kisses me as softly and sweetly as morning dew kisses the grass.

* * *

A WEEK AND A HALF LATER, TESS COAXES ME SLOWLY THROUGH THE stretches our royal healer, Avi, concocted to keep the muscles in my chest from seizing. Even magic can only do so much. The sunset light shines through my gossamer curtains, illuminating the bedroom I grew up in.

Once all the wolfsbane fled my system, we returned to Sundrop Gem—with Anwen—for my convalescence. Everybody agreed the cold weather would be no help, though I was sorry to say goodbye to the friends I'd made. Candace and Raven both promised to write.

"A wedding is only one day," Tess says comfortingly. "You have the rest of your lives to behave as you wish."

I sigh as she pushes my arm higher above my head. "It is the one day dedicated to the declaration of our love. I wish that could be important."

"Well, having it here will certainly be more relaxed, won't it?" Tess smiles. "You won't have to contend with Bright."

I smile back at her, but it fades quickly. "I simply wish I was looking forward to my own wedding. There is far too much pressure, inviting all the other kingdoms and ensuring the people of Sundrop Gem understand Anwen's commitment to them."

"It really is just one day."

"I will tell you that once I promote Orion, and we will see how you like it then." I shake my head. "But a Luna owes her people. Shall we start with the guest list?"

Tess nods. "I did not like the Lilywind people. Must we—"

Mother steps into my room. "What are you girls talking about?"

"My wedding." I force a smile as Tess releases me from the final stretch. "I am well enough that we should begin planning."

"Why?" Mother asks.

I frown. "Because I would like to be wedded to my mate."

She shakes her head, a smile twinkling at the corners of her lips. "I mean, why are you doing that when your wedding is already planned?"

"What?" I ask breathlessly. "How?"

Tess grins. "Go with her if you want to find out."

Mother offers me her arm. I take it and step, wide-eyed, into the unknown.

5 8

THE OASIS

Anwen

"Wish you could still be my Beta." I fix my hair in the mirror again. "I was looking forward to being able to boss your ass around."

Baz grins. "How do you know that wasn't why I changed packs in the first place?"

I snort. I should've known he was gonna move with me when I saw him at that party. There's nothing he likes better than a good time. But I didn't realize the Alpha's Beta here could only be natural-born Sundrop. Baz is just going to be another subject from here on out.

"Stop fucking with your hair," he says. "You're just gonna drive yourself insane."

Another subject, and the best friend a guy could ask for.

"Can you blame me for wanting to look good?" I turn to him with a smile. "It's a special night."

"Yeah, yeah." He hops up with a roll of his eyes. "I'd better get mated during the next Haze, or I'm really going to regret moving."

"Because Dun's Crossing was working out so well?" I shake my head. "Do you have them?"

"Of course." From an inside pocket of his deep purple tunic—his only concession to Sundrop's style—Baz produces a small, carved wooden box.

I take it and open it immediately. Just in case.

There, nestled into the velvet cushion, sit two rings of carved moonstone. It's the one Dun's Crossing tradition I wanted to bring with me, and an echo of the tattoos Estrella and I already have. The carvings catch the light—on each, one half of a heart shines.

"Damn," Baz says. "They are nice."

"Nice?" I snap the box shut. "They're fucking perfect."

"Somebody's gotta keep your ego in check." He grins. "You're sure you don't need me there?"

My smile softens. "We don't need anyone else."

He claps me on the shoulder, fixes my hair one last time—the bastard—and pushes me out the door.

The Sollabella palace is easy to navigate after all the years I spent learning Solberg Castle. Wide hallways, open to the air more often than not. Thin curtains wave in the nighttime breeze.

As I step out into the courtyard and see her, all my nerves disappear.

Estrella stands between her mother and Castor wearing a simple —for Sundrop—wrapped dress that shines alternately red-orange and gray when she twists to look at me. A cape of the same fabric drapes down to the floor. Her hair curls, loose and wild, around her shoulders. Dark ink charting the night sky covers her exposed arms and blends with the faded, black veins still reaching up from the neck of her dress. The court healer thinks they'll probably scar like that. She cried when he first told her, but in the days since, we've agreed they make her look badass.

That's the last word on my mind right now. I don't even know if there is a single word. All I can think is that she looks so much better than she did in her wedding dress—even though I never saw it without some blood.

"Good evening," I say.

Estrella grins. "Good evening? Are we truly affecting you so much already?"

I laugh. "What am I supposed to say? Welcome to our wedding?"

"Here?" She looks around, her brow furrowing.

And there goes any last worry. She's been thinking about my perfect wedding as much as I have.

"Just the first part," I say. "Dowager Suniva, you—"

"Dressed her according to the old customs." She smiles and runs a hand along her daughter's arm. "Now, she can take the old life with her into the new."

Estrella smiles up at her mother, bittersweet. "What about the final blessing?"

The end of her question hangs in the air between us. According to Sundrop tradition, her father should do this part. For the original wedding, her whole family was going to, but there was no time to set that up now. I had the damned idea three days ago, when she first mentioned we should probably reschedule our wedding and looked like she was going to cry.

"That falls to me." Castor nods at me—we're in a truce since I saved her life—and smiles at her.

"Oh." Estrella covers her mouth with one hand, tears sparkling in her eyes.

I take her other hand. The tattoos on our pinkies line up again.

He pulls a small scrap of paper out of his sleeve. "I found this in Father's desk, and I just want to read it. When the Moon Goddess created us, she split us down the middle," he says. "Until we come of age, we live half a life. We learn, grow, develop, but something is always missing—our mate. But when we know who we are alone, She reunites us. The reunion might not be easy"—Castor grins—"but She knows best. She knew I—Father—needed your mother to keep my feet on the ground when my head scratched the clouds. She knows you need your mate. I hope he bandages your bleeding heart and tempers your stubbornness. I hope you show him how deep love can truly run and encourage him to see the beauty in life. I hope you are happy, my darling. May She always light your path, even when you cannot see it."

My chest tightens. King Isai was an incredible man. Someone who would've been really helpful to have around while I figured out how to deserve his daughter.

Estrella releases my hand to throw her arms around Castor and whispers something to him that I can't hear.

"I know," he replies. "I love you."

Dowager Suniva looks at me. "My husband seems to have developed the gift of prophecy."

"Thanks," I reply.

"Thank *you*." She kisses me on both cheeks.

Estrella lets go of Castor and swipes at her tears. "Where is Yana?"

I smile. "Waiting for us. Come on."

She exchanges a final, brief, goodbye with her family, and we race off into the night.

The way to the oasis is much longer on foot, so I arranged to have two horses waiting. Estrella rides like an extension of the animal, her hair flowing around her in the wind. Finally, though, we arrive at the oasis where we first truly talked to each other. Where I realized I was in love with her.

Yana, the holy woman, kneels in front of the pool. She looks up with a gentle smile when we dismount.

Estrella squeezes my hand. "You were right. This... this is perfect."

"I figure we can do the big royal thing in a couple weeks, if we need to," I reply. "But I wanted our actual wedding to be ours."

She kisses me, then steps into the oasis with Yana and kneels before her. I take my spot at her side. Exactly where I belong.

"The Moon Goddess offers us great freedom," Yana says. "We may, at any time, ignore Her guidance. Ignore the skills and gifts She sets before us. For this reason, we have both the mating mark and the wedding. The bite is instinctual—it is Her promise that the one you find in the Haze is yours, that you are intended to love each other. But the ceremony, which binds your souls forever, is a choice. You have chosen to sit before me today and pledge yourselves to each other."

I catch Estrella's gray gaze. Tears shine in the moonlight, but the smile she gives me is all confidence. She's a queen worthy of the people I've already started to care about. I grin back at her.

Yana nods. "Anwen, the offering?"

I pull the box out and open it.

Estrella inhales sharply. "They're beautiful."

"Ready?" I take the ring carved to perfectly fit over her tattoo and hold it out.

"I have been for a very long time."

"Repeat after me," Yana says. "I, Anwen, pledge my love and life to you, Estrella."

"I, Anwen, pledge my love and life to you, Estrella." I slide the ring onto her finger. "The other half of my heart."

Yana smiles indulgently. "Now, Estrella?"

She plucks the other ring from the box and studies it for a long moment, then speaks. "I, Estrella, pledge my love and life to you, Anwen. The other half of my heart."

Estrella slips the ring into place on my hand. The moonstone glimmers a pale rainbow. I've always liked these rings, but our promise feels steadier with the tattoo underneath. No matter what happens—if they break, get lost, anything—we'll always have proof of our commitment to each other.

Yana joins our hands then pulls a length of silvery ribbon out and wraps it around us, up onto our arm. Estrella's palm is warm and soft against mine.

"Both of you now," Yana says. "I thank the Goddess for joining our hearts across all time."

In unison, we repeat, "I thank the Goddess for joining our hearts across all time."

"The Goddess thanks you for brightening the world with Her love." Yana bows her head, then stands.

I frown and tug slightly at the ribbon. "Aren't you supposed to untie us? And tell us to kiss?"

"Those are Dun's Crossing traditions," Estrella murmurs. "Here, we unbind ourselves. In privacy."

The low rasp of her voice shoots straight to my cock.

Yana mounts one of the horses, grabs the reins of the other, and rides away. We're alone, back where I first believed we could actually make this work.

Fuck it. I don't want to be any farther away from Estrella than I am right now. As soon as the sound of hoofbeats dies out, I tackle her in a kiss.

59
FOREVER

ESTRELLA

ANWEN DIVES AT ME, THE RIBBON TYING US TOGETHER TUGGING AT MY skin, and I lean closer rather than away. Our mouths crash together. Those beautiful rings scrape lightly against each other. My emotions threaten to overflow yet again, a cup being filled over and over again. When he first described this wedding, I thought it sounded lovely. I had no idea how truly, totally spectacular it would be. Just us, alone under the Goddess's eye.

He licks along the seam of my lips, and I open for him. With my free hand, I begin fumbling at the folds of my dress, the folds of the tunic and pants he wore in proper Sundrop style. There is no rush—we have years upon years of falling into the same bed or escaping the palace to return to this place ahead of us. But the idea of being separated from my mate by even a few layers of fabric suddenly feels painful. I squeeze his hand within the ribbons holding us together. This is how close I always want to be.

The folds crumble quickly under my practiced hands. Fabric

loosens. Slivers of skin peek free, burning hot where we touch. Anwen starts to pull back, clearly trying to help.

'No.' I sink my teeth into his lower lip. '*Don't go any further.*'

'*I love you,*' he says through mind-link, his voice tinged with amusement.

The feeling of him, inside my head for the first time, crashes through me in a bright wave. I release his lip to laugh with the sheer delight of it.

Anwen, always the opportunist, seizes his chance to shove away the long strips of fabric separating us. The ground beneath my back offers up the barest hint of the day's warmth. Before I can grow cold, I pull him close again.

'*I love you too,*' I reply.

He smiles against my wanting mouth.

Pleasure courses through my limbs as I tangle myself with him. Wrap one leg around his, ensnare my free fingers in his hair, tighten my grip on our entwined hands. Our chests press so close that I can only inhale when he exhales, filling the space he leaves behind. Even though his cock stiffens against my leg, even though I can feel wetness forming between us, I don't do anything but kiss him. Chase his tongue back into his mouth. Savor the spark when he nips my lip. Swallow his breath and move with him like the moon and the ocean waves.

This, I truly could do forever.

Anwen breaks the kiss first but only to drag his mouth along the line of my jaw. I arch up into him with a moan. He nips my earlobe then begins to kiss down my neck.

I stiffen. He's so close to the sickly scars Avi says I'm likely to have for the rest of my days. I know Anwen believes them impressive—how many can say they've had a brush with wolfsbane and survived?—and I've conceded they could be politically useful. Only. but

'*Don't worry,*' Anwen says.

'*How can I not?*' No one has touched them other than Avi. Not even myself. They feel like someone else's body, foreign territory I cannot invade, especially now that I am home.

'Because I love you,' he says simply, hesitating a breath away from the scars. *'There's no part of you I won't love, no matter how it becomes part of you.'*

'Even my stubbornness?' I smile.

He huffs a laugh against my neck. *'If that was a dealbreaker, the deal would've broken already.'*

I shove him gently. But his words make sense. We've both changed so much in only the few short weeks we've known each other. If we are truly to complete each other, to spend the rest of our days together, it would be ridiculous to expect we will always be exactly as we are right now. We have to be able to bend, to grow with each other. Perhaps that is why the Goddess split us, at the beginning. So that we might learn how to grow in order to do it once we are reunited.

'All right.' I shut my eyes.

Anwen's lips brush, feather-light, over the still-taut skin of my neck where I know the sickened veins lie. I shudder. The sensation is… different. Muted, yet sharper. Just on the edge of painful, but not quite unpleasant.

'You okay?'

I nod. *'You may continue.'*

He laughs again, but his next kiss is harder. The feeling crests into pain, and I yelp.

Anwen stops instantly, worry painting his face.

'Gently,' I pant.

He nods and runs his free hand over the scars softly. Once again, it returns to muted near-pain. I lean up and capture his mouth again.

Anwen responds eagerly, his fingertips lingering on the scar. He traces down its length, making space for his hand between us. It's a teasing reminder of what I endured. What we both endured. I may never understand how he ran through the castle twice while feeling what I did. I will certainly never stop being grateful.

He strokes it rhythmically, slipping to either side now and again to toy with my breasts and tease my nipples to peaks. The agonizing memory alchemizes into something sweeter under his touch. There is so much to be grateful for—too much to simply lie here and receive.

I roll us over, pressing his back to the sand, and drop deep kisses on his neck. Early stubble scrapes my cheeks. Salt clings to his skin, mingling with the taste of him on my tongue. Anwen moans and clutches my hand inside the ribbon. I rock my hips against his, feeling his hardness.

'For luck,' I tell him, 'we should keep our hands bound for at least the first orgasm.'

'Happily.' He wrenches our joined hands up, over his head, knocking me off balance.

I flatten even closer to him, and my breasts land within reach of his mouth. His talented tongue plays over my nipples. I reach back to line up his cock with my entrance. There is so much time between us and dawn. I want to feel him.

We moan in harmony when he sinks deep inside me.

I begin moving my hips wildly, savoring every inch of his skin on mine. He offers all the feverish warmth the desert night denies. My breasts bob in and out of his reach, but he holds my gaze whether he can taste me or not. His blue eyes are as rich and deep as the sky above, no sign of the ice I saw in him so long ago.

Anwen folds his legs so his knees press into the base of my spine. The change in angle drives him even deeper—and allows me to roll my hips against him, chasing friction without ever moving out of the reach of his mouth. My full weight rests on him. Our limbs twist in complex knots. He pulses inside me, already racing toward the apex of pleasure, and my clit scrapes against his coils of hair. A throaty moan pours from my lips, more than such gentle pressure would usually elicit.

The burst of pleasure ricochets through me, and Anwen jerks his hips, pulling another wild exclamation out of me. We become an endless loop, linked in explosions of want. My desire drives his, just as his hope gave me the strength to stand when I was certain Floyd had already killed me.

We will share all the sweetness of life just as we share the pain.

Tonight, though, we simply erupt over the precipice together. My vision goes white, and my limbs shake as pleasure greater than anything I've felt before overwhelms me.

A few moments later, I blink my eyes open to find myself on my back, staring up at the sky. Anwen pants heavily next to me, and the ribbon still keeps our hands entwined.

'Wow,' he says.

I nod. Tears slip down my cheeks once more.

'Estrella?' he asks.

'That night, at the peace ball... I did not believe I could ever feel like this again.'

'Like what?'

I turn onto my side and look at our bound hands for a long moment. Then, I drag my gaze up to his face. His smile softens the angular lines of his face. The man I first saw when he woke me from my nightmare, the man I fell in love with, has completely consumed the one I first met. The one I still turned to after Father died. Because this man was always inside him, even if he hadn't yet found the way to him.

'Happy,' I say.

Anwen gathers me to his chest, one-armed and awkward. 'I figured I'd find out what "happy" was when I took the throne.'

I don't need to ask what throne he's talking about. The moment when I honestly believed he was using me for my title feels so silly now.

'I don't think I would've, if you're curious,' he adds.

'But now?'

'Now, I'm looking forward to my coronation.' He grins. 'But I'm already pretty sure I'm the happiest motherfucker alive.'

I smile back at him.

'Or I will be, when we take this ribbon off.' He rubs his arm against the ground as if itching it. 'Have we gotten all the good luck we need out of it?'

Something in my chest squeezes. When we untie ourselves, we

will return to our normal lives. To being royals, leaders, people others depend on. Our wedding will end, and our life will begin. Our wonderful lives, which I'm looking forward to. But—

'Let's leave it,' I say. 'Just a little longer.'

'Whatever you want,' Anwen agrees.

60
IN A HAZE

Candace

Seven months after Anwen left to become Alpha King of Sundrop, I struggle to focus on the embroidery in my lap as the carriage bounces along a rutted road.

"She was here for a week!" Ingrid laughs. "You can't be that excited to see her again."

I stick out my tongue at my younger sister. "How do you know I'm not excited to see Anwen and Estrella again?"

"Because you've been up in the rook, sending letters back and forth with Lady Eva every fucking week?" Finn replies.

Ingrid and I both flinch at his profanity. That feels sillier and sillier, the more time passes since Kieran took the throne. It was Mother's rule—fine ladies do not swear, nor do they endure swearing. But it's an old habit that's dying harder than I hoped.

"We're friends," I mumble. "It's not my fault you didn't meet anyone when all the delegates were here."

Finn scoffs, but there's nothing he can say to that. He *didn't* meet anyone. And Ingrid, as usual, didn't even try. I don't know why. She's beautiful, talented—everyone would love her. But every time people start showing up at the castle, Ingrid basically locks herself in her room until they leave.

I rub my temples. A headache brews behind my eyes, and I wonder if I'll have the dream again tonight. For two weeks, almost every night, it's been the same. Just like before Raven's Haze, I'm in the forest. I think it's the one outside the castle, but there's something weird about it. I haven't been able to put my finger on what. But in this forest, the Haze descends. And then... there he is. My mate. Huge and powerful against the trees, his coat so dark I can't tell whether it's black or something else in the night. I put my hand on his shoulder—and it's sticky. When I pull my hand back, it's covered in blood. And then I wake up.

Ingrid nudges me. "You all right?"

I nod and pick up my embroidery again.

'Do you see that?' Kieran asks through mind-link.

He and Raven rode ahead of the rest of us. She needs to set up some kind of supplies or something—I've really been trying to pay attention, but it's hard to understand when she gets excited about this potion she and Estrella have been working on.

'No?' Finn replies.

I try to peer through the curtains, but it just looks like every other bit of rocky land we've passed through since leaving for the border of Escuro.

'What is it?' I ask.

'It looks like the Haze.'

My stomach drops. That's not possible. I just turned twenty a couple of weeks ago. That's a bit early for a Haze to have an affect, but it's not impossible. Still, I figured the dream was... I don't know, an early warning. There was no sign of the Haze rolling in.

'That should make things more exciting,' Raven says tiredly.

She really shouldn't be out here in the first place. She's so desperately pregnant I expect her to give birth any moment, and sure, the nausea has stopped, but she's as big as a boulder and just as slow. But of course, she refused to wait when she had the ability to help her people.

It was Anwen's idea to invite all the other kingdoms. He and Estrella were already going to be there representing Sundrop, so he said it was only reasonable to make it an international event. A formal gesture of peace. So the Haze is rolling in right before a dozen or more kingdoms arrive.

I fix my hair, like the other delegations can already see me, and wish I could see the color of my mate's pelt in the dreams.

* * *

When the carriage finally rolls to a stop, Finn and Ingrid pile out. It takes a lot of focus not to grab Ingrid and fix her dress and hair as well. But she's nineteen now. Old enough to make her own decisions. So I sit alone in the carriage, fixing myself in a small hand mirror until I'm perfect.

I snap the mirror shut, climb out, and am immediately greeted by a flurry of deep blue fabric. When it wraps itself around me, I recognize Eva by smell—cinnamon and jasmine, underpinned by the iciness of all Snowcrest nobles, like the scent of the air a few hours before it snows.

"I missed you!" she squeals.

I hug her back. Ingrid accuses me of being overly social, but very rarely do I connect with someone like I did with Eva. "I missed you. There's been no one to talk to about the birds around the castle."

Even though I can't see her, I can feel Ingrid roll her eyes. She also says birdwatching is weird and lame.

"By the Goddess, do I have things to tell you." She pulls back and grins at me. "The sparrows started migrating early."

"Really?"

Before she can reply, a hush sweeps over the crowd. Snowcrest isn't the only delegation here, judging by the assortment of colorful tents I can barely see through the fog already collecting—the Haze is going to happen tonight. I'm sure of it. And the only thing that can make everyone fall silent at once trundles up behind me.

A heavy-looking, barred prison wagon. Raven had one additional request—that Mother witness the revitalization of Escuro with everyone else. She can't show Father anymore, but she admitted to me that she needed the people who did this to know their stain on the world could be removed.

Eva blinks and turns to Hollis. Through the angle of the sun, I didn't even realize he was standing next to her. He doesn't look at me —he's always a tough nut to crack, but he's got a nice laugh when I do —and his face is as impassively unimpressed as usual.

I don't want to hear their thoughts. While she's distracted, I slip away to find our tent.

* * *

THAT NIGHT, I LAY ON MY COT, TRYING TO DROWN OUT THE FIRST howls splitting the night with my thoughts. I am stronger than the fire trying to burn me alive from the inside out. I am—

'What are you doing?' Ingrid asks.

Wasting my time. Like a chisel in the dam of my self-control, Ingrid's question sends me flying out of bed, shedding clothes in my wake.

'Good luck!' she calls.

But I can't hear her anymore. I can't hear anything but my thudding heartbeat and the howling. Fire burns through my chest and out, throwing me into a shift. Fine, white fur explodes out of my skin. My smell sharpens to almost painful clarity. I never realized the Haze itself had a scent, something cool and pleasant like clean water or fresh clothes. Instinct sends me pounding away from the tent, one among dozens, maybe hundreds of young wolves.

I follow my nose.

Nothing appeals to the east, where the bulk of Escuro is staying. Nor to the west, where most of the delegates—

There. Pine, amber, snow. I turn to the north and sprint toward my mate.

Time ceased to mean anything as soon as I shifted, but I can feel it stretching. It is taking a long time to reach him, longer than it should. In the morass of instincts and want, I just put my nose to the ground and run faster. His scent grows more intense with every step. He has to be here. I can almost taste him.

I explode into a clearing at the same moment he does. He's exactly as I dreamt him, and I can't imagine waiting, trying to find a tent now. Still in a daze, lost in the Hazy, I shift into my human form skid to a stop in front of him.

Just like in my dream, I put a hand on his shoulder. Just like in my dream, it comes away sticky. Before I can worry, he shifts and crushes his mouth onto mine.

He tastes even stronger than he smells. I lick along his lips, trying to soak up every morsel. He opens his mouth and plunges his tongue into mine, possessive and insistent. His muscles tense as he wraps his arms around me—he's strong, even as a human. He lifts me, and I wrap my bare legs around his waist. My center rubs against the ridged surface of his stomach, sending sparks I've never felt before skittering through me. I moan, and he groans in response.

The world shifts, and I realize he's laying us down in the grass. My back touches the dew. I cling to him, digging my nails into his skin to make sure he can't release me. I can't let him. I need him.

Thick fingers swirl across the apex of my legs, and I nearly scream. I've never even touched myself before, but he feels so right. I roll my hips into his touch.

He growls and rips himself away from my mouth to bury his face between my legs. The touch of his tongue is even more intense than his fingers, more targeted on the spot that makes me see stars and babble wordlessly.

I scream, and my whole body tenses as hot, bright pleasure rips through me. But the Haze isn't done with either of us yet. He lowers my hips back to the grass, and I throw myself at him before he can even think to stop. We tumble to the ground together, and I land on top. That fire inside me burns even brighter as I take in the array of shallow scratches covering his arms and part of his chest, all dribbling blood.

A howl tears from my human lips. Whoever hurt my mate is in danger. Just as soon as I finish making him mine.

I line my hips up with his and spear myself on him. There's a single second of pain as I stretch to fit—then, nothing but the scent of him and fire. He grabs me and lifts me, then drops me back down. More want sears through me. With a roll of my hips, I let him fuck himself with my body. Being handled like this is tantalizing, spurring me ever higher.

His rhythm grows uneven. He releases one of my hips and fists a hand in my hair to pull my torso down against his. I immediately put my mouth on him. His blood turns his taste to copper, but I won't let go. Not when I can feel a second peak curling in my gut, when he cups one of my breasts and plays with it like a toy.

He grunts. His body goes stiff. And his teeth sink into the skin around my collarbone with a rush of sweet pain. With it, I careen over the edge and bite into the meat of his shoulder.

Euphoria washes through me. I slump onto his chest, boneless, and instantly fall asleep.

Mated to Four Alphas

Threats Against the Breeder

At War for the Breeder

The Stolen Breeder

Four Alphas, Four Babies

Becoming the Luna Queen

Descendants of the Breeder

Desired by the Devil series

Whispers of the Devil

Banter of the Devil

Murmurs of the Devil

The Mafia Kings series

Indebted to the Mafia King

<u>Loved by the Mafia King</u>

Claimed by the Mafia King

Secrets of the Mafia King

Burned by the Mafia King

Kidnapped by the Mafia King (coming soon!)

Dark Stalker Romance series

Tempted by Sin

Fated to Sin

Secret Billionaires series

Finding the Secret Billionaire by Olivia Bhelle Kildare

Falling for My Secret Billionaire by Bella Moondragon

Driven by the Secret Billionaire by ID Johnson

Wolf Shifter Alpha Kings series

Ravens and Ruins

Sundrops and Shadows

Snowflakes and Sabotage

The Vampire King's Feeder series

Claiming the Alpha's Daughter

Loving the Alpha's Daughter

Finding the Alpha's Daughter

Writing as B. Moon

The Boy Who Died

Sign up for Bella's newsletter here.

Or get a free novella from The Alpha King's Breeder series when you sign up here: The Beta and the Maid

Follow Bella on Facebook here.

Follow Bella on Bookbub here.